2015

AMERIKAN EAGLE
The Special Edition

Brendan DuBois

writing as Alan Glenn

Createspace Edition Copyright 2015 by Brendan DuBois.

Cover art by Jeroen ten Berg

ISBN: 151476203X
ISBN-13: 978-1514762035

To my parents and my wife, Mona Pinette.

ACKNOWLEDGMENTS

The author wishes to express his deep thanks and appreciation to Chief Lou Ferland and Deputy Chief Stephen DuBois of the Portsmouth, N.H., Police Department for their assistance in the research of this novel. Thanks as well to the library staffs in Portsmouth, Exeter, at the Phillips Exeter Academy, and at the University of New Hampshire.

Thanks as well to my agent, Nat Sobel, and his associates, for their extraordinary devotion and advice, and to my editor, Kate Miciak, for her sharp eye and unflagging enthusiasm for this novel, as well as to Randall Klein. I would also like to thank Hilary Hale, Donald Maass, Freddie Catalfo, and Liza Dawson for their thoughtful and helpful suggestions. In addition, thanks to Erin Mitchell, for literally bringing this book to life.

PROLOGUE

Miami, Florida, Wednesday, February 15, 1933

His whole life had been focused on keeping secrets, and after the twelve-day voyage south here on the Nourmahal, a luxury yacht owned by Vincent Astor—his neighbor from Warm Springs, Georgia—the newly elected president of the United States looked at the swarms of people meeting him at Bayfront Park this warm evening, and amid all the waves and jokes to his aides and puffs on his cigarette, he thought, Children. They are all children, frightened at what has happened to them, what has happened to their families, what has happened to their country. That was his latest secret, then, that he looked at the 140 million Americans out there and thought of them as children, even the twenty thousand who had gathered to see him tonight. Children who needed to look to a strong father who would promise to make everything right again. He grimaced, wondering what Colonel McCormack and his damnable Chicago Tribune would do with that particular thought. Which was why... secrets, so many secrets to be kept.

But oh, how that made sense, seeing all these people as children. Their dreams, their lives, everything torn apart since Black Tuesday nearly four years ago, as the stock market crashed and the grinding Depression followed. Despite all the soothing words of Hoover and his administration, it had gotten worse month after month, year after year. Factory after factory shutting down. Farmland turning to desert. Unemployment lines and soup kitchen lines and relief lines stretching for miles through hushed and fearful cities.

So here he was. New York state senator, former assistant secretary of the navy, failed vice presidential candidate in 1924, two-term governor of New York, under a month away from being inaugurated the thirty-second president of the United States, and already he knew he would have enormous power and the authority to use it once he was in the White House. During the leisurely cruise south to Florida, as he fished and talked and drank his own well-made martinis, the work had been under way. He was picking his cabinet, conferring with his smart young men, eager to go to Washington to make the necessary and overdue changes. From getting people back to work to ending the embarrassment that was Prohibition to finally chopping out the rot in the capitalist system that allowed a depression to shatter so millions of lives... There was so much to do!

The heat was oppressive, he thought as the motorcade rumbled its way through the crowds, the excited people reaching out to touch him, he waving at them, enjoying their attention, enjoying, too, the trust they were putting in him. Such a time to be alive. The problems of this blessed and rich and desperately troubled country were not unique in the world and weren't even the worst.

Japan was in Manchuria, ruthlessly slaughtering thousands of Chinese every day, hurtling threatening remarks about the Pacific and the Philippines. And Europe—ah, Europe, that would have to be faced once again, under two decades after the Great War. The global depression was devastating England and France and Germany. Now, Germany, that was a place to watch. An Austrian beer-hall rabble-rouser had just been named chancellor of Germany, and though elections were to be held there on March 5—the day after his own swearing- in—there was little doubt that Herr Hitler and his Nazi sons of bitches were going to seize power.

And speaking of sons of bitches, there were a handful here he needed to keep an eye on, like Senator Huey Long from Louisiana, the Kingfish himself. Just last week Long grabbed control of the state's banking system—even though, as a U.S. senator, he had no authority to do so. But the governor there, a weak character named Oscar Allen, did what the Kingfish told him to do—and Long still ran that state as his own private kingdom. Long had campaigned hard for Roosevelt, but he still didn't trust the man, not for a second. And there was A1 Smith from New York, the former governor who believed he should have been the nominee last year. Keeping his enemies and friends in fine was going to take a lot of a work, a lot of work, indeed. Certainly not one term; two terms, at least. And in the future, well, why not a third term? There was a tradition of only serving two terms, but the depth of the ' crisis—banks closing across the country, county judges lynched to prevent farm foreclosures, desperate streams of refugees going from state to state looking for work, looking for a new life, looking for hope—would surely allow for tradition be tossed aside.

He was now sitting on the rear seat of his halted green Buick convertible, helped up by Gus Gennerich, head of his Secret Service detail, his legs with their ten-pound leg braces dangling uselessly before him. Yet another secret, his paralysis of nearly twelve years, a secret he was determined to keep from those who didn't need to know. This was a time to be alive, but the millions of people who had voted for him might have hesitated had they known just how crippled he was.

The mayor of Miami introduced him, to thunderous cheers and applause. As the microphone was handed down to him, though he had no prepared speech, he would say a few words that would make everyone happy.

The crowd calmed as he talked about how many times he had visited Florida on his old houseboat, the Larooco, and how he'd had a wonderful time fishing. But he wouldn't bore them with fishing stories, he told them, and after a few more words and some laughter from the people, he was done. He passed the microphone back to the mayor, and the crowd surged some more, and now there was a familiar man joining him in the convertible, breathing hard, face subdued. Anton Cermak, mayor of Chicago and one of Al Smith's fellows. Cermak was here to kiss and make up—the poor man had twenty thousand schoolteachers who couldn't be paid—and he was also here, hat in hand, to seek federal aid. Politics was politics, and there was always a price to be paid, but he wouldn't let those teachers suffer because their mayor ' had backed the wrong horse at the Chicago convention last year.

Times had changed. Times were changing. The problems of a town or city or a state could no longer be settled by the locals. It was time for the federal government to take control, to improve things, to change the economy and rescue capitalism from its corrupt overseers, to give those poor children out there the flickering hope that things would improve, that something new would come, yes, that was it, the New Deal he had announced last year at the convention, a New Deal for the American people, the New Deal that would—

Noises.

Shouts.

Firecrackers?

God, his chest hurt.

He looked down, touched his white shirt. His hand came back bloody. Not firecrackers. Gunshots. Fired at him! More screams, and he felt the Buick begin to move, heard the shouting voice of Gus Gennerich telling the driver to move, move, move!

3

Now he was in the seat, on his side, his shoulders gripped by someone... Tony Cermak, it seemed like, telling him it would be all right, that he had to live, that he couldn't leave them, not now, that this was wrong, so wrong, and the pain in his chest flared, and as the darkness grew, he tried to fight back because... it was wrong\ There was so much to do, so much...

The darkness descended upon him. The voices grew distant. Even the pain seemed to subside.

Oh, there was so much to do.

PART ONE

Partial transcript, phone call received 01 May 1945, FBI Officer in Charge, Boston Field Office, Federal Bureau of Investigation, from Confidential Informant "Charlie":

Cl Charlie: ...sorry, it didn't work out.

FBI OIC: What do you mean it didn't work out?

Cl Charlie: It didn't work out. He's dead. That's it.

FBI OIC: Did you recover anything from the body?

Cl Charlie: Not a goddamn thing.

FBI OIC: Were you seen?

Cl Charlie: I don't think so.

FBI OIC: There's going to be hell to pay.

FBI OIC: And you should know, something huge is coming down the pike in less than a week and in your neck of the woods. You and your crew better be ready. You can't afford to screw up again or you'll be a dead man for sure, along with whoever else gets in the way or screws up.

Cl Charlie: But there's going to be a police presence on this, I'm sure—

FBI OIC: What, you think a local police badge protects anyone nowadays?

Cl Charlie: Oh, Christ.

CHAPTER ONE

Portsmouth, N.H., Monday, May 1,1943

Through the gloom and driving rain, Inspector Sam Miller glimpsed the dead man sprawled beside the railroad tracks, illuminated by the dancing glow from flashlights held by two other Portsmouth police officers. Sam had his own RayoVac out, lighting up the gravel path alongside the B&M tracks. The metal flashlight was chilly in his hand, and a previously broken finger was throbbing. It was raw and cold and he was hungry, having been called out just as he sat down to supper, but dead bodies demanded the presence of a police inspector, and Sam was the only inspector the department had.

Minutes earlier he had parked his Packard next to a Portsmouth police cruiser, back at the nearest spot open to the tracks, the dirt parking lot of the Fish Shanty restaurant. In his short walk to the scene, he had gotten soaked from the rain, and his shoes were sloppy with mud. His umbrella was safe and dry back home. The two police officers waited, flashlights angled, black slickers shiny with rain.

The path was getting rougher, and he had to watch his step past the wooden ties. When he was young, he'd found railroads exciting, romantic and adventurous. In the bedroom he shared with his brother, late at night, the steam whistle would make him think of all the places out there he'd visit. But that was a long time ago. Now trains still did their work, but the passenger trains were crowded, tramps often overwhelmed freight cars, and there were other, secretive trains out there that spooked him and so many others.

Near the two cops standing in the middle of the tracks was another figure, hunched over in the rain. Beyond the tracks, grass and brush stretched out about twenty feet to the rear of some warehouses and storage buildings. To the right, another expanse of grass melted into marshland and North Mill Pond, a tributary from the Portsmouth harbor. Farther down the tracks, Sam saw the flickering lights of a hobo encampment, like the campfires from some defeated army, always in retreat.

Thirty minutes earlier he had been dozing on the couch—half-listening to the radio, half-listening, too, to Sarah talking to Toby, warm and comfortable, feet stretched out on an old ottoman, and he had been... well, if not dreaming, then just remembering. He wasn't sure why—and maybe it was the onset of his finger aching as the temperature dropped—but he was remembering that muddy day on the football field of Portsmouth High School in the finals of the state championship in November, he the first-string quarterback... an overcast autumn day ten years ago, wind like a knife edge with the salt tang from the harbor... the wooden bleachers crowded with his neighbors and schoolmates... slogging through the muddy field, aching, face bruised, and the first finger of his right hand taped after an earlier tackle, no doubt broken, but he wasn't going to be pulled out, no sir... down by three points against Dover, their longtime rival... knowing that a pretty cheerleader named Sarah Young was watching him from the sidelines, and Mom, Dad, and his older brother, Tony, were there, too, in the nearest row of the stands, the first time Tony and Dad had ever come to one of his games.

Slog, slog, slog... minutes racing away... only seconds left... and then an opening, a burst of light, he got the ball tight under his arm, raced to the left, his finger throbbing something awful... dodging, dodging, focusing on the goalposts... a hard tackle from behind... a faceful of cold mud... his taped finger screaming at him... and then quiet, just for an instant, before the whistles blew and the cheers erupted.

He scrambled up, breathing hard, ball still in his hands, seeing the scoreboard change, seeing the hand of the clock sweep by, and then a gunshot... game over. Portsmouth had won... Portsmouth had won the state championship.

Chaos... shouts... cheers... slaps on the back... being jostled around... looking at the people, his high school, his playing field... pushing... taking off the snug leather helmet, his hair sweaty... and there, Mom clapping, her face alight, and Dad had his arm around Tony's shoulders, Tony standing there, grinning... Mom saying something, but he was staring at Dad, waiting, desperate for him to say something, anything, as so many hands patted his back... hands trying to get the game ball away from him... his broken finger throbbing.

Then Dad spoke, and Sam could smell the Irish whiskey on his breath. "Great news, boy, great news! Tony got into the apprenticeship program at the shipyard. Like father, like son... ain't that great?"

Sam's eyes teared up. "We won," he said, despising himself for the humiliation in each word. "We won."

Dad squeezed Tony's shoulder. "But that's just a game. Our Tony, he's got a future now... a real future." And that winning, confident grin of Tony the school dropout, Tony the hell-raiser and hunter, Tony whom Dad cared about... not the other son, the winning football hero, the Eagle Scout, the one who—

A series of bells rang somewhere. Something nudged his foot. Sam opened his eyes.

"That was the station," Sarah said. "Someone's found a body."

The taller cop said, "Sorry to get you wet, Sam. You okay with that?" His companion laughed. The tall cop was Frank Reardon, and his shorter and younger partner was Leo Gray. The third man stood behind them, silent, arms folded, shivering.

"I'll be just fine," Sam answered. The body beside the tracks was splayed out like a starfish, mouth open to the falling rain, eyes closed. The man had on black shoes and dark slacks and a white shirt and a dark suit coat. No necktie. No overcoat. Sam stepped closer, stopped at the gravel edge of the tracks. The man lay on a stretch of ground that was a smooth outcropping of mud, with just a few tufts of faded grass.

"How long have you been here?" Sam asked Frank.

" 'Bout ten minutes. Just long enough to make sure there was something here."

"That our witness?"

"Yeah." Frank grabbed the third man by the elbow and tugged him forward. "Lou Purdue, age fifty. Claims he found the body about an hour ago."

"An hour?" Sam asked. "That's a long time. Why did it take you so long to call us?"

Purdue was bearded and smiled with embarrassment, revealing bad teeth. He wore a tattered wool watch cap and a long army overcoat missing buttons and held together with safety pins. "I tried, I really tried." His voice was surprisingly deep. "But the Shanty place, I went there and asked them to-call, and they wouldn't. They wouldn't even give me a nickel for the pay phone. So I went out in the street and waited till I saw a cop car come by. I waved them down, that's what I did."

Sam asked Frank Reardon, "That true?"

"Yeah, Sam. Almost ran over the poor bastard. Said there was a dead guy by the tracks, we had to come up to see it. We came up, saw what was what, then I sent Leo back to make the call. And here you are. Pulled you away from dinner, I bet."

"That's right," Sam said, playing the beam from the flashlight over the body. The man's clothes were soaked through, and he felt a flicker of disquiet, seeing the falling rain splatter over the frozen features, the skin wet and ghostly white.

The younger cop piped up. "Who was there? The mayor?"

Sam tightened his grip on his flashlight, then turned and played the beam over Leo Gray's face. The young cop was smiling but closed his eyes against the glare. "No, Leo. The mayor wasn't there. Your wife was there. And we were having a nice little chat about how she peddles her ass to pipefitters from the shipyard 'cause you waste so much money on the ponies at Rockingham. Then I told her I'd arrest her if I ever saw her on Daniel Street at night again."

Frank laughed softly, and Leo opened his eyes and lowered his head. Sam, feeling a flash of anger at losing his temper to the young punk because of his father-in- law, turned back to the witness. "How'd you find the body?"

Purdue wiped at his runny nose. "I was walking the tracks. Sometimes you can find lumps of coal, you know? They fall off the coal cars as they pass through, and I bring 'em back. That's when I saw him over there. I figured he was drunk or something, and I kept trying to wake him up by callin' to him, and he didn't move."

"Did you touch the body?"

Purdue shook his head violently. "Nope. Not going to happen. Saw lots of dead men back in the Great War, in the mud and the trenches. I know what they look like. Don't need to see anyone up close. No sir."

The wind gusted some and Purdue rubbed his arms, shivering again, despite the tattered army overcoat. Sam looked back at the Fish Shanty, saw a flashlight bobbing toward them from the parking lot. "What's your address?" he asked Purdue.

"None, really. I'm staying with some friends...you know." He gestured to the other end of the tracks, where the hobo encampment was clustered near a maple grove. "Originally from Troy. New York."

"How did you end up here?"

"Heard a story that the shipyard might be hiring. That they needed strong hands, guys who could take orders. I took orders plenty well in the army, and I figured it was best to come out here. Maybe they'd be a veteran's preference. So far—well, no luck. But my name's on the list. I go over every week, make sure my name's still there. You know how it goes."

Sam knew, and spared a glance at the lights staining the eastern horizon. The federal Portsmouth Naval Shipyard, set on an island in the middle of the Piscataqua River, an island claimed bitterly by both New Hampshire and Maine for tax purposes, and busily churning out submarines for the slowly expanding U.S. Navy. The world was at war again, decades after this filthy soul before him and Sam's father had suffered to make the world safe for democracy. Some safety.

"Yeah," Sam said. "I know. I might need to talk to you again. How can I do that?"

"The place—you know the place down there. Just ask for me. Lou from Troy. I can be found pretty easy, don't you worry."

"I won't. Hold on." Sam reached under his coat, took out his wallet, and slipped a dollar bill out of the billfold, along with his business card. He folded the dollar bill over the card and passed it to the soaked and trembling man. "Go get some soup or coffee to warm up, okay? Thanks for grabbing a cop, and thanks for not disturbing the body. And call me if you think of anything else."

The dollar bill vanished into the man's hand. He snickered and walked in the direction of the camp, calling back through the darkness, "Hell, a damn thing for that guy to end up dead. But hell. That's a lucky walk, you've got to say, finding a body like that and making a buck... a hell of a lucky walk."

Frank shuffled his feet, "So the bum gets to go someplace dry. You gonna look at the dead guy some, or you gonna keep us freezing out here?"

"Going to wait a bit longer," Sam replied. "Don't worry. The coffee and chowder will be waiting for you, no matter the time."

"What are you waiting for, then?"

"To record history, Leo, before we disturb it. That's what."

Frank muttered, "Ah, screw history."

"You got that wrong, Frank," Sam said. "You can't screw history, but history can always screw you."

Another minute or two passed. From the distance, near where the fires of the hobo camp flickered, came a hollow boom, and then another.

"Sounds like a gunshot, don't it," Frank said, his voice uneasy.

The younger cop laughed. "Maybe somebody just shot that hobo for the dollar you gave him."

Sam looked to the thin flames from the hobo camp. He and the other cops stayed clear of the camps, especially at night. Too many shadows, and too many angry men with knives or clubs or firearms lived in those shadows. He cleared his throat. "We got one dead man here. If another one appears later, we'll take care of it. In the meantime, you guys looking for extra work?"

The other cops just hunched their shoulders up against the driving rain, stayed quiet. That was the way of their world, Sam thought. Just do your job and keep your mouth shut. Anything else was too dangerous.

CHAPTER TWO

From the rainy gloom, another man stumbled toward them, swearing loudly, carrying a leather case over his shoulder, like one of the hordes of unemployed men who went door-to-door during this second decade of the Great Depression, peddling hairbrushes, toothbrushes, shoelaces. But this man was Ralph Morancy, a photographer for the *Portsmouth Herald* and sometime photographer for the Portsmouth Police Department.

He dropped the case on the railroad ties and said, "Inspector Miller. Haven't seen you since your promotion from sergeant to inspector, when I took that lovely page- one photo of you, your wife, the police marshal, and our mayor."

Sam said, "That's right. A lovely photo indeed. And I'm still waiting for the copy you promised me."

Ralph spat as he removed his Speed Graphic camera from the case. "Lots of people ahead of you. Can't do your photo and be accused of favoritism, now, can I?"

"I guess not. I remember how long it took you to get me another copy of a photograph, back when I was in high school."

The older man rummaged through his case, clumsily sheltering it from the rain with his body. "Ah, yes, our star quarterback, back when Portsmouth won the championship. How long did it take for me back then?"

"A year."

"Well, I promise to be quicker this time."

Sam said, "Just take the damn photos, all right?" Ralph put a flashbulb in the camera with ease, like a magician performing the same trick for the thousandth time. "Anything special, Inspector?"

"The usual body shots. I also want the ground around the body."

"Why's that?"

"Because I want photos of what's not there," Sam said.

Frank Reardon stirred. "What's not there? What kind of crap is that?"

Sam played the flashlight beam around the corpse, the raindrops sparking in the light. "What do you see around the body?"

"Nothing," Leo said. "Mud and grass."

"Right," Sam said. "No footprints. No drag marks. No sign of a struggle. Just a body plopped down in the mud, like he dropped from the sky. And I want to make sure we get the photos before the body's moved."

He kept the flashlight beam centered on the corpse. The rain fell in straight lines, striking the dead man's face. To Sam, the dead man looked like a wax dummy. There was a sudden slash of light, and Sam flinched as Ralph took the first photo. As Ralph replaced the bulb, he groused, "Plenty of time for me to make tomorrow's edition."

"No," Sam said. "You know the arrangement, Ralph. We get twenty-four hours, first dibs, before you use any crime scene photos in the paper."

Another flash, and Sam blinked at the dots of light floating before his eyes. "Come on, Inspector, give me a break," Ralph muttered. "Twelve hours, twenty-four hours. What difference does it make?"

"If it's twenty-four hours, it makes no difference at all. If it's twelve hours, the department makes arrangements with another-photographer. You're an educated man, Ralph, you know what the jobless numbers are like. You really want to dick around with this sweet deal?"

A third flare of light. "Some goddamn sweet deal, getting rained on in the cold, taking photos of a dead bum." Sam gave him a gentle slap on his back. "Just the glamour of being a newsman, right?"

"Some fucking glamour. My boss got a visit last week from some jerk in the Department of the Interior. Wanted to know how we'd survive if our newsprint ration got cut again next month. So my boss got the message— tone down the editorials, or the paper gets shut down. Yeah, that's glamour."

Sam said, "Spare us the whining. Just get the photos." "Coming right up, Inspector. I know how to keep my job, just you see."

This was Sam's first untimely death as an inspector. As a patrolman and, later, sergeant, he had seen a number of bodies, from drowned hoboes pulled from Portsmouth Harbor to sailors knifed outside one of the scores of bars near Ceres Street. But as a patrolman or a sergeant, you secured the scene and waited for the inspector to arrive. That had been old Hugh

Johnson, until he died of bone cancer last year.

Now it was Sam's job, and what he did tonight could decide whether he got to keep it. He was on probation, a month left before he turned in the silver shield of an inspector on tryout, before getting the gold shield and a promised pay raise that would give his family some breathing room, a bit socked away in savings, something that would put them at the top of the heap in this lousy economy. So far, all of his cases had been minor crap, like burglaries, bunco cases, or chasing down leads for the Department of the Interior on labor camp escapees who had ties to the area. But if this turned out to be a homicide, it could help him with the Police Commission and their decision on his ultimate status.

As Ralph made his way back to the restaurant's parking lot, Frank spoke up. "Sam, looks like this is a lucky night for all of us."

"Not sure what you mean."

Frank played the light over the corpse. "Doesn't look like a political hit, which means it won't be taken away from us. This'll be a good first case for you, Sam."

"Sorry, what in hell's a political hit?" Leo asked. Frank answered, "What I mean, kid, is that sometimes bodies pop up here and there, mostly in the big cities, where the guy has his hands tied behind him and he's got two taps to the back of the head. None of those cases ever get solved. So it's lucky for us that this guy's arms are nice and spread out. Means nothing political is involved. We can just do our jobs, and nobody from Concord is going to bother us."

Sam squatted, winced as a cold dribble of rainwater went down the back of his neck. He looked about him: a dead body, possible homicide, his first major case. Even in the rain and darkness, everything seemed in sharp focus: the two cops and their wet slickers, the mud, and the sour tang of salt water. The scent of piss from the dead man before him, the one who'd brought him here.

The man was thin, maybe fifties, early sixties. The skin was pale and the hair was a whitish blond. No cuts or bruises on the face. Sam touched the skin. Clammy. He went through the pockets of the suit coat, taking his time. No money, no paper, no wallet, no coins, no fountain pen, no cigarettes, no lighter. He sensed the other cops watching him, evaluating him, a feeling he hated.

Sam raised each shirtsleeve, looking for a watch or jewelry. "Frank," he said. "Bring the light closer, down to his wrist."

Frank lowered the light, illuminating the skinny white wrist. There. A row of faint squiggles on the skin. Numerals. Sam rubbed at the numerals. They didn't smudge or come off.

15

A row of numbers, tattooed along the wrist. Portsmouth was a navy town, and Sam had seen every kind of tattoo, from Neptune to mermaids to naked hula girls, but never anything like this.

The numerals were blue-gray, jagged, as if they had been quickly etched in:

911283

"Frank? You see those numbers? You ever see anything like that before?"

Frank leaned forward, and rainwater poured off his hat brim. "Nope, never have. Maybe the coroner, maybe he's seen something like that. But not me."

Though it didn't make any difference to the dead man, Sam lowered the shirtsleeve. "Leo. Give me a hand here. We need to roll him over."

"Cripes," Leo said, but he was a good cop and did as he was told. They rolled the corpse on its side, and Sam checked the front and rear pockets of the trousers. The fabric was sopping wet, but the pockets were empty. The stench from the body grew stronger. Frank was right. No bullet wounds to the base of the skull. Sam and Leo rolled the body back.

"No money, no wallet," Sam told them, standing up. Leo said, "Maybe he was stripped, robbed, by one of the bums from the camp."

Frank laughed. "Shit, kid, don't be dumb. There'd be footprints. Nope, the way he got here is the way he arrived: no cash and no belongings. Still, Sam..."

"Go on, Frank."

"Those clothes. They look pretty good. You know? Not from somebody riding boxcars or hitchhiking, looking for work. No patches, no rips. Not brand-new but not... well, not beat up."

There was noise again from the Fish Shanty parking lot, and Sam looked up to see the hearse from the Woods funeral home roll in. Saunders from the county medical examiner's office shouldn't be too far behind, so the body could be moved and they could all get out of this damn rain. Sam was hungry, and it was getting late, and Sarah and Toby were waiting for him at home.

Two attendants carried a canvas stretcher from the hearse, the men holding the stretcher by its side so water didn't pool in the canvas. Sam didn't envy them having to haul this corpse back to the hearse, over the gravel and railroad ties, but it was their job. As everyone said nowadays, it was good just to have a job.

Frank stared at the approaching attendants, stumbling a little in the mud, and said, "Hey, Sam. All right if me and the kid take off after the body's removed?"

"Yeah, but first I want the two of you to do a check of the buildings on this side of the tracks. See if anybody saw anything."

"They're mostly stores. They're all closed by now." "Then it won't take long, will it?" Sam told Frank. "If anything of interest surfaces, call me at home. If not, write up a report. Leave it on my desk when your shift's over."

Frank said, "All right. But hey, remember, there's a Party meeting tomorrow night. You've missed the last two. You don't want me to make a report to the county director, now, do you? Or have one of Long's boys start asking you questions?"

"Just do the search," Sam said. "Write something up and put it on my desk. Don't worry about me and the Party."

"Sam, that's the wrong attitude, you know it is." Frank's tone had sharpened. "Now, I give you a break 'cause you're on the force and all, but you better be there, no foolin'. I'd hate to make a formal report. Especially with you being on probation and all. Hate to have something like that affect your promotion."

Sam folded his arms, flashlight in his right hand, forcing himself not to move, forcing his voice to come out slow and deliberate. "I'll be at the damn meeting. Okay?" Leo was grinning, a rookie cop glad to see his mentor give the new detective a hard time. "Your brother be there, Sam?"

Sam aimed his RayoVac at the young cop's face. "You know my brother?"

"No, but I know where he is," Leo said. "In a labor camp up in New York."

Sam kept quiet as the wind rose up, water striking his face, keeping the flashlight beam steady on the younger man. "Then I guess he won't be there tomorrow night, will he, Leo."

"Hey, Sam, just a joke. That's all. Don't you know how to take a joke?"

"Sure, Leo. I'm an inspector. I know a lot of things. Know how to question people. How to look at a crime scene. And how to recognize jerks when I meet them." Frank started to say something, but Sam turned away. "Party or no Party, brother or no brother, you're both still beat cops, and I'm an inspector. In a couple of minutes, I'm going to be nice and dry, and you're still going to be out here in this shitty rain, doing what I told you to do. That's what I know. Anything else?"

"Yeah," Frank said. "Now I wish this fucking guy had been a political. At least we could get out of the rain sooner."

"We all have wishes, don't we, Frank," Sam said.

CHAPTER THREE

Ten minutes later, Sam sat in the warmth of the Fish Shanty, writing up his notes while trying to ignore the smell of fried seafood, mixed in with the smoke from cheap cigarettes and cigars. Sarah was waiting at home with his supper, and woe be to him if he went home without an appetite.

He sat on a stool at the lunch counter, and off to both sides, booths filled up with shipyard workers, a scattering of locals, and sailors getting a fast meal into them before heading out for a night of whoring and drinking.

Unbidden, an empty white coffee cup was placed on the counter, and Sam looked up from his notes to see a smiling red-haired waitress wearing a black and white uniform that was just a tad too tight. Donna Fitzgerald, a few years younger than Sam, a local girl who had hung out with him and other kids years ago, having fun, raising hell, until high school and the Depression had scattered them. He smiled back.

"Having a busy night, Sam?"

"Just working a case. How are you doing, Donna?"

"Doing okay. Last night here at the Shanty, thank God." Her smile broadened, displaying the dimple on her left cheek.

"Really?"

"Uh-huh," she said, filling up his cup from a dented metal coffeepot. "I start tomorrow at the Rusty Hammer, in town. Oh, it's still waitressing, but you get a good lunch crowd with the businessmen, with better tips. Here, well, most of the customers are tight with their money, saving it for...other things." She winked and put a freckled hand on top of his. "Now, Sam, how come you never asked me out when we were in school together?"

"Oh, I don't know, Donna. The age difference, I guess. Being in different classes."

"Age doesn't make much of a difference now, does it?" Her hand was still on his.

He smiled. "Guess it doesn't."

There was a shout from the kitchen; she took her hand away. "Time to get back to work. Good to see you, Sam...And did you hear? My man Larry is getting released from the camps in Utah. He should be back here in Portsmouth by the end of the week."

"That's... that's good news, Donna." For the briefest of moments, when her hand had touched his, there had been a little spark, a jolt.

She winked at him, and he remembered how pretty she'd been at fifteen. "Certainly is. You take care, Sam, okay?"

"I will," he promised, and he watched her walk away, admiring the way the uniform hugged her hips and her other curves. He saw at the far end of the counter, sitting by themselves, a man and woman and small boy. They sat with cups of tea before them and nearly empty plates, a paper check on the countertop near the man's elbow. They were well dressed and quiet. He knew the look. Refugees. French, Dutch, Brits, or Jews from everywhere else in Europe. Like lots of port cities up and down the Atlantic Coast, his hometown was bursting with refugees. The family had probably come here for a hot meal, and they were stretching out the comfort of food and being warm and dry. Sam knew they were here illegally. He didn't care. It was somebody else's problem, not his.

He looked down at his notes again, trying to get Donna out of his mind. Not much in his notes. Dead man, no identification, nice clothes, and a tattoo: 9 1 12 8 3. What the hell did that mean? A series of numbers so important they couldn't be forgotten? Like what? A bank account? A phone number? Or if they were added in some sort of combination—or did they stand for letters? He did some scribbling on his pad, substituting each number with the corresponding letter in the alphabet, and came up with LAABHC. He tried rearranging those letters and came up with nothing. So maybe it was just the numbers.

But why go to the trouble of having them tattooed?

Sam looked up from his notebook and watched the boy at the other end of the counter whisper something to his mother. She pointed to the rear of the diner. The boy slid off his stool, then walked away from the counter, toward the bathroom. The boy was about Toby's age. Sam wondered what it must be like to be that young and torn from your home, to live in a strange land where sometimes the people treated you nice and other times they arrested you and put you in a camp.

He took his wallet out, looked inside. Sighed. Being a cop meant a paycheck, but not much of one. Still...

For the second time this night, Sam slid out a dollar bill. He waited until the boy came back out, then let the bill fall to the linoleum. As the boy went by—Sam noted the sharp whiff of mothballs from the boy's coat, probably a castoff from the Salvation Army—he reached out and caught his elbow. "Hey, hold on." The child froze, and Sam felt the sudden trembling of the thin arm.

"Sir?" the boy said.

Sam pointed to the floor. "You dropped this on the way over."

The boy—brown-eyed with olive-colored skin—shook his head gravely. Sam reached to the dirty floor, picked up the dollar bill, and pressed it into the boy's palm. "Yes, I saw you drop it. It belongs to you."

The boy stared, looked at Sam. Then his fingers curled around the bill and he ran back to his parents. The father started whispering furiously to the mother, but she shook her head and took the dollar bill from her boy. She picked up the check and nodded at the Shanty's owner, Jack Tinios, who had just ambled out of the kitchen. He pocketed both the check and dollar bill, then came over to Sam, wiping his hands on a threadbare towel.

Like most of the restaurant owners in this stretch of New Hampshire, Tinios was from Greece but had moved here before the Nazis overran his country back in '41. His real first name began with the letter J and had about a dozen syllables; he and everyone else made it easier by calling him Jack. His face was florid, his mustache damp with perspiration, and his arms and hands were thick and beefy. He had on a T-shirt and stained gray slacks, an apron around his sagging middle.

"Found a body on the tracks a hundred yards or so away," Sam said.

Jack grunted. "So I hear."

"Guy in his sixties, maybe a little younger. Thin blond hair, wearing a white shirt, black suit, no necktie. He come in here today?"

"No."

"You sure?"

"Guys in suits come in here, I notice. I don't notice no guy in a suit."

"Okay, then," Sam said. "Another guy came in here about two hours ago, wanting to use the phone to call the cops. He didn't have a suit. You notice him?"

"Sure. Bearded guy, long coat. Told 'im to beat it." "You wouldn't even let him use the pay phone?"

"Bum wanted a nickel. You know what happen, I give 'im a nickel to make a phone call? He runs out. I never see him, never see nickel again."

"You might have impeded an investigation, Jack. We might have gotten here earlier if you'd let him make that call."

"Hell with that. One dead man, what do I care? What I do care is those bums down the tracks, living like animals, pissing and shitting in the woods, always breakin' in my place, goin' through my trash, lookin' for scraps to eat, dumpin' it all on the ground. Why don't they get cleaned out? Huh? I'm a taxpayer. Why don't they get cleaned out?"

Sam dropped two quarters on the counter. "Priorities, Jack, priorities. One of these days..."

Jack said something in Greek and palmed the coins. "You sound like the President. One of these days. Every man a king. One of these days."

"Sure," Sam said, "and make sure Donna gets that tip, okay?"

"Yeah, I make sure."

The door opened and another Portsmouth cop came in, his slicker glossy with rain. He held his uniform cap in one hand, shaking off the water to the wet floor. Rudy Jenness was one of the oldest cops on the force and the laziest, but because his brother ran the city's public works, he was safe in his job as shift sergeant. He walked over, his face splotchy red and white. "Sam, glad I saw your car parked out there." Without a word, Jack pressed a cup of coffee into Rudy's palm.

"Yeah, lucky me, what's up?" Sam said.

"Marshal Hanson, he wants to see you. Like now."

"He say why?"

Rudy noisily drained the cup and then slapped it on the counter. "Shit, you got a dead son of a bitch, right? Hanson wants to chat you up about it."

Sam felt a voice inside saying, *Not fair, dammit, not fair, this case is less than a half hour old, I don't know enough to brief my boss.* Rudy added, "Nice job you got there, Sam. Being warm and all. Me, I'm back on the streets for another three hours."

Sam said, "Good place for you, don't you think?"

Rudy smiled, and Sam saw a patch of stubble on his chin where the razor had missed shaving. "You can have your inspector job. Lots of bullshit a guy like me don't have to worry about, and I'll be getting mine when I retire. See you in the funny papers, Sam. Thanks for the coffee, Jack."

After Rudy left, Sam folded his notebook shut, put it inside his coat, and got up from his stool. The door banged open and two young men stumbled in, noisy, already drunk, swaying. Their cropped hair was wet from the rain, and they were dressed almost identically, in leather boots, dark blue corduroy pants, and leather coats. On the lapel of each coat was a small Confederate-flag pin, and Sam stood still, watching them stumble by and sit down at the counter.

The two jokingly passed a menu between them, and Sam started to the door, just as one of the men yelled out to Jack Tinios, "Hey, you old bastard, get over here and take our order! What the hell are you, a lazy Jew or something?"

The coffee shop fell silent. One of the sailors set his fork down. Sam looked to Jack, who looked back at him, eyes sharp. No one dared look at the two men who had just slammed in. Donna stood by the kitchen doors. She had a plate of food in her hand, and even at this distance, Sam saw her eyes tear up. In the restaurant window was a faded sign: we support share the wealth. One of the ways to get along, not to make waves, even though Sam knew Jack detested the President.

The rain was pelting down, but Sam took his time after he went outside. He looked at each of the cars parked in the dirt lot until he found the one he was looking for, a '42 Plymouth with Louisiana license plates, a pelican in the center of the plate. The front fenders and windshield were speckled with insect carcasses from the long drive north. Two members of the President's party—Long's Legionnaires, they were called in some of the braver newspapers—sent north as reverse carpetbaggers, to install Party discipline with a fierce loyalty for their Kingfish. Up till recently, Portsmouth had been spared such visitors, but in the past few weeks they'd been here, setting up shop, doing their bit to extend their President's control.

Sam looked back at the rain-streaked windows of the small restaurant, saw the two young men sitting there, laughing. Then he knelt down, took out his pocketknife, and gently slit the two rear tires.

INTERLUDE I

With Vermont behind him, it took him nearly a week, but he finally made it to this isolated farmhouse on the New Hampshire side of the Connecticut River. Standing in the trees at dusk, he had watched the place for almost an hour before reaching a decision. Sweet wood smoke rose and eddied up from a metal smokestack set in the sagging roof of the one-story home next to an empty barn. He rubbed his hands. It was probably warm in that snug old farmhouse. He couldn't remember a time when he'd last been warm. Only when it was dark, and someone lit a kerosene lamp from inside, did he make his move.

He walked up to the rear door, going as fast as he could, limping from last winter's injury, when a pine tree he'd cut down had fallen the wrong way. When he got to the door, he gave it a good thump with his fist.

No answer.

His breath snagged as he thought, *A trap?* When he thumped again, the door creaked open an inch.

"Yeah?" came a voice from inside.

"Just passing through," he said.

"So?"

He hesitated, knowing it would sound silly, but still, it had to be said. "Give me liberty..." He waited for the countersign, wondering if he could run fast enough back to the woods if it went wrong.

The man on the other side of the door replied, "Or give me liberty."

His tight chest relaxed. Only someone he could trust would have the correct countersign. Only then did he recognize how tense he had been. There were two men inside, the one answering the door, another sitting at a wooden table, where the kerosene lamp flickered. Both wore faded flannel shirts and denim overalls grubby with grease and dirt. The man at the table held a sawed-off shotgun pointing at his gut. He stopped on the threshold, and the man put the shotgun down on the table. The armed man was in his thirties, the other man—who walked over to an icebox, opened it, and came back holding a plate with two chicken legs and a mug of milk—was in his fifties. His face was scarred on the right, and the eye on that side drooped. A lit woodstove in the other corner warmed the small room.

"Thanks," he said, sitting down, picking up a chicken leg and starting to eat. "Been a long time."

The older man sat across from to him. "You can spend the night, but Zach here"—he gestured in the armed man's direction—"will get you into Keene tomorrow. From there, someone will get you to the coast."

Amazing how quick it was to finish off one chicken leg, and it seemed he was even hungrier when he picked up the other. "Fair enough."

Zach asked, "How's things where you came from?" "Tough," he replied. "How's things here?"

Zach laughed. "Used to have the best dairy herd in this county before milk prices turned to shit. Lost money on each gallon of milk I sold, so I slaughtered my herd and make do where I can. Still, not as bad as Phil here." "True?" he asked Phil.

Phil rubbed at stubble on his chin. "I went out to the Midwest back in '28, got a job at Republic Steel. A tough place. Management treated us like shit, got worse after the Crash. Then we went on strike in '37."

He nodded, remembering. "Yeah. The Memorial Day massacre. You were there?"

"Sure was. Hundreds of us strikers marching peacefully, lookin' for better conditions and wages, then reachin' a line of Chicago cops. More than twenty were shot dead by those bastards, whole bunch of others were wounded, the rest got gassed. I got hit in the face by a tear gas canister. My wife... didn't make it. So I came back here... found... something else to do."

He didn't know what to say. He finished his milk. Phil studied him and said, "You know what you got ahold of, don't you?"

"I do."

"You're settin' to kill one of the most guarded men in the world. You think you can do it?"

"I wasn't picked for my damn charming personality, was I?"

Zach laughed again, softly, but Phil didn't. "Understand you might got family issues. That going to be a problem?"

He shook his head. "No, it'll all work out."

"It better."

Outside, he thought he saw a light flicker, and his hands tensed on the mug. He said, "What the hell do you mean by that?"

Zach was silent and so was Phil. A floorboard creaked. Phil said, "Not sure if you're goin' to be tough enough to do what has to be done. I know you heard all the plans. Most likely, damn thing is goin' to be a suicide mission when it all gets wrapped up and the shootin' stops. So. I got to know. Are you tough enough?"

Another flicker of light. He leaped up, grabbed the shotgun from the table, and burst out the rear door, with shouts and the sounds of chairs being upended behind him. Even with his bum leg, he could move quick, and he was around the other side of the farmhouse, yelling out, "Don't you move again, you son of a bitch!"

The light jiggled and someone was crashing through the brush. He raised the shotgun and pulled the trigger. There was a loud *boom* that tore at his ears, a kick to his right shoulder, a flare of light, and a scream. Zach and Phil were behind him, Zach holding up the kerosene lamp. The three of them tore through the underbrush. A man lay on his back near the trunk of a pine tree, moaning, his pant legs torn from the shotgun pellets.

He went up to the man, kicked at his torn legs. Blood was oozing through the shredded dungarees, and the man jerked. "Who the hell are you? What are you doing here?"

From the yellow light of the lamp Zach held, he saw that the injured man was clean-shaven and young, wearing a brown jacket over a buttoned white shirt. He looked up, eyes brittle as glass, and said, "Screw you."

"Bring the lamp down here," he said, and Zach reached down. Hidden behind the lapel was a Confederate-flag pin. "I'll be damned," Phil whispered.

He stood up, shotgun firm in both hands, and in three sudden, hard, vicious jabs, brought the stock of the gun down against the man's throat, crushing it. The man spasmed, then was still.

Breathing hard, he passed the emptied shotgun with the bloodied stock over to Phil. "You were saying something about how tough I was?"

Phil took the shotgun, looked to the other man. "All right, then. Everything gets moved up. Zach, get the truck. Our man goes to Keene now. And take a good last look about this place. Me and you, we can't come back." "Won't miss it much," Zach said.

Phil looked down at the murdered man, then at him. "Sorry about what I said back there. You got a tough job ahead of you, sure enough."

Thinking of his family, such as it was, he answered, "We all do."

CHAPTER FOUR

Surprisingly — maybe because of the rain — the lobby of the Portsmouth Police Department was empty except for a desk sergeant, hands folded across his belly, eyes closed, head tilted back. The police station was in a brick Victorian at the corner of Daniel and Chapel streets, sharing its quarters with City Hall. The county jail was just around the corner on Penhallow Street.

Sam went up to the second floor, where his boss had his office. Most cities had a police chief, but Portsmouth was always a bit different, even in the colonial days, and had a city marshal instead.

Sam's desk was in a corner just outside of Hanson's office, facing a brick wall. There was a cluster of filing cabinets, another desk for the shift sergeant, and a third desk that belonged to the department's secretary, Linda Walton. The door to Hanson's office was open, and Sam went up to it, looked in. His boss waved him inside.

"Have a seat, Sam," the marshal said.

Harold Hanson was sixty-three years old, had been on the police force for nearly four decades. He'd seen the force grow and shed its horses and get Ford patrol cars and the very first radios and an increasing professionalism, trying to break the grip of the payoff pros who ran the bars and whorehouses at the harbor.

Oh, there were still juke joints and bawdy houses on the waterfront, but if they were discreet, and if nobody made too much of a fuss, they were ignored. As far as who was on the take nowadays, Sam didn't ask questions. He didn't care what was going on with the other members of the force, what shameful secrets they kept, for Sam had his own. But keeping quiet and staying away from whatever money was being passed around also meant that when he was a shift sergeant, he always had the night and weekend shifts. The price, he knew, of doing what he thought was right.

Hanson's pale face was pockmarked, he wore brown horn-rimmed glasses, and his usual uniform was a three- piece pinstriped suit. Tonight the coat was on a rack, and his vest was tight across his chest and belly. His pant legs were darkened with rain splashes, but his shoes were dry and freshly shined. On the wall were framed certificates and a few photos: Hanson with a series of mayors over the years—including the most recent, Sam's father-in-law — a couple of New Hampshire governors, a U.S. senator, and in a place of pride, the President himself, taken three years ago on a campaign swing through the state. And there was a photo of Hanson wearing the uniform of a colonel in the state's National Guard, where he was one of the top officers in the state, working for the adjutant general. In addition to being the city's lead cop, he had connections among the politicians in D.C. and in Concord, New Hampshire's capital.

Hanson sat in his leather chair, and Sam sat across from him in one of the two wooden captain's chairs. Hanson said, "I heard about the dead man over at the tracks by the Shanty. What do you know?"

"Not much," Sam said. "A hobo from the encampment spotted him and flagged down Frank Reardon, and then I was brought in."

"Cause of death?"

"Don't know," Sam replied. "The body's been picked up for transport to Dr. Saunders's office. I'll find out tomorrow."

"Not run down by a train?"

"No."

"Nothing else apparent, then. Gunshot wound, knife wound."

"No, nothing like that," Sam said.

Hanson leaned back in his chair, the wheels squeaking.

His face was impassive, and the lack of expression made Sam shiver a little.

Sam knew his promotion to inspector was due to political play among the police commission, his father-in- law, the mayor, and Hanson—other candidates were unacceptable, and Sam was a compromise—and he still wasn't sure if Hanson was on his side. Hanson was loyal to his fellow officers to a point, but it was known that Hanson was loyal to Hanson, first, second, and always.

"All right." Hanson leaned forward, picking up a fountain pen. "Any ID?"

"No papers, no wallet. Just a tattoo on his wrist, some numbers." In his mind's eye, Sam saw those numbers again: 9 1 12 8 3.

"Luggage? Valise? Anything in the area that might have belonged to him?"

Sam knew he was disappointing his boss but couldn't help it. "No."

A tight nod. "All right. What next?"

"Right now Frank Reardon and Leo Gray are conducting a canvass, and I expect their report later tonight. When we're through here, I'll type up my notes, give you a copy, send a telex to the state police. Tomorrow I'll check in with the medical examiner."

Another nod. "Good. We'll talk again tomorrow. And Sam? If it's just an untimely death, if there's nothing to indicate foul play, drop it."

Sam shifted in his seat. "But...it might take some time. Blood work from the ME, looking for witnesses, getting him identified—"

Hanson's lips pursed. "I meant what I said. Drop it. You've got enough on your plate with the car thefts, the amount of bad paper that's been passing lately in town. Not to mention the store break-ins, for which your father-in-law continues to ride my ass. So if that dead guy is just a dead guy, you drop it. Understand?"

"Yes. I got it."

"Good. Now here's something that just came up..." Hanson touched a slip of paper and grimaced. "I just got back from a state Party meeting in Concord. We've been directed to look for any evidence of an Underground Railroad station in town. There have been reports of people passing through the Canadian border who've been sheltered here in Portsmouth."

Sam made sure his hands stayed still in his lap. "Sorry... Underground Railroad? I know Portsmouth was a stop back in the Civil War, but now?"

Hanson dropped the paper, annoyed. "Yes, now. Dissidents, protestors, Communists, Republicans, all heading north to Canada so they don't get tossed into a labor camp, where they belong. So if you see anything suspicious, people who don't belong, word that there's human smuggling going on, check it out. Report it to me immediately. The Party is really pressing me on this."

Sam fought to keep his voice even. "I would think that checking in to an Underground Railroad station here would belong to the FBI. Or the Department of the Interior."

Hanson said, "Yeah, you would think. But they're stretched thin, and stuff like that is getting tossed to the local departments. And speaking of stuff being tossed our way, when you go home, I need you to make a delivery for the DOI. They have a prisoner over at the county jail, and he's due to head out on a train later tonight. Their Black

Maria broke down again, so I said we'd do them this favor."

"And nobody from the patrol division is available?" "Well, I understand two are performing a canvass on your behalf, which leaves two others, and there's a brawl being broken up on Hanover Street as we speak. So no, Sam, nobody's available."

"It can't wait?"

"No, it can't wait. And I want you to do it. Don't worry, it's not some hobo. A well-dressed fellow. I'm sure he won't piss in the backseat of your car. Get going so you can go home to that pretty wife of yours."

Sam got to his feet, feeling his face flush at being made into a delivery boy. As he turned toward the door, Hanson said, "Oh, one more thing," which Sam had expected. Nobody got to leave the city marshal's office without a "one more thing."

"Sir?"

Hanson leaned back in his chair, the wood and leather protesting. "The Party meeting tomorrow tonight. Make sure you attend, all right?"

"It's a waste of—"

His boss raised a hand. "I know you think it's a burden, not worth your efforts, but in these times, it's necessary for all of us to sacrifice a bit, to get along, to keep things on an even keel. So. To make myself very clear, Probationary Inspector Sam Miller: You will attend the Party meeting tomorrow night. Have I made my point?" Once upon a time there had been two political parties, the Republicans and the Democrats. But when Huey Long was elected back in '36... well, now there was pretty much one political party in the country.

"Sam?" Hanson pressed.

"Absolutely. But it's still a goddamn waste of time. Sir."

"It certainly is, but you'll be there. And I'll be thankful for it. And so will your father-in-law. Now get going." Sam went out. He slammed the door behind him.

CHAPTER FIVE

At his desk outside the marshal's office, Sam carefully slid three sheets of paper, separated by two sheets of carbon paper, into the Remington. Before he started to type, he allowed himself a quick shake, a quiver of nerves. The Underground Railroad in Portsmouth. Holy Christ. He shook his head and got to work.

At 1910 hours on 1 May 1943, INSPECTOR SAM MILLER was notified of a possible homicide victim located near the B&M railroad tracks west of the Fish Shanty parking lot off of Maplewood Avenue. MILLER arrived at the scene at 1924 hours and met with PATROLMAN REARDON and PATROLMAN GRAY, who pointed out the location of the body. Said body was discovered at approximately 1800 hours by LOUIS PURDUE, age 50, of Troy, NY., currently residing at an encampment off of North Mill Pond. PURDUE said he discovered the corpse while walking the tracks.

Sam paused in his typing. No point in saying what Lou Purdue was doing, for he was sure that in addition to retrieving lumps of coal, Lou was also checking out how strongly some of the B&M boxcar doors were locked, up at the collection of sidings just over on the other side of Maplewood Avenue, near the B&M station. Let the B&M cops handle it.

The body is that of a white male, approximately fifty to sixty-five years of age. There is no apparent sign of trauma. There is also no apparent cause of death. A preliminary search of the body revealed no possessions save for clothing and no identification. The tattoo 9112

83 was found on the man's wrist. Photographs of the scene were taken by photographer RALPH MORANCY, on contract to the Portsmouth Police Department. The body was placed into the custody of DR. WILLIAM SAUNDERS, Rockingham County Medical Examiner's Office, and was removed by attendants of the Woods funeral home.

A teletype with the dead man's description has been transmitted to N.H. state police headquarters in Concord.

Sam read and then reread the report after taking the sheets of paper from the typewriter. He signed each sheet and put one sheet in a folder for this case, gave another to the department's secretary. The third sheet he placed in Hanson's mailbox. He looked at a clock on the far wall, shook his head, and left to play errand boy before getting home to Sarah and Toby.

As his boss had promised, the prisoner was well dressed, a tall man with a fleshy face and wavy hair. The left leg of his fine trousers was torn open, exposing a bloody knee. His hands were cuffed in front of him and his eyes were unfocused, as if he couldn't comprehend what was happening to him. He kept silent as Sam bundled him into the rear seat of his Packard, ducking down from the continuing onslaught of heavy rain. The prisoner's paperwork was tucked inside Sam's coat, unread, since he had no interest in knowing why this guy had been arrested. All Sam cared about was getting this piece of crap work done as soon as possible.

Sam started up the Packard, and as he backed out into the street, the man said from the rear seat, "Are you FBI? Or Interior Department?"

"Neither." Sam switched on the wipers, wondering why it was his luck to be out tonight in such a nasty downpour. "Local cop being a taxi driver, that's all." "What's your name?"

"Miller."

"Mine's Lippman. Ever hear of me?"

"Nope."

"I've written some books, used to be a newspaper columnist down in New York...hell, even worked for President Wilson during the last war... now look where I am. Do you have any idea why I've been arrested?"

Sam braked at a streetlight. There was a small fire in a nearby alleyway in a metal drum. Three men in shabby clothes were clustered by the drum, holding their hands out over the flickering orange flames. He had a feeling that the men would be there all night, just trying to stay warm.

"No," Sam said. "I don't. Look, I'm just bringing you to the train station and—"

Lippman said, "Suspicion of income tax evasion. That's the catchall charge so they can hold you until something better comes along. But the real reason—the real reason is that I kept on writing against that damn man and his administration, even after being fired from my newspaper job. That's my story, friend. Arrested and sent away because of my opinion."

The light changed to green. Sam let up on the clutch and headed down Congress Street, to the local station of the Boston & Maine railroad. His eyes ached and his car now held a smell of old smoke and sweat. Lippman cleared his throat. "This has nothing to do with you, does it?"

"What's that?"

"My arrest. That's not a local charge, not even something your state police would care about. Look, you seem like a good man, Mr. Miller. I mean, this is a lot to ask, but... you didn't look happy, bringing me out of my cell. I'm sure you don't like being pushed around by the FBI, the Interior Department. So why not do something about it?"

"Like what?" Only a few stores were open on this main city street, their lights brave against the rain and lack of customers.

A nervous laugh from the prisoner. "Let me go. It's the proverbial dark and stormy night... .just help me out of the car, and I'll just disappear. I'll make my rendezvous up in Maine. I know it's asking a lot, Mr. Miller... but maybe I can rely on you. A simple thing, really. A prisoner escaping? Happens all the time, doesn't it? And why am I a prisoner? For what crime?"

Another red light. Even though there were no other cars or trucks out, Sam eased the Packard to a halt. A hell of a thing, to be arrested for an opinion. Sam remembered a time when that hadn't been a crime. And Lippman was right—it would be easy just to open up that rear door, have the guy tumble out, and let him take his chances...

Yeah. And then what?

"Sir?" came the voice. "Please. I... I don't think I could handle a labor camp. Not at my age. Please. I'm... I'm begging you to look into your heart, to help me out..."

The light changed. Sam made a turn onto Maplewood Avenue, past the Shanty, and one block later, he was in front of the stone and granite building of the B&M railroad station, just off Deer Street. There, parked in front as if it belonged, was a black Buick van with whitewall tires. No insignia or lettering on the side or doors. The Black Maria didn't need such markings. Everyone knew what it was and what it carried. The Buick's hood was open and someone was working on the engine, and standing nearby, in long trench coats and slouch hats, were two lean-looking men who looked up as Sam's Packard approached.

"Sorry," Sam told Lippman, tightening his hands on the steering wheel. "I can't do it." He got out and opened the rear door and helped his prisoner out.

Standing in the cold downpour, Lippman said hoarsely,

"I suppose it was my bad luck to be transported by a man with no heart or soul."

Sam said, "No. It was your bad luck to be transported by me."

He turned Lippman and his paperwork over to the Interior Department men and finally went home.

His home was a small light blue house on Grayson Street, which ran parallel to the Piscataqua River, separating this part of New Hampshire from Maine and eventually emptying into the Atlantic Ocean. He pulled his Packard into an open shed, dodging a Roadmaster bicycle lying on its side in the driveway, and walked out in the rain, feeling sour over his completed errand. The tiny rear yard ran down to a low hedge; beyond the hedge was the river, a tidal river: Four times a day, the rear yard overlooked a smelly mudflat.

He looked at the house again, felt disappointment in his mouth. To be his age and have one's own home, in this time and place, was a miracle. He remembered how, a couple of years after getting married, when Sarah was pregnant with Toby, he had promised to get the three of them out of a downtown apartment that had plumbing that knocked and leaked, and rats and roaches scurrying around, even during the day. He had done everything possible, gone to the banks, measured up his savings, went without beer for months... but when the time came, he was short five hundred dollars.

Don't ask how he knew, but his father-in-law, Lawrence Young, the mayor of Portsmouth and the owner of the city's biggest furniture store, that greasy bastard knew what was going on and had offered a loan. That's all—a loan that could be paid back by Sam working weekends at the store, under Lawrence's supervision, of course, and under the bastard's eye and thumb.

He didn't do it. Couldn't do it. He had found another way — a way that still disturbed his sleep, a way that made sure coming to his home at night gave him little joy, for the money he had finally gotten for the down payment had been dirty money.

Up onto the sagging porch, past the wooden box for their weekly milk deliveries, and after unlocking the front door, he went in. Sam remembered a time when doors were always unlocked, but that was before thousands of hoboes had taken to the rails.

A small brunette woman was curled up on a small couch, reading the daily *Portsmouth Herald*. All the local news in ten pages for a nickel, and not much news at that. Like the photographer Ralph Morancy had noted, the news had to be the right news, or else the federal pulp-paper ration would be cut back. Sarah looked up and studied him for a moment. Then she said, "You're late. And sopping wet, Sam Miller."

"And you're beautiful, Sarah Miller," he said, taking off his coat and hat, hanging them both in the vestibule. He unbuckled his shoulder holster and slid the .38 Smith & Wesson Police Special revolver on the top shelf, away from curious hands.

The radio was on, tuned to Sarah's favorite station, WHDH out of Boston, playing ballroom dance music. The couch, two armchairs, the Westinghouse radio, a crowded bookshelf, and a rolltop desk filled most of the room.

Sarah got up from the couch and came to him, a blue lace apron tied around her tan dress and slim waist. Her dark hair was cut in the over-the-eye look of Veronica Lake. Sarah one time said she thought she looked like the Hollywood actress, and in certain lights, her head tilted a certain way, Sam would agree. He had met her in high school, the oldest story in romance magazines and movie serials, she the head cheerleader, he the star quarterback.

Now he was a cop and she was still at school, a secretary for the school superintendent, and they were among the lucky ones in town, to have reasonably safe jobs.

A quick dry kiss on the lips and she asked, "Was it what they said when they called you? A dead man by the tracks?"

"Yeah," Sam said, thinking of what he had to say in the next few moments, wondering how that pretty face in front of him would respond to the news. "One dead man. No ID. A real mystery."

"How did he die?" she asked.

"Don't know yet," he replied absently, still working through what had to be done. "Doc Saunders will probably let me know tomorrow."

Sarah said, "Sounds interesting. And Sam, I just saw in the paper, Montgomery Ward's has a sale on, men's dress shirts for a dollar forty-four apiece. Do you want me to pick you up a couple next time I'm downtown? With your promotion, you've got to have more than just two."

"Yeah, I guess... Look, we've got to talk."

He took her hand and led her back to the couch. He sat his surprised wife down and looked around, then turned up the radio's volume. The thumping joy of some big- band orchestra grew louder, the trumpet piercing. Harry James, playing "I've Heard that Song Before." He leaned over to her and said, "It has to stop, Sarah. Now."

Her eyes widened. "What has to stop?"

His chest was tight, so tight it hurt. "The Underground Railroad. It has to stop now. Tonight. This instant. And we've got to empty out the basement of any evidence."

His hand was still in hers, and her fingers felt cold. "What's wrong? Who found out?"

"Damned if I know how, but the Party knows there's a station operating here in the city. Marshal Hanson asked me to keep an eye open for any evidence. Pretty damn ironic, right?"

"Sam, this could be a good thing. You could pretend that you couldn't find anything, the heat would be off, and—"

"No. Not going to happen, Sarah. It's one thing to look the other way when you and your friends set the station up in our basement. But I can't jeopardize my job, or you and Toby, by going along with a cover-up. It's not going to happen. Promise me the station shuts down. Tonight." She withdrew her hand gently. "I promise we'll talk about it. All right? That's all I can do right now." Her cheeks were flushed.

"Sarah, please. It's been a hell of a long day."

She stood and reached over to snap the radio off. "I'm sorry to say, but your day's not over yet."

In the silence that followed, he didn't want to argue any more about the Underground Railroad. Sam didn't know how much the Party suspected, but he did know the Party had amazing wiretapping abilities when they had the desire, and lately, they'd had plenty of desire. "How's that?" He tried to keep his voice even.

"Your ham loaf and potatoes are ready, but you need to talk to Toby first."

"Don't tell me we've got another call from his principal."

"No, nothing like that. He just wants you to say good night to him. And Sam—he wants to know if he can get rid of the rubber sheet. He's terribly upset about wetting the bed last week."

"All right. I'll talk to him."

"And there's Walter, Sam—"

"Damn," he said. "What now?"

She rolled her eyes in the direction of the ceiling. "Said his sink is clogged. Wants to know if you can fix it before you go to bed."

"A clogged sink? Again? Can't the man fix a damn clogged sink?"

"He used to be a science professor at Harvard. How smart can he be?"

"I don't know. He's living with us because you're friends, so you tell me."

"Please," she said. "Can we not get into that now? He's paying us rent, we need the money, and he needs his sink unclogged. Can we just leave it at that, Sam?"

He recalled what he had said to the snide young cop about knowing things. "Yeah, I guess so. Okay, Sarah— Toby first, dinner second, and Walter third."

Her mood changed suddenly; Sarah smiled at him, a welcome sight after their talk about the Railroad. "Care to think of a fourth, Inspector Miller?"

"I certainly do, Mrs. Miller, and look forward to it."

She slapped his rump and pushed him away. "Only if you get your boy to sleep and play plumber. So get to it. And Sam... we'll talk about the other thing later. Promise."

He went through the kitchen and past a new Frigidaire refrigerator, an anniversary gift from his father-in-law. He hated receiving something so extravagant from a man he despised, but Sarah loved getting rid of the icebox and the never-ending task of emptying the floor drain pan, so that had been that.

He eased open the door to his son's room. The night-light illuminated the narrow bed and a bookcase that held a cluster of books and toy trucks, one, he always noted with a smile, a police cruiser with Portsmouth markings. On the other side of the bookcase were a Gilbert chemistry set and a fossil collection.

From the ceiling, model aircraft hung from black thread and thumbtacks pushed into the plaster: Great War aircraft like a Sopwith Camel and a Fokker triplane, and a German zeppelin and U.S. Navy blimp. All made from balsa wood and tissue paper, each one carefully pieced together with his boy on lazy Sunday afternoons.

He sat on the corner of the bed and touched Toby's silky brown hair with his hand. His boy stared up at him sleepily.

"Dad."

"Hey, kiddo. Why aren't you sleeping?"

Toby yawned. "I wanna make sure you were home. That you were okay. That's why."

"Well, I'm back. And I'm okay."

"Why did you have to leave?"

"There was a case I had to investigate."

"What kind of case?" Toby rolled on the mattress, making a rustling noise from the rubber sheet underneath the cotton one. Just last week the boy had awakened screaming from a nightmare, having wet the bed.

"A... dead man was found. I had to check it out." "Was it a murder?"

"I don't know yet."

"Oh..."

"Toby, are you scared of something?"

"I dunno. I worry sometimes about bad men. Spies, killers. Bad men hurting you. Hurting Mom. Stupid, huh?"

"Not stupid," Sam said firmly. "But I promise you: No bad men are going to hurt you. Or Mom. Or me. Ever."

"You sure?"

"Yes. I promise."

"Dad... I don't like this rubber sheet. It's for babies."

Sam repressed a sigh. "Just a little while longer, pal."

His boy turned his head. "Dad, you're sure about that? That there are no spies?"

"There's no spies," Sam said firmly. "We're safe, pal, you and your mom and me."

How many fathers out there had had the same talk with their sons hours before being seized, arrested, their families broken up, their children sent to state homes? Sam thought, *Oh, there are so many bad men out there, how in God's name can I protect you from all of them?*

Sam cleared his throat. "Now make us both happy and go to sleep, okay? And no more nightmares."

" 'Kay, Dad."

"And keep doing good in school, okay? No more notes from your teachers, all right?"

"I'll try, Dad," Toby murmured, already falling asleep. Sam kissed the soft brown hair, got up, and went to the door. A small voice said, "Dad? Can I listen to my crystal set for a while?"

The crystal radio set, made as a project in the Cub Scouts. Let him listen to music or a western or a mystery... or no, his bright little boy would probably listen to the news of the bad men butchering little boys in Manchuria and China and Indochina and Russia and Finland and Burma and—

Sam felt adrift. What he really wanted to do was talk to his son, to tell him there was a time when the radio wasn't full of news about wars overseas, that the President was someone to admire, that people had work and unemployment wasn't approaching 40 percent. When newsprint wasn't a rationed government resource. And that even though the country had managed to stay out of the bloody wars in the Pacific and in Europe, it now

37

seemed to be endlessly at war with itself, with arrests and detentions and labor camps, all orchestrated by a man who wasn't fit to inhabit the house once lived in by Abe Lincoln and Teddy Roosevelt and Woodrow Wilson.

But for tonight..."No," he answered. "I don't want you listening to your radio. You go to sleep now, okay?"

" 'Kay, Dad."

Sam closed the door behind him, softly.

CHAPTER SIX

The ham loaf had dried out, and the potatoes were cold, but he ate them greedily as Sarah sat with him and asked him about the body. He grunted in all the right places, trying to hurry things along so he could go to the upstairs apartment and fix the sink and get this long day and long night behind him. Once during dinner the phone rang— one long ring and three short rings—and they both ignored it. Their ring on this local party line was two long and two short; the other ring belonged to the Connors down the way.

He pushed his chair back, kissed her cheek, and said, "Back in a bit, girl. Boy's asleep and—"

She started picking up the dishes. "Get along, Inspector. You still have work to do, and that boy had better still be asleep if you want to get lucky."

"Lucky is the day you said yes to me," he said, making it a point to look down the front of her dress when she bent to reach for his plate.

Another fleeting smile, and she moved her hand in a fluttering motion as if to shoo him away from leering. "You know what, Inspector? You are so right. Now make me proud and get to work."

"Hope it's not all work," he retorted, but she was already at the sink, running the hot water. It was if she was now ignoring him. That was Sarah. Sometimes bubbling with childish enthusiasm, sometimes quiet, and now silent, thinking of who knew what. Her change of mood was as though a window had been opened, letting in a cold draft, and he knew it had to be about the Underground Railroad. He couldn't help himself, but he thought of Donna back at the Shanty, her eager smile and sweet body, and he remembered just... how simple Donna was. No, that wasn't the right word. Donna was uncomplicated. That's all. Just uncomplicated. Sarah... now, she was complicated.

So why hadn't he dated Donna back in school?

Forget it, he decided. That was then, this is now.

He went downstairs to the dirt-floor cellar, past the coal furnace and outside bulkhead, where he grabbed a canvas bag of tools from his workbench. In one corner, near the coal furnace, hung an old sheet. He pulled the sheet back. A cot was pushed up against the stone foundation. There was a pillow at one end and a green wool blanket folded at the other. He looked at the cot and thought, *Well, that's it for charity work*. That was their private joke about this Underground Railroad station. But it was one thing to do what you could, when trouble was down in D.C. or Baton Rouge. It was another thing when trouble was on your front doorstep, especially delivered by your boss. What did Sam know about the Underground Railroad here in Portsmouth?

A hell of a lot, he thought. A hell of a lot.

Bag of tools in hand, he climbed upstairs, went through the living room and then outside. The rain had finally stopped. He went around the rear of the house, where an open stairway led up to the second floor. Up the creaking stairs he went, and at the top, he knocked on the door. He had to knock twice more before it opened.

"Inspector Miller!" boomed the familiar voice. "So nice of you to make it here." The door swung open.

The apartment was even tinier than the rooms downstairs and really shouldn't have been an apartment at all, but he and Sarah needed the extra income after promised pay raises for both of them fell through last year. Through a friend of Sarah's at the school department—who was once a student of Walter's—Walter Tucker had come into their lives. Blacklisted from a science-teaching position at Harvard University for refusing to sign a loyalty oath, Walter was in his late forties, heavyset, almost entirely bald. His fat fingers always clasped a stubby cigar. Tonight his eyes, behind horn-rimmed glasses, were filmy, and he was wearing worn slippers and a frayed red plaid bathrobe.

The room had cracked yellow linoleum and had been turned into a kitchen of sorts, with a scarred wooden table and three unmatched chairs. There was a wooden icebox in the corner and a hot plate on a small counter. Off to the right was a bathroom with a toilet and the offending sink. Open doorways led to two other rooms: a bedroom with an unmade bed and an office that had a desk made of scrap lumber that bore a large typewriter. Everywhere in the apartment were books and pulp magazines and copies of *Scientific American* and *Collier's*.

A radio next to the hot plate was playing swing music, Benny Goodman, it sounded like. Sam went into the bathroom and sighed at the gray water in the sink. "What now, Walter? What did you do?"

"Nothing, my dear boy. Just preparing my evening meal. Nothing out of the ordinary, but there you go. The sink overflowed, and I wanted to make sure it was repaired before it started leaking on your head."

"Thanks," Sam muttered. "Do you have a coffee cup or something I could borrow?"

"Absolutely." Walter waddled off. He came back with a thick white coffee mug with a broken handle, and Sam started bailing the water out of the clogged sink. As he worked, Walter leaned against the doorjamb and lit a cigar. "What news of the Portsmouth Police Department?"

"Had a body out on the railroad tracks tonight. By Maplewood Avenue."

"A suicide?"

"Don't know right now."

"How fascinating. Maybe you've got a real murder on your hands, Sam."

Sam paused, the mug slimy in his hand. "What are you doing, Walter? Research for a detective story?"

Walter studied his cigar. "No, son. Detective stories are a tad too realistic for me. You know what I write. Science fiction and fantasy. That's where my degraded tastes have led me. Stories about rockets and robots. Evil wizards."

"Speaking of which, rent's due on the fifteenth. Just so there's no misunderstanding."

The older man grinned. "No misunderstanding. I received a check from Street and Smith yesterday and expect another one shortly. The rent will be paid in full and on time."

"Best news I've gotten today." The sink was empty. He squatted down and said, "Can you get me a saucepan or something?"

"Certainly."

Minutes later, Sam undid the U-joint with a wrench, and brown water rushed into the pan. He reached in with his fingers and winced in disgust as he pulled out the clog, greasy lumps of potato peelings. He dropped them in the saucepan, put the piping back into place, and worked the wrench, then stood up.

"Don't peel your potatoes in the sink, please, Walter. Do it someplace else, okay? It just clogs the sink. You did the same thing last month."

"My thanks, Inspector, my warmest thanks."

"You're welcome, Walter." Sam dropped his tools into his bag, saw a worn leather valise on the floor nearby. He never saw Walter without the leather valise, in which the former professor carried letters, manuscripts, and God knew what else. On the table was a stack of magazines with names like *Thrilling Wonder Stories* and *Amazing Stories* and *Astounding Stories*. He picked up *Astounding Stories*, studied a garish spaceship, fire spewing from its nozzles. There were three names on the cover, and he was startled to see one he recognized: Walter Tucker. He set the pulp magazine down. "How's the writing gig going?"

"It's a living of sorts. I'm sure the overpaid and quite cowed professors at Harvard would turn down their noses at what I do, but it can be a lot of fun, frankly. You have to tell a story quickly and to the point. Actually, I've learned an extraordinary amount the past few years. About astronomy, biology, atomic theory, and archaeology. Among other things. Anyway, once you've been blackballed, that's it. Even industries that need workers with a scientific background won't touch me. And the secret satisfaction of science fiction and fantasy is that you can also write about forbidden topics without worrying about censors and critics with handguns and nightsticks."

Sam was silent, thinking about how tired he was.

"If you write a story about a suppressed group of knights who are working hard to overthrow a king from a swampland who has usurped the throne from the rightful king, who was murdered before his time, and how this swamp king has put his lackeys into places of power around the kingdom... and how they fight to return the kingdom to the old and free ways... then it's just a fantasy. A tale that no overseer or censor will worry about... a tale that won't get the author into trouble."

"Or into a labor camp."

"Exactly," Walter agreed, dropping the magazine back on the table. "Speaking of labor camps, how's your brother?"

The second mention of Tony in one evening. Must be a record. "Got a postcard from him last month. Seems to be doing well."

"Glad to hear it. And I'm glad he has a brother who's handy with tools."

"I've got to get going. Remember, no potato peels in the sink."

"Duly noted. No peels in the sink. Thanks again, Inspector."

"You're welcome. And make sure that you—"

"Yes, yes, I know. The rent on the fifteenth."

Outside, the night air was damp and chilly. The lights from the shipyard reflected yellow and white against the low clouds, and he could now make out the faint sounds of workmen putting together the latest class of navy submarines. He stood there, seeing a place that had built ships for a century and a half, a place his father had worked after his service in World War I and a place his brother, Tony, had worked until... Sam again felt that flush of embarrassment of a law officer having a brother who had been arrested three years ago and charged with illegally trying to unionize the shipyard workers. A quick star-chamber-type trial, and now Tony was serving a sentence at a federal labor camp near Fort Drum, New York. Besides the shame and concern for his older brother, there was also anger, for he was certain his brother's arrest had very nearly sidetracked his promotion to inspector.

The crack of a gunshot down the street startled him, the hollow *boom* echoing and re-echoing about the frame houses. He didn't move. Another example of what was called by his fellow cops "a shot in the dark." Like the gunshot at the railroad tracks, these firearm discharges— scores being settled, somebody being robbed, an argument ending—were ignored unless they were officially reported. Not a way for a good cop to respond, but he had no choice. Besides, he had his hands more than full with a corpse, the pile of paperwork on his desk, and his convict brother.

One could pick one's friends, but one could never pick one's relatives. Or in-laws. And both were giving him a headache.

At the bottom of the steps, he tripped over a small shape. He turned on the back porch light and stooped to see what had tripped him.

By the steps were three rocks piled on top of one another.

Three rocks.

He was positive they hadn't been there when he had gone up to Walter's apartment.

He bent down, picked up the rocks, then tossed each as hard as he could out into the darkness. Two fell within the yard, and he had a moment of satisfaction as the third splashed into the Piscataqua River.

The radio was off, as were most of the lights, and he moved through the silent living room and into the kitchen and to their bedroom. The only light came from the bedside radio, which was on. Sarah liked to fall asleep to the sound of the radio, music or news or a detective tale. He, on the other hand, couldn't fall asleep if the radiator was ticking.

Sarah had laid his pajamas out on his side of the bed. He changed clothes and slid in under the sheets. Sarah murmured and he leaned over and pressed his lips against her neck. "Sony," she murmured. "I know you had something in mind tonight... I just couldn't stay awake..."

"Don't worry, dear, I'll take a rain check—if you offer one."

She sighed, took his hand, and placed it on her breasts, the soft lace of the nightgown pressing against his palm. In the darkness, he smiled. Sarah could stretch a food budget or a utility budget, but she never skimped on nighties and lingerie. She called them her tools for keeping Sam in place, and he had to admit they did a very good job of at least keeping him in bed.

"Rain check offered, then," she murmured. "Just make sure you use it and don't lose it."

He moved up against her, his hand on the softness of her flesh and the delicacy of the lace. "Rain check accepted, and it won't be lost. Not ever. Good day at the school department?"

"Not bad. Getting ready for another round of budget cuts."

"Anything I should know about?"

He felt her tense under his touch. "The usual."

"Sarah..."

"I've been careful, honest. Nothing going on just right now, though we've heard rumors of a refugee roundup sometime soon. Have you heard anything?"

"No. But watch yourself. Leaflets stuck under windshield wipers, registering new voters, dropping off pamphlets at the post office at night. That's one thing for you and your fellow revolutionaries."

He waited for a reply and heard nothing but cold silence from her and soft music from the radio. He gave her a squeeze and said, his voice a low whisper, "But Sarah... being a stop on the Railroad, that's another. We've got to close it down. Now. Besides the marshal dropping that big-ass hint to me earlier, we've got Long's Legionnaires in town, watching things. I ran into two of them tonight, at the Fish Shanty. Two losers and they made everyone in the restaurant freeze in their seats, scared out of their wits."

Unexpectedly, she turned her head and kissed him, hard. "Sam... I don't know what I can do. There's one in the pipeline coming to Portsmouth in the next couple of days. I just got word this afternoon."

"Can you delay it?"

"I don't know. I can try, but sometimes it's hard letting the right people know."

"You've done enough already. Time for somebody else to take up the burden. We can't take the chance, Sarah. We've got to close it down."

She sighed. "Sam, I said I'd try. It's not like I can make a phone call and stop it cold. And look, we're just a bunch of schoolteachers. And secretaries. That's all."

"There's a whole bunch of schoolteachers from Hyde Park in New York, breaking rocks in the Utah desert because they were suspected of harboring FDR's widow, Eleanor. Your pretty hands and face won't last long in the desert." He heard the cruelty in his voice and winced. "Look, Sarah, I worry about you. We need to think of Toby."

She moved some, and he thought she was rolling over in anger, but she surprised him again by raising up her face and giving him another, deeper kiss. "All right, Sam, I'll be careful. I'll try to stop the visit here. You be careful, too, Inspector."

"I'm always careful."

"If you're right about what the marshal said and those damn Legionnaires being in the area, then I don't know. Even the careful ones can get into trouble."

Sam lay there, blankets and sheets pulled up to his chest, as his wife's breathing slowed. The radio was on his side of the bed, the shallow glow of light from the dial reassuring. He could reach over and shut it off, but instead, he listened. It was the top of the hour, and time for the news. He closed his eyes, started to feel himself doze away, while the headlines droned on through the static.

"... bombing raids upon Berlin by a number of long-range Ilyushin bombers took place tonight. Officials reported that no military targets were struck but that a number of homes and hospitals were destroyed and scores of civilians were killed.

"On the Russian front, house-to-house fighting continued in the city of Stalingrad, while Russian armored units have reportedly engaged German panzer groups on the outskirts of Kharkov.

"In London, Prime Minister Mosley met again with German Foreign Minister von Ribbentrop. The talks were conducted to review terms of the armistice agreement signed between Great Britain and Germany two years ago. One of the main areas of disagreement, according to Washington diplomatic sources, is the number of German troops allowed to be based in Great Britain and some of her overseas possessions.

"In Montreal, a surprise visit from a trade delegation from the Soviet Union raised suggestions in some quarters that the government of Canada may be seeking closer ties to its neighbor to the west.

"Closer to home, President Huey Long signed a bill today ensuring that all Americans receiving federal assistance of any type sign a loyalty oath to the government, guaranteeing, as the President said, that patriotism will continue to thrive during his second term. The bill, called the Patriot Enhancement Act, will be enacted into law immediately. A violation of the loyalty oath will mean an automatic prison term.

"On Capitol Hill, Treasury Secretary Henry Morgenthau, fresh from his attendance at a meeting of the World Jewish Congress, was unsuccessful in his attempts to convince Congress to increase the number of Jewish refugees allowed into the United States this year.

"Also from Washington, unemployment figures released from the Department of Labor indicate that more Americans are working today than at any time before and that—"

Sam reached out and switched off the radio. News of the world. Mostly lies, half-truths, and exaggerations. Everyone knew that the unemployment numbers were cooked. Every month more and more Americans were supposedly working over a decade after the stock market crash. But he saw with his own eyes what was true, from the hobo encampments by the railroad tracks, to the rush of unemployed men at the shipyard gates when a rumor spread that five pipefitters had been killed in an accident, to the overcrowded tenements in town.

That was the truth. That desperate numbers of people were still without jobs, without relief, without hope. And nothing over the radio would change what he knew. He rolled over, tried to relax, but two thoughts kept him awake.

The thought of three stones piled up on his rear porch.

A series of blurry numerals, tattooed into a dead man's wrist.

Both mysteries. Despite his job, he hated mysteries.

INTERLUDE II

Now he was back in the shadowy streets of old Portsmouth, where there were lots of homes from the 1700s, with narrow clapboards, tiny windows, and sagging roofs. He kept to the alleyways and crooked lanes, ducking into a doorway each time he saw an approaching headlight. When he got where he had to be, he crouched beneath a rhododendron bush, waited some more. He thought about these old homes, about the extraordinary men who had come from this place, had gone out to the world and made a difference. Did they feel then what he felt now? The history books claimed they were full of courage and revolutionary spirit. But he didn't feel particularly full of anything; he was just cold and jumpy, knowing that behind every headlight could be a car full of Interior Department men or Long's Legionnaires.

Across the street, the door of an old house opened and a man stepped out, silhouetted by the light. The man looked around, bent over, put two empty milk bottles on the stoop, then went back inside.

In the darkness beneath the bush, he smiled. All clear. One bottle or three, and he would have left. But two was the sign. He crossed the street, through an open gate to a picket fence, then to a cellar door. He opened the door and went down the wooden steps. The cellar was small, with a dirt floor, an exposed rock foundation, and three wooden chairs set about a wooden table. There were two men in the chairs, only one of whom he recognized, and that was a problem.

The man on the left had a thick mustache and swollen hands, scarred with old burn tissue. The owner of the house, Curt Monroe. He looked to him and said, "Curt."

"Boy, I'm glad to see you, pal," the scarred man said.

He said, "You tell me who this other guy is, Curt, or I'm out of here."

The other man had thinning hair and a prominent Adam's apple. Curt said, "This is Vince. He's all right." He thought about that. Then he took the spare chair and sat down. "How's he all right?"

Vince said, "Look, I'm—"

He stared at the second man. "I don't remember asking you a goddamn thing."

Vince shut up. Curt tapped his fingers on the table. "I used to date Vince's sister back when I was working, before my hands got burnt. I know him, he's okay, and he can get what we need."

Now he looked to Vince. "Where?"

"Huh?"

He had to struggle to keep his temper under control. "We need something particular. Something that's hard to get nowadays, with the latest confiscation laws for firearms. So. Where the hell are you getting it from?"

"A guy up the street from my sister. He's got a ready supply. I already paid him with Curt's money. You just tell me where you want it."

He thought about that and said, "I want it delivered to Curt."

Vince was confused. "I...that wasn't the deal. The deal was, I get paid half for making the buy and the other half for delivering it where you want it."

"Fine. And I want it delivered here, to Curt."

"But—"

He stared right at him. "Bud, last time I'm going to say this. I know Curt. I worked with him back when we were both employed. I was one of the first guys to get to him when his hands got burnt. So me and him, we got a history. You, I don't know shit about you. Curt's vouched for you, but I'm a suspicious bastard, you know? Last time I trusted somebody I didn't personally vouch for, I got my ass arrested. So the deal's changed. All right? You deliver it here. You get paid. And then you forget this all happened. Got it?"

Vince looked to Curt, and Curt shrugged, and then Vince got up and left, going up the wooden steps, his feet thumping hard. Curt said, "Pal, you're even a bigger prick since you've gotten out."

"All that government attention will do it to you," he said. "Be back in a sec. Don't leave."

"What?" Curt asked, but by then he was at the cellar door, swinging it open. There was movement out on the street, and he followed Vince in the shadows as he strode away, hands deep in his pockets, shoulders hunched forward, moving fast. *Idiot,* he thought, trailing him with no difficulty at all. *Damn fool isn't even checking who might be behind him.*

Vince walked four blocks, then stopped at a corner. This part of town was more commercial, with two bars and a corner grocery and an abandoned bank building, the former Portsmouth Savings & Trust, one of many abandoned banks across the country. He stood in a doorway, watching. Vince took a cigarette out, stuck it between his lips. It took three tries to light it up. *Nervous twit*, he thought, and then a sedan came down the street and stopped.

Vince tossed the cigarette into the gutter and got into the rear of the sedan. The vehicle quickly drove off. It was too dark to see the license plate or who was inside the car, a model he didn't recognize, knowing only it was a pricey set of wheels.

He stayed for a few moments, looking at the now empty street corner. He started walking back to Curt's place, thinking of another chore that had to be done later the next day.

Revolutions were so damn tricky.

CHAPTER SEVEN

The dingy lobby of the Portsmouth Police Department was crowded the next morning with poorly dressed men and women checking on family members or friends picked up the previous night for the typical offenses in a hard-drinking and hard-living port city. Upstairs at his desk, Sam found a note propped on his typewriter: *Sam. See me soonest. H.* There was also a single sheet of brown paper with a penciled handwritten note:

TO: Inspector Sam Miller

FROM: Patrolman Frank Reardon, Badge Number 43

A canvas of a 2 block area surounding the dead man discovered on May 1 determined that no witnesses could be produced that had any now ledge of the dead man, his identity, or any other clues to facilitat your investigation.

There was a scrawled signature, also in pencil, on the bottom of the sheet. Sam shook his head at the memo's misspellings. He was sure Frank and his young partner had spent ten minutes walking around in the rain before coming back to the warm station and spending an hour on this report. Sam put the useless report down, looked again at the note.

Sam. See me soonest. H.

H being Harold Hanson. Something about last night had gotten Hanson's attention—what was one dead guy, even if it was a possible homicide? He looked over to Hanson's secretary, a woman whose gray hair was always tied at the back of her head in a severe bun, and who wore vibrantly floral dresses no matter the season. He called out, "Mrs. Walton? Is he in?"

Linda Walton looked up from her typing, eyeing him over her black-rimmed reading glasses. She had been working for the city for decades; nobody knew her husband's name, and the jokes were that she actually ran the department, a joke nobody had the balls to mention in her presence. She was also responsible for religiously maintaining a leather-bound book known as The Log, a record of where every senior police officer was day or night, week or weekend. With the city in a continuous budget struggle, The Log also made sure the city wasn't cheated on its meager salaries.

"Yes," she said, looking down at her telephone and its display of lights. "But he's on the phone and— Oh, he's off now."

He lifted the note as though it was a hall pass and she were a high school geometry teacher. "He says he needs to see me."

"Then go see him already." She went back to her typing. He got to his feet, not liking the way she talked and knowing he would do nothing about it. Cops who irritated Mrs. Walton often found their overtime hours mysteriously went away at a time when scraping for overtime meant the difference between soup or ground round for dinner. He went past her, detecting a scent of lilac, and after a brief knock on the door, went in.

Hanson looked up from his desk, and if it weren't for his clean shirt, he would look like he'd spent the night there. He told Sam, "This won't take long. Have a seat."

Sam sat, and Hanson said, "I take it you made the prisoner transfer successfully last night?"

He thought about that poor man pleading to be let free and how he had delivered him as ordered. "Yes, it was successful. And I don't want to ever do it again."

"Sorry, Sam. Can't promise you that."

He kept his mouth shut, and his boss said, "Did Frank and Leo find anything concerning your dead John Doe?"

"Not a thing."

"You're on your way to see the medical examiner?"

"In just a bit," Sam said.

"Good. Let me know what you find out. And remember what I said last night. If this guy died from hunger or cheap booze, leave it be. Now. I need to ask you something else. You were at the Fish Shanty last night, am I right?"

"Yes, I was."

Hanson picked up a sheet of paper, and Sam felt uneasy, as if a tax assessor were about to double his property tax bill. "An interesting coincidence, then, since about the same time you were at the Fish Shanty, two fine members of Long's Legionnaires said they exited the restaurant and found two tires on their car slit. I suppose you have nothing to tell me about this."

"That's right, sir. I don't have anything to tell you."

"Fine." Hanson crumpled up the paper, tossing it in his wastebasket. "Goddamn Southerners forgot who kicked their ass back in '65. Look, knock it off, all right? So far, we're doing all right here. We don't want another South Boston incident. Understood?"

Sam had heard a few rumors about South Boston and saw his opening. "What South Boston incident?"

Hanson hesitated, as if judging whether he could trust Sam with the information. Then he said, "Some of Long's Legionnaires were in South Boston two months ago, trying to instill a little freelance Party discipline. Fighting broke out, got escalated, and before you know it, you had barricades in South Boston with a couple of squads of Legionnaires on one side, and some Southie Irish cops on the other, shooting at each other. Ended up with three dead, scores injured, and one police precinct burned down. Only by the best of luck did the mayor avoid having martial law declared and National Guard platoons sent in. And what I just told you is confidential."

"I understand."

"I hope you do. I also hope you didn't forget that other matter from last night. About the Underground Railroad."

Sam wondered what he could say, for he was out on a very long limb, and his boss was holding a very sharp saw.

"Suppose I found out there had been a station? But that the station had stopped operating... was no longer sending criminals north? What then?"

Sam's heart was racing at the gamble he had just taken. From the other side of the closed door, Mrs. Walton kept on slamming at her typewriter keys. Hanson lowered his head and said, "Officially, I want you to prepare a report—in your spare time, of course—on what you learned about the station. Unofficially, I'd be very glad to hear there's no longer any illegal activity attracting the attention of the Party."

Hanson's tone changed. "All right, that's enough for now. Let me know if you find anything out about that dead man, and remember that Party meeting tonight."

"Yes, sir. Party meeting tonight."

Hanson picked up a fountain pen. "You got anything else for me?"

"Just one thing, if I may."

"Go ahead."

"I heard a... a rumor, actually, that there might be a crackdown coming down on the refugees. That we might be used to clear them out and turn them over to the Department of the Interior."

"Who told you that?"

Sam thought of Sarah and fought to keep his voice steady. "Nobody... well, nobody of importance, sir."

"I see," Hanson said, writing something down. "Well, I won't press you for your source. But I'll tell you I don't know anything about a crackdown, and you know how your father-in-law and I feel about it, that being one of the few things we agree on. It's the federal government's mess. Not ours. And speaking of your father-in-law, go see him right after you get out of the building. The honorable Lawrence Young is being a pain in the ass and requires an immediate visit from you."

"But the case—"

"The man's dead right now, he'll still be dead an hour from now, but your father-in-law will still be a poisonous bastard today and tomorrow and for some time to come. So go see him and solve something, and get him off our collective asses. And Sam—after tonight's meeting, I want you to plan to become more active in the Party. It would be a great help to the department and to me personally if we knew what was going on with the mayor and his allies. Just... information, that's all. There are factions, groups within the Party, jockeying for funds and influence, and any information you could provide about the mayor would be very helpful to me and my friends. Do you understand?"

Sure, Sam thought with cold disgust. Be more active in the Party and be a rat as well.

"Yes, I do," he said. "I don't know, but I promise I'll think about it."

"Good. Now get out. You've got a full day ahead of you."

As he left, Sam noticed the smile on Mrs. Walton's face. She had no doubt listened to every word.

CHAPTER EIGHT

Outside, the sky was gloomy, threatening more rain. Sam walked up Congress Street, where he passed a man setting up a table on the sidewalk with a rough wooden sign that said homemade toys for sale. He didn't look long at the man—who had two well-dressed little girls in blue dresses and cloth coats with him, sitting on wooden milk crates—for guys like that came and went like the seasons, selling apples in the fall, gadgets and toys during the spring and summer, and—

"Hey, Sam," came a voice. "Sam Miller."

He stopped and looked back. The toy peddler had on a coat that was a size too small, a battered fedora, and his sunken face was unshaved. Sam stepped closer and, with a flush of embarrassment, said, "Brett. Brett O'Halloran. Sorry, I wasn't paying attention."

Brett smiled shyly. "That's okay, Sam. I understand." Sam looked to the table and picked up one of the toys, a wooden submarine. Brett told him, "I get scrap wood from here and there, carve it at night, then paint it. Not a bad piece of work, huh?"

"No, Brett, not a bad piece of work at all." He balanced the submarine in his hand, not wanting to look at Brett. He had been an officer in the fire department until last year, when someone found a pile of magazines and newspapers in the bottom of his locker at the fire station. *PM, The Nation, The Daily Worker*—just printed words, but by the end of the day, he was gone.

Brett said, "Relief ended a long time ago, so I do what I can. I mean, well, nobody wants to hire me, considering I'm trouble, you know?"

"Yeah, I know," Sam said, throat tight, and Brett said, "These are my twin girls. Amy and Stacy. They were in the same class as your boy... Toby, right?"

"That's right."

Brett reached over and rubbed the top of the smaller girl's head. "They should be in school, but I sell more if they're out here. Tugs at the old heartstrings. Not a fair trade, but—"

Sam reached into his pocket. "How much?"

"Free for your boy. He always treated my girls okay."

Sam shook his head. "No dice." He laid down a handful of coins, pushed them across the table, slipped the wooden submarine into his coat pocket. "It's really good work, Brett. Really good work."

The coins were scooped up with a soiled hand. "Thanks, Sam. I appreciate that. You get along now, okay? And my best to your boy."

Sam walked away, looked back one more time at the former city firefighter. His pretty girls, perched on either side of him, gently rocked their legs back and forth, lightly kicking their heels against the crates.

Two blocks away from the police station, the toy submarine weighing heavy in his coat pocket, Sam reached a storefront that had a green and white sign hanging overhead: YOUNG'S FINE FURNISHINGS.

The dangling bell on the door announced his presence, and once again, he was struck by that soul-deadening smell of new furniture. He wasn't a snob, he knew people needed furniture, but having to spend hours in a showroom like this, deciding what fabric went with the wallpaper and between that sofa or that settee... Christ, he'd rather be hauling drunken sailors stained with piss and vomit back to the Navy Yard. On a counter by the door was a pile of President Long's own newspaper, *The American Progress*. He ignored the papers and looked around, saw a customer come out of an office at the rear of the store, holding a brochure.

Sam tried not to smile. The man was dressed in a shabby brown suit with dirty brown shoes, the old soles flapping as he walked. His gray hair was a mess, and as he went to the door, he noticed Sam.

"Inspector," he said. Sam nodded back, as Eric "The Red" Kaminski made his way to the door. Eric was a passionate rabble-rouser, passing out leaflets or holding up a sign in front of the post office protesting the government, though a stint last year in a Maine labor camp had cut back on his public appearances. He was also the brother of Frank Kaminski, the principal at Toby's school, and a source of unending frustration for his straitlaced brother. One day Sam should have a cup of coffee with the principal, he thought, maybe trade frustrating brother stories.

"Eric," Sam said, holding the door open. "Didn't know a man of the people needed new furniture."

As he went past, Eric said sharply, "You don't know me, and you don't know shit about the people, Inspector."

"You're probably right," Sam replied cheerfully as Lawrence Young came out of the office, wearing gray slacks, a crisp white shirt, and a black necktie. His thick black hair was sprinkled with gray about the temples. As always, a little thump of irritation jumped up in Sam's throat. From day one Lawrence had never hidden his dislike that Sam came from a poor family and wanted to many his only daughter. Over the years that dislike had only grown.

"It's about time, Sam," he said.

"Larry," he replied. "What can I do for you?"

"Well, Inspector Miller—or should I say, Probationary Inspector Miller?—I was hoping you could give me an update on last month's burglaries."

The thump of irritation was now beating in him as if it were an extra heart. "Like I told you and the other store owners, it doesn't make sense to have the best locks on your front doors and a hook-and-eye fastener for the rear door."

"So it's our fault that our stores are being robbed?"

"No, Larry, it's not," he answered evenly. "What I'm saying is that you've all got to do your part to cut down on the opportunity. I've asked the shift sergeants to increase patrols, I've interrogated the pawnshop owners up and down the seacoast, and I've talked to your fellow businessmen. If we all do our part, we'll cut down on the crime."

"I see," Larry said.

Sam checked his watch. He was going to be late for the county medical examiner. "Larry, that's nothing new, and you know it. So now, if you've proven your point, I'll get back to work."

His father-in-law offered him a chilly smile. "And what kind of point is that?"

"The point being that as mayor, you can haul my ass over here any time you want."

"I'm sure you're right. But there's other work that needs to be done. As important as your position in the police department. Political work."

Sam counted to five silently before he said, "I'm not interested."

"Too bad. I've received assurances you'll be at the Party meeting tonight. That's good. Your past absences have been noticed, and I've gotten a fair amount of grief about how my son-in-law doesn't meet his obligations to the Party."

"Larry, I do my job, and I go to Party meetings when I can. What else do you guys want?"

"You should be more active. Take part in the county or state committee. Make a name for yourself. I could put you in touch with the right people, and—"

Sam turned. "I'll think about it, okay? But I've got real work to do."

Larry called out, "Then think right, and think of Sarah and Toby. Think what might happen to them if you don't get your promotion, if you're demoted or even lose your job. I may be the mayor, Sam, but I don't control the budget committee. The police department is always a favorite target."

At that he swiveled. "A threat?"

"It's a recognition of what's going on. Who you know in the Party is going to be more important than the job you do. Even if the commission approves your promotion, it makes good sense to have important allies in your corner. And I could use you a man like you in the department ... letting me know what the marshal is up to."

"I don't care about politics, I just care about my job," Sam said, thinking, *Oh, Christ, what a world, asked to be a rat twice in one day.*

"Yeah, well, politics will sure as hell care about you. Better think about it, Sam. Do more with the Party: It's a good career move."

Sam stared directly at the man's smug face, remembering a time last year when that face hadn't been so smug. Sam had been across the river in Kittery, accompanying the cops and the Maine state police when they raided a house that had hourly paying guests. One of the guests being led out had been his father-in-law, and after Sam had a quick word with a Kittery detective, the cuffs had come off and Larry had run into the shadows. For Sarah's sake, Sam had kept his mouth shut about what he had seen.

"Like I said, I don't care about politics. I'm going to just do my job."

Larry shot back, "If you don't cooperate, if you end up losing your job, if bad things happen to Sarah and Toby, it'll be your fault. I'm trying to be a reasonable man and show you a path to a brighter future, and take care of my daughter and grandson."

"No, Larry, you're trying to be a jerk."

Out on the street, it seemed as if Larry yelled something out after him. Sam kept on walking.

In the daylight, the crime scene looked smaller and less sinister. He kicked a stone onto the railroad tracks, frustrated after his drive here. His meeting with his father- in-law had made him late to see the county medical examiner, who was now down the coast in Hampton, looking at a body that had washed up from the Atlantic. So the autopsy report would have to wait until tomorrow. He stood on the tracks, saw the gouges in the mud where the funeral home boys had retrieved the body. How in hell did his guy end up here, dead and alone?

Funny, he thought, how John Doe was now his guy. Well, it was true. Somehow he had turned up dead in Sam's city, and Sam was expected to do something about it. He was going to find out who this guy was, and his name, occupation, and what had killed him. That was his job.

9 1 12 8 3.

The newly disturbed mud yielded no clues. He started walking in a slow circle, staring down at the dirt and the grass. An hour later, all he'd come up with was an empty RC Cola bottle, four soggy cigarette butts, and a 1940 penny. He kept the penny.

Now what?

Two men emerged from behind one of the small warehouses, moving deliberately up the railroad track. Both wore tattered long cloth coats and patched trousers. They stayed to the side of the tracks as they came closer.

Sam looked around. He was alone.

"Got any spare change, pal?" the man on the left called out.

"No, I don't."

"Here's the deal, pal. You turn out your pockets, give us your wallet, your shoes and coat, and we'll let you be." The first man moved his hand from behind his coat, showing a length of pipe. "Or we don't let you be. Whaddya think?" The second man grinned, showing gaps in his teeth, and also the length of the pipe he was carrying.

Sam pulled his coat aside, reached up to his shoulder holster, pulled out his .38-caliber revolver. Then, with his other hand, he took out his badge. "I think we've got another deal going on here."

The men froze, and Sam said, "Am I right, guys?"

The one on the left gave a quick lick to his lips. His companion said, "Yes, sir, I guess we do."

"Then drop the pipes, why don't you. How does that sound?"

"Hey, bud," the one on the left whined as his pipe length dropped to the ground. "We was jus' foolin', that's all."

"We're jus' hungry, that's all," the second man said. "That a crime now? Bein' hungry?"

Sam kept his revolver leveled on them. "Here's our new arrangement. Lucky for you clowns, I got a busy day ahead of me. So I'm not going to haul you in. But you two are going to turn around and start walking. You ever show up here again in Portsmouth, I'll shoot you both and dump you in that pond over there. You got it?"

He could see them looking at him, evaluating him. Then they turned away. He kept his revolver up to make sure they weren't going to change their minds. Only when they had gone about fifty yards did he return the gun to its holster.

Christ, he thought, what a week.

To the east he could make out the roof of the B&M railroad station and its sister freight station. There was also a smell of smoke in the air, and he looked down the tracks, away from Maplewood Avenue, down by the grove of trees.

He started walking.

The encampment was built on a muddy stretch of ground, up against the marshland that bordered the shallow North Mill Pond. There were automobiles and trucks parked near the trees, and from the condition of most of the tires, it looked like the vehicles had made their final stop. Shacks made from scrap lumber and tree branches were scattered around, most with meager fires burning before them and women tending them. The children playing about were shoeless, their feet black with dirt. The women, with their thin dresses soiled and patched, looked up at him, eyes and expressions dull. It made him queasy, thinking about Sarah and Toby safe and warm back home. He shivered, knowing that one mistake, one bad run-in with a Long's Legionnaire or some other screw-up, could easily put his family here.

A skinny old man came over, his white beard down to his chest, his skin gray with grime, his leather shoes held together by twine. "What are you lookin' for, fella?"

"Looking for Lou from Troy. Is he around?"

"Depends who's askin'. You a cop?"

"I am."

"Town cop, railroad cop, or federal cop?"

"Town cop. Inspector Sam Miller."

The old man spat. "Haven't seen Lou since yesterday. He in trouble?"

"No. I just want to ask him a few questions."

"Huh. Sure. Well, he's not here. Just me and the kids and the womenfolk. That's it."

Sam took in the encampment once more. "Where are the other men?"

"Whaddya think? Out in town. Day jobs. Looking for work. Other stuff."

Other stuff, Sam thought. Rummaging through trash bins, looking for swill or food scraps. Or collecting bottles or cans. Or, like Lou, scavenging for coal lumps to cut the cold at night, when your wife and your children shivered in the rags as you lay there with them, in despair and rage, wondering again how you had ended up here, a failure as a father, a husband, a man.

"Look, last night, there was something loud coming from here... like gunshots. You know anything about that?"

The old man spat again. "A couple of fellas were drunk, got pissed at each other, fired off a couple o' rounds. Missed, o' course. But shit, you tell me you're worried about that, somethin' that happened twelve hours ago? Why didn't you come earlier?"

Sam said, "Other matters had priority, and—"

"Yeah, that's crap. You cops, you don't give a shit. If you did, you woulda been here last night instead of comin' out here the next day to pick up the pieces. Well, the hell with you."

Without warning, the man took a swing at Sam, the blow landing hard on his left cheek. Sam, stunned, stepped back and, with two hands, shoved the old man in the chest. The old man fell on his butt, snarling, "Fuck you, cop. You and your kind don't care about us. I was a stonecutter from Indiana, made stone that built this country, and look at me and my family— livin' like animals, beggin' for scraps. So get the fuck out of here, leave us be. Shit, better yet, you want to arrest me? Go ahead. I'll be fed better and will sleep better tonight in your damn jail."

Sam touched his cheek, then turned away. Suddenly, he heard a man laughing. From one of the shacks a man stepped out, buttoning his fly. A shipyard worker, probably, Sam thought. The man strolled away, whistling, lighting up a hand-rolled cigarette, and then a woman in a gray dress emerged from the shed, holding a dollar bill, an empty look on her tired face. When she saw Sam, she ducked back into the shack, and he heard her say something he couldn't make out.

He looked at the rails again. Hearing that woman's voice, a memory had come to him of a time when he had been a patrolman. Along these very tracks, not far from here, he'd been part of a search party seeking an old man who had wandered off when a train rumbled by unexpectedly. Not a B&M train, just a dark locomotive with a series of closed-off boxcars, and from those boxcars, Sam remembered hearing... noises. Voices. Scores of voices, crying out desperately as the train shuttled through the night, going God knows where.

Voices he couldn't understand.

He looked back at the trampled spot where the dead man had been found.

"Who are you?" he said. "And where in hell did you come from?"

Then he continued back to his Packard, rubbing his sore cheek.

CHAPTER NINE

Dinner was a bowl of chicken stew and some chunks of homemade bread, and while Toby drew doodles on scrap memo paper from the department, Sarah sat on the other side of the table, silent and looking paler than usual. There was a faint crackle to the air, as though a thunderstorm were approaching.

When she spoke, there was a listlessness to her voice, as if she were preoccupied with something.

"You were out late last night with that dead man, Sam. You shouldn't have to go out again tonight. The marshal should give you a break. Especially since you got in a fight. Your cheek is really bruising up."

"It wasn't much of a fight, and tonight's a Party meeting," he told her. "You know how it is."

She spooned up some of the stew. The radio was playing a repeat sermon of the famed radio priest Father Charles Coughlin, out of Chicago. In his musical accent, Coughlin said, *"The system of international finance which has crucified the world to the cross of depression was evolved by Jews for holding the peoples of the world under control..."*

Sam frowned. He despised the priest. "Why are you listening to him? I thought you liked the music from that Boston station."

"It went off the air yesterday. The FCC yanked its license."

The priest went on. *"...from European entanglements, from Nazism, communism, and their future wars, America must stand aloof. Keep America safe for Americans and the Stars and Stripes the defender of God."*

"I'm finished. May I be excused?" Toby asked breathlessly.

Sam looked to Sarah, and she said, "Yes, you may."

"Thanks!" He pushed his chair back with a screech and ran for his room, and Sarah called out, "And no radio until your homework gets done, got it, buster?"

"Yep!"

With Toby gone, Sarah picked up her spoon. "Sam, are you sure you can't stay home tonight?"

"Honey, I've missed two Party meetings in a row. I can't afford to miss a third. I start missing meetings, then somebody will start looking in to me. And if that happens, maybe they'll find out about your little charity work, right?"

"Sam, I know we called it charity work, but it was much more than that," she said sharply. "It is—*was* --- very important to me. It was once important to you, too. You always supported me before. I don't like that you've changed your mind."

"I haven't changed my mind. Other things have changed. And if I miss one more meeting, I can get put on a list. And I'm still on probation. You know where that toy sub came from, right, the one for Toby? An unemployed firefighter selling wooden toys on the street because someone ratted him out for reading the wrong newspapers. If there are cutbacks next budget season, I could lose my job. Or end up chopping down trees with my brother if they find out what's been going on in our basement."

"You won't be on any list like that. You know that. Please knock it off. You're just trying to scare me."

"Don't be so sure. And something else you should know. I saw the marshal and your dad separately this morning, and they want the same thing: me to be more active in the Party, so I can be a rat and tell them what the other is up to. Isn't that great? The marshal and your dad have such a high opinion of me that they both want me to be a rat."

Sarah wiped her hands on a napkin. "Maybe you *should* be more active in the Party. I mean, with the Underground Railroad station closed, my friends and I, well, if you could tell us things ahead of time—"

"Dammit, woman, it's bad enough my boss and your dad want me to be a rat, you want me to do the same for you and your half-baked revolutionaries and concerned schoolteachers? "

Sarah's eyes flashed at him. "Don't insult us by calling us that. It's people like my friends who can make a difference. And I wish you would stop being so mean about my dad. I don't like it."

"I'm sorry you don't like it, but you know he can be a jerk."

"Jerk or not, he's just trying to help his son-in-law, me, and our son. What's wrong with that? You know how he helped us with the furniture, and he wanted to help with the down payment for our house. I still don't know why you didn't let him."

"Because I don't want to be under his goddamn thumb, that's why!"

She glared at him, and noisily clattered the dishes together. "But it's all right to sleep in a bed that he provided us at cost, isn't it, Inspector Miller?"

"Look, Sarah—"

His wife made a point of looking up at the kitchen clock. "I don't want to talk about it any more. You're going to be late to your precious Party meeting."

The meeting was held in American Legion Post #6, off Islington Street, nearly a dozen blocks away from the police station. The air inside was blue-gray with smoke. Most of the men were smoking cigars or cigarettes; the bar was open, and bottles of Narragansett and Pabst Blue Ribbon were held in a lot of fists. Sam went up to a table near the entrance, where he paid his fifty cents and his name was checked off a list. *There*, he thought, *I'm here, dammit, and I won't be back for another month, no matter what the marshal or the mayor wants.*

There was a burst of laughter in the corner, and Sam noted a freckle-faced man holding court. Patrick Fitzgerald, father of his friend Donna. Remembering his chilly dispatch from home, he thought again of Donna and her sweet smile, and... *Why hadn't he asked her out back in school?*

Frank Reardon came toward him, giving him a satisfied nod. Unlike the other night by the train tracks, Frank wore civvies and had an American Legion garrison cap tilted on his head, as did a number of others.

"Glad to see you made it, Sam. What the hell happened to your cheek?"

"Walked into a door."

Frank grinned. "If you say so. Look, anything new about that body? Any ID yet? Or cause of death?"

"Nope," he said. "Still working it. Should get a report from the medical examiner tomorrow."

"Sounds good. But I bet you a beer that you find out that dead man's a hobo who stole those clothes and got clipped by the train some way."

"Maybe," Sam agreed, and Frank said, "You watch. One beer."

Frank wandered off, and Sam decided one beer was a good idea. There was a stir amid the crowd, and two young men came in from the rear of the room, laughing. Blue corduroy pants, leather jackets, and even in the crowd, Sam felt alone and exposed, as if he were in a crowded church and feeling like the pastor was staring right at him when sermonizing about the wages of sin. Long's Legionnaires, the same creeps from the other night at the Fish Shanty. They dragged chairs over near an empty lectern and sat there, legs stretched out, arms folded. Here to keep an eye on the locals. Sam looked away and went up to the wooden bar, where he managed to get a Narragansett. Then there was an elbow in his side and a voice in his ear: "Inspector, I sure hope you don't drink like that on duty."

A short man with red hair stood grinning up at him. Sean Donovan, former ironworker from the Portsmouth Naval Shipyard and now a clerk at the department, who spent most of his days burrowed in the files in the basement, trying to clean up a backlog of misfiled papers and case reports. Most cops ignored him—what the hell was a guy doing in a broad's job, anyway?—but Sam liked Donovan's quick wit and ability to find some obscure bit of paperwork in just a few minutes.

"Didn't know you were so interested in politics, Sean."

"I'm interested in keeping my job, my belly full, and a roof over my head. That means decisions, compromises, and the occasional sacrifice that would make your stomach roll. If I was in Berlin, I'm sure I would be a fully paid member of the Nazi Party. If I were in Moscow, my party card would be red. In England, Mr. Mosley would have my allegiance; in Italy, Signor Mussolini; and in France, Monsieur Laval; but here I am in Portsmouth, New Hampshire, eager to once again swear undying fealty to the Kingfish."

Sam clinked his bottle against Sean's. "And then go home to curse him out in private."

"You know me too well, Inspector. But I'm sure you're not here out of any particular love or duty to the Party. Just here not to rock boats, am I right?"

"And now, because you work for the cops, you're a mindreader?"

"You'll be amazed at what I've learned. Ah, I see our boys from Baton Rouge are here to keep an eye on us." Sam looked again to the two young Southern men, and there was Marshal Harold Hanson, talking to them. Hanson went to the other side of the room, took a seat. Then one of the Legionnaires raised his head, and his chilly blue eyes seemed to look right through Sam. The Legionnaire nudged his companion, and now they were both staring at him. Sam raised his bottle in a salute and gave them a smile, and for that, he got frozen gazes in return. Fine. *To hell with you bastards*, he thought.

"Looks like two of Long's finest don't like your Yankee hospitality," Sean remarked.

Sam kept a smile on his face. "The little crawfish bastards should crawl back to their bayous or swamps or whatever the hell they call them."

"Now look who's talking sedition. Hold on, it looks like the show is about to begin."

A large man wearing a Legion cap and a dark blue suit that pinched at every seam stood behind the lectern. Teddy Caruso, city councilor and a Party leader for the county. Caruso's loud voice carried out into the mass of men—the women had their own Party auxiliary, which met at a different time—and there were some grumbles from the crowd as he said, "Come on, come on, find a seat, find a seat, we wanna get going here…"

Lawrence Young walked in, with his sharp smile that suggested a fondness for the rough-and-tumble world of politics. He joined Teddy for a moment, whispering into his ear. Both made a point of smiling at the two Southern men sitting near them.

Sean said, "I see your sainted father-in-law is up front, member of the ruling class, ready to oppress us workers. Why don't you go up and give him a big ol' handshake?"

"And why don't you mind your own damn business?" Sam shot back.

"Tsk, tsk, it seems Mr. Young and his favorite son-in- law don't get along," Sean said cheerfully. "If that's the case, take a number. You're not the only one in the room who despises him. Like our boss, for example."

"Really? I know they're not best friends, but—"

"Oh, come on, Sam. There's more to police work than being out on the street. You've got to look beyond the streets to the offices overlooking them and the men who inhabit them. Like our mayor and the marshal. Both men who crave power, who like being in the Party, and who neither trust nor like each other."

"Even if they're both Party members?"

"Especially if they're both Party members." Sean said it firmly. "Sam, m'lad, listen well and learn. In all fascist organizations, there are factions within that battle each other. Over in Germany, it's the SS versus the Gestapo. Here, it's the Nats versus the Staties."

From the crowd came another roar of laughter. Sam said, "The Nats versus the what?"

"Nats and Staties. Nats are short for National, Staties slang for States. The Nats believe in supporting the Party organization no matter what, subordinating the needs of their states and their own people. The Staties believe in supporting their people and their state first and foremost. Hanson is a Nat. The mayor is a Statie. So there you go. The mayor thinks the marshal listens too much to the national organization, and the marshal thinks the mayor listens too much to the poor foot soldiers out there in the streets. They're jockeying for position, Sam, looking for allies, to be in total control of the county Party organization and then, eventually, the state."

The beer now tasted flat. He knew for sure what had been going on earlier with his boss and his father-in-law: As Sean said, both the marshal and the mayor were looking for allies to help them in their struggle, and why not have Sam Miller on the inside, working to betray the other?

"Too much politics for me, Sean. Look, let's just find a seat, okay?"

Sean said, "Sure, Sam. Look. Let the dedicated ones go up front. We hang back, that means we're the first ones out when this breaks up."

"Sounds fine to me," Sam said. He waited with Sean until most of the crew had taken folding chairs, and then they walked to the last row. Sean walked with a pronounced limp, revealing the true reason he worked at the police department instead of the shipyard. Two years ago, a falling piece of welded metal had crushed his left foot, putting him in the hospital for three months. As Sean once told Sam, that piece of metal had "accidentally" been tipped over by someone, someone whose brother took Sean's job the very next day.

Sam took his seat, remembering something else Sean had said: When it comes to jobs or your life, always watch your back, Sam.

CHAPTER TEN

Once everyone in the hall sat down, they stood right up again as an overweight man made the audience stand for the Pledge of Allegiance. Sam shuffled to his feet—a few rows up, there was loud cursing as somebody kicked over a beer—and looked to the far corner of the hall, where an American flag hung from a pole. Joining the other men, Sam held out his arm straight in the traditional salute as the ritual began.

"I pledge allegiance...

"To the flag...

"Of the United States of America...

"And to the Republic...

"For which it stands...

"Indivisible...

"With liberty and justice for all!"

As they sat, Sean leaned toward Sam's ear. "Unless you're an immigrant, a Jew, a Negro, a Republican, intellectual, communist, union organizer, or—"

"Sean, shut up, will you?" Sam snapped, and Sean sniggered softly.

Up front, Teddy pulled a sheaf of papers from his pocket. "All right, c'mon, fellas, can I have some quiet back there? All right? Good. I hereby call the meeting of the Portsmouth District of the Rockingham County Party meeting to order. I move that the reading of last month's minutes be waived. Is there a second? Good. All in favor? Good. Okay. Second agenda item, the Daniel Webster Boy Scout Council is looking for a donation of...."

And so it went. Sam crossed his feet and glared at the rear of the chair before him, stenciled with the A.L. #6 logo. He let his mind drift as Teddy went on, running the meeting as expertly as the Kingfish ran the Louisiana Legislature and then the Congress. Motions were made, seconded, and passed within seconds. He remembered reading somewhere—*Time* magazine, maybe?—that the record for bill passing was forty-four in just over twenty minutes, down in Baton Rouge, while Huey Long was senator and still running the state, before the assassination of FDR, the disastrous single term of Vice President Garner, and the triumphant election of Long in '36 and his reelection in '40.

He shifted in his seat. A cynical thought but a true one: Democracy might be dying, replaced by whatever was going on here and around the globe, but at least its death made for quick meetings. Teddy droned on, then said, "All right, only three more things left on our agenda tonight. First of all, we're lookin' for your help for some information."

There was a stir in the room. "There are index cards being passed out now, okay? We've all been asked to write down on those cards three names of people you think need to be looked at. Okay? Neighbors, coworkers, people down the street, we're lookin' for anybody who talks out of turn, insults the President and his people, or anybody else that needs to be looked at because of subversive activities or words. Okay?"

Some murmurs, but nobody protested. Sam felt queasy, as though the chicken stew from earlier had spoiled. Sean whispered something about how stoolies were the only growth industry in this administration, but Sam ignored him. He was thinking about his own status as a stoolie, being pressed by both his boss and father-in-law to be a rat. And he thought suddenly about that terrified writer he had put into the hands of the Interior Department last night.

When a card was passed to him, he took out his fountain pen, scribbled down three names—*Huey Long, Charles Lindbergh, Father Coughlin*—and then passed the card forward. There. Up front somebody laughed— "At last my idiot cousin will get what's coming to him"— and then Teddy collected the cards, breathing a bit hard, and passed them to one of the Long Legionnaires.

"Okay, item number two, some remarks from President Huey Long that we're gonna play right now. Hank? Got the Victrola ready?"

There was a smattering of applause. Sam sat still, thinking about the other names on those cards. Sixty or seventy city residents were going about their business tonight, not realizing or imagining that they'd just been put on a list, a list that would eventually destroy them. Just like that firefighter O'Halloran, carving toys from scrap wood, peddling them on the street. Something cold seemed to catch in Sam's throat. Maybe his own name was on that list.

He folded his arms tight as the man named Hank fiddled around with a Victrola set up in the corner, and from two speakers set up on chairs, there was a crackle of static and then the familiar Southern drawl of the thirty-third president of the United States:

"But my friends, unless we do share our wealth, unless we limit the size of the big man so as to give something to the little man, we can never have a happy or free people. God said so! He ordered it.

"We have everything our people need. Too much of food, clothes, and houses—why not let all have their fill and lie down in the ease and comfort God has given us? Why not? Because a few own everything—the masses own nothing.

"I wonder if any of you people who are listening to me were ever at a barbecue! We used to go there—sometimes one thousand people or more. If there were one thousand people, we would put enough meat and bread and everything else on the table for one thousand people. Then everybody would be called and everyone would eat all they wanted. But suppose at one of these barbecues for one thousand people that one man took ninety percent of the food and ran off with it and ate until he got sick and let the balance rot. Then nine hundred ninety-nine people would have only enough for one hundred to eat, and there would be many to starve because of the greed of just one person for something he couldn't eat himself.

"Well, ladies and gentlemen, America, all the people of America, have been invited to a barbecue. God invited us all to come and eat and drink all we wanted. He smiled on our land, we grew crops of plenty to eat and wear. He showed us in the earth the iron and other things to make everything we wanted. He unfolded to us the secrets of science so that our work might be easy. God called: 'Come to my feast.'

"Then what happened? Rockefeller, Morgan, and their crowd stepped up and took enough for one hundred twenty million people and left only enough for five million, for all the other one hundred twenty-five million to eat. And so many million must go hungry and without these good things God gave us unless we call on them to put some of it back..."

Sam kept his hands fisted in his pockets as the record ended and most of the men in the room applauded. Not moving his hands was a small protest, but it was the best he could do. Sean sat next to him, head nodding forward, and Sam jabbed him with an elbow.

"Huh?"

"Speech over," Sam said. "Look suitably enthusiastic."

Sean covered a yawn. "Sorry. Dozed off. Must've listened to that same speech a half dozen times, starting ten years ago. Rockefellers and Morgans too rich. Everybody else too poor. A new Homestead Act. No man a slave, every man a king." He looked about at the mostly smiling faces. "The same blah-blah-blah. If the Kingfish wants to get elected next year to a third term, he's gonna have to do better than reusing the same old speech."

"If it works, it works."

Teddy, the Party leader, came back to the lectern and took another folded sheet of paper from his coat. "All right, all right, all right. Last item on tonight's agenda. I gotta list here of some names. When I read out the names, you can leave the hall. For you, the meetin' is over. We'll see you next month. Okay, here we go: Abbott, Alan, Courtney, Delroy..."

It was as if the temperature in the hall had abruptly dropped. Sam saw that the others near him felt the same way, moving in their seats, looking around. No matter what Teddy said, this was unusual, this wasn't right. Sean whispered gleefully, "That's how it happens in the occupied lands. You get separated out. One group lives, the others get shot. Wonder what group we're in."

"Sean, nobody's going to get shot."

"Maybe so. But you got your revolver with you?"

"Why?"

"If there's shooting, I want to be next to you. I get the feeling you wouldn't go without a fight."

Sam kept his mouth shut. He knew where his revolver was. Safe back at home. Teddy droned on, "Williams, Young, and Zimmerman. Okay, get a move on, get a move on."

The sound of chairs being scraped and men walking away and the doors swinging open quieted down, and Sam saw that about a fourth of the room had filed out. Now the place was so quiet, he could hear a steam whistle blowing from the shipyard.

Teddy cleared his throat. "Okay. Now. The rest of you fellas, get ready for somethin' important, okay?"

Sam looked at the rear door. It was unmanned, no sergeant at arms standing by. He could bail out right now and hit the street and—

Teddy carefully unfolded another sheet of paper. "Okay, these orders come straight from Party headquarters in Concord and Washington. Understand? Good. It's been decided that the National Guard has to be expanded for future challenges. All the men that left, they're already members of the Guard. You fellas aren't. So you're gonna volunteer this evening to join the New Hampshire National Guard. Understood?"

A voice came from the back. "Hey, Teddy! The hell with you! I got a bum knee! I ain't gonna join the Guard, march around, and sleep on the ground. The hell with that!"

Teddy nodded, fat lips pursed. "That's your right, then. And you know what happens next. We take note of who gets in and who doesn't, right? Right. And then things happen. Maybe your uncle gets kicked off relief. Maybe your kid doesn't get a summer job from the city And maybe your boss, maybe he gets word that you're not cooperative, that you're not part of the team."

The silence fell across the room like a cold, wet blanket. Teddy was right: Everyone knew what the threat meant. Not being part of the team, not being cooperative, meant you could get fired. Just like that. Whatever thin thread you were living by could be cut in an instant. No job, no government relief, no charity, and in a manner of weeks, you and your desperate family would be scratching out a living in the hobo camp out by Maplewood Avenue. Or selling cheap toys on the sidewalk.

Teddy looked about the hushed room. "Good. That's more like it. I don't want the word to get out that the Portsmouth district didn't get one hundred percent enlistment. Good. Now. All you guys, stand up, raise up your right hand."

There was the barest hesitation among the men, and Sam felt like here and now maybe somebody would make a stand, maybe somebody would push back. But nobody did. The room was still, and then one man got up, looking at his feet. He was joined by the man sitting next to him. A third man stood up, and another, and then the rest of the room joined in. Sam stood up with the rest, thinking, *Not right, this is not right,* and he realized with a sour taste in his mouth that it was just another step in that long descent into whatever was now passing for civil society, where you were conscripted and it was called volunteering, when the poor and homeless were called bums, and when you lied over the radio and it was called a frank talk with the American people.

So Sam raised his hand, his voice low and quiet, as he joined his fellow men in the American Legion hall in swearing to uphold and defend the constitutions of the state of New Hampshire and the United States, and to defend both the state and the country against all enemies, foreign and domestic.

Teddy folded the paper. "Okay. Word is, a couple of weeks, you'll report to the armory to get a medical exam and get issued gear. More training will happen down the road. For you guys with bum knees or whatever, don't fret, there'll be something for you to do. We all pull together and we'll do just fine." He went through the quick and formal phase of dismissing the meeting, and by then Sam was out of his chair, joining everyone else to crowd out the rear door.

It seemed there was one more bit of business left undone. Two Long's Legionnaires were blocking the door, holding up their hands.

"Jus' hold on a second there, fellas," the one on the left said. "We got somethin' special for y'all."

The other Legionnaire reached under his leather jacket. There was a slight gasp from someone, wondering what was going on as the man's hand slipped in, and Sam watched, the hand came out, holding a—

A paper sack.

The tall young man jiggled the paper sack, held it out. "As you leave, boys, take one, okay? Gonna be a nice way to find out who our friends are up here."

The first man up put a hand into the paper sack, came out with a flash of metal. Sean whispered, "Oh, crap, look at that," and Sam saw "that" was a Confederate-flag pin. The two Legionnaires grinned.

"Welcome aboard," the one on the left said.

With the flag pin in his hand, Sam rushed out of the meeting hall, his stomach sick, his head aching. He stood on the sidewalk, sucking in the cool air.

"Can you believe this?" Sean demanded, holding the pin up. "Just like Russia, just like Germany. Show your loyalty to nation and party by wearing a bloody pin." He dropped his pin in an open drain grate. Sam, without even hesitating, did the same thing. It felt good, hearing the clink as the pin fell into the shadows.

"And another thing," Sean raged. "Did you hear the oath we just took? It's not the foreign enemies I'm worried about. It's the other half. The *domestic*. Pretty big fucking blank check, if you know what I mean. That's one of the reasons why our fair President got to keep control in Louisiana when he started out. He had the Guard in his pocket. Now we're part of his shock troops. We do his dirty work wherever he wants us."

Sam knew exactly what Sean meant. The National Guard was a trained reserve to help out the army overseas during a war, but more and more, it was used for other things. Breaking strikes in the big industrial cities in Pennsylvania and Illinois and Michigan. Burning down hobo encampments when they got too large outside of New York and Los Angeles and Chicago. Shooting at mobs when the relief money ran out in Seattle and Miami and Detroit. And now he and the others in that smoky hall were part of it.

"Christ, Sam." Sean's voice was harsh with anger. "What's going to happen to us?"

"Damned if I know," Sam said, moving away, wanting to get away from the hall, to get away from Teddy, to get away from the Party and everything else.

Just to get away.

But when he got to his Packard, he was brought back to ground very quickly.

As he opened the door, the overhead dome lit the front seat, and there, lined up in a row, lay three bound grass stalks. He froze. He started to crumple them but then gently placed the stalks back in the car, got in, started up the big engine, and motored home.

CHAPTER ELEVEN

Sarah and Toby were both asleep, Sarah with the radio on low, Toby snoring, cuddled tight against his pillow. Out there was the Party, out there were the hoboes, out there armies and air forces and navies were grappling in the dark, men and women and children blown up, shot, drowned, burned...

Here it was peace. Inside this little frame house in this old port city, here was peace. A peace built on illusions, based on him doing his job, keeping his head down, not getting involved, and so far, the illusions were working.

But for how long?

He walked into the living room to the small bookcase. Among the books was a well-worn thick paperback with a faded green cover. The Boy Scout Handbook. His very own, and one that Toby liked to look through even though the boy was only old enough to be in the Cub Scouts. He opened the flyleaf, saw the little scrawl. Sam Miller. Troop 170. Portsmouth, N.H. Nearly twenty years ago.

A small black-and-white photo slipped out, a photo of Sam and his brother, Tony, in their Boy Scout uniforms, standing in front of their house. Sam was smiling at the camera, Tony was glum, no doubt at having to share the photo with his younger brother. Sam was struck again by how alike they looked. There were only two years' difference between them, but in the right light and at the right distance, they could pass for twins. Brothers who really got along probably could have had fun with that as they grew up, confusing teachers and friends. Sam never remembered having any such fun with Tony.

He put the photo back and flipped through the pages until he found what he was looking for.

Secret messages to your troop mates. Danger. To alert your troop mates of danger, draw three lines in the dirt.

Or pile three stones.

Or gather three bundles of grass.

He closed the handbook, put it back on the shelf, and went over to the rolltop desk where the checkbook and the utility bills were kept. He looked into one of the wooden cubbyholes and found the small collection of postcards, the newest one on top. The card was postmarked from last week. Like most places, Portsmouth got its mail delivered twice a day.

His address was handwritten in the center, and in the upper left was a preprinted return address:

IROQUOIS LABOR CAMP
U.S. DEPARTMENT OF THE INTERIOR
FORT DRUM, N.Y.

He flipped the card over and reread the message.
There were three printed lines.

AM DOING WELL.
WORK IS FINE.
YOUR FOOD PACKAGES MOST WELCOME.
TONY.

The postcards arrived once a month, with unerring regularity and with the same message. All outgoing and incoming mail at the camp was censored, of course. He rubbed the edge of the postcard and sat there in the darkness, hearing the frantic tap-tap from upstairs as Walter Tucker, former Harvard science professor, entered his fictional universes, a place where loyalty oaths and labor camps didn't exist.

"Sam?" Sarah came in so quietly he hadn't heard her. She was wearing a light blue robe, her hair tousled. "It's late. How did the meeting go?"

"As well as could be expected. We were all drafted tonight."

"Drafted? Into what?"

"Into the damn New Hampshire National Guard, that's what."

"How did that happen?"

A good question. How to explain that choking feeling in the smoky room, feeling desperately alone even in the midst of that crowd? "We all stood up like good little boys, raised our right hands, took an oath, and now I'm in the Guard. Along with practically every other able- bodied male in the city."

Sarah sat down heavily on the ottoman. "And everyone went along? Nobody put up a fuss?"

"Sarah, your dad was there. Marshal Hanson was there. Hell, two of

Long's finest were sitting up front. It wasn't a place for anyone to be brave."

"Oh, Sam... And you're not going to like this, either. We're going to have a visitor tomorrow night. Sam, it's just for the night and—"

He shoved Tony's message back into the desk so hard the cardboard crumpled. "You heard what I said last night, right? No more. We've got Legionnaires in town, the Party and my boss know there's an Underground Station here, and you want to keep shuttling people north? Sweet Jesus, Sarah, do I have to make it any clearer? I even went out on a limb today with Hanson, telling him I knew the station was shut down. Hell, what more do you want? Do you want to see me standing next to Brett O'Halloran, begging strangers to buy wooden toys?"

"No, I don't want that." Her voice was frigid. "I know you're trying to protect me and Toby. But I told you there was one in the pipeline, and I couldn't do anything about it—"

"Oh, come on—"

"What happened to that guy I knew back in high school? The one who kept on playing football even with a broken finger? Where did he go?"

"He grew up, Sarah, and got a whole bunch of responsibilities. Back then the worst thing would have been losing the finals. Now... Have you been to the hobo camp lately? Children barefoot in the mud? Moms and dads starving so they can give their kids whatever food they can scrape together?"

"I've been to the camp. All of us at school have, with used clothes and some extra food. We do what we can, to fight back, and part of that is our little cot down in our basement. I'm sorry, Sam, he's coming. The last one, I promise. It's an emergency and—"

The choking feeling was back, as if he had no choice in anything. "Fine. Last one. An emergency. Whatever you say."

"Sam, please, keep it down. Toby—"

"Sure. Don't want to wake him. Okay, one more, tomorrow night. Who is he?"

She said, "I don't know. Some famous singer named Paul. On the arrest lists for sedition. Usual nonsense. He'll be here tomorrow night; I promise he'll leave before dawn. You'll never even know he's here."

He looked at his wife, his very smart and pretty wife who would sometimes have afternoon card sessions with fellow secretaries and teachers from the school—"the girls," she called them—where they would talk and gossip about marriages and births but also about politics and Long and Stalin and Marx. Her face was impassive, and for a terrifying moment, he looked at her and it was like looking at the face of his boss, Harold Hanson, not having a clue what was going on behind those eyes.

Sam took a breath. "So this guy, this stranger, is important to you. To get him to Canada, to keep him out of jail, is important enough to you to endanger my job, our house, and our son. Is that what you're telling me?"

Her cheeks were flushed and her lips were tight, and he braced for the inevitable blowup, but instead she nodded and said, "Yes. He's that important. And... I thank you. With him, we're done. This Underground Railroad station is closed. I swear it to you."

He waited for a heartbeat. Then he said, "How long have you known?"

"Sam?"

"This wasn't a surprise sprung on you in the past few hours. So how long have you known?"

She hugged herself, seemed smaller. Her robe slipped open and he noted the long smoothness of her legs, felt a flash of desire despite his anger. "A... .a few days. I told you about him being in the pipeline."

"But you knew there was no way to stop it. And still you've kept it secret from me, haven't you?"

"I... I was afraid you'd say no. So yes, I'm sorry. I kept it a secret."

"I see. And you thought by letting me know now, in the middle of the night, that I couldn't do anything but say yes."

"Sam—"

"I've got to go out for an hour or so. Don't wait up."

"Why?" she asked, bewildered. "What's going on?"

Sam didn't look at her as he put his coat and hat on, reached for the door. "Sorry, sweetheart. It's a secret."

Twenty minutes later he was in his Packard, rumbling over a wooden bridge to Pierce Island, in Portsmouth Harbor. Earlier he had paid a quick visit to a truck stop on Route 1, just before one of the bridges going over into Maine. In the rearview mirror he could make out the apartment building where he, Tony, Mom, and Dad had lived years back. The Packard's headlights carved the small brush and trees out of the shadows. The steering wheel shook violently as he turned off the dirt road.

He left the engine running and the headlights on as he sat there. Three stones. Three bundles of grass. Nothing much to anyone else, but... it meant a lot to him. And to somebody else.

Sam switched off the engine and stepped out onto the dirt. Crickets chirped in the darkness. He folded his arms and sat against the Packard's fender. Out before him stretched the harbor and the lights of the city and the shipyard. The island was a piece of city property that had never been developed. Over the years it had been a popular place during the day and night for a variety of people and purposes. In daylight it was a destination for fishermen, for the young boys who climbed the trees and played along the shore, for picnickers who managed to enjoy the view while ignoring the stench from the mudflats and marshes.

At night a different crew came in. Hoboes. Drunks. Men looking for satisfaction from other men, needing secrecy and darkness to do their illegal business. Sailors from the shipyard who didn't have enough cash for a room but had enough money for a quick fumbling date in a grove of trees. Every now and then the city council would bestir themselves to ask the marshal to clean up the island, and sure enough, there would be a handful of arrests, enough to satisfy the Portsmouth Herald and the do-good civic groups.

There was a thumping sound coming from the shipyard.

Sam straightened and saw a shape by the dark trees. "You can come out," he called. "I'm alone."

The man stepped forward. Even in the darkness, Sam recognized the walk. Something in his chest seized up, and he was a rookie again instantly, facing his first arrest, a drunken punk from one of the harborside bars, wondering if he could do it, could actually make that leap from being a civilian to being a cop.

"Hello, Sam," came the voice.

"Hello, Tony," he answered, greeting his older brother: welder, illegal union organizer, and escaped prisoner from one of the scores of labor camps across these troubled forty-eight states.

PART TWO

State Party Headquarters Concord, N.H.

May 3, 1943

For Distribution List "A"

Following note was received through mail slot entrance of Party headquarters last night:

Dear Sirs,

My name is Cal Winslow and I am a public works employee at the city of Portsmouth. I wish to report that last night, during our Party meeting at the American Legion Hall, there was a time when it was requested of people there to submit three names on file cards for future investigation. I was assigned to help collect and assemble these cards.

What I wish to report is that one card listed the following names: Huey Long, Charles Lindbergh, Father Coughlin, as an employee of the city, I used to work as a janitor at the police department. I recognized the handwriting on this card and am certain it belongs to Sam Miller, an inspector for the City. I wish to denounce him as a subversive.

C. Winslow

P.S. For more information, please contact me at home, not at work. Please also advise what reward I might receive. Thank you.

CHAPTER TWELVE

Tony came up next to him, and Sam noted the smell of sweat, of coal, of old clothes and bad meals and long travel along back roads and rails.

His brother held out a hand, and without hesitation, Sam took it and gave it a squeeze. The hand was rough from all of the outdoor work his brother had done in the camp. Sam reached into his coat pocket, took out a waxed-paper package he had gotten from the truck stop for twenty-five cents, and passed it over. Tony tore open the package greedily, started eating the roast beef and cheese sandwich. Sam let his older brother eat in silence. When he finished, Tony said, "God, that tasted good. Thanks," and then sat down next to Sam on the Packard's wide fender.

"You're welcome."

Tony wiped a hand across his mouth and Sam asked, "How long have you been out?"

"Just over a week."

"You okay?"

"Stiff. Sore. Hope I never pick up an ax again for the rest of my life. And you?"

"Doing all right."

"How's Sarah? And my nephew?"

"Doing fine."

"Good. Glad to hear that. You know... well, you get to feeling odd up there in the camps, wondering how family and friends are doing. All those months dragging by, every shitty day the same as the one before. And Sarah and Toby... good to know they're doing well. Up there... means a lot to think about family."

Sam said, "I know they worry about you."

Tony crumpled the waxed paper and tossed it into the shadows. "Those food packages, they make a hell of a difference, even though the guards steal a third of everything. If it wasn't for those packages, it'd be stale bread and potato soup every day."

"Glad to hear the packages make a difference."

"You know, where the camp was built, it's gorgeous country. Would love to try hunting in those mountains one of these days, if things ever change. Christ, that's another thing I miss, heading out into the woods for a quiet day of hunting."

Sam remembered how Tony always seemed happier fishing or hunting than doing chores or being at school. "How long are you staying here?"

"Don't know yet."

Sam knew what he had to say next and was surprised at how it felt, like he was twelve again, trying to stand up to his older brother. "Then you should know this: You can't stay long."

"Why's that?"

"You know why."

"Enlighten me, little brother."

Little brother. "Tony, you're a fugitive. You stay here, you're going to get picked up, sure as hell. Portsmouth's the first place the Department of the Interior and the FBI will look. Once they publicize a reward on your head, there are damn few places for you to stay out of sight in this town."

"Maybe I don't have a choice, you know? On the road after getting out, this was the only place I could go, at least for now. And tell me, what's got you worried? Me getting arrested? Or you getting the heat for me being caught in your backyard?"

"I don't want you to get arrested, and I'm also trying to protect my family. If you think so much of Toby and Sarah, you'll be going someplace else tonight."

"You're my family, too, little brother."

"If I get picked up because of you, Toby and Sarah will suffer. You ever take a moment to think about that?"

No response, just the old and complicated silence between two brothers who were never really friends. Sam felt like kicking something. It was always like this, always, "like he and his brother were two radio stations endlessly transmitting past each other on different frequencies.

"I'll be along in a while, I promise you that. All right?" Tony's voice had softened, as if he recognized Sam's frustration and was trying to make amends.

"Really? You got something going on? Something planned?"

"Yeah, that's right. Me in my smelly clothes, my feet covered in blisters, no money, no place to sleep, oh yeah, I got plans, brother. Lots and lots of plans."

Sam felt ashamed, thinking of how Tony must feel, finally being free after years of being in a work camp and not getting anything but grief from his younger brother, save a cheap truck-stop sandwich.

Tony asked, "How's Mom doing? Any change?"

"She has good days and bad days. Depends on when you visit her at the county home."

"Next time you see her, if she's with it, tell her I said hi. And Sarah, she still working at the school department? And Toby still a hell-raiser?"

"Yes on both counts," Sam said. "You telling the truth about moving on in a couple of days?"

"Yeah, I am."

"I can put you up someplace, if you'd like."

"Am I hearing you right? A minute or two ago, you were so shook up you were going to hand me over to J. Edgar Hoover himself. Now you're offering me a hidey-hole? A hell of a change of heart."

"No, it's not," Sam said. "It's being realistic. You stay on the streets, it's easier for you to get picked up. I can get you in at a boardinghouse; a landlord I know owes me a few favors. What do you say?"

"If I say no, will you arrest me?"

Something thickened the air between them. There was a cry of something out in the woods being hunted and killed. Sam said quietly, "I should. I should grab you right now and see that you transported back to Fort Drum tomorrow. You've always been a pain in the ass, you've always thought you were better than me, but I won't turn you in. It's... it's bad now, Tony, but not bad enough to turn in my own brother."

Tony nudged him with an elbow. "You wouldn't believe the number of guys back at the camp who were ratted out by family members, either for a reward or to save their own hides. You're a better man than a lot of folks."

"Not sure what kind of man I am, but I won't arrest you."

"So you got both of my messages."

"Hard to ignore them," Sam replied. "I'll always remember what you or me would do, whenever Dad got into one of his tempers, to warn the other."

"Yeah, three stones or three sticks on the porch, and haul ass to Pierce Island to wait until his mood changed. Or he fell asleep in his chair. Or Mom told him to go to the cellar to sleep it off. Tough times but good times, brother."

"Well, if that's how you remember it. I just remember Dad drunk a lot, beating on us and making Mom cry."

' "He worked hard for us, you know that. The job ended up killing him."

"That's history, Tony."

"The hell it is. It's the reason I got into trouble back at the yard. Family can mean more than blood, you know? I wanted to reorganize the union, get better health care for the workers, increase the number of docs on shift…you know, the yard doc, back when Dad started coughing and coughing, didn't even know about Dad's service in the first war. So he told Dad to stay away from dust, told him his lungs would get better. Some fucking diagnosis. It killed him."

Sam said, "That wouldn't have made any difference, and you know it."

"Oh, my cop brother, he's a doctor now, huh? Don't you ever think that if Dad hadn't gotten sick, then he wouldn't have drunk as much, wouldn't have been so mean to Mom and us over the years? Don't you?"

"Oh, hell, I don't know," Sam said, hating to be put on the spot in the same place he had been so many times before.

"All I know is that what happened to Dad shouldn't happen to anyone. And trying to do something about it got my ass in a labor camp."

"Now your ass is out of a labor camp. Where exactly do you plan to take your ass, Tony?"

"You asking me as my brother? Or as a cop? Somewhere I can make a difference. Where else?"

"Yeah, you're right. You're always right, Tony, and that's always been your problem."

"And your problem is that you've always taken the safe and easy way out, Sam," he shot back. "Star football player, Eagle Scout, cop, kiss-up to the mayor, and good little son-in-law. Or so you think."

"What do you mean by that?"

"Even in labor camps, news gets around. Met a guy out in the woods once, bundling brush. We got to talking, and when I told him I was from Portsmouth, that made him take notice. Seems he had a sister—an organizer from Manhattan, the ladies' garment union—and she was on an arrest list. Got out of Manhattan ahead of Long's goons, got on the Underground Railroad, and spent a night in Portsmouth. Should I go on?"

"Do whatever you want."

"So she spent the night in Portsmouth in the basement of a little house. A little house that was near the river and across from the shipyard. "

"Tony…"

"So don't use the Goody Two-shoe defense. You're in the same fight as me."

"No, I'm not."

"Oh, yes, you are. Different tactics, but trust me, your tactics—letting people sleep in your basement on their way up to Canada, that's not going to change things. Direct action, getting people in the streets, fighting this government hand to hand—that's what's going to change things."

"Sure it will," Sam said. "It'll change a lot of living people to dead people."

"Better to die on your feet than live on your knees."

It always ended like this with Tony, with one or the other losing his temper until all that was left were savage words and corrosive memories.

"Look, if you're going to stay here for more than a day or two, the offer of that room still stands."

"Please, no favors, all right? I know how to keep my head down from the feds and the screws. So go back home and be safe, and I'll be out of here in a few days. Look, we all have our jobs to do. My job is other things."

"Such as?"

"Such as I'm not going to tell a cop, even if he is my brother. I'm outta here, Sam. You take care of you and your family, and I'll take care of my own things."

Tony started walking away and Sam said, "I'm glad you're out, but I'm not glad you're here."

His brother called back, "You know, you make this big old act of not liking me that much, and I know that's so much bullshit."

"You do? Why's that?"

"Because of your boy. And his name."

"I don't know what you mean."

"Christ, for a police inspector, you can be dense. Yeah, his name. Where did you get it? A relative on our side of the family? On Sarah's side of the family?"

"I don't remember," Sam said. "It just seemed...just seemed right."

"Your boy and me share the same first and last name, except for one letter. Tony and Toby. You can call it coincidence. I won't. In a way, I think the two of you named him after me."

Then the shadows swallowed him. Sam listened for a moment, then called out, "Tony!"

There was no answer.

INTERLUDE III

After he saw his brother's Packard leave the parking lot, he started walking to the city. He stood on the wooden bridge going from Pierce Island to the mainland, looking over at the shipyard lights. That's where it had started, that's where he thought it had ended, but now it was starting again. Organizing, fighting... back then he thought he was making a difference, but he realized it was just preparation. Preparation for that special day, the day when he would be there to make one shocking difference in this world, to make it better.

Sam was too much of just living in the day-to-day, not looking about him, not looking at the world that needed saving, that needed changing. His brother had no idea what was coming at him.

He squeezed his hands on the guardrail, thinking of his time in the labor camp, recalling all the things he had learned, remembering most the correct way to cut down a tree. Funny, in a time like this, with so much at stake, that you remembered how to slice at the trunk with an ax, knowing it was a delicate job no matter how clumsy it looked, hammering away at the tree, for how you cut it meant how it would fall.

If you judged wrong, a couple of tons of lumber were coming down straight at you, so you learned pretty quick which way to jump to save your life.

He resumed his walk into his old hometown, heading back to Curt's place. Which way to jump. Except what do you do when there's no safe place to jump?

CHAPTER THIRTEEN

The next morning Sarah had toast and coffee for breakfast, while he and Toby had cream of wheat. He and Sarah talked about random things—including a request for him to take the boy to school, since Sarah had to go check on her aunt Claire, who was feeling sickly yet again—but Toby kept on kicking his feet against the table legs while working on a drawing.

Finally, Sam said, "Kiddo, you knock that off right now and get ready for school or you'll lose your comic books for the week. Savvy?"

"But I wasn't doing anything!"

"What, you think I can't hear? You've been kicking the table all morning, so cut it out."

Toby said, "Fine!" and clambered off the chair, heading to his bedroom.

"What is up with that boy?" Sam asked. "For the past month, he's been a handful. Notes from school, the bed-wetting, and now this. What's going on?" Sarah poked the crumbs on her plate and didn't meet his eyes. "I don't know. I wish I did, Sam, I wish I did. If I could, I'd tell you."

"Sarah, look, it's—"

She reached over, touched the back of his hand. A nice surprise. "I'm sorry about yesterday. Sorry about not telling the truth. It won't happen again. But... please... just tonight. I swear it's over."

"Sarah, Tony's out."

"What?" Her face grew pale. "Paroled?"

"No, escaped."

"Oh, Sam," she said, drawing her hand back. "That's why you went out last night."

"He left a signal for me. Something from our Boy Scout days. I went to see him at Pierce Island."

She kept quiet for a moment. Then she said, "You're not turning him in, are you?"

"For God's sake, what do you think? I can't believe you asked me that."

Her eyes moistened. "I'm sorry. It's just that... lately I don't know what to think. There's a teacher at the school, he has a son who's in the National Guard, was about to get promoted. The son found some anti-Long flyers in a closet in his father's office, and the son turned him in. Can you believe that? The son turned his own father in! Just so his promotion would go through."

"Tony and I, we've had our rough patches. We're not like those fun brothers you see at a Mickey Rooney movie. Sometimes I think I don't even like him much. But I'd never betray him."

"Then what's going to happen?"

"I offered him a place to stay. He said no. He said he'd be leaving in a few days. It's just that— Dammit, is there any way you can cancel tonight's visitor?"

"No, I can't, Sam. You know how dangerous phone calls can be. Messages sometimes get passed hand to hand, through couriers. There isn't time."

"We could lock the bulkhead door."

"And do what?" she said. "Force him to sleep in the bushes? Try his luck at the hobo camp? Picked up, maybe, by one of your brother officers for loitering? He's my responsibility."

"All right. The last one. And Tony—forget I mentioned him. Officially, he's still in prison. Any questions from anyone, that's all you know. I'm sure the FBI or somebody will be checking up on him. You haven't seen him, you don't know where he is. And that's the God's honest truth."

"Days like this, you surprise me, Inspector. Just when I'm going to give up on you and think you've been seduced by Long and his people, you come back and stand up for something."

Sam thought of Tony's critique of him and said, "I'd rather be seduced by you than anyone else, Sarah Miller, and that includes the President. Don't forget about that rain check."

Sarah looked tired but pleased, may be because the argument about their upcoming guest was over. "Oh, sweetie, that's one rain check that will never expire. Here, I'll even show you where it's being stored." She brought her hands to the hem of her skirt, slowly drew it up past her thighs. He moved his hand under her skirt, on the smooth stockings. He slid his fingers up, past her thighs. Sarah played a little game with him, squeezing her thighs tight, but as he pushed ahead, past the top of the stockings and the garter snaps, she moved her legs open. The skin of her thighs was soft indeed, and he heard her take a sharp breath as he moved his hand higher and—

Toby thumped out, carrying his book bag, eyes downcast. His parents straightened up, Sam breathing hard. "I'm sorry about kicking the table, Dad. I'm ready for school. And here. See? I finished my drawing. What do you think?"

The paper showed some sort of stick figure with a big head. There was a star drawn in the middle of the torso. "See? It's you, Dad. Do you like it?"

"I sure do," Sam said.

"Mom?"

"You made his head too small," Sarah said.

Sam looked at his former cheerleader. "How about his heart?"

"Not big enough," she said, smiling back, her gaze warming him despite all that had gone on before. Still... he had the feeling that all of this had been some sort of act, from the pleadings to the upraised skirt. The cast of her eyes didn't match the brightness of her smile.

Toby sat next to him on the big front seat of the Packard, his school bag gripped with both hands, prattling on about a new lady at the cafeteria who kept on dropping mashed potatoes on the floor during lunchtime. Sam thought about the day ahead of him, about his John Doe, about Tony out there in the woods or maybe now in the city, and about their illegal guest coming tonight.

As they went down to the end of Grayson Street, there was movement off to the right at a house that had been empty for a month. It once belonged to the Jablonski family. One day the family vanished, just like that, and no one knew why. If anyone had seen a Black Maria come up to the house late at night, no one was talking.

There was a freight truck backed up to the house, a couple with two young boys standing nearby, huddled together, as three Long's Legionnaires directed the movers bringing in boxes and furniture. That's how it went sometimes, in other places. But not in Portsmouth, not until today. Somebody had been denounced to the authorities, and the denouncers got to move into the house of the deported as a reward.

Sam stopped at the yellow and black stop sign and looked into the rearview mirror, watching his new neighbors move in. Then he put the car in gear and drove on. "Ask you something, Dad?"

"Sure, sport, go ahead."

"You're not a rat, are you?"

He turned. Toby looked up at him, his face serious.

"A rat? What made you ask that?"

"Oh, some of the guys at school say cops are all rats. That they put dads in jail for made-up stuff. That they take money from bad guys. Stuff like that. Some guys at recess yesterday, they said you were a rat."

His wife, operating an Underground Railroad station in their basement. His brother, living God knew how five miles from here, and he, a sworn peace officer, letting him be. Family versus duty. Good guy versus rat. And just how did we get the money to buy our house? he thought.

"No, Toby, I don't take money from anybody except from the city for my paycheck. I only put bad guys in jail, for real things, not made-up things."

His son kept his mouth shut, toying with the buckles on his school bag.

"Toby, you believe me, don't you?"

"Sure, Dad, of course I do." Toby didn't say anything more until Sam drove up to the squat brick building of the Spring Street School. Across from the school was a small grocery store. Glistening red on the store's cement wall was a painted red hammer and sickle, and below that, in sloppy letters, DOWN WITH LONG. Toby looked out the window and said, "See that kid, Dad? Over there by the fence, the kid with the brown coat? That's Greg Kennan. He told me you were a rat. I'm... I'm gonna tell him how wrong he is."

"Don't get into any trouble, Toby, okay?"

"I could take him, you know. If we had a fight." The look in his eyes, the look of the devil that sometimes reminded him of Tony.

"Don't have a fight."

"I just want to stick up for you, that's all."

"And I want you to behave and do good, okay?"

Toby's lips trembled. "I don't like getting into trouble.

I don't. I... sometimes it happens. I can't help it. Mom understands. Why can't you?"

"Understand what?"

Toby opened the big door and climbed out, a little figure running toward the fenced-in asphalt courtyard. Two boys wearing short jackets and knickers were bouncing a ball off the side of the brick wall of the school. Nearby was a small parking lot for those teachers and administrators fortunate enough to own automobiles. Three girls were on the sidewalk, playing with yo-yos. Out in the yard was Frank Kaminski, the brother of the local agitator Eric. The owner of the grocery store came out with a bucket of whitewash and a paintbrush, standing in front of the red hammer and sickle, his shoulders sagging.

"No, Toby," Sam said to himself, shifting the Packard into drive. "I'm not a rat. And you don't have to stick up for me."

In the basement of the Portsmouth City Hospital, seven blocks south of the police station on Junkins Avenue, the Rockingham County medical examiner had a small office and work area next to the morgue. The walls were brick and cement block painted a dull green. The lights flickered as Sam opened the door. The medical examiner sat behind a desk covered with papers and folders, the usual debris of an overworked and underpaid county employee. On the walls hung framed photographic prints of the White Mountains, photos taken by the doctor, a hobby he was proud to show off.

"It's about time you got here," William Saunders said.

The doctor's voice was raspy—an old throat wound from his time on the Western Front during the last world war.

"Couldn't be helped," Sam replied. "Yesterday both my boss and the mayor had to have a piece of my butt."

"Hell of a thing, to be so popular," the medical examiner said. He was tall and thin, with a thick thatch of gray hair, and as he stepped up from his chair, he remained stooped, as though working in the basement of the hospital had permanently weighed him down. "But I won't give you any more grief, Inspector. You've given me a delight this fine morning."

From a rack he pulled down a black rubber chest-high apron, which he tossed over his head and tied behind him. Sam followed him.

The examination room, like the office, was cluttered. On the far wall were three heavy refrigerator doors. Three metal tables stood centered on the tile floor, the middle one occupied by a sheet-covered lump. Saunders picked up a clipboard and started flipping through the sheets of paper. Sam imagined bits of bone, flesh, and brain tissue stuck in the cracks and grooves of the tiles and metal equipment.

"Why is it a delight?" Sam asked.

"You know what my customers are like day in, day out? A hobo from one of the encampments with a knife wound. A drunk pulled from a car crash. Or some wretched fisherman who fell into the harbor and was found a month later. Do you know how much a body in the water swells and decomposes after a month?"

"I have a hunch," Sam said. "You still haven't told me why this body is a delight."

"Because the bodies I usually get are boring. They're traditional. They're easy. Lucky for me, no corpses have come by with their hands tied behind them and two bullets in their skull." Saunders tapped the clipboard on the feet of the body on the metal table. "This John Doe, this one is a mystery. I've been with this good man for hours now, and I've only come up with a few crumbs of information."

"So tell me what your crumbs are."

"Ah, the crumbs." Saunders tugged the sheet down. The dead man looked ghastly in the yellow basement light, the Y-shaped incision ugly on the pale skin of his sunken chest. "What we have here is a malnourished white male, approximately fifty to fifty-five years in age. There was no identification in his clothing, and his clothing had no store tags, no laundry marks."

"Yeah, I know. I noticed that when I first examined him."

"Something, isn't it, Inspector? It was like someone— either him or somebody else—wanted to make sure that identifying him would be impossible. Which is probably true. But you see, this poor dead man has one distinct advantage."

Sam really wanted Saunders to pull the sheet back •over the body, but he didn't want to show a weakness. "And what's that?"

"He ended up in my county and faced me, that's what. Any other county in this state, he'd be in a potter's field. But here, not quite yet. First of all, I believe the man is European."

"Why?"

"Two reasons. One, the clothing. The stitching is different, the quality of the cloth. Second, his dental work. There's a difference in American and European dental work—the amount of gold and how it's used, for example."

"Can you be more specific? French? English? German?"

"They're all German now, aren't they? Sorry, no way to tell which occupied land this man is from."

"You said he's malnourished. What do you mean by that?"

"There's a scale you use when you have a male subject of a certain height and certain age. This gentleman should have weighed between one hundred sixty pounds and one hundred seventy pounds. He actually weighs one hundred twenty. Almost skeletal."

"Did he have cancer or TB?"

Saunders shook his head. "Internal organs were distressed from being underweight, but there was no obvious sign of disease. I sent his blood out for analysis, but it seems to me, odd as it sounds, that your friend here hadn't eaten a good meal in a very long time. Some of the hoboes I've examined over the years have been underweight, but nothing like this man. It was like he was deliberately starved. However, just to advise you, his lack of eating didn't kill him."

Sam felt frustrated, like he was being lectured to. "So you don't know what killed him. Good for you. Then what was the cause of death?"

The medical examiner stepped up to the dead man's head. "His neck was snapped."

"Broken neck. All right, accident or homicide?"

"Homicide, without a doubt. Here"—Saunders pointed to the neck and jaw with a pencil—"and here, there are bruises that indicate to me your John Doe was forcibly grabbed from behind. He had his neck snapped. By someone taller and stronger than he. Left-handed, I have no doubt. To be fair, in his frail and malnourished state, a teenage boy could have probably killed him. There you have it. One older European male, neck snapped, and dropped right in your lap."

"There was a tattoo on his wrist. A bunch of numbers. Did you see any other tattoos?"

"Not a one," Saunders said. "But it's intriguing, isn't it?" He lifted up the left arm. "Six digits in a row. I've never seen anything like it."

"Any guess what it can mean?"

"Who knows? Mother or girlfriend's birth date. A safe combination or a bank account number. Like I said, intriguing. In the meantime, I'll write up a preliminary report and have it sent over this afternoon. I won't officially put down the cause of death—I want to wait for blood work—but you can be sure it was murder."

Despite his earlier frustration, Sam was pleased. Saunders could be a pain in the ass with his lecturing style, but he knew his job. "Appreciate the work, Doc."

"Let me know how this one turns out before it appears in the newspapers. Half-starved European with a broken neck dropped off in our fair city. Before you go, would you care for a bit of advice from someone who's been on the job longer than he should have been?"

"Depends on the advice, I guess,"

Saunders slowly tucked the sheet back into place, as tenderly as if preparing the dead man for a long nap. "This is an unusual case, and unusual cases tend to have something sinister attached to them. Be careful, Sam. So many think that the story ends here, with a dead man on a slab. More often than not, this is where the story begins."

CHAPTER FOURTEEN

Back at his desk at the police station, Sam typed up another memo, in triplicate, while Mrs. Walton sat glumly nearby, working at her own typewriter.

TO: City Marshal Harold Hanson
FROM: Inspector Sam Miller

An autopsy performed by Rockingham County Medical Examiner DR. WILLIAM SAUNDERS has determined the cause of death for the unidentified male found last night by the B&M railroad tracks to be a HOMICIDE. According to DR. SAUNDERS, his autopsy results have not yet been finalized, although he is confident in his finding of HOMICIDE.

No progress has yet been made on the victim's identification, although the investigation continues.

It was time to notify the state. In New Hampshire, the state's attorney general was brought in for all homicide cases, and for the first time in his career—feeling just a bit nervous, despite the giddiness of having a murder case before him—Sam picked up the phone, got an operator, and placed the call to Concord.

A bored-sounding woman on the other end of the line informed him that all available assistant attorney generals were at court, with the state police, or otherwise engaged. She promised a return phone call later today or perhaps tomorrow. Depending.

Sam hung up the phone, feeling oddly satisfied. Fine. He would continue the investigation on his own, which suited him perfectly. Next to his typewriter was a manila envelope with the return address of the

Portsmouth Herald. Opening the envelope, he slid out a handful of black-and-white photographs of his John Doe, sprawled on that bare stretch of mud. How in hell did he get there? Dropped? Thrown? From where? And why?

He picked up the phone again and dialed a four-digit number from memory. In seconds, he was talking to Pat Lowengard, the station manager in town for the Boston & Maine railroad.

"Sam, how are you today?" Pat's voice was smooth and professional, as though it belonged over a station's PA system.

"Fine, Pat, fine. Looking for a bit of information."

"Absolutely. What do you need?"

Sam picked up his fountain pen. Pat and the cops had a long and cooperative relationship. The department and its officers got a break on ticket prices to Boston and New York, and the railroad station got a break from automobiles parked illegally on side streets.

"What trains did you have come by two nights ago?" Sam asked.

"Can you narrow it down a bit?"

"Yeah. Hold on." He looked at his notes. "Anytime before six PM."

"Just a sec. Let me check that day's schedule."

Sam leaned back in his chair until Pat came on the line again. "Got two in the afternoon. One at two-fifteen PM., the other at five forty-five PM."

Two-fifteen in the afternoon? No, too early. The body would have been noticed way before Lou Purdue stumbled across him. So it had to be the later train, for if it were a train that went to the Portsmouth B&M station, it would have slowed before stopping. Which meant maybe John Doe was murdered on the train and tossed off. From there, start checking the train, the passenger manifest, the conductors and the train crew, and you could start making some effort to finding out just who in hell had been—

"The five forty-five pm.," he said. "A local?"

"Nope," Pat said. "Express. Straight shot from Boston to Portland."

Damn, he thought. So much for that theory. "How fast does the express go?"

"Through town? Thirty, maybe forty miles an hour." Sam looked back at the glossy prints of his John Doe, lying peacefully in the mud. At thirty to forty miles an hour, the body would have been tumbled in a mess of broken limbs and torn clothes. But there he was. No broken bones, no smears of mud on his clothes, no identification, half starved...

He rolled the fountain pen between his fingers. "Any unscheduled trains come through yesterday? Trains associated with the Department of the Interior?"

A pause, as though the connection had been broken, and then Pat's voice returned. "No, nothing like that, and please never ask me that again over the phone, all right?"

Sam dropped his pen on his blotter, hearing the sudden fear in the station manager's voice. "Sure."

After a quick stop in the grubby men's room, Sam went back to his desk. The phone started ringing and he picked it up as he sank into his chair. "Miller, Investigations."

"Inspector? Inspector Miller?" From the rumble of traffic over the wire, he could tell the call was coming in from a pay phone. "It's me. Lou Purdue. Lou from Troy. You was lookin' for me earlier, weren't you?"

Inadvertently, Sam touched his sore cheek. "Yes, I was."

"Good, 'cause I want to see you again. The other night you said to call you if I remembered somethin'. And I did." Lou coughed. "Shit, I know I only got a couple of minutes 'fore the pay phone hangs up on me. Look, meet me over at the camp, okay? I'll be there in five minutes. Hey, will I get another buck from you?"

"You'll get more if you tell me what you remembered." Another cough, and in the background, the sound of a truck driving by.

"Like this, I remember standing there in the rain, waitin' to see if a cop car was gonna come over, there was another guy waitin', too. So what, right? But now I remember. His shoes were all muddy... and they was nice shoes, too... but they was muddy like he had walked down the side of the tracks, just like me and you and those cops. Made me think maybe he knew somethin' about that dead guy."

"What did he look like?"

"Oh, a nice-lookin' fella, you could tell that—"

Click.

"Hello? Lou? You there?"

Nothing save the hiss of static. The operator had cut him off after the first three minutes.

"Dammit!" he said, banging the phone back into the cradle, shoving back his chair and grabbing his coat, leaving the station and Mrs. Walton to her typing, before she could say a word.

Back to the encampment he went, making that long walk after parking in the Fish Shanty lot. Like before, the old man who was the unofficial mayor stalked up to him and said, "You, the cop. Lookin' for another slug?" Sam poked him in his skinny chest with his index finger. "Are you?"

The old man laughed. "Like I said 'fore, cop, arrest me, I don't give a shit, and—"

Sam stuck out a leg and then tripped him. He fell to the ground and squawked. Sam pressed his boot down on his left wrist, bent, and said, "I gave you that last one, pal, but don't think you can screw with me again, all right? And maybe I'm not in the mood for arresting you, maybe I'm in the mood for breaking a finger or two, so shut up, all right?"

The old man grimaced, and Sam knew he should feel guilty, but he didn't. He looked around at the worn-out cars and trucks, the shacks and lean-tos, the smoky fires and the children, children everywhere, thin and too quiet. "Lou from Troy. Is he around?"

The old man spat up at Sam. "Nope. He was here a few minutes ago. But he's gone now. Jesus, step off my arm, will ya?

Sam saw three men, joking and talking by one of the shacks, ignoring him and the man on the ground. "Where did he go?"

"Lucky son of a bitch got himself a job. Ran into camp, grabbed his bundle, said he had a job up north, won't be back for a month. A month! Lucky bastard."

Damn, he thought. Damn it all to hell. "Did he say where he was going?"

"Nope. Jus' that he was gone, it paid okay, and he'd be back."

Sam stepped off the old man, who scrambled to his feet, rubbing his wrist, eyeing Sam, spit drooling down his chin. Sam slid a business card from his wallet, passed it over to the old man with a quarter and a nickel. "You save that nickel and call me the minute Lou comes back. Okay? You do that and I'll pay you a dollar."

The old man shook his head. "Think you can bribe me, that what you're thinking?"

Sam said, "Yeah, that's exactly what I'm thinking."

"Mister, that there's a deal, no matter what you call it." A man emerged from one of the shacks, laughing. Sam watched him go over and josh some with his coworkers— oh yeah, they were Navy Yard guys. The four of them—in dungarees, work boots, and heavy shirts—looked at him as he approached.

"Fellas, time to leave," Sam said.

A pudgy guy said, "Hey, take your goddamn turn, okay? We got here first."

Sam held out his inspector's badge. "I got here last, and you're leaving now, and you're not coming back. Unless you want your names and pictures in the paper." Eyes downcast, they moved away hastily, and as Sam left, a woman yelled at him, "Who the hell are you, huh? Mind your own goddamn business!"

He looked at the shack, saw it was the woman he'd seen before, the one collecting her dollar from the visiting dockworker. She said, "You gonna make up for these guys not comin' back here? Huh? Are you? You got money for me, a job for me, you got anything, you bastard?"

Sam shook his head and walked on.

Parking outside the police station and walking up the sidewalk, Sam felt as though he could use a bath. The size of the camp ebbed and grew depending on the weather and the availability of jobs, but it had been in that spot by the cove for years. In other places, such as Boston and New York and Los Angeles, the camp populations were in the thousands, or so he had heard. One never saw the camps on the newsreels.

Up ahead, Sam was surprised to see who was coming toward him: his upstairs tenant, Walter Tucker, with a tentative smile, his leather valise firm in his hand.

"Hey, Walter, everything okay?"

"Oh, yes, things are fine." Walter's watery eyes flickered behind his eyeglasses; a soiled blue necktie fluttered in the breeze through his open coat. "You see, I was walking to the post office to mail out my latest opus, and I thought I'd come by and take you out to lunch. My work habits aren't the best, but I do get to the post office every day at noon. So. A lunch to thank you for cleaning out my sink the other night."

"Walter, really, you don't have to—"

"Please, Samuel. A free hot meal that doesn't come from a relief or a soup kitchen. Doesn't it sound attractive?"

Sam paused, thinking maybe Walter wanted to become more friendly in exchange for a rent reduction, but to hell with it. The curse of being an inspector was being suspicious all the time. "Sure, Walter," he replied. "Lunch sounds swell."

They walked three blocks from the police station, joining the thin lunchtime crowd from the shops and. businesses. A few of the men in the crowd were sandwich men, sad-looking fellows wearing cardboard signs on their front and back. One said CARPENTER WITH 10 YEARS EXPERIENCE. NO JOB OR PAY TOO SMALL. PLEASE HELP I HAVE 3 CHILDREN. Sam looked away. The signs were different, but the men all looked the same: unshaved, thin, clothes and shoes held together by tape or string. The sky was slate gray, a sharp breeze bringing in the salt air from the harbor. Walter said suddenly, "Let's cross the street, all right?"

On the other side of State Street, Sam saw the problem. A squad of Long's Legionnaires was outside a shuttered and closed synagogue, slapping up posters with buckets and brushes dripping glue, laughing as they plastered the paper over the dull red brick. The large posters showed President Long's grinning face, and each poster had one of two slogans: EVERY MAN A KING or SHARE THE WEALTH.

They walked on. After a moment Walter said, "Well, it's not ein Volk, ein Reich, ein Führer, but it'll do. Sam, do you miss your Jewish neighbors that much?"

"I was just a patrolman when they left back in '36. My dad said we lost the best deli in town and the best haberdasher. That's all I remember. There were only twenty or so Jewish families in town at the time."

"Can't really blame them for leaving. When Long was elected, you could smell trouble was coming, somehow. So the Jews self-ghettoed themselves in Los Angeles and New York and Miami. Easier to help defend one another if you're in one place. Still, a hell of a thing. Makes you wonder if they thought it through. Being in one place makes it easier to round you all up, and if that's one thing this and other governments have learned, it's how to round people up."

The Rusty Hammer was a restaurant set on the corner of State Street and Pleasant Street, with a quick lunch service, and Sam hated to admit it, but he was pleased that Donna Fitzgerald turned out to be their waitress. Her uniform was tight and pink, the skirt a bit above the knees, and with a zippered top she had undone some, exposing the tiniest scrap of a white lace bra when she leaned over to give Walter his menu.

"So good to see you, Sam," she said, putting a warm hand on his shoulder when she gave him his menu.

"You, too, Donna," he said.

"Any news about Larry?"

A wide smile, the same dimple flashed. "Yes, he came home early. And my, it's so good to see him, but he's tired and thin, and he can't sleep that well. But I'm trying to fatten him up, and I hope I can get him a job here when he's stronger, maybe even as a dishwasher, so long as he stays out of politics."

"That'd be great," Sam told her, and with a wink she went back to the kitchen. Walter eyed him, and Sam just stared back until he looked down at the soiled tablecloth.

Where they sat overlooked the street through a set of bay windows in a quiet corner. In the windows, as in so many other windows in the city, was a sign that said WE SUPPORT SHARE THE WEALTH. A radio in the kitchen was playing Rudy Vallee's "As Time Goes By." Donna came back with fried haddock chunks for Walter and a cheeseburger for Sam. She gave

Sam another smile and another warm touch on the shoulder, which pleased him.

When lunch was finished, Walter delicately dabbed at his lips with his napkin and cleared his throat, "Despite all my problems, I've come to love Portsmouth. Here, you have one of the oldest port cities on the East Coast, a place where John Paul Jones stayed as one of his ships was being refitted. Nearly forty years ago, it was one of the great diplomatic triumphs of this new century."

"Sorry, you lost me at that last one," Sam said.

"What do they teach young'uns nowadays? The Treaty of Portsmouth, ending the war between Russia and Japan. Big doings here in 1905. Teddy Roosevelt was behind it all and got the Nobel Peace Prize for his efforts."

"Some efforts," Sam said. "Russia and Japan are still at war."

"Hah," Walter said, "but not with each other now, right?"

"True," Sam agreed.

"You know, speaking of history, a more recent history happened here just over a decade ago, about three blocks away. Do you remember that, Sam?"

"No, but I'm sure you're going to enlighten me."

Walter moved in his chair, looked out the window, as if trying to catch a glimpse of whatever had been there ten years earlier. He said quietly, "Roosevelt came here for a campaign rally in the summer of '32. A funny place for a Democratic candidate to be, since New Hampshire's been solidly Republican since... God, probably since Lincoln's time. But FDR was here and gave a little talk about the different times he had visited New Hampshire, and the Navy Yard, and just a bit of gossip. It was a Sunday, and Market Square was packed... and you know what? He could have read from the telephone directory and he would have been cheered. He had such magic in his words, such power."

"Sounds like you were there," Sam said.

"I was," Walter said simply. "Took the train up from Boston. He had... he had energy, a confidence, a style that was just what we needed. He won in a landslide. And then, just before he was inaugurated in '33, he was assassinated. Murdered by Giuseppe Zangara, an Italian with a grudge against power and powerful men."

Sam checked his watch, was sure that Mrs. Walton was now back from lunch and was keeping careful track of his absence from the office in her all-important Log. "I'd just gotten out of high school. Don't remember much about the assassination... more interested in girls and trying to get a job to help out my mom and dad. Walter, he was just a man. Okay? Just a man. He didn't become President. Somebody else did. Life goes on."

"Inspector, I'm sure you are correct about many things, many times, but you're wrong about Roosevelt. He was what this country desperately needed. Hell, maybe even what the world needed, a real strong leader, and he was taken away before he could do one damn thing. And the man we got after his murder, his Vice President, was a Texan nonentity who bumbled through his four years and did nothing of note except clear the stage for our current glorious leader, a two-bit demagogue from Louisiana who loves being on the stage, loves crushing his enemies and jailing them, loves eating and drinking and whoring and doesn't do much of anything else except drive this nation deeper into our own little red-white-and-blue brand of fascism. Don't ever think one man can't make a tremendous difference."

"Maybe so, but I don't have the benefit of your college education," Sam said.

His companion smiled wearily. "Not many do. Tell me, Sam. Did you vote for the son of a bitch?"

Sam toyed with his napkin and said, "My first vote for President. And who else was I going to vote for? It was even tougher back then. My dad, he was getting sicker, needed help... and none of the hospitals or relief agencies could help him. He died at home, coughing his lungs out. So yeah, I voted for Long. He promised change so old guys like my dad wouldn't have to die without medical help."

"It was meant to be, Long being elected the first time around," Walter said reflectively. "Unemployment was thirty percent, factories were cold, grass was growing in city streets, people were literally starving. When people are scared, they'll give power to anyone they think will protect them. So he promised change, and we certainly got a whole lot of change. And none of it good. We could have been a great generation, you know, something for the history books, instead of what we've become."

Sam thought of the dead man, thought about his own job. Do your job and try to keep your head down. That's all that really mattered in these days of the Black Marias and political killings and lists.

"And me," Walter quietly went on. "Blackballed from Harvard, and all because of something I did back in 1934 that put me on a list."

"In '34? You were an early hell-raiser, then."

Another faint smile. "Me and a few dozen others. We were protesting the fact that our learned institution was honoring one of its famed alumni, Ernst Hanfstaengl, who had graduated twenty-five years earlier. Good old Ernst, varsity crew rower, football cheerleader, performer at the Hasty Pudding Club, and in 1934, devoted Nazi, head of foreign press operations for the Third Reich. That Nazi bastard even had tea at the home of James Conant, the Harvard president, even though everyone knew the terror he and his friends were beginning against the Jews and others. So I protested, got on a list, and when I refused to sign that loyalty oath a couple of years ago, that's all it took. Now here I am, back in Portsmouth—"

He stopped, as Donna dropped off the check on the table and said, "Thanks for coming by, Sam. And even with Larry back, don't be a stranger, okay?"

"Sure," Sam replied. "And good luck to the both of you, all right?"

"Thanks, hon," she said. Walter watched her walk back into the kitchen, and so did Sam. "Walter, I'm sorry, I've got to go."

"Oh. Excuses, I'm terribly sorry. One of the many curses of being a writer. You forget other people have jobs and responsibilities and places to be."

The college professor reached for his wallet, and Sam thought of something. "Walter, you've been my tenant for more than a year. This is the first time you've ever had lunch with me. What's going on?"

Walter seemed to struggle for a moment and then leaned over the table, lowering his voice. "I'm... I'm sorry to say this, but I was hoping I could ask a favor of you."

"You can ask," Sam said. "Doesn't mean I'll say yes."

Walter took that in and nervously looked around again. "It's like this. In my time in Portsmouth, I've made a number of friends with our... our foreign guests. Guests who might not have the proper paperwork. I was thinking—hoping, actually—that if you were to hear word of a crackdown, you might, well, see your way through to—"

"Walter." Walter's face was expressionless, as though he knew he had pressed too far.

"Yes?"

"Pay the check. I've got to get back to work."

Walter examined the bill, and the next few moments were excruciating, as the older man counted out three singles and then a handful of change. Sam felt a twinge of guilt. Being a police inspector didn't earn much, but at least the pay was regular. Depending on money to arrive magically in your mailbox from magazines in New York had to be a tough life.

"Let me help you with the tip," he said, and Walter's face colored, but he said nothing as Sam pulled out his wallet. On the sidewalk, Sam said, "Walter, no promises. But I'll see what I can do if there's a crackdown. Now. Here's a question for you: Do any of your refugee friends have tattoos on their wrists? Tattoos of numbers?"

"No, I've never heard of such a thing. Why do you ask?"

"I can't say," Sam said. "Sorry. But I've really got to go now."

"Very good, Sam. It... it was a pleasure."

A shiny black Buick wagon with whitewalls went by, two men in the front seat. It seemed as though Walter shivered, standing next to Sam. "A Black Maria, on its rounds," the older man said. "Such evil men out there, to drive and use such a wagon."

"Yeah," Sam said to his tenant. "Such men." He quickly crossed the street and almost bumped into another man. This time the sign said EXPERIENCE IN PLUMBING & HEATING. PLEASE HELP CHILDREN HAVE NO SHOES. The man looked up at him, chin quivering, cheeks covered with stubble, and Sam murmured a quick "excuse me" and briskly walked back to his own job.

CHAPTER FIFTEEN

Outside the City Hall and police station, a slight man was pacing back and forth, stopping when he saw Sam approach. He was dressed in a dark brown suit that had been the height of fashion about ten years ago; it had exposed threads at the cuffs. A soiled red bow tie was tied too tight about the shirt collar. The man nodded, licking his lips quick, like a cat that had been caught stealing cream. His face was sallow, as though he had spent most of his life indoors, which he no doubt had, since the man before Sam was one of the best forgers in the state.

Kenny Whalen said, "Inspector, please, a moment of your time?"

"What's the matter, Kenny? Still upset that I arrested you last week?"

"Price of the business I'm in, including paying for my bail. But please, a word in private?"

"Just for a minute. I've got to get back to my desk." Sam led the forger down an alleyway and stopped by an overflowing trash bin. He said, "Kenny, I still don't know why you were so stupid to forge those checks for your brother-in-law. The idiot tried to cash them at the same bank, all at the same time. He gave you up about sixty seconds after I arrested him."

Kenny grimaced. "If one has a shrew of a wife, one does what one cap to soothe the home fires."

"All right, what do you want?"

"What I want... Inspector, you have me charged with six counts of passing a forged instrument. If I'm convicted on all six counts, I'm looking at five to six years in the state prison in Concord."

"You should have thought about that earlier."

"True, but if I may... if I were only charged with *five* counts of passing a forged instrument instead of six, then my charge would be of a lower class. If convicted on all five counts, I'll be facing one to three years, and if I'm lucky, at the county jail across the street. Not the state prison in Concord. Easier for friends and family to visit, you understand."

"I still don't know what you're driving at, Kenny."

"You're a man of the world, you know how things work. If, for example, one of the charges were to be dropped or forgotten, it would make a world of difference for me and my family. And in return, well, consideration could be made. Favors and expressions of gratitude could be expressed. And, um, so forth."

"This is your lucky day. I've decided to review your charges, just like you've asked. And you know what?"

"What?" He asked it eagerly.

"I've decided not to charge you with attempted bribery along with everything else. Forget it, Kenny. Leave me alone." He started out of the alley, and Kenny muttered something. Sam turned and said, "What was that?"

The forger looked defiant. "I said you've got a price, just like everyone else in that station! Least you could do is tell me what it is."

"Wrong cop, wrong day. Can't be bought."

"Bullshit."

"Yeah, take care of yourself, too, Kenny," Sam said. "Drop me a postcard from Concord if you get a chance." Out of the alleyway, the sunlight felt good as he went up the police station's front steps. He should have felt a bit of pride for turning down a bribe—and this hadn't been the first time on the force he had done that—but the small victory tasted sour.

The house, a voice inside him whispered, *remember the house...*

Up on the second floor, he saw a chilling sight: the city marshal sitting at Sam's desk. Harold Hanson was leaning back, hands across his plump belly, looking up at him from behind horn-rimmed glasses. Mrs. Walton was at her desk, lips thin, no doubt distressed at seeing the order of the ages upended by the city marshal sitting at a mere inspector's desk.

"Inspector Miller," Hanson said. "There's a gentleman from the FBI in my office, along with another... gentleman. They're here to see you."

"About what, sir?"

"I don't know. What I do know is one of Hoover's bright boys, with another bright boy accompanying him, are here. You're going to use my office, talk to them, cooperate, and when they depart, I expect a full report."

A voice inside him started to nag. *Do it now,* it said. *Tell the marshal about your brother. Don't try to cover it up. Give up Tony and you can salvage your career, your life, your future. You can tell the FBI you were surprised last night, which is why you didn't give up Tony earlier.* Now, the voice said, more insistent. *Give him up now and maybe they won't dig more, find out about the Underground Railroad station running out of your basement, and all will be good, and—*

"I understand what you want, sir," Sam said.

"Good. Now get your ass in there and do what you have to do so I can have my goddamn office back."

Sam hesitated. Could he trust Hanson to contact Sarah, tell her to grab the boy and leave town before the FBI shipped them off to Utah in a boxcar? And if he asked his boss to do something like that, wasn't he admitting he was guilty and—

Could he trust Hanson? Or anyone?

Sam walked to the door. He didn't bother knocking. He just opened it and went in, keeping his head high.

CHAPTER SIXTEEN

He entered the marshal's office into a dense fugue of cigarette smoke. One of the visitors was sitting in Hanson's chair. He was a ruddy-faced, large-framed man with dark wavy hair. He had on a loud gray and white pinstriped suit that said flashy big city to Sam, and his black wide- brimmed hat was on the marshal's desk. Sitting in one of the captain's chairs was a second man. His suit was plain dark gray, and his blond hair was fine and closely trimmed. Unblinking light blue eyes looked out from behind round wire-rimmed glasses. His own black hat was in his lap.

"Inspector Miller?" asked the man in the pinstriped suit. He stood up from Hanson's leather chair, holding out a hand.

"That's right," Sam replied, feeling the strong grip as he shook the man's hand.

"Special Agent Jack LaCouture, FBI, assigned to the Boston office." LaCouture's voice was Southern—no doubt Louisianan, for the Kingfish made sure a lot of his boys were sprinkled throughout the federal government.

"Glad to meet you," Sam said, knowing his tone of voice was expressing just the opposite. LaCouture motioned to his companion, who stood up. Sam froze, knowing the mild-looking guy, who resembled a grocery clerk or something equally bland, must be with the labor camp bureau of the Department of the Interior. In a very few seconds, he knew, everything was going to the shits.

So be it, he thought.

But Tony wasn't mentioned at all. Instead, the FBI man said, "Allow me to introduce my traveling companion. Hans Groebke, from the German consulate in Boston." Groebke gave a brisk nod, and his hand was cool as Sam did the usual grip-and-release. Sam made out the faint scent of cologne.

"A pleasure," the German said in a thick accent, and he turned to

LaCouture and rattled off something quick in German. LaCouture listened and said to Sam, "Hans says he's glad to make your acquaintance and hopes you will be able to assist him in this matter. He also apologizes for his rough English. He doesn't *sprechen* the King's language that well, you know?"

They all sat down and Sam said, "What kind of matter are you interested in?"

LaCouture answered, "The dead man by your railroad tracks the other night. We'd like to know how your investigation is proceeding."

"I'm sorry," Sam said, feeling his head spin: the body, not Tony, not the Underground Railroad, that was why the FBI was here! "Why is the German consulate concerned about a dead man?"

LaCouture smiled, revealing firm and white teeth. "First of all, it appears your body may be that of a German citizen, perhaps here illegally. Second, the German consulate doesn't give a crap about the body. But Herr Groebke does, as a member of the *Geheime Staatspolizei.*"

"The *Geheime...* I'm sorry, what's that again?"

"*Geheime Staatspolizei,*" LaCouture repeated patiently. "The Secret State Police. More commonly known as the Gestapo. Hans is stationed at the Boston consulate."

How many lurid newspaper stories had Sam read and potboiler movies had he seen, all about the sinister Gestapo in Berlin and Vienna and Paris and London, keeping track of illegals, Jews, anybody opposed to the Nazi regime? Dark stories of torture, of the midnight knock on the door, to be dragged out of your home and never seen again. The Gestapo had replaced the bogeyman to scare little boys and girls at night.

But Groebke looked like an accountant. Nothing like the ten-foot monster in a black leather trench coat, slaughtering innocents across a half-dozen occupied countries in Europe.

Sam said, "I didn't know the Gestapo were here in the States."

"Sure," LaCouture said. "All the embassies and consulates have the Gestapo kicking around. The long arm of Hitler reaches lots of places, and there's a fair number of Germans who live here. The Gestapo likes to keep their eyes on everything, make sure they're good little Germans, even in the States."

Groebke said something in German to the FBI man, and LaCouture snapped something back. "Sorry, Inspector. Hans is a bit impatient. Krauts like everything to be neat and tidy and all official. So, let's cut to the chase: Did you have a body pop up here two days ago?"

"Yes, we did. An old man, no identification. A homicide. Found near railroad tracks down by a cove off the harbor."

"Any suspects?"

"No," Sam said.

"Did he have any luggage with him?" LaCouture asked.

"No."

"Any papers or photographs?"

"Nothing."

LaCouture translated the last few answers for the German. Then he said, "How was the body found?"

"A hobo walking the tracks found it. He also thought he saw someone in the area who might be of interest, but I haven't been able to recontact him."

LaCouture rattled off another string of German and then said, "Go on."

Sam looked at the blank, smooth face of the German and thought, *Sure, an accountant, a bank accountant who could toss a family from their home for one late mortgage payment without blinking an eye.*

He said, "That's about it. No other witnesses, not much information. I think the body—"

LaCouture interrupted. "I'm sure you were quite thorough. But from this moment forward, this matter is now under the jurisdiction of the FBI. All right, Detective?"

"Inspector," Sam corrected dryly. "My position within the department is inspector, not detective."

"My apologies, Inspector." The FBI guy smiled without a trace of remorse. "We'll be talking to your local medical examiner later today, and we want a copy of your report."

"You'll get what you want," Sam said, "but I'd like to know why you're so interested in this body. And how did you find out about it?"

"You sent a telex to the state police," LaCouture said. "We get copies of all those kinds of telexes. The Germans had been looking for this particular character for reasons they've kept to themselves."

"So you can't say who he is and why he was here illegally?"

"Even if I could, I won't, because it's now none of your business," LaCouture said. "Because we believe the body is that of a German illegal, it's a diplomatic matter, and because the investigating arm of the German government is the Gestapo, it's a Gestapo matter. And because we don't like the Gestapo traipsing across our fair land without an escort, it's also an FBI matter. Do I make myself clear?"

"Quite clear, but I still want to know—"

LaCouture folded his large hands, and Sam saw the man's nails gleamed with polish. "You seem to be a curious man. So am I. And I'm curious how a patrol sergeant like you became a police inspector while your older brother is serving a six-year sentence in a labor camp. A labor camp in New York, correct? The one near Fort Drum? The Iroquois camp?"

The German looked like he was enjoying seeing the two Americans sparring. Sam felt his mouth go dry. So Tony's name was going to come up after all. "Yes," Sam said. "My brother is serving a six-year sentence. For organizing a union. Used to be a time when that wasn't illegal."

"There was a time when booze was legal, became illegal, and then became legal again. Who the hell can keep track nowadays?" LaCouture chuckled.

Sam looked at the German and said, "You'll get my report. I'll have Mrs. Walton type up a copy, should be ready in under an hour. But I still want to know something."

"I don't care what you want to know, I don't have anything more to say to you."

"The question's not for you," Sam said. "It's for the Gestapo, if that's all right."

LaCouture glanced at Groebke. Then he said, "Go ahead, Inspector. But make it snappy."

Sam said, "This man was half starved. And there were numbers tattooed on his wrist. The numerals nine-one-one-two-eight-three. Can he explain that?"

LaCouture spoke a sentence or two to the German, who nodded in comprehension. Groebke said something slow and definite, and LaCouture told Sam, "He said he doesn't know the man's eating habits. As to the tattoo, perhaps someday you will be in Berlin, at Gestapo headquarters at Eight Prinz-Albrecht-Strasse, and then he may tell you. But not here, and not now."

"Not much of an answer," Sam remarked.

LaCouture motioned to the German, stood up, and grabbed his hat. "Only one you're going to get today. Now, this has been cheerful and all that, but you mind not wasting our fucking time any longer?"

Sam could feel his face burning. "No. I don't mind." The German made a short bow. "Herr Inspector, *danke*. Thank you. Goodbye."

"Yeah. So long."

After they left, Marshal Hanson came right in and reclaimed his seat with a look of distaste that somebody else could have occupied his place of honor and polluted his office with cigarette smoke. He folded his hands and said, "Well?"

"The FBI guy's name is LaCouture. His buddy there is from the

Gestapo. Groebke. They say the body from the other night was a German illegal."

"So they've taken the case from you. Now a federal matter. Good."

"Good?" Sam asked. "What's good about it? They waltzed right in here and took my case away... a homicide! You know how the FBI operates. We're never going to hear anything more about it."

"We're cooperating," Hanson said gruffly. "Which is the smart thing to do, so we don't piss off the wrong people and the FBI and Long's Legionnaires leave us alone. I know this was your first homicide, and you wanted to see it through. But I also know what your caseload is like. If you spend more time on your caseload and less time worrying about a matter now belonging to the Germans and the feds, then I'll be happy, the people of Portsmouth will be happy, and so will the police commission. Got it?"

"Yeah. I do."

"Fine. Now, about the other night. I was glad to see you at the Party meeting. Have you thought about what I said—about becoming more active?"

"No, I really haven't. With this John Doe investigation, I haven't considered it much."

"Do you think I was joking, Sam? This is no longer a request. Soon I'll be putting in your name for the county steering committee. There's a vote, but it's just a formality. And I expect a return favor from you concerning your father-in-law."

Sam felt as if the day and everything else were slipping away from him; he thought about what Sean had said. Nats versus Staties. "But the mayor, he's said something similar about me—"

"Divided loyalties, Sam? Or do I have to remind you who signs your time sheet?"

"No, you don't have to remind me."

"I didn't think I'd have to," Hanson said, looking triumphant. "What's ahead for you?"

"I told the FBI they could have copies of my reports later today. And that Mrs. Walton would type them up for them."

Now Hanson didn't look happy. "Since when you do start making commitments for my secretary?"

Sam stood up and pushed the chair back toward the desk. The legs squeaked gratingly against the wooden planks. "Since you told me to cooperate, that's when," Sam replied.

CHAPTER SEVENTEEN

Sam spent a few minutes at his desk, staring at the piles of paperwork. Then, restless and irritable, he headed for the stairs. Mrs. Walton—frowning because of the extra typing—called, "Inspector?"

"Off for a walk," he called back.

She smirked. "A walk."

"Sure. Put it in your log. W-A-L-K. A walk."

He went down the wooden stairs two at a time, through the lobby, and then outside. It was cloudy, and the salt smell from the harbor was strong.

His very first homicide, taken away from him. And not by the state police; no, by Hoover's own SS, the FBI. With the assistance of the Gestapo. And the assistance of his boss. Who would have thought?

Dammit.

He started walking away from the police station, heading south. Before him, a small gang of truant boys were huddling around something in the gutter. When they saw him approach, they looked up but kept at work, each holding a paper sack. Cig boys, picking up discarded cigarette butts to strip out the tobacco and then roll their own, selling them for a penny apiece on the streets.

Not much of a crime, but still.

"Beat it, guys," Sam said. "You're blocking traffic."

They scattered, but one boy with a cloth cap and patched jacket and black facial hair sprouting through his pimples said, "Screw you, bud," and lashed out with a fist.

Something struck Sam's right wrist. He grabbed at his arm and stepped back, but by the time he reached for his revolver, the boys were gone, racing down a trash-strewn alleyway. He looked at his wrist. Part of the coat sleeve was torn; the little thug had sliced at him with a knife! He pushed the tattered threads together and looked down the empty alleyway, holding his arm.

A few feet in another direction... could have been buried in his chest.

He lowered his arms, kept on walking. He couldn't do anything about those little bastards. Too much was going on. Damn Tony for breaking out and making everything even more dangerous. To add to the fun, he had been drafted twice this week: for the state National Guard, and now the county steering committee for the Party. What would Larry Young do when he heard his political rival was sponsoring his son-in-law?

Crap. Where the hell was he going?

Up ahead was the Portsmouth Hospital on a slight rise of land. It was as if his mind were directing him where to go.

Sam found William Saunders sitting at his desk, smoking a cigarette. The doctor looked up from a sheaf of papers. "Inspector Miller, to what do I owe this pleasure?"

"Looking to see if you've had any special visitors lately."

Saunders tapped some ash from the cigarette. "Alive or dead?"

"Alive, of course."

"Yeah, I have," he said. "Two thugs. One working for a gangster called Hitler, the other working for a gangster called Long. Charming visitors."

"Mind if I ask what they did here?"

"Hell, no," Saunders said. "The usual crap about autopsy, cause of death, that sort of thing. Stayed all of five minutes and then went on their way. But one interesting thing...They didn't want the body or his clothing. Funny, huh? You'd think a murder case that has the interest of the feds and the Gestapo would mean they'd want the body. At least to have smother autopsy done by a fed coroner. Nope. Our John Doe stays with the county."

Sam said, "I'd like to look at him again."

Once again, Sam followed the medical examiner into the autopsy room. Saunders went to the wall of refrigerator doors. The one in the center said JOHN doe.

Saunders opened the center door and reached in. The metal table slid out, making a creepy rattling noise. Saunders pulled down the soiled white sheet.

Sam stared at the dead man. Once upon a time this man walked and talked and breathed, was maybe loved, and had ended up here, in his city. Murdered.

Who are you ? he thought.

As if he were watching someone else, Sam reached down, turned over the stiff wrist, examined the faded blue numerals again.

9 1 12 8 3.

"Inspector?" Saunders asked. "Are you through here?"

"Yeah, I am," Sam said. He put the wrist down and wiped his hands on his coat. The sheet was placed back over the body, the tray was slid back in, and the door was closed.

"So what now?" Saunders asked.

"The FBI and the Gestapo have taken my case. This John Doe belongs to them. Question is, what do you do with the body?"

"Potter's field, where else? But if need be, I can keep him here for a while. If you'd like."

Sam remembered something from a couple of years back about old Hugh Johnson, his deceased predecessor. Hugh had been holding court one night in one of the local taverns when he loudly announced that the most important part of the job was closing the case. That's it. Close the case and move on. Closed cases meant no open files, no pressure from the Police Commission, and a good end-of-the-year report, to keep your job for the next year.

Just close those cases, boys, Hugh had said. *Close 'em up and move on.*

"That'd be great, Doc," Sam said. "Because I'm still going to work the case. It's mine. No matter what my boss says. Or the FBI and the Gestapo."

Saunders scratched at his throat, where the shrapnel scar from the Great War glistened out. "Your boss? The FBI? The Germans?"

"Yeah?"

"Fuck 'em all," the county medical examiner said.

"That's an unpatriotic response, Doc."

"Glad I surprised you. You get this old, sometimes that's the only joy you get—that and ticking off the powers that be."

Sam said, "What are you driving at?"

Saunders raised a hand. "Enough. Leave me be with my dead people, okay? Christ, at least they have the courtesy to leave me alone most hours."

When he left the city hospital, Sam knew where to go next. He walked the eight blocks briskly, thinking and planning. The Portsmouth railroad station stood at Deer Street, almost within eyeshot of his crime scene. It was an old two-story brick building with high peaked roofs, which looked as though the architect who had designed it had been frustrated that he hadn't been born during the time of the great European cathedrals. The last time Sam had been here had been as an errand boy, dropping off that Lippman character for the Interior Department.

Sam made his way past tiny knots of people buying tickets to Boston or Portland or checking on arrivals. He went through a glass door that said manager and took the chair across from Pat Lowengard. Pat was a huge man with slicked-back hair who looked like he couldn't stand up without his office chair sticking to his broad hips. He had on a tan suit and a bright blue necktie and looked surprised to see Sam. His desk was nearly bare, and on the walls were printed displays of train schedules for northern New England.

"Something more I can do for you, Sam?"

"Yeah, there is," Sam said. "I'm looking for more information about that five forty-five express from Boston to Portland."

"What kind of information?"

"Let's just say... is there anybody working at the station who might have been on that train?"

Lowengard rubbed at his fleshy chin. "Gee, I'm not sure..."

Sam waited, but Lowengard kept silent. Sam said, "Well?"

"Huh?"

Sam said, adding a bit of sharpness, "Then find out, will you? I need to know if anyone here was on that train. The sooner the better, Pat."

The man's face flushed. He picked up the phone, started talking to his secretary, made a second call. Sam sat there patiently. From outside there was the sharp whistle of a steam engine heading out, its engine hissing and grumbling.

Lowengard put the phone down. "You're in luck. A stoker named Hughes was on that train. He's in the marshaling yard. I told his boss to send him over. That all right?"

"That's perfect."

Sam waited, took out his notebook. Lowengard said, "Heard there was a corpse found two nights ago near our tracks. I hope you don't think we hit him, Sam. Even though the express goes through here pretty fast, our engineers would notice something like that."

Sam said nothing. Lowengard wet his lips with his tongue, as if he couldn't stand having his mouth being dry.

There was a knock at the door. Lowengard called out, "Come in!" and a man about Sam's age came in, wearing greasy overalls and a denim cap. His skin was soiled as well, especially his big hands, and when he entered the office, he took off his hat. There was a white stretch of clean skin on his forehead, making it look like an errant paintbrush had struck him.

Lowengard told Sam, "This is Peter Hughes. Peter, this is Sam Miller. He's an inspector from the Portsmouth PD. He'd like to ask you a few questions."

Hughes blinked and looked at Sam. "Is...Am I in some kind of trouble? Sir?"

Sam said, "No, not at all. I'm conducting an investigation, and I have some questions about the Portland express."

Hughes was twisting his hat in his big greasy hands. "An investigation, sir?"

"A police investigation," Sam said, flipping open his notebook. "You were on the express two nights ago, from Boston to Portland?"

"Yep."

"Did the train hit anything when it came through town?"

"No, sir. Not at all."

"You sure?"

" 'Course I'm sure. When we got to Portsmouth, hell, even if we did hit somebody, it probably wouldn't've hurt 'em bad, anyway."

Sam lowered his fountain pen. "I'm sorry, say that again."

Hughes looked to Lowengard as if for reassurance, but Lowengard's face had paled and Hughes found no reassurance there. He said, "Well, we were coming through town at a crawl."

"You were? How fast was the train going?"

"Oh, crap, who knows. Three—maybe four—miles an hour. A nice slow pace."

Lowengard said, "What the hell do you mean, four miles or hour? You're supposed to be traveling much faster through there. Was the engine having problems?"

"No, the engine was fine, Mr. Lowengard. It's just that, well, there was an auto on the tracks. On Market Street. Damnedest thing you ever saw. An auto, just sitting there pretty as you please. A yellow Rambler. Stan Tompkins, he's the lead engineer, he hit the brakes and we slowed damn fast, and then the car drove off the tracks and headed downtown. Damn thing slowed us down right, that's for sure. We had to pour on the steam somethin' awful so we'd make our schedule to Portland." Sam looked at Lowengard. "And you didn't know this?"

"No, I didn't," he said, indignation in his voice.

"Really? Station manager for Portsmouth and a train is forced to slow way down by a conveniently parked car, and this is the first you know of it?"

"If the train hit the car, fine," Lowengard said. "Then I'd know. But a train slowed down by a car? Christ, Sam, every day something slows down the train. Kids playing on the tracks. A stuck truck. I don't know everything about every damn train that comes through. This is the first I heard of it. Honest to Christ."

Sam knew what both men were thinking: In these days, companies had no patience with anyone getting noticed by the law. If you caused a problem, any problem at all, you were out. Plenty of talented people were out there in the dole lines, begging for a job.

He said, "Mr. Hughes, thanks for the information. You can go."

In an instant, the railroad worker was out the door. Sam said, "Pat..."

"Yes?" The station manager's face was still pale.

"I want the passenger manifest for that express train."

"That might be hard to get." Lowengard frowned. "Lots of paperwork. Ever since the new law about internal transportation records kicked in a couple of years back, you wouldn't believe the stacks of paper—"

"How long?"

A shrug. "Lots of paper. A week. Maybe two."

"All right," Sam said. "Two it is."

The station manager grinned with relief. "Thanks for understanding. "

"Sorry, maybe you didn't understand me. When I said two, I meant two days."

"Days? Two days? That's impossible!"

"Well, it's going to have to be possible. Or there're going to be lots of parking tickets around this station in the future. Got it?"

"Yeah, I got it," Lowengard said, and Sam noted his forehead was shiny with sweat. The phone on the desk rang, and Lowengard grabbed it before the second ring. After listening for a few moments, he grunted a "yeah" and tossed the receiver back into the cradle. "There's a train here that's not on the schedule, that needs to be watered up. You wouldn't believe the crap I have to put up with, Sam. Would not believe it... and then you waltz in here and add to it."

"I'm investigating a homicide, Pat," Sam said.

Lowengard picked up the phone again. "And I'm trying to run a train station and trying to keep my ass out of said train. Grace? Get me dispatch right away."

Outside, Sam spotted some cars parked at the other end of the station, blocking the entrance. People were running away from the cars, heading to the tracks. A few of them were yelling, raising their arms, as other cars braked, two with steam spewing from their radiators.

He followed the noise to a fence blocking off the tracks. The men and women and some children were up against the chain-link fence, holding on to it with their hands, looking out to the train yard, to a parked locomotive, eight boxcars trailing and—

Sam saw National Guardsmen standing outside the train, carrying rifles with fixed bayonets. No wonder Lowengard had been so upset. A labor camp train, stopping here for coal or water before going out west or up north or someplace where the communists, the labor leaders, the strikers, any and all enemies, foreign and especially domestic, were dumped. Something cold tickled at the back of his neck. Those people in that train... they were heading to a labor camp for choices they had made, people they had associated with, organizations they had supported.

Choices. The cold feeling increased. And what kind of choices was he making now?

"Saul Rothstein!"

"Hugh! Hugh Toland!"

"Sue! Sue Godin! Are you in there?"

One heavyset woman with a blue scarf tied about her head turned to Sam, tears in her eyes. "Sir? Can you help? Can you?" She gestured at the train. "That train... it left Brooklyn two days ago. We followed it, best we can, they no tell us where it's going. Now we just want to bring food and drink. That all."

Brown paper grocery sacks lay on the cracked sidewalk. There were barred windows at each end of the boxcar, and hands were poking out between the bars, waving. Sam looked up and down the fence, spotted a gate. A B&M railroad detective, dressed in a brown suit, with a badge clipped to the coat pocket, was standing on the other side.

"Hey," Sam said. "How about opening the gate, let these folks bring some food over to the train?"

The detective shifted the toothpick in his mouth. "Hey. How about you leave me the hell alone?"

Sam pulled out his badge, pressed it up against the fence. "Name's Miller. I'm the inspector for the Portsmouth Police Department. What's your name?"

"Collins," he grudgingly replied.

"Look, Collins, let these people go in there. And tell you what: For the rest of the month, you can park anywhere you want, speed anywhere you want, and no Portsmouth cop will ever bother you. How does that sound?"

Collins said, "Boss'll get pissed at me."

"I can handle Lowengard. C'mon, let these folks go over, drop off the food, be a nice guy for a change."

Collins shifted the toothpick again. "What's it to you, then?"

"Guess I like being a nice guy sometimes."

Collins scowled and spat out the toothpick, but stepped back. The crowd watched silently as he unlocked the gate. In a brusque voice, he said, "You folks go up there, pass over the stuff, then leave. Any funny business, you'll be thrown in the boxcar with those slugs, and you'll be in a labor camp tonight!"

Sam felt the crowd swirl about him like water parting around a rock, and there was a touch on his arm, the woman with the scarf, who whispered something foreign—Yiddish, perhaps?—and said, "God bless." She joined the other family members streaming to the parked train, rushing over the railroad tracks. Within moments grocery sacks, bottles of Coke and Pepsi, and sandwiches were being passed up to the barred openings, the eager hands reaching down, grasping for life.

Sam walked away. Maybe Walter was right. Maybe one man could make a difference. But for how long?

He stopped and looked back at the train, thinking again of the train that had sped through late one night, the one that was sometimes in his dreams. It was similar to this one but different—there were no openings allowing air and sunlight to come in. Those boxcars had been shuttered closed, as if those in charge didn't want anyone to see what was inside.

But they couldn't hide the voices, couldn't hide the screams.

And one more thing. The train that night, speeding through the darkness, had gone past a streetlight, illuminating the shuttered boxcars and...

And what else?

The paint scheme. The cars in front of him were dark red. The special train from that night was a dark color as well, but there was a difference.

Yellow stripes had been painted on the sides of those special trains.

What the hell did that mean?

Nothing, that's what, and nothing that was going to solve this murder for him.

He went to his desk, ignored Mrs. Walton, and when she got up to powder her nose, he picked up his phone, got an operator, and made a call to Concord again, this time to the motor vehicle division of the Department of Safety. He quickly found out it would take a week to get him a listing of all yellow Ramblers registered in the state. A week... well, what the hell. Make it thorough. Maybe it was an accident, maybe it was deliberate, but the train slowing down in Portsmouth was a question mark, and he wanted that question answered. Was the train slowed on purpose so the body could be dumped?

After the phone call, he was going through his old case files when a familiar voice spoke up.

"Inspector," said the man. "You look like you could use some hooch. And since this department is officially dry, how about a cup of joe instead?"

Sam swung about in his chair, saw a smiling Sean Donovan before him, holding two white mugs of coffee. Sean limped over and pulled a chair closer to Sam's desk. "I understand you've had quite the busy day."

"I have," Sam said, sipping the coffee. Sean had made it the way he liked it: black, with two sugars.

Sean nodded. "No doubt dealing with the forces of darkness. I'm surprised you didn't go home and take a bath after spending time with those two G-men."

"Only one was a G-man," Sam said. "The other was— Oh, I get it. A joke. FBI guy and Gestapo guy. Both G-men."

Sean raised his mug to his lips. "So now we both have something in common, having spent time with these G-men."

Sam swung around in his chair, glad Mrs. Walton wasn't back yet. "They've talked to you, too?"

"I'm not sure if 'talk' is the right word," Sean answered. "This was more like requests made, requests complied with. The FBI man wanted some files, which I happily passed over to him. And he seemed pretty eager to share what he had with his goose-stepping friend." Sam said, "What kind of files?"

"Hmmm," Sean said, sipping. "Anybody else in this building, I would say none of your business. But since you're more than the average cop, I will tell you this. Personnel files."

"I thought the FBI would be looking into active cases. Not personnel files."

Sean laughed. "That's a good one. Sam, why would the FBI give a shit about criminal cases at the Portsmouth Police Department? Drunk driving? Hookers? Break-ins? Oh, I know they've taken away your homicide, but the real crimes the FBI and their German friends are interested in are the new ones: disloyalty, lack of enthusiasm for the new order, thought crimes like that."

Sam heard footsteps, saw Mrs. Walton ambling her way back. He leaned over to Sean. "So. Whose personnel files were they asking for?"

"You really want to know?"

"Of course."

Sean smiled. "Yours."

120

CHAPTER EIGHTEEN

That night Sam and Sarah went out to the movies. He was eager to slip into a make-believe world for a while, a world without the FBI or Gestapo or the Underground Railroad or rats or the Party. Sarah had tsk-tsked over the slash the knife had made in his coat sleeve, and had promised to mend it later. Still, Jesus, what a day.

Though a small city, Portsmouth boasted three movie theaters, and tonight they went to the Colonial, up on Congress Street. Throughout Sarah's pre-movie dinner— fish stew—he kept up a steady patter of conversation, playing the good husband, playing the good father (definitely not playing the rat!), though he had hardly any appetite at all. He had a cold feeling about the meeting with the FBI earlier today, about how close he had seemed to losing it all because of Tony. If that wasn't enough, another Underground Railroad passenger was going to spend the night in their basement. Talk about living dangerously.

And then there was that train, ready to depart Portsmouth, to drop off another load of prisoners, where there was always room in other trains for one more dissident, one more family.

During dinner Sarah had seemed more cheerful, as though determined to gloss over what was going to happen in their home later that night. And when he had mentioned the visit by the FBI and the Gestapo, Sarah paused at that, ladle held in the air. "Gestapo? Here?"

"That's right," he had said, buttering a piece of bread. "Assigned to the consulate in Boston. It seems my dead man was from Germany, here illegally. So it's not my case anymore. The feds took it away."

Sarah glanced at Toby and dipped the ladle in the stew. "It's impossible to believe the Gestapo are here in Portsmouth. It's bad enough to have Long's Legionnaires here, but the Gestapo..."

"That's what the papers and newsreels say. But this German didn't look that evil to me. More like a paper shuffler, a cop like me."

Sarah shook her head. "No. You're wrong, Sam. I don't care what he looks like. The whole bunch of them— Nazis, Gestapo, SS—they're pure evil. Mrs. Brownstein at the school, some of the stories she's told us about what they did to her relatives over in Holland..."

Sam had raised his eyebrows, glancing at Toby taking in every word, and Sarah had changed the subject. Then they had left, with their tenant Walter in charge as a babysitter. Toby had that devil look in his eyes. Sam hoped Walter was in a mood to be tested by an eight-year-old.

Now they were sitting in the darkened theater, most of the men nearby smoking, a paper bag of greasy popcorn between them, Sarah cuddled against his shoulder. Tonight was a Judy Garland musical, and though Sam enjoyed being out, he had to work to pay attention. The FBI—and the Gestapo!—were looking at his personnel files. For what? Not much was in there, nothing that the FBI probably already didn't know, but maybe the Kraut wanted to learn more about Sam and—

He was suddenly poked in his ribs. "What?" he whispered to Sarah. "What's wrong?"

"I said something, and you're not listening to me," she whispered back.

"Oh, sorry. Mind drifted. What did you say?"

"I said I hope Walter does a better job babysitting. Last time he fell asleep on the couch and Toby tied his shoelaces together."

Sam said, "At least he's free. You remember what happened with that bobby-soxer Claire. She charged us two dollars, brought her boyfriend over, and Toby got a quick lesson in make-out sessions about five years ahead of schedule."

"Shhh," someone in the audience scolded, and then the films began.

There were a couple of previews of coming attractions, and then a Bugs Bunny short, and Sam felt himself unwind as he joined Sarah and the others in laughing at the antics of that wascally wabbit. Then came the familiar trumpet tunes of Movietone, showing the bloody world in its black-and-white glory.

Up on the screen, thick smoke was rising up over a village, and a line of panzer tanks was crossing a field. The narrator said, *"As spring continues and summer beckons in the fields of Russia, fresh fighting continues while German and Russian tank divisions grapple once again for supremacy. The third year of fighting in Eastern Europe continues afresh, with most observers predicting another fierce struggle for each side to gain the upper hand. Unless there is a dramatic change in the fortunes for Nazi Germany or Red Russia, experts say to expect another year of bloodshed before the snows come."*

As the narration continued, the familiar newsreel shots of tanks on the move, Stuka aircraft dive-bombing, and German soldiers on the march were repeated, but Sam noticed that now, as opposed to during their blitz-krieg victories in '40 and '41, the Krauts looked exhausted, faces dirty and grim.

Trumpet tone, change of view, showing more troops, this time Japanese, swarming across rice paddies. *"The Empire of the Rising Sun, "* the narrator went on, *"continues its expansion west as it fights to secure some sort of stability in Manchuria and China. Forces loyal to Generalissimo Chiang Kai-shek and Communist leader Mao Tse-tung continue their guerrilla warfare, making sure the soldiers of the Japanese emperor battle for every inch of ground lost in China. "*

Sarah whispered, "I'm so sick of this foreign news.

Let's see the movie already." He squeezed her leg as a familiar cherubic face popped up on the screen, to the assortment of scattered boos and a few cheers. A rotund man who was smoking a cigar walked through a hotel lobby through a barrage of camera flashes and questions from a mob of reporters. The man held up two fingers in the shape of a V

"Former British prime minister Winston Churchill, in New York City this week, continues to meet with supporters of the so-called British government in exile. "

Churchill stopped before a set of radio microphones and said in a tired, lisping tone, *"We are fighting to save the whole world from the pestilence of Nazi tyranny and in defense of all that is most sacred to man. This is no war of domination or imperial aggrandizement or material gain; no war to shut any country out of its sunlight and means of progress. It is a war, viewed in its inherent quality to establish, on impregnable rocks, the rights of the individual, and it is a war to establish and revive the stature of man. "*

Another trumpet tone, another switch, and even more cheers and a few boos as the President appeared on the screen, shaking hands with a dour-faced man wearing formal clothes.

"In our nation's capitol, President Huey Long completed discussions this week with the German ambassador over future relations between the American republic and the Third Reich. Neither man had anything to say for reporters, but word around the capitol is that a new era of peace and understanding lays ahead for American democracy and the Third Reich. "

There was a quick jump in the newsreel to a bald man in a suit, hurrying past photographers in a polished corridor. *"Also in Washington, Treasury Secretary Henry Morgenthau was again unsuccessful in his attempts to expand the number of Jewish refugees allowed into this country by Congress. "*

A shout from a male in the audience: "Leave the kikes where they belong!" and a couple of others laughed; Sam sat still, embarrassed at the outburst.

Another jump to a number of gray-suited men with matching gray faces, standing in front of some government office.

"From our friends in the north, an unexpected trade delegation from the embattled Soviet Union has paid a surprise visit to Montreal, refusing to even go to that nation's capital of Ottawa. What areas of discussion were made with the Canadian government remain a secret, but some observers believe the Reds are looking for assistance from their neighbors across the North Pole. "

One more trumpet tone and a few more cheers and whistles as the Hollywood sign came up on the screen, and then a swimming pool, and some sort of talent contest involving young lovelies in bathing suits standing under palm trees. It was hard to hear what the narrator was saying over the wolf whistles. Sarah nibbled his ear. "Like what you see, sport?"

"Like who I'm with," he said. "How's that?"

She whispered, "Glad to hear it. Here's a taste of what's yours."

He looked down, felt a warm tingle expand from the base of his neck. Sarah had daringly pulled her skirt up past her thighs, showing the top of her stockings. She gave a soft laugh and pushed the skirt back. Sam whispered, "Never get tired of tasting that, sweetheart."

That earned him another kiss. He bit her ear and she sighed. He whispered, "Remember the times back up in the balcony when we were dating, learning to French?"

One more kiss and she warned, laughing. "You keep it up and I'll drag you back up there, Inspector."

He squeezed her leg. "No room. I already checked. We'll have to save it for later."

"Deal," she whispered back, fingers flickering over the front of his trousers. "Now be a good boy and watch the movie."

He sat back in his seat, feeling warm and almost happy, despite all that had gone on this day. The feature film started, a cowboy musical called *Girl Crazy*, with Judy Garland and Mickey Rooney. The thought nagged at him as the credits unrolled up on the screen that it seemed unseemly, with the world at war and in chaos, with empires bloodletting for survival, that what got everybody's interest here in the States were Hollywood starlets.

It was, he thought, like living in an apartment building. When the screaming from the neighbors started, when the bottles were being tossed and the punches thrown, you just turned up the radio and pretended everything would be all right.

When the movie let out, they joined the other patrons spilling out onto the sidewalk. Standing by the entrance, waving, was Donna Fitzgerald. Sam gave her a wide smile and saw a skinny man standing next to her, Donna's hand firmly clasped in his. Sam thought, *Welcome home, Larry. Welcome home from the camps.*

Somebody else called out, "Sam! Hey, Sam!" Standing by the theater door was Harold Hanson, accompanied by his wife. Hanson waved Sam over, and Sarah's hand tightened on his arm. "Oh, God, his wife... I forget, what's that shrew's name?"

"Doris," Sam murmured. "Come on, we'll make it quick."

The marshal's wife—a tiny woman with gray hair tied back in a bun and a pinched expression—stood up on her toes and whispered something in her husband's ear, then ducked back into the movie theater. When they reached him, Hanson held out his hand to Sarah and said, "Dear, so nice to see you out tonight."

Sarah said properly, "And so nice for me to have him for a night. Without being called out on a case. Or going to a Party meeting. Or something else."

Hanson seemed taken aback. Then he nodded. "Well, yes, we all have duties and obligations to perform, including the Party. Sam, I wanted to thank you for your cooperation today with the FBI and his German friend. They said they got everything they needed."

Sam said, "Did they tell you who the dead man was?"

"No, they didn't. And it's not our case anymore, so let it be. They promised to inform us if they have anything we need to know."

"I'm sure," Sam said, and Sarah squeezed his arm again. She could sense the sarcasm in his voice, but Hanson didn't seem to pick up on it, for his expression lightened and he said, "If you excuse me, Doris said she had to go powder her nose, and you know how long that can take."

"Good night," Sam said, and Hanson smiled down at Sarah and went into the theater.

"Sam, what was that all about?" Sarah asked him.

"I'm being warned off."

"Warned off what?"

"That dead man by the tracks. The case supposedly isn't mine. And I think the marshal saw me tonight and decided to remind me of that."

She stopped, making him stop as well, in front of a Rexall drugstore. "What do you mean," she demanded, "supposedly? Are you off the case or not?"

"Officially, yes. Unofficially, Sarah, it's my first murder case. I'm not going to just give it up."

She looked up at him, and there was something going on with her eyes. He couldn't decipher her expression. Then she seemed to make a decision. "All right, Sam. Do you what you have to do. You're still on probation... and well, I don't think either of us can stand it if you get bumped down back to sergeant. Just be careful."

"I will."

She surprised him by kissing him on the lips. "That Harold Hanson... if he and the rest of them only knew how lucky they were to have you, Sam Miller."

He put his arm around her, squeezed her tight, and kissed her. "As lucky as I am to have you."

And then her mood lifted, as if changing a frock, and she chattered on about the musical they had just seen, but he was distracted as they walked up to the Packard. He always prided himself on being able to gauge Sarah's moods. But back there, when she was asking about his case, it was as if he were looking at a blank wall.

What was going on with Sarah? That had always been part of her allure, that at one moment she could joke about dragging him up to the balcony for some loving and then be hard as stone when it came to running the Underground Railroad station. A lover and a fighter, all mixed in one pretty, exasperating package.

Sam knew he should ask her, but now her mood was cheerful, upbeat, and he wanted it to last. He also wanted to stop thinking of Donna and that sweet, uncomplicated smile.

CHAPTER NINETEEN

When they got home, Walter tottered back upstairs, declaring Toby had been a peach of a boy. Sarah went to check on their son as Sam hung up their coats. When Sarah came back, he walked to the cellar door. "Going to the basement for a second."

"All right. And it's the last one. Promise. And be nice to him, whoever he is."

"I'll be nice," he replied, trying to keep his voice even. "And you're the one telling me to be careful, my little revolutionary."

He was rewarded with a smile. "When you come back up, sweetie, I'll show you just how dangerous I can be." As he turned the knob, the doorbell rang. Sarah stopped, shocked. He said more sharply than he intended, "Any chance there's been a foul-up? That your passenger thought he had to come to the front door?"

Sarah had paled. "No, impossible. They all know the routine."

The doorbell rang again, followed by a pounding at the door and muffled voices. To his wife, in a low and determined tone, Sam said, "No argument, Sarah. No discussion. Go to Toby's room now. If you hear me shouting, grab him. Climb out the window. Go to one of the neighbors and call your dad. Do you understand?"

Lips pursed, she left the room. Sam went to the vestibule, looked at the upper shelf, where his service revolver rested.

"Just a sec," he called out. He switched on the porch light and opened the door.

Before him stood two Long's Legionnaires.

He took a breath. "Something I can do for you?"

He'd never seen these two before. They looked so alike that they could have been brothers. But the one on the left was taller and carried a clipboard, and the other one was shorter, squatter, and had his arms crossed across his uniform jacket, as though he was impatient about everything.

127

"Evenin', sir," the one carrying the clipboard said. "My name is Carruthers. This here is LeClerc. We're doin' a survey of our local Party members, lookin' for some information."

Sam held the doorknob tight. "What kind of information?"

An insolent shrug from LeClerc. "Stuff. You know how it is."

"No. I don't know how it is."

Carruthers said, "All right if we come in?"

"No, it's not all right. It's late. My boy's in bed, and my wife is getting ready to retire."

LeClerc made a point of leaning to one side, looking over Sam's shoulder. "Your wife gettin' ready by goin' into your cellar? Door's open."

Sam didn't move. "I was just down there, checking on the furnace."

LeClerc said, "With the light off?"

"I turned the light off when I came up, when I heard you fellows ringing and banging on our door. Now, if you don't—"

Carruthers smiled. "Well, sir, we do mind, if you don't mind me sayin', and we'd like to come in and ask a few questions..."

LeClerc started moving forward. Sam stayed where he was, blocking the doorway. "It's late," he said. "You know who I am and where I work. If this is so damn important, you can talk to me there. Otherwise, get the hell off my porch."

Carruthers glanced to his companion, then looked at Sam. Sam tensed, wondering if Sarah was ready; if these two clowns made one more step in his direction, he was going to start throwing punches, and—

The Legionnaire on the left—Carruthers—smiled. "If you say so, sir. We'll try to get to you tomorrow. At the police station. Tell your wife and boy good night, now, okay?"

Their heavy boots clattered on the worn planks, as they went down the porch stairs. Sam closed and locked the door, then switched off the light. He realized his hands were shaking.

The door to Toby's room was open, the night-light on. Sarah sat on the end of the sleeping boy's bed. Sam said in a quiet voice, "They're gone."

"Who are they?" Sarah whispered back.

"Long's Legionnaires. Two of them."

"Oh, Sam..."

"They said they were conducting some kind of survey. I told them to come to my office tomorrow."

"Sam—"

"I'm going to the cellar," he said curtly. "I'll be up in a bit. And Sarah..."

that was a damn close thing. I hope you know just how damn close it was."

His frightened wife just nodded, not saying a word. 'He went through the open door to the cellar, walked down a few steps, then switched on the light. The basement snapped into view, and there, behind the hanging sheet, he could make out a shape.

"Hey there," he called, descending the rest of the stairs. "You okay?"

A hand came up to draw the blanket aside, and Sam stopped. The man was a Negro, huge, with penetrating eyes and... hard to put a finger on it, but a presence.

"Hello, and thank you for your help," the man said. His voice was deep and unexpectedly cultured. Sam came closer, tried not to stare. In this part of the world, one didn't see too many Negroes.

"You're welcome," he said. "Is there anything you need?"

"No. I'm told that my travels will continue in just a few hours, and by tomorrow evening, I should be in Montreal."

Just a few seconds earlier, Sam had been ready to dislike the man who was putting his family in jeopardy, but that feeling was now— inexplicably—gone. He said, "I hope it works out all right."

The visitor laughed, a full sound that echoed in the old root cellar. "Ironic, isn't it, that I should find myself here. My own father was a slave on a plantation in North Carolina. He had high hopes for me, he did, and now here I am, a hunted man on a new Underground Railroad. I was in Britain for a while, working before the Nazis invaded, and I came back here, hoping to continue the fight. And look where I am. Alone, hunted, just like my daddy, like a fugitive slave from the last century, on the run from the South. All because of that man in the White House." Sam looked at the man closely. Damn, he looked familiar. Hadn't he seen him in a newsreel or a newspaper? He wanted to ask but didn't want to pry. "You take care. I've got to go back upstairs to my wife and boy." He held out his hand to the Negro. "Sam. Sam Miller."

The man shook his hand warmly. "Nice to meet you, Sam. I'm Paul. Paul Robeson."

The name was familiar, but it was time to go.

"Good luck, Paul."

"Thank you, Sam. I appreciate that."

Sam left the man and went back upstairs.

Sarah was in bed, the radio off, and he changed into his pajamas and slid under the sheets. Sarah gently touched his chest, and he rolled to her. "Close. We were that close to being arrested and sent away. Do you understand, Sarah?"

"Yes," she murmured. "I promise, Sam. He's the very last one."

"It's too late," he said. "Somebody knows, somewhere, that there's an Underground Railroad station here. And I don't mean the marshal. He was just giving me hints earlier. This is much more serious."

"How can you tell?" she asked softly.

"Because those two Long's Legionnaires, they saw an open door, and they knew it led into the cellar. They know, Sarah, they already know. At some point, the hammer's going to fall hard."

He kept silent for a bit, and then she pressed against him, perhaps frightened more by his silence than the threat the two uniformed men at their door presented. He kissed her cheek, her lips, and she said, "Sam... thanks for keeping them out, for standing up for us." "

My wife... my little revolutionary... we're in this together, okay? No matter what. You and me and Toby. The three of us. Always."

"Yes, Sam. Thank you. The three of us. Always."

He fell asleep with her sweet scent all about him.

PART THREE

Eyes Only

Report from Party Field Officer H. LeClerc:

On the evening of 4 May '43, I beg to report that while conducting loyalty check and survey operations on Grayson Street in Portsmouth, New Hampshire, me and fellow Party Field Officer T. Carruthers encountered Party member Sam Miller. Miller refused to answer our questions. Miller refused to allow us entry into his home. Based on our earlier instructions, we were therefore unable to gain entry into his home at this time and perform further loyalty check investigations of the residence.

In light of Miller's response and lack of cooperation, I recommend the future detention of Miller and family to determine the status of Miller and his home.

Respectfully submitted,
H. LeClerc Party Field Officer Badge #4166

CHAPTER TWENTY

Sam got up early, his sleep restless and churning with bad dreams he couldn't recall. He threw on some clothes without waking Sarah, then went downstairs. The cellar was empty. He took a breath, tore down the sheet, and folded up the cot, tossing the blanket to the floor. With cot and sheet in hand, he climbed a short set of stairs to the cellar bulkhead, which he shouldered open. Outside, it was cold and raw, the thin lawn glittering with frost. It was high tide. He moved to the hedge separating his yard from the Piscataqua River and, in one heave, tossed the cot and the sheet into the river.

He stood there, chest heaving, and then he went back into the house.

Maybe it was the exhilaration of having made it through the night without a Black Maria rolling up in the driveway, but breakfast that morning was full of smiles and laughter. Even Toby got into the act, finding a straw and blowing bubbles in his orange juice, announcing to his parents that these were "Florida farts" because orange juice came from Florida. Despite Sam's bad dreams, the sight of Sarah smiling and making their morning meal cheered him. A couple of times he patted her bottom as he squeezed past her in the kitchen, and she laughingly retaliated by squeezing him back, though in a much more sensitive area that made him yelp and made her grin.

After the dishes were cleared and Toby had gone to his room, Sam spotted a paper bag by the stove. He looked in and saw a couple of old shirts and a pair of pants that had been torn but were now repaired by needle and thread.

He looked up at Sarah. "Another clothing run?"

She wiped her hands on a washcloth. "Yes, during our lunch break. A few of us from the school department are going over to the hobo camp."

He closed up the bag. "Good. Just don't go there alone. And I'm glad you're doing it in the middle of the day."

Sarah put the cloth down. "And that's it, Stun. Just this... what we can do."

He went over to her, kissed her, and held her tight. "Before day's end, some folks who don't have anything to wear will be in better shape, thanks to you. Just be careful, all right?"

She tugged at his ear. "I heard you twice the first time, Inspector. Now get going and stop cheating the taxpayers."

Sam drove out alone to work, passing a horse-drawn wagon from one of the local dairies, detouring his way to Pierce Island, going over the wooden bridge. He found the dirt parking lot empty. He stepped out, maneuvered around the broken glass from some shattered beer bottles, saw a flaccid piece of rubber draped over a rock.

Sam looked around. "Tony! You out there?"

No reply. Just the cries of a few seagulls and the whistle of a piece of equipment out in the shipyard.

Sam reached into the Packard, took out a bag of sandwiches he had made quickly while Sarah and Toby got dressed. He went over to a path that led into the woods and, in a few moments, fashioned three sticks that pointed to the left. Another old Boy Scout message. Look to the left. And to the left, at the base of a large pine tree, he dropped the sack of sandwiches. Waited. Waited for movement out in the brush and the trees. One hand went into his coat pocket, about a set of handcuffs.

If Tony came out right now, Sam could get control of one problem. Get him back to his house, toss him in the cellar... So much going on, and to have his escapee brother roaming around...

Waited some more, checked his watch, and then went back to his Packard.

When he got to his desk, he was pleased to see that Mrs. Walton was out sick that morning. He hated having her nearby, listening in on what he was saying over the telephone, reading his notes and paperwork when he went away, and generally being the nosy woman that she was, keeping track of him and the others in The Log.

He had another pleasant surprise when he settled in his chair: an envelope on his desk with his name scribbled on the outside, and a stamped return address of Boston & Maine Railroad. Portsmouth Station.

Portsmouth, N.H.

The envelope felt heavy in his hand. To do the smart thing, to be a smart fellow, would mean tossing the envelope into the trash without opening it. The case now belonged to the FBI and the Gestapo. It didn't belong to him. But that old man, that tattooed man... Sam remembered what the medical examiner had said. Fuck 'em all. He leaned back in his chair, slit the envelope open. A thick sheaf of papers came out, with a note clipped to the top:

Sam—

Happy to get this to you quicker than I thought. Let me know if you need anything else.

—Pat

Sam looked at the papers. A collection of blurry carbons listing the passenger manifest of the train from Boston to Portland, the one that just might have been carrying his John Doe.

He dialed the local four-digit number for the B&M station, and when Lowengard got on the phone, Sam told the station manager, "Pat, you did good. Thanks. The department owes you one."

Lowengard's voice was shaky, but he seemed happy to be praised. "So glad it worked out, Sam. Is there anything else I can do for the department?"

"Yeah, there is."

Silence. Just the sound of the heavy man's labored breathing.

"Only a question, Pat. According to the new internal transport laws, there's got to be a manifest for the passengers, right? And the manifest is checked by a railroad cop assigned to that particular train?"

"That's right," Pat said carefully.

"Good. Now. According to the law, shouldn't the manifest be checked when the train arrives? To match the number of people getting off the train against the master list?"

"Sam, please don't hold me to this...I really don't want to say anymore. I mean, look, I'm in an awkward position and..."

"Pat, whatever it is, you won't be in trouble from me. I'm just trying to find out if my John Doe got tossed off that train to Portland. If there's a name on the list that didn't get checked off in Portland, then there's a pretty good chance that's my man."

No answer.

Sam said, "Things get busy, don't they? Paperwork gets sloppy. Train pulls in late, nobody wants to hold up the passengers, checking off names. So people look the other way. Maybe there's a favor. Someone doesn't even make the list. A good guess?"

"A very good guess, Sam."

"Then tell me who to call up there in Portland, your counterpart. On the off chance that the paperwork was done right."

"George Culley," the station master said. "He should be able to help you."

"Thanks, Pat." But by then Sam was talking to a dead phone.

Sam took a quick bathroom break and then came back to his office, saw a note among the papers. It was from Sean Donovan, records clerk, and all it said was *See me ASAP, v. important, Sean.* Sam called down to the records department. No one picked up the phone.

Later, then, for now it was time for real police work. After going through the local New England Telephone operator, getting a long-distance line, he got hold of George Culley of the Portland office of the Boston & Maine. Culley's tough Maine voice sounded as though he belonged on a lobster boat and not in a train station, but when Sam told him what he needed, the Mainer's voice became conspiratorial, like that of a child who had spent too much time listening to Dick Tracy.

"Really?" George asked. "A murder investigation?"

"That's right," Sam said. "I believe the murdered man was on the express from Boston to Portland three days ago. I have the manifest of those passengers who boarded in Boston. If you have the manifest of the departing passengers, then—"

"Then we can find out who didn't get checked out up in Portland, and you know who your dead man is! Hold on, let me get that paperwork."

There was a thud of the phone being dropped. Sam looked about his tiny work area and was thankful again that Mrs. Walton was out.

"All right," George said.

"I've counted the number of passengers on this manifest, and I came up with a hundred and twelve. What do you have?"

He could hear Culley murmuring, and then his voice came back, excited. "One hundred eleven. I counted it twice. One hundred eleven. So my manifest must have your John Doe."

"Okay, let's start, and remember, just the male names. Don't need the females."

"Sure," George said. "First name on the list, Saul Aaron."

Sam looked at the blurry carbon. "Check."

"Okay, Vernon Aaron."

"Check."

Sam yawned. It was going to be a long afternoon.

CHAPTER TWENTY-ONE

About thirty-five minutes later, they found it.

"Wynn. Roscoe Wynn." George's voice sounded tired. Sam rubbed at his eyes, looked again.

"Repeat that, George? What was that name?"

"Wynn. Roscoe Wynn. With a Y."

He checked the fuzzy letters once more. There was a Roscoe Wynn, but another name was listed before it. "Not Wotan? Peter Wotan?"

"No. It goes from Williams to Wynn. No Wotan. You think that's it?"

"Not yet," Sam said. "Let's be thorough. It looks like there's only a dozen left."

Which was true, but at the end, as he felt a thrill of excitement course through him like a drink of cold water on a hot day, he knew who his dead man was.

Peter Wotan.

No longer John Doe.

Sam looked at the list again.

Peter Wotan.

Let's find out who you are, he decided.

An hour later, he didn't know very much more.

Using the long-distance operators, calls to the B&M office in Boston confirmed that Peter Wotan had boarded the express train from there to Portland. Sam even got a home address, 412 West Thirty-second Street, Apartment Four, in New York City. But a series of additional operator-assisted long-distance calls to various police precincts in New York City—he shuddered to think of what Mrs. Walton would say about next month's long distance bill—revealed that the address was a fake.

Fake address.

Fake name as well?

Where to next?

He looked to the clock on the near wall.

Time to go home, that's what.

Toby was a handful at dinner, wanting to bring an Action comic book to the table and trying to sneak it in during a dessert of lime Jell-O. Distracted, Sam spoke sharply to him, sending him to his room in tears. Toby stormed out, yelling, "You never let me have *any* fun!" It took everything for Sam not to go after him and swat his butt. Sarah had asked him questions about his workday all during dinner, and he found himself giving her one-word answers.

Finally, when Toby had gone to bed and they were in their own bedroom, he stood by the door and remembered again what had happened just over twenty-four hours ago. "That was a real close run last night."

"I know, I know," she said. She was sitting on the edge of the bed, brushing her hair. The radio was on. It seemed like Sarah had found a new dance station, though it was peppered with bursts of static. Then the dance music stopped and was replaced by Bing Crosby singing "Oh, What a Beautiful Morning."

"Do you?"

She turned, put the hairbrush down, her eyes teary. "Yes, I do. I truly do. I know I went too far with the last one, and it won't happen again. I... Hearing those Legionnaires at the door really scared me. It really did."

"All right, then, it's done. If we're lucky, they just came by scare us."

She picked up the hairbrush, lowered it again. "If so, they did a good job, didn't they? You know..."

"Go on."

"There was a time when getting involved in politics... it was fun. Innocent. Like back when Dad first ran for city councilor, right after Mom died. He needed to get out of the house, stay busy, and I was so proud of him. Not even a teenager, and I was passing out leaflets and sliding brochures under doors. We'd stay up late at night at City Hall, watching the ballots get counted. That's when I got the first taste of it, you know. By working on Dad's campaigns, I knew one person could make a difference."

"Still can," he said, thinking that she was echoing what Walter Tucker had said.

She shook her head. "Not like before—not after Long got elected. Now you can still make a difference, but you can end up in jail. Or worse. And clothing donations— after the Underground Railroad, that's all I have the taste for."

"That sounds good. Look, what's going on with Toby? Why is he acting up?"

"I wish I knew. Sometimes"—she looked at him, smiling—"I think the little guy takes after his uncle. A real hell-raiser."

"Lucky us," he grumbled. "It's going to be a long ten years before he's old enough to be on his own."

She didn't say anything, and then he turned away, and she looked surprised. "Sam, where are you going?"

"Just going to make sure the doors are locked," he answered. He went through the house, taking his time, checking everything, making sure every window and door was locked, but he knew it was a futile gesture. Nothing was safe anymore, not your life, not your job, not when Legionnaires could show up on your doorstep on a whim.

When he got back to the bedroom, the light was off, the radio was off, and in the darkness he stripped and pulled on his pajamas. It took him a long time to fall asleep. Slipping away, he heard Sarah whisper, "I do love you so, Sam." He reached up to her hand, gave it a loving squeeze, and then fell asleep.

INTERLUDE IV

As Curt promised, a side door in the small industrial building was left unlocked, and the all-clear sign was there, said sign being a burnt-out lightbulb over the door. The doorknob spun easily in his hand and he walked in, hearing the hum and feeling the vibration of the printing presses overhead. About him, stacked in huge piles up to the ceiling, were massive rolls of newsprint, with a tiny path between the rolls. He went in.

Two men stood there, not looking particularly happy; he didn't particularly care. He recognized both but knew only the shorter one. The bulkier one he knew from a blurry photo passed to him weeks ago in New York, at the camp. But he was glad they were known to him and trusted.

"You're late," the man on the right said. He had on soiled khakis and a black turtleneck sweater, and at his side was a small table cluttered with cameras and other photo gear. He was the staff photographer for the *Portsmouth Herald*.

"Sony, Ralph," he said. "Decided getting here without getting arrested was more important than keeping a schedule. I don't have to tell you what's crawling around out there."

Ralph said, "No, that's not news to me, and it's not news to our friend."

He looked at the other man. He was stocky, with a bull neck and a nose that looked as if it had been broken once or twice. His clothes hung oddly. He was sure it was because this guy was used to wearing a uniform, not a uniform of the American or German armed forces or police.

Ralph added, "You or me get picked up, it's a labor camp. For... Ike here, it's a quick military trial and then a firing squad."

"Yeah, well, we all got problems," he said. "Can we get on with this?"

"Sure," Ralph said, going to his photo gear, but then Ike spoke up, speaking English with only a hint of a Slavic accent. "Yes, we all have problems, and I'm here to make sure you will do what it takes to solve at least one of them."

He stared at Ike. "I don't need to be reminded, pal."

Ike stared right back, and he imagined the guy wished he were back at Moscow's Lubyanka prison, where he and his kind ruled the roost. Ike said, "Then I'll remind you of this: We have gone to great trouble to assist this... effort. And we want to ensure what we've done will not go to waste."

"It won't," he said.

"How can you guarantee it?"

"Pal, I can't guarantee we all won't be shot tomorrow, but I can guarantee we're going to do what it takes to get the job done. Either me or somebody else. The job will get done."

Ike looked to Ralph, who was busy with his photo gear. Ike said, "I've come here just to see what is what, and to tell you that there will be an announcement shortly from your capitol that will severely restrict the movements of people here. Our intelligence services have confirmed this information."

"We've been anticipating that, too," he said. "We've got our own people telling us stuff, even from D.C. So what else is new? That's why I'm here."

Ike said, "We need to know that you've made arrangements to have you and whatever else you need to be in place—or to otherwise be able to have freedom of movement, to get the job done."

"Like I said, that's why I'm here, guy, to get that taken care of. Anything else?"

Ike cocked his head as though hearing a whisper, far off. "This job... it should have been handled professionally, but we are forced to deal with you... amateurs. And we need to know that when the time comes, you will follow orders. You will do what it takes, no matter what."

He gave the man a good hard stare. "I sure will. But know this. About the only thing we admire about you is that you're fighting fascists over there, and you're helping us fight fascists over here. For that you have our thanks. But we're going into this with open eyes."

The Slavic man demanded, "What do you mean by that?"

"I mean this—we're no starry-eyed lovers of you or your system. Maybe, a while ago. Some years ago I even filed an application with your Amtorg Trading Corporation down in New York City. I was tired of the crap around here, thought I'd have a better life shipping out overseas. But two things changed my mind. The first was that I decided I wasn't going to cut and run. I was going to take part in the struggle here."

From the next floor up, there was a sharp whistle, and then the humming of the printing plant seemed to slow. Ike asked, "What was the other thing that changed your mind?"

"The other thing is that I had a couple of buddies go through Amtorg and get jobs at the Ford plant being built at Nizhny Novgorod, the one called the Gorky Plant. They went there and disappeared. Never to be heard from again. Crap like that, I wasn't going to chance it. So here I am. And bud, I'll follow orders and get the job done. Don't you worry."

Ralph spoke up. "Can we save the debating society for later? We got work to do." He picked up his camera. "By the bye, I saw your brother last week."

Not wanting to bring his brother into the conversation, he said, "Big deal. Let's get this done."

Ralph reached down to the open bag, pulled out a shirt and necktie. "Put these on, and then we'll start. Amateurs ... hah, we'll see about that."

Ike said to the photographer, "You, then. Why are you helping, eh?"

Ralph stopped and then rubbed the roll of newsprint next to him. "There was a time when this wasn't rationed by the government. When we had a free press. When we could write what we wanted, print any photos we wanted. Sure would like to see that again."

He stepped over, took the shirt and tie from Ralph. "I'm sure two out of three of us here would agree." At that, Ike suddenly laughed, and then so did Ralph, and seeing the dark humor in it, he joined in as well.

CHAPTER TWENTY-TWO

The next morning Sarah was cheerful and smiling, fixing him and Toby bacon and eggs—a weekday splurge—and Sam ate well, even though he had a headache from not sleeping well. At one point, when Toby was busy drowning his scrambled eggs in ketchup, Sarah leaned in to Sam and said, "Like I said last night, I do love you so." Her lips brushed his ear.

Even with his headache, he smiled up at her, feeling relieved as it came to him: no more overnight guests, no more Railroad, and by God, if they kept their heads down, all might just be all right.

"And I do love you back, even though you keep giving my clothing away to strangers."

That brought a laugh from her and a snicker from Toby. He took Toby to school, as Sarah once again had to visit her sick aunt. Sam took Toby's hand as they walked out to the shed where the Packard was parked.

"I'm sorry for being a brat last night, Dad," Toby said suddenly. "Sometimes... sometimes I just get mad. Like at school. When the other guys call you a rat. It just happens. Mom understands. I really, really wish you did, too." Something caught in Sam's throat. It was times like these that his boy reminded him most of Tony. "Just be a better boy, all right? At least for your mother."

"Dad? Have you ever arrested a spy?"

"A spy? No, never have. Why do you ask?"

"Nothing. Just thinking."

Sam was going to say something and stopped. "Toby, where did you get that pin?"

His son rubbed at the Confederate-flag pin on his coat lapel. "I got it at school yesterday. Some kids were passing them around."

"I see," he said. "Did they tell you what that flag means?"

"It's the flag from the South. And the President likes this flag, so it's like a club, you know? Next week a couple of guys are coming at recess, and everyone who wears the pin will get free ice cream. Isn't that neat?"

Sam said, "Give me the pin, Toby."

"Ah, Dad, c'mon "

"I'll tell you later what the pin means, okay? And if there's ice cream that day, I'll make it up to you."

Toby's face turned sour, but he undid the pin and passed it over. Sam pocketed it and opened the door to the Packard, and Toby clambered sulkily up onto the big front seat, holding his dark green book bag. "Mom said something about you this morning when she came in to wake me up."

"Really? What was that?"

Toby looked so small in the wide front seat. "She said that Daddy was a good man, no matter what other people said."

Sam shifted into first. "Thanks for telling me, Toby. And for that, you get ice cream no matter what."

When they reached the Spring Street School, Sam pulled to the curb and let Toby out. He sat there, watching his serious little boy walk to the old brick building, as though entering a place that had been his work site for decades. Sam thought about what kind of world Toby was inheriting, a place where the dwindling number of free men and women were under brutal assault, day after long damn day, all over the world. At the grocery store nearby, the owner hadn't done such a good job of whitewashing the graffiti from the other day. The letters that said DOWN WITH LONG and the hammer and sickle were still faintly visible, as if the idea or protest just wouldn't go away.

He reached for the gearshift. Woolgathering. Time to get to work.

And then a flash of color caught his eye.

Yellow.

He moved in the seat, saw a car make its way up the street.

A yellow Rambler.

Just like that railroad guy had noted from the other day. The car that had made the train slow down the night the body was discovered.

Coincidence or part of a plan?

A plan to make sure that Peter Wotan—or whoever the hell he was—was dumped and later found in Portsmouth.

He put the Packard in reverse, backed up the street dodging one kid going to the school, the transmission whining, and when he came to the intersection, looked both ways.

Gone.

Gone for now, he thought. But how many yellow Ramblers could there be in the Portsmouth area? He should be hearing soon from the motor vehicle division about the Rambler listings, and it wouldn't take much to match that list with addresses in Portsmouth.

The blare of a car horn made him curse.

A Portsmouth police cruiser drew up next to him, engine idling, and he rolled down his window. An older officer leaned out, a guy named Mike Schwartz, with a thin, drawn face. "Sam, I don't know what the hell's going on, but we've all been recalled to the station. On shift, off shift, even those on vacation. Everybody to report in."

Sam shifted the Packard into first. "What's going on?"

"Who the hell knows? But it sounds important, and I'll be fucked if I'm going to be late."

The cruiser pulled away, and after performing a highly illegal U-turn, Sam followed him in.

At the station, he was stunned at what he saw: every patrolman, sergeant, and officer in the department was milling about in the crowded lobby. Frank Reardon stood by the door, and Sam went up to him. "What the hell's going on?"

"Cripes, who knows." Frank cupped a lit cigarette in one hand. "Got a phone call, just a few minutes ago. Everybody to report to the station. Even the guys on shift are rolling in. Shit, now's gonna be a good time for every second-story guy or bank robber to hit us."

Sam looked around for a certain young cop. "Where's your buddy Leo?"

"You didn't hear?" Frank replied. "Gone. Two nights ago a Black Maria came by his apartment and took him away."

"You've got to be kidding."

"Wish I was. Kid obviously screwed up along the way, and he got picked up. You saw him back at the tracks. Liked to ask lots of questions. That's always a dangerous habit."

"You going to do anything to help him out?"

Frank dropped his cigarette butt on the dirty tile floor, crushed it under his heel. "Like what? Too late for Leo. That's just the way it goes. Asking questions, poking around, just leads to more trouble. Leo was okay, but I'm not putting my ass on the line for him. You know how it is."

"Yeah, Frank, I know how it is." Sam broke away from Frank, knowing very much how it was. Stay out of trouble. Keep your head down.

There was a loud murmur of voices that went on for a few minutes, and he was going to head up to his desk when Marshal Hanson appeared, carrying a large Philco radio. Mrs. Walton was with him, notepad in hand. Hanson put the radio on the desk sergeant's counter and raised a hand. "Okay, listen up, fellas, all right? Christ, shut your mouths back there." The room fell silent. Hanson looked satisfied and turned to the desk sergeant. "Paul, plug her in, will you?"

"Hey, boss, what's up?" came a voice from the rear of the room. "We at war or something?"

"Or something," Hanson said, pulling out his pocket watch from his vest and checking the time. "All I know is I got an urgent message from Party headquarters in Concord that there's going to be a national announcement coming across at nine A.M., an announcement that everybody—and I mean *everybody!*—needs to hear. Okay, my watch says it's one minute till, so everybody keep your yap shut. Paul, put that radio on and turn the volume on high."

There was a faint crackle and then a click as the switch was thrown, a hum as the vacuum tubes warmed up. Then a shot of jazz music burst from the speaker, making a couple of the guys laugh, but Sam didn't feel like laughing.

The music suddenly stopped, replaced by the familiar three musical tones for NBC, and a voice said, *"We interrupt our morning program with this special news bulletin. Flash from Washington, D.C., we bring in our special correspondent Richard Harkness. "*

A burst of static, and then the voice, fainter, began to speak, and in a split instant, Sam knew just how accurate the phrase was that you could hear a pin drop. In a crowded room with nearly thirty men and Mrs. Walton, the only sound was coming from the radio.

"This is Richard Harkness, reporting from Washington, D.C., with a special news bulletin. It is being announced simultaneously today in Washington and in Berlin, Germany, that a treaty of trade and peace has been reached between the government of the United States and the government of Germany. This treaty will put into place a framework of peace and cooperation between the United States and Germany and will also see an immediate increase in trade between the two countries, with a substantial rise in employment and the stimulation of the American economy."

"Christ," someone muttered.

"As part of this new trade agreement, Germany has announced that it will immediately begin purchasing substantial new armaments from the United States, including tanks, fighter planes, and bombers, to replace those German armaments being expended in the Eastern European war. In exchange, the United States will seek to improve relations with the government of Germany, including an understanding on the stationing of naval forces in the Caribbean and Atlantic, and new provisions associated with the criminal extradition treaty. "

A cop behind Sam whispered, "Such a deal. We get jobs paid for by stolen treasure from Europe, help kill millions more Russians, let the Krauts turn the Atlantic and Caribbean into their playground, and oh, by the way, if you're here in the States illegally, we'll help the Gestapo grab your ass and stick it in a concentration camp back in Europe."

Someone told the whisperer to shut up, but somebody else griped, "Shit, you woke me up to listen to this crap? Who cares?"

And, Sam thought, in a matter of seconds, everybody within listening range of the radio instantly knew why they should care.

"To officially approve this treaty, a summit meeting will take place between President Huey Long and Chancellor Adolf Hitler seven days from now at the Navy Yard in Portsmouth, New Hampshire, site of the—"

What was being said on the radio was instantly drowned out by the burst of voices coming from the cops.

INTERLUDE V

Since coming back to Portsmouth, he had lived in Curt's attic. It was stuffy, tiny, with a sleeping bag on the floor and not much else save boxes of junk and a low roof that meant he banged his head at least twice a day. There were two small windows at either end of the attic, and even though it had been a cool May, it got stiflingly hot in the afternoon. Once in the morning and once in the evening, Curt let him out to use the bathroom and to grab a bite to eat, as plans and plots moved ahead here in Portsmouth and other places.

This morning he tried to stretch out his legs and arms after waking up, when he heard movement in the hallway underneath him. He froze, wondering if Curt was back early, and then there was a flare of light as the trapdoor in the middle of the attic floor came up. He looked around frantically for something, anything, to grab as a weapon, then almost burst out laughing at his fear.

A well-dressed woman slowly came up through the square opening, her eyes blinking from the dust. "So there you are, as promised," she said, smiling.

He knelt and took one of her hands in both of his. "My God, I can't believe it's you."

"I can't stay long. I need to be at work. But here." One of her hands went down and came back up with a brown grocery sack with twine handles. "Some more food. I know Curt is feeding you, but he's a bachelor. This should be better. I'm sure what he gives you gets dull after a while."

He picked up the bag and lowered it to the floor. Everything just seemed all right. The visitor before him was the prettiest thing he had seen in years.

"You doing all right?" he asked.

Her happy expression faltered. "I'm... I'm holding up. There's a lot of danger out there. But it's you I'm worried about. From what little I know about what you're up against..."

He said, "That's it. Don't worry about me. Worry about yourself, worry about what we're all doing. You do your job, I'll do mine, and in the end, it will all work out." As she bit her lower lip, her eyes became weepy. "Okay, I hear you, but I'm still so scared for you." She swiped at her eyes with one hand. "This is when... when I think about what might have been if you had been first to ask me out in high school instead of Sam. I know that's a horrible thing to say... I mean, damn, I'm all mixed up. I just worry about you and miss you awful. And I think of you a lot."

"Stop that," he said. "If I had been with you back then, you would have been arrested, too. And you wouldn't have that wonderful boy, my dear nephew. And my brother... he's crazy about you. So please don't say any more."

She wiped her eyes again. He bent down, kissed the top of her head. "It's all right. You get going now... and thanks. This was the best gift you could have given me." She smiled up at him through her tears. "It's not much. Just some sandwiches and—"

"I wasn't talking about the sandwiches. Now go." She started to descend, and he thought of something. "Sarah?"

"Yes?" his sister-in-law asked.

"Stop thinking about the past, about what might have been. Think about the future. Toby... we're doing this for Toby and the world he gets to grow up in. No matter what happens, no matter how much you and Sam and even I suffer, remember that."

"I will," she promised, and she closed the trapdoor, and the attic suddenly got dark again.

CHAPTER TWENTY-THREE

An earsplitting whistle cut through the chatter as somebody brought fingers up to his mouth. Hanson held up his hands and said, "Guys, I'm just as surprised about this as you are. Christ... Look, for now all days off are canceled. In fact, all time off is canceled. We'll put cots in the basement because I know it's gonna be a long haul between now and then. Okay, I want to see all the sergeants in my office, pronto, along with Captain Stackpole and Inspector Miller. Guys, this is going to be a hell of a thing. By the end of today, this city is going to be crawling with radio newsmen, newsreelers, newspaper reporters, and every nut with a grudge. I know you got questions, but I don't have the answers. We'll have a department meeting at ten o'clock, and we'll know better then."

A voice from the rear of the room: "Boss, all right if we go home, wrap a couple of things up, then come back?"

"Yeah." Hanson nodded. "That makes sense. You officers on duty, go back to work. The rest of you fellas, if you need to go home, check in with the wife, or whatever, that's fine. Just be back here by ten o'clock. And pack some clothes and essentials." He slapped his hands together. "Let's get a move on. There's plenty of work to be done."

Moving through the crowded lobby, Sam went upstairs, where Hanson's door was open and Mrs. Walton was on the phone, desperately fielding message after message. The three shift sergeants and Art Stackpole, the sole police captain, were clustered around Hanson's desk. Hanson was on the phone, nodding, saying, "Yeah, yeah, yeah" while writing something down. The sergeants and Stackpole ignored Sam as he entered. Four of his fellow officers, and four men who figured they should have had the inspector's job instead of him.

Hanson hung up the phone. He tore off a sheet of paper and passed it over to Sam. "Change of plans, Inspector. Rockingham Hotel. Room Twelve. Get over there right now."

"What's going on?"

"What's going on, Sam, is that FBI character you met the other day is still here, and he's going to be part of the federal task force running the summit security. He wants a liaison officer with the department, and guess what, you just got picked."

"But I can do more if—"

"Sam, just do it," Hanson cut in impatiently. "Okay? Look, in the last five minutes, every goddamn newspaper, radio station, and newsreel outfit within a hundred miles called me. Not to mention the governor's office and our two distinguished senators and two representatives. I've also got to see your father-in-law in about ten minutes. Then there's the matter of coordinating everything with the Navy Yard and about a hundred other things have just landed on my desk, so please, Sam, just shut up and do this. All right?"

Sam folded the piece of paper, stuck it in his pocket. "I'll take care of it."

"Good. And one more thing. Here." Hanson passed over an embossed piece of cardboard, and Sam glanced at it, saw a bad photograph of himself pasted on one side, and a drawing of an American eagle, and some lettering. Hanson said, "Your new commission in the New Hampshire National Guard. Congratulations. Stick it in your billfold, and for God's sake, don't lose it."

"It says I'm a lieutenant. How in hell did that happen?"

"What? You got problems with being an officer and a gentleman?"

One of the other cops snickered, and Hanson sighed. "Don't worry about it, Sam. Automatic official rank and all that, reflecting your position in the department. Understand now?"

"Yes, I do."

"So glad to hear it's all clear for you, Inspector." Hanson reached for his phone. "And if you can get to the Rockingham ten minutes ago, that would be goddamn delightful."

Sam turned and left. As he passed Mrs. Walton in the outer office, he heard her say, "I don't care if you're NBC Red, NBC Blue, or NBC Pink, you can't speak to the marshal. And he's not a chief, he's a—"

He took the stairs down to the main lobby two at a time.

CHAPTER TWENTY-FOUR

The Rockingham Hotel was under a two-minute ride from the station, on State Street, and for Portsmouth it was an impressive building, brick, five-story, with two sets of narrow granite steps leading up to the wide swinging oak doors of the lobby. On either side of the steps was a massive stone lion, staring blankly out into the street.

The phones were ringing at the main desk, as people started calling in, demanding rooms, demanding reservations, demanding everything and anything for the upcoming summit. As Sam took the carpeted stairs up to the first floor and Room Twelve, he still found it hard to get his mind around what had just happened. His hometown, his Portsmouth, was hosting a summit between the world's two most powerful men, Long and Hitler. It was one thing to grow up with history about you— the royal governors, the John Paul Jones house, the revolutionaries—but it was something else to know that history was going to happen here in the next few days and that you were stuck in the middle of it.

At Room Twelve he knocked on the door. A male voice invited him in.

"Inspector," said Jack LaCouture of the FBI, standing up from a cushioned chair. "So glad to see you again. You remember my German traveling companion, don't you? Herr Groebke."

Groebke didn't bother standing up. He stared at Sam through his cigarette smoke, his glasses obscuring his eyes. Both men wore white shirts. Both also wore holstered revolvers. Sam waited till LaCouture sat down, then sat and said, "So. How goes my homicide investigation?"

"Who cares?" LaCouture asked. "One dead guy here illegally. I only care if Hans here cares." LaCouture said something in German and Groebke replied, and LaCouture said to Sam, "See? Hans said there are priorities, and the current number one priority is this summit meeting. So the dead guy will have to wait. You got a problem with that?"

Peter Wotan. The dead guy had a name. Peter Wotan, and I know that, Sam thought. *I know that and you can't stop me from finding out more.*

Aloud he said, "No, I don't have a problem with that."

"Your chief, he tell you why you're here?"

"Marshal Hanson mentioned something about being a liaison with you. He didn't say anything about the Gestapo."

LaCouture frowned. "Sorry if working with the Germans pisses you off, but I really don't give a crap. We've got about a month's worth of work to do in seven days, and we need to do it right. I just got a phone call a bit ago from God Himself to make sure nothing gets screwed up."

"President Long?"

"Hell, no. J. Edgar Hoover. Chances are, Long won't be President forever, but I can tell you that Hoover intends to be FBI director until the sun burns out. A phone call from that bastard can send you to either D.C. or fucking Boise, can make you or break you, and I'm not one to be broken. So let's get to it."

Sam was silent.

"Your boss probably told you boys in blue how important the next few days are going to be, a chance to do good, to shine, blah, blah, blah," LaCouture continued. "Well, that's just so much bullshit. The next few days belong to us and the Germans, the Secret Service and the Navy. You Portsmouth guys are going to be controlling crowds and traffic. And you, my friend, you're gonna go out now and get us info on traffic choke points, lists of restaurants and places that can maybe hold all the goddamn visitors that are going to be streamin' in here. That's it. Savvy?"

Sam watched Groebke stub out his cigarette, light another one. He thought of what he could be doing with the Peter Wotan case. Instead, he'd become a glorified errand boy. "Yeah, I savvy."

"Super. Here's something to hold on to." LaCouture flipped over a white business card. It had the FBI seal and LaCouture's name and a handwritten notation on the front with the Rockingham Hotel's address of 401 State Street and phone number of 2400. On the back was another note: *Bearer of card detached to federal duty until 15 May.*

Sam looked up at LaCouture. "A get-out-of-jail card?"

The FBI man did not smile. "It's a card that makes sure you don't get your ass *into* jail. By nightfall this city is going to be cordoned off, there will be troops in the street, and I don't need my liaison having to explain to some army captain why he needs to take a dump somewhere."

"Look, I just want to—"

The phone rang. The FBI man swore and got up to answer it. "LaCouture. Hold on. Yeah. Yeah. Crap. All right, I'll be right down." He slammed the receiver down. "Having a problem with the manager about the number of rooms we need. Look. I'll go straighten it out. You two can stay here and improve German-local relations or something." •

LaCouture grabbed his coat and left, slamming the door behind him. Sam sat still, the white business card pinched between his fingers. The Gestapo man stared at him, smoking. Sam thought about the stories in *Life* and *Look* and the newspapers, the radio shows and Hollywood movies. This was how it ended for so many people over in Europe. Alone in a room with a Gestapo agent. The German had no power over him, but a part of Sam felt paralyzed by that rattlesnake gaze, the cool stare of a man who had the power of life and death, didn't mind using it, and rather enjoyed having it.

Groebke stubbed the cigarette out in his ashtray and said, "You look... unsettled."

"First time I've ever been alone with the Gestapo," Sam said.

"Most of what we do... most of what I do.. .just like you," Groebke said with a shrug. "A cop." His English was impeccable but thickly accented.

"Maybe you think so. I find that hard to believe."

Groebke stared at him.

"You don't like Germans," he said.

"Doesn't really matter, does it?"

Groebke cocked his head like a hunting dog catching a far-off scent, a sound of something rustling in the grass that must be chased and killed. "Have we hurt you in some way?"

"Yeah," Sam replied, feeling his chest tighten. "You killed my father."

The head moved again, slightly. "I think rather not. I have not had much experience with Americans. So I do not think I have killed your father."

"Maybe not, but you and your people did."

"Ah. The Great War, am I correct?"

"Yes, you are correct."

"It was wartime," the German said. "Such things happen during war."

Sam thought, *Oh yeah, such things, and mostly from the Germans.* Flattening cities like Rotterdam or Coventry. Sinking passenger liners. Being the first to use poison gas. But this man was Gestapo, friends with the FBI and who knew whom. So Sam said, "Yeah. War. Not a good thing."

"And your father," Groebke persisted, apparently unoffended. "What happened to him?"

"He came home from the war, lungs scarred from German gas. Then he coughed his lungs out for another fifteen years before dying in the county home."

"That was a long time ago, for which I am sorry. But what do you think of us now?"

Sam didn't want to go any further with this German. "I'd rather not say. For reasons I'm sure you know."

Groebke relaxed as if he knew he was winning this conversation. "I think I know Americans. You believe our leader is a dictator, a tyrant. Perhaps. But what of you? Hmm?"

Sam kept quiet. Wished LaCouture would hurry up and get back.

Groebke's eyes narrowed. "Of you, I will say that your President is a fool and a drunkard. I will also say that my leader—he will be known as the greatest leader of this century. He took a country shattered by war, shattered by an economic depression, and brought it back in a brief time, to seize what was rightfully ours. Can you say that about your President? Your Depression still cripples you... your armed forces are an international joke... the Japanese are raping China and you stand by doing nothing... They are pushing you out of the Pacific by bribing you to abandon your bases, like the one at Guam... and you lifted not a finger when the Low Countries, France, and finally England itself fell into our laps."

"You leader is a murdering bastard," Sam said quietly.

Groebke was about to reply when LaCouture slammed in, banging the door behind him. "Nearly had to strangle the son of a bitch at the front desk, but it's settled. Good. You guys okay up here?"

Groebke took his pale eyes from Sam and looked at the FBI man. "*Ja*. We are."

"Good," LaCouture said. "Now, if you'll excuse us, Inspector..."

Sam got up and went to the door just as somebody knocked. LaCouture said, "Shit, see who it is, will ya, Miller?"

Sam opened the door, saw two Long's Legionnaires standing there, cocky grins on their young faces. Carruthers and LeClerc, the ones who had come by his house last night. "Oh, it's you," LaCouture said. "Get your asses in here and let's get to work."

As he went past Sam, LeClerc bumped Sam with his shoulder, then laughed as Sam did nothing. Carruthers called out, "Oh, yeah, bud, we haven't forgotten about that survey!"

Sam closed the door behind him, shutting out more Southern-tinged laughter.

CHAPTER TWENTY-FIVE

Nine hours later, Sam was back at the Rockingham Hotel, his notebook filled with scribbled notations of what the FBI was looking for—traffic control spots, restaurants to feed the arriving masses of federal agents, and rooming houses to lodge them all—but to his surprise, LaCouture and Groebke were gone. At the front desk, the harried clerk—working on a switchboard that wouldn't stop ringing—pulled out a note and said, "Oh, Inspector Miller. Agent LaCouture said to meet him... let's see here, meet him by the hobo encampment off Maplewood. He said you'd know where that was."

Ten minutes later, Sam was right back where this had all started, walking up the railroad track past the Fish Shanty, past the spot where his tattooed John Doe—no, Peter Wotan!—had been found, and up to the hobo camp, the place where Lou Purdue and the others lived, the place where—

Smoke was billowing up from where the camp had been.

Sam quickened his pace, heard the low growl of diesel engines, saw black clouds billowing up. Two bulldozers from the Portsmouth Public Works Department scraped the charred ground into a burning pile, moving the crumpled boards and shingles of what been people's homes. LaCouture was standing by a polished black Pierce- Arrow, watching the action. Groebke stood closer to the flames, talking to a Long's Legionnaire.

LaCouture turned to Sam, looking satisfied underneath the brim of his wide black hat. His pinstriped suit was immaculate, as always. Even his shoes were unscathed. "Inspector. So glad you could join us."

"What's going on?"

"A little cleanup, what do you think?"

The bulldozers growled, and he watched a bureau, a chair, a child's doll get shoved into the flames. Smoke kept billowing up, oily and stinking. "What's the point?"

LaCouture laughed. "What the hell do you think, boy? In a week, the

President hisself is going to be coming up these railroad tracks. Do you really think we're gonna want him and the press to see a bunch of bums and their filthy shacks?"

Sam watched the orange flames do their work. A bulldozer grumbled by, scooping up trash, some dirt. Riding the top of the dirt was a Roadmaster bicycle, just like the one Toby had. Sam stared at the bicycle, willed it to fall to the side, safe, unharmed, but then the bulldozer bucked and the bicycle fell under the treads, was crumpled, chewed up, destroyed. His chest ached. What kind of place was he living in?

"There's not enough bulldozers in this country to clean up all the places like this," he said.

"Don't matter none," LaCouture said. "So long as it's clean around here, that's all I care about."

"What about the people? What happened to them?"

"Trespassers all," LaCouture said. "Those Long boys took care of 'em. Sent off to some transit camps, far away from the newsreel boys come summit day."

Sam's witness, Lou Purdue, had lived here, but he knew that wouldn't get any sympathy from LaCouture. To the FBI, that matter was done.

LaCouture said, "All right, then, tell me what you got for me today."

Sam took out his notebook, flipped through the pages, started telling LaCouture what he had learned. After a minute, LaCouture held up a hand and said, "All right, all right, type up your notes and pass it along. We'll deal with it later."

Sam closed the notebook. The smoke and the flames were finally dying down. The bulldozers and their operators had moved off to the side, the diesel engines softly rumbling. Talking with the Long's Legionnaire, Groebke laughed, tossed his cigarette into the smoldering embers.

LaCouture leaned back on the fender. "You don't like me, do you, Miller?"

"I don't know about that," Sam said. "You're here, I'm working for you. Why don't we leave it at that?"

"You know, I don't give a bird's fart if you didn't vote for the Kingfish, but he is my President and yours, too, no matter if you don't like him or me. Just so you know, I grew up in Winn Parish, down in Louisiana. You know Winn Parish?"

"That's where Long came from."

"Yep," the FBI agent said. "That's where he came from, and man, he never forgets that. I grew up in Winn Parish, too, barefoot, poor, Momma dead, and Daddy, he never finished grammar school. Could barely read and write. Worked as a sharecropper, barely makin' it year to year. And that was gonna be my life, Inspector, until the Kingfish came to power."

"You were lucky, then."

"Yeah, you can call it luck if you'd like, but when Long became governor, he started taxin' Standard Oil and the other fat cat companies, and he got me and my brothers free schoolbooks, built hospitals and roads. You got good roads up here. Down home, it was dirt tracks that became mud troughs every time it rained. When the Kingfish became our governor, there weren't more than three hundred miles of paved road in the entire state, and when he became senator, that had changed to more than two thousand miles. He took care of his folks in Winn Parish, he took care of the great state of Louisiana, and believe you me, he's takin' care of this great country."

"Sure," Sam said. "Lots of new roads, lots of new labor camps, and lots of new railway lines to help fill 'em up."

LaCouture's eyes flashed at him. "The voters here wanted change. They wanted to make things better. If that means some losers get put away, that's the way it's gonna be. And for those of us he helped, those of us who got an education and got to be somebody, there's nothin' the Kingfish can do wrong. Maybe I serve two masters, Long and Hoover, but they both are doin' what's right for this country. Don't you forget that."

"I'm sure I won't," Sam answered.

On the coals, the child's doll burst into flame.

"Good," LaCouture said. "You talk to your marshal when you get back to the police station, Inspector Miller, and you tell him to contact Randall at Party headquarters. It's on for tomorrow night, and that's all you need to say. Your marshal can figure out the rest."

Groebke joined them, smiling. He gave a crisp nod to Sam and said in English to the FBI agent, "That was nice, *very* nice. Herr Roland, over there, has just returned from a term of service with the Waffen-SS George Washington Brigade. He spent some time on the Estonian front with other Legionnaires, getting needed experience."

Sam turned away from the smoldering pile of debris and wreckage that had meant so much to people who had so little. "Yeah," he said. "Takes a lot of experience to burn things."

Groebke gave him a stiff nod. "Fire is wonderful. It cleans, it purifies, it makes everything...clear."

LaCouture grinned at his counterpart. "Christ, we get a job done, you get all philosophical on us, Hans. Inspector, you believe in philosophy?"

"Not today," Sam said.

Minutes later, he was back at the police station pushing past people moving in and out of the lobby, newsreel cameras already setting up shop outside, reporters buttonholing him as he went inside. He shrugged them all off and went upstairs. Mrs. Walton said, "He's busy talking to the governor. And when he's finished with that call, the governor of Maine wants to talk to him. So he can't see you for a while."

Sam went back to his desk and started going through the top stack of file folders and—

File folders.

Records.

Dammit. Sean had wanted to talk to him.

"I'll be back in a couple of minutes," he called out to Mrs. Walton. He took some satisfaction in ignoring her when she called after him.

The records were kept in the basement. Sean's desk was empty. Stretching out into the darkness were file cabinets and boxes, and Sam heard a squeaking noise approaching him. Clarence Rolston, the janitor and overall handyman for the police station, was coming toward him. A bucket of water on rollers was before him, and he was pushing it forward with the mop inside.

Clarence was the older brother of a city councilman. He'd once supposedly drunk some poisoned rotgut during Prohibition, and his brain had been slightly scrambled ever since.

Sam said, "Clarence."

The man looked up. His gray hair was a tight ball of fuzz about his head. "Sam... I'm right, aren't I? Sam."

"That's right, Clarence. Good job. I'm looking for somebody."

The janitor shook his head. "My brother Bobby? I tell people all the time, I can't help you. I can't get you to see Bobby. Bobby does his own thing and I do my own. If you need a job or relief, then I can't help you, I'm sorry."

"That's fine, Clarence, I'm not looking for your brother."

"Oh." The janitor looked relieved. "What is it, then?"

"I'm looking for Sean, the records clerk. Can you tell me where I can find him?"

A shake of the head. "I can, but I shouldn't."

"Why's that?"

"Because they told me not to say anything, that's why."

"Who?"

"The G-men, that's who."

"Are you telling me that Sean's been arrested by the FBI?"

"Darn you, you tricked me. You tricked me into saying something I shouldn't've. Oh, darn it, I'm going to lose my job..."

Tears were trickling down Clarence's cheeks. Sam grasped his upper arm gently. "Clarence. Look at me. I'm the police inspector here. And I know a lot of secrets. This is going to be one more secret, all right? I won't tell anybody I was here, won't say a word about you. You won't lose your job, your brother won't get into trouble, nothing like that's going to happen. Just calm down." Clarence was smiling as he wiped away the tears. "That's nice. That's right nice of you to say something like that, Sam. Thanks a lot."

"Not a problem," Sam said.

Back upstairs he was pleased to find Hanson alone, no phone up to his ear. Sam took a seat and Hanson said, "Tell me what you've got."

Sam spent the next fifteen minutes describing the requirements of LaCouture and Groebke. When he finished his briefing, Hanson pushed aside his notes and said with disgust, "Glorified travel agents and traffic cops. That's all the damn feds and Krauts need us to do. All right, we'll do what we're told. Not like we have any goddamn choice in the matter. Anything else?"

"Two more things," Sam said. "Agent LaCouture told me to tell you to contact Randall at Party headquarters in Concord. That something is on tomorrow night and you would know what that means. Do you?"

Hanson's face seemed to lose color. "Yeah. Yeah, I know what that means. Shit. You and everyone else in the department ... we have a dirty job set for tomorrow night." From the bleak look on Hanson's face, Sam knew what was going to happen. The long-rumored and long- threatened crackdown on refugees was about to begin.

"What time?" Sam asked.

Hanson scribbled something in his notepad. "Probably early evening. Damn. Okay, you said two things. What's next?"

"Sean Donovan. He's been arrested by the FBI. Do you know why?"

"Not my business and not yours," Hanson said. "Donovan was taken into federal protective custody two days ago. That's all I can say."

"And Leo Gray? Picked up by the Interior Department the other day?"

"Same answer. Not your business. You've got enough to do."

"But Sean Donovan and Leo Gray, they work for you, work for the department, can't you—"

Hanson glared at him. "Right now I have the big- name correspondents from the radios and the newsreels wanting a piece of me, the governors of two states, the FBI, the Gestapo, the German diplomatic corps and the State Department and the President's people in D.C. and Concord. If you think I've got time to worry about a file clerk and a rookie cop, you're seriously wrong. They've both been charged with federal offenses, it's nothing I can fix, that's it. None of us are above being rousted by the feds if they're in the mood for trouble. Got it, Inspector?"

Sam tasted ashes in his mouth. "Got it, sir."

"Good. Remember, you're liaison, so if the FBI and the Gestapo are finished with you, go on home and get some rest. Check in with them tomorrow and see what they want."

"And what might that be?"

"How in hell should I know?" Hanson exploded. "If they want you to strip naked and dance the Charleston in Market Square, do it! If they want you to fly to Hollywood and bring back Mae West for the Fuhrer's entertainment, do that, too!"

Sam got up and left without another word. So much going on, so very much, and right now he was late for dinner.

Outside of the police station, there was a crowd of people trying to come in, trying to be seen. There were a few children holding the hands of a mother or a father, crying, not wanting to be here on such a cold night. Under a streetlight, watching with amusement, stood another squad of Long's Legionnaires.

INTERLUDE VI

In the dirt-floor basement, once again, Curt spread a set of cards and papers on the table. He examined them and said, "Damn fine job. Ralph did great with the photos, but my compliments to whoever finished this."

Curt grunted. "I'll make sure to pass that along if any of us make it alive through the next week."

Up above, the cellar door opened and the man from before, Vince, clumped down the stairs, carrying a long cardboard box that said fresh flowers in a pretty script. Vince put the box on the table. "There you go. As promised."

He pulled the box over, lifted the top. Inside was a long object wrapped in brown paper and twine. He pulled it out, undid the twine, and unwrapped the paper. A bolt-action rifle with attached telescopic sight was revealed, along with a small paper sack. Inside the sack were six rifle cartridges.

Curt said, "Do you recognize it? Will it work?"

He felt the cool metal and smooth wood of the rifle. "Sure. It's a U.S. Army model 1903 .30-06 rifle. Nice and accurate. Holds eight rounds. Has a sweet Weaver 2.5 scope. Will do the job perfectly." He picked it up, worked the action, held it up to the light. Nice light sheen of oil, no rust or specks of debris.

"Well?" Vince asked.

"As advertised," he said. "Good job."

"You know, I can still deliver it if you'd like, won't be a problem at all, and—"

He put the rifle down, got up, and kicked out with his good leg, catching Vince at the back of the knees. Vince fell hard to the dirt. He rolled him over and put his knee at the base of the man's spine, reached down to the man's chin and top of his head, twisted, and pulled. There was a dull crack, a spasm of his legs, and that was that.

He stood, brushed his hands together.

Curt said sharply, "Damn it to hell! Was that really necessary?"

"Afraid it was," he said. "He wouldn't give up trying to find out where I wanted the rifle stashed. I think he was a snitch. And whoever he's working for...they only know I have the rifle. They don't know where it's going to end up." '

Curt said, "Think or know he's a snitch?"

He remembered the other night, seeing Vince entering a nice new sedan. "Know."

"Suppose you're wrong?"

"Then he died for his country."

Curt seemed to struggle with that for a moment. Then he said, "Now what?

He went hack to the rifle and cartridges, and in a few moments, everything was back in the flower box. He handed it over to Curt. "You leave now, and soon as you can, put it where I want it, along with one or two other things. But you need to make sure you're not followed. You're smart enough, you've been at this long enough, but Curt—you can't be followed."

"I won't be followed."

"One more thing," he said. "Once you make the delivery, get the hell out of town. Don't come back home. Don't go to anyone you know, any place you've been before. Just get in the car, pick a compass point, and start driving."

Curt looked at him, his eyes moist. "You.. .you think you can do this?"

"I was born in a revolutionary town," he said, trying to put confidence in his voice. "I can do it."

CHAPTER TWENTY-SIX

At home, Toby had gone to bed and Sarah was in the kitchen, slicing up some cold roast beef from last Sunday's dinner as fried potato pancakes splattered and sang in the frying pan. She had on a light blue cotton dress, and her white apron was snug around her hips. She turned, a length of hair falling across her face, smiling at him.

He remembered a cold fall day back in '31 when he came off a muddy field, football helmet in hand, and for whatever reason that day, he saw that face, saw that smile, and instantly knew he would do almost anything to see it again.

"Sorry I didn't call, tell you I was going to be late," he said.

"I understand," she said, turning back to the stove. "I heard over the radio what's going on. My word, Sam, President Long and Adolf Hitler, coming to our town. I can't believe it."

He shrugged off his coat, took off his hat, and deposited them in the front closet along with his revolver and holster. "Believe it. It's going to happen, and this place is going to be a zoo for the next week."

Back in the kitchen, he came up behind her, grasped her slim hips, and kissed the back of her neck. Sarah made a quick purring noise, like a cat happy for the attention, and she leaned back up against him, her buttocks warm against his groin.

"I'm going to be helping the zookeepers," he told her. "I'm now the liaison between the police department and the FBI. As things happen, it's the same FBI guy from before, the one on my John Doe case. Accompanied by his German secret-police buddy."

He kissed her again and went to the sink to wash his hands. Sarah said, "So what does that mean for you?"

"It means lucky me, I get to be the feds' errand boy until this summit is over. Finding places to sleep and eat for all the government types coming into Portsmouth over the next week. Lots of FBI and Secret Service, people being rounded up, I'm sure... and damn, speaking of rounding up—you remember Sean Donovan?"

She turned, spatula in hand. "Sure. That crippled guy who works in records?"

"He got picked up two days ago. Off to a labor camp."

"Can't the marshal get him off?"

"It's a federal charge. And Hanson can't do much with something federal, as much as he'd like to. One other thing: As long as I'm being an errand boy, I won't be able to investigate my John Doe case."

She put the slices of roast beef on a plate. "What a world, what a time... and here in Portsmouth. I can't believe it. Why Portsmouth?"

Sam yawned. He couldn't help it. "I heard from somebody in the state police that Hitler hates the water, hates ships. He didn't want to spend a day more on the water than he had to. So instead of New York or D.C., he's coming to Portsmouth. A quicker trip. Plus, the Navy Yard's an easy place to secure."

Sarah put the potato pancakes on a plate, brought it over to the table. "Security, hah. Maybe if we're lucky, a crane will fall on Long and Hitler at the same time. Make the world a safer place."

He picked up his knife and fork as she sat across from him. "Maybe so, but if Long goes, some other creep takes over. What's-his-name. That senator from Missouri. Same with Hitler."

She placed her chin in her hand. "Oh, I don't know. I don't get the feeling our Vice President likes being Long's lackey, the poor son of a gun. And I heard that—"

He put his silverware down, looked at the cheerleader who once won his heart, no longer listening to what she was saying. He thought of the boy at the Fish Shanty with the dollar in his hand. Sean warning him to watch his back. The train of prisoners heading up to Maine. The families outside the police station, the children crying. His brother, Tony, on the loose. Donna Fitzgerald and her man, Larry, back together. Leo Gray being picked up by the Black Maria. The visit last night from the two Long's Legionnaires, who made a point of knowing the door in his living room led to the cellar. And what Hanson had said not over an hour ago.

No one was safe.

Her head came up. "Everything all right? Sam?"

He kept his face calm, picked up his knife and fork again, then laid them down. "Sarah... the next few days are really going to be hell around here. The FBI, the Secret Service, army and navy, you name it, they'll be here. Not to mention Long's bully boys."

"I'm sure you're right. What's wrong, then?"

"You and Toby need to leave town during the summit."

"Sam, you can't be serious."

"I'm very serious. There's going to be roadblocks, protestors. People out in the streets. Lots of chances for punches being thrown, people getting arrested, maybe even people getting shot. I don't want you or Toby caught in the middle."

"We could just stay home."

"And suppose the Secret Service or the Department of the Interior do some digging, talking to people, and hear about you and your school friends? Or if the Long's Legionnaires decide to finally act on what they know about the cellar? You two could be in a boxcar headed west before I knew it, before I could do anything about it."

"Sam..."

"Look, a department employee just got himself arrested, and his boss, the city marshal, couldn't do a damn thing. Someone who *worked* for him! How much pull do you think I'd have if anything happened to you and Toby?"

"But my dad—"

"Sarah," he interrupted. "Your dad, he could help. His summer place up at Lake Winnipesaukee. In Moultonborough. It would be a good place to stay for a few days. Quiet, remote, far away from this madhouse."

"Take Toby out of school? And not go to work?"

"Schools are going to be closed, Sarah. You know it makes sense. With my brother out there, the place crawling with cops and feds and all that..."

She sat back in the chair. "Sam...okay, we'll talk about it later, okay? After you eat."

"Sure," he said. "But you know it makes sense. Just for a few days. That's all."

She took a breath. "Okay. For now—I hate to say this, but after you're done, I need you to go upstairs and see Walter."

"Why? What's up? His typewriter too loud?"

"No, nothing like that. He's got a visitor up there, and they were talking loud a while ago, keeping Toby awake. You know Walter promised to keep quiet. Could you just remind him, please?"

"Sure," he said. "Anything else I should know?"

"Yeah. I hate it when you're right."

That should have brought a witty response, but he kept his mouth shut. They ate silently for a little bit, and then, remembering something from the morning, he said, "Sarah, do you know anyone from school who drives a yellow Rambler? Four-door, a big car."

She sliced a piece of meat. "No, I don't think so. Why?"

He hesitated. Should he tell her the car was connected to his murder investigation? And if he did that, suppose it belonged to someone in the Underground Railroad movement—could he trust her to keep quiet? Sarah might warn this person and—

"Oh, just something that happened when I dropped off Toby this morning," he led quietly. "Yellow Rambler came up the street, nearly clipped me. Ticked me off a bit, that's all."

"Oh," she said, bringing her fork up to her mouth. "I see."

No, he thought, you don't. What you don't see is that earlier, when you didn't tell me about Paul Robeson coming to our house, you had kept it a secret from me. And now I don't know what other secrets you might be keeping. And if 1 don't trust you, then our marriage has just taken a big hit, but I can't say that to you, because then there would be more and more questions, voices and tempers raised, and I just don't have the energy for it.

So he kept quiet, as a good inspector—and lousy husband—should.

CHAPTER TWENTY-SEVEN

After Sam finished dinner, he grabbed his coat and went to the outside staircase. He trotted up the steps and knocked on the door, calling out, "Walter! It's Sam. Open up, please."

It took three more knocks before Walter opened the door. "Sam!" he said a bit too enthusiastically. "How good of you to join us. Of course, I assume you're here as a landlord and neighbor and not as part of your duties in the constabulary... constabulation... the police force."

"Walter, can I please come in?"

"But of course!"

Walter opened the door wider, and Sam stepped inside. A one-legged man was sitting at Walter's table, smoking a cigarette, crutches leaning against his wooden chair. He had on a shapeless black sweater and khaki trousers, the right leg of the pants folded over and pinned just above the knee. His brown hair was cut very short, and the way he held his cigarette said "foreigner" to Sam. "Sam, may I present my guest... my boon companion for the evening...Reginald Hale, late flying lieutenant in His Majesty's Royal Air Force. Reggie, this is Sam Miller, inspector for the Portsmouth Police Department, good neighbor, and kindly landlord. Gentlemen."

Reggie said in a drawling British accent, "Charmed, I'm sure."

"Hi, yourself," Sam said.

Walter put both hands on the back of a chair, as if depending upon it for support. On the chair was his leather valise. "Reggie is helping me with a bit of technical advice. You see, I'm working on a story in which the hero is a fighter pilot suddenly transported in time to the future, where civilization is under siege and the civilized ones have forgotten how to fight and—"

The professor must have noticed the look on Sam's face, for he swallowed hard and continued, "But of course, my plotting means nothing to you. What was important was knowing the technical details of flying, which the good lieutenant"—Walter pronounced it in the British fashion, "leftenant"—"was going to help me. And then we started listening to the news about this wonderful bit of bloody diplomatic business that the butcher of Europe and the Kingfish of Louisiana managed to pull off, and well, a bottle emerged and other tales were told."

"I see," Sam said. "Walter, look, no offense, but Sarah heard some loud noises up here, Toby's trying to sleep and—"

The RAF man stubbed out his cigarette in an overflowing ashtray, struggled upright, reaching for his crutches. "Not a problem, Inspector, it was time for me to leave anyway. Professor, thank you for your hospitality." He hopped, grabbed his crutches, and Sam didn't know whether to keep looking or glance away. So he did nothing. The crutches went underneath the man's arms and Sam said, "Do you need a hand getting down the steps?"

"Thanks awfully, but I've had lots of practice. Months and months, if you must know. First time I've ever met an American copper. You wouldn't be interested in my immigration status, would you?"

"No, I wouldn't, but others might."

Reggie smiled, leaned on his crutches. "Bloody awful, this. Hopping around like a toad. Once upon a time I was somebody important, one of those knights of the air, ready to do battle against the invading Hun. We were the last hope for our island, and we were going to repulse those bloody bastards. That was the plan, at any rate. Too bad nobody told Jerry about the plan. They had their own ideas. Bomb the shit out of our airfields and radar sites, clearing the way for the paratroopers to seize ground and hold it for the follow-up invasion troops. Still, we fought, against terrible odds... It sounds strange, but I was the lucky one. Lost my leg after an ME-109 jumped me, and managed to get out on one of the evacuation ships."

Reggie made his way to the doorway, turned awkwardly, and said wistfully, "We might have made it, you know. If Winnie hadn't been tossed out, if the Cabinet hadn't sued for peace after the first landings, if the king hadn't died in the bombings, if you... if you bloody Yanks hadn't sat on your hands and decided not to help us. We might have made it. And then Herr Hitler would be fighting both us and the Bolshies."

"Bunch of us thought we had done enough last time," Sam said. "It just looked like another European squabble, and the last one didn't end well. So most of us didn't want to get involved."

Reggie shook his head. "Oh, you'll get involved. Maybe not this year or next year, but I guarantee this, Inspector: Once that fucking German housepainter gets the Reds hammered down, he's going to turn west again.

And your mighty wide ocean won't help. Maybe then you'll wish you had helped us."

Walter opened the door, and Reggie hobbled out. Cold air came in, and when the door was shut, Walter turned to Sam and said, "I'm sorry again for disturbing your lovely wife."

"Apology accepted, Walter. There's one more thing... and I swear to God, you haven't heard it from me." Sam never thought he would do this, but after the past few days, he couldn't stay quiet any more. "Tomorrow night. You might want to tell Reginald, and any other similar friends, that they shouldn't be in their usual haunts. Something's going on. Do I make myself clear?"

"As clear as crystal. Sam...I cannot tell you how much I owe you, this is going to be—"

"Walter, I have no idea what you're talking about. And neither do you."

His tenant grabbed his arm. "I'm not a religious man, but God bless you for what you've done."

Sam broke free from the man's grasp. "I think God's got His hands full enough without worrying about me."

Before going to bed, Sam checked in on Toby. His boy had his crystal radio set on low; thankfully, it was just playing soft dance music from someplace where people had enough money and time to go dancing. He reached down to unplug it, and Toby stirred and said, "Dad?"

He sat down on the edge of the bed. "Yeah, sport. What is it?"

"Mmm, Mommy said we're gonna go on a trip tomorrow ... up to Grandpa's camp."

He touched Toby's hair. "That's right. Just a few days. You and Mom."

"And I won't get in trouble at school?"

"No, no trouble at all."

"Good. I've been in trouble enough."

His boy's breathing eased, and Sam stood up to leave. Toby stirred and said, "I told 'em, you know. That my dad wasn't a rat. I had to tell 'em you're not a rat. So I did okay. I didn't fight, Dad, but I didn't let him get away with it, either..."

Sam went out, closing the door softly behind him.

He slid into bed next to Sarah, who rolled over and nuzzled up against him and said, "You win."

"Thanks."

"Don't thank me yet. Dad's coming to pick me and Toby up tomorrow."

"He'll get over it," he said, kissing her and feeling the silkiness of lace on her body. She kissed him back and then pressed her lips against his ear and whispered with urgency, "Sam... forgive me, will you?"

"For what?" he whispered back. Both of them kept their voices low from habit, being so close to their dozing son.

"For who I am. A disappointment... a shrew... and... oh, just forgive me."

He kissed her again, deeper, as she moaned and moved underneath him. "Forgiven, Sarah, always forgiven. Though I don't agree with what you just said."

"Shhh," Sarah replied, lowering her hand on his belly, "let's stop talking for a while. Here's the rain check I promised you from a long time ago, big guy."

In the darkness he sighed at the touch of his cheerleader. "Not that big."

Her warm hand lowered some more. "Just you wait."

CHAPTER TWENTY-EIGHT

At breakfast that morning, his heart nearly broke at the sight of the two suitcases—one large, the other small—at the door, huddled there like frightened children. It was wrong, it was awful, but he knew it was the right thing to do.

Sarah had made a good breakfast for them all, pancakes and bacon. Toby kept on asking if the water was warm enough up at Grandpa's camp, could he do some swimming when he got there if Mom was there to watch him?

Sam said, "If your mother says so, then it's fine."

Now the dishes had been gathered and he stood behind Sarah, hands on her hips, and kissed the curve of her neck, and said, "Leave them. I'll do them later." "Please. It gives me something to do. Something to keep me busy. All right?" Her voice quivered.

Sam ran his hands up and down her slim hips, recalled with delight the passion that these same hips had brought him last night. He brought his lips to her ear and said, "What did you mean last night, asking for forgiveness? Where did that come from?"

In an instant, her body tensed, as if she had heard something disquieting. She shook off his hands with a sharp movement. "Can we not talk about this now, please? Dad will be here any moment, and I need to get the dishes done."

Message received. Once again he was struck by the contradiction that was his wife: the passionate lover of last night and the irritated housewife this morning. Sam went out to the living room to get his revolver, coat, and hat and, through the front window, saw his father-in-law, Lawrence Young, striding up the walkway as if he owned the damn place, which he once wished to do. Back during those long days and nights as a newlywed, when Sam had struggled to come up with the down payment, Larry had hinted at how his new son-in-law could get the desperately needed money: Sam's ass working weekends at the furniture store.

Larry had never gotten what he wanted, Sam thought. But Sam had gotten something else. Bloody hands and a memory that would never leave him.

Larry came in, dressed in a fine dark gray overcoat, looking pleased with himself. "Morning, Sam."

"Hello, Larry."

"I understand my daughter and grandson need some protection."

"In a manner of speaking," he replied.

"I thought that was your job."

Sam felt his shoulders tense. "It is. Which is why I'm getting them out of town during the summit."

"Maybe you're getting them out of town, but I'm putting them up, driving up there and back, taking the better part of my workday. I hope you appreciate that." From the kitchen, Sarah came out, smiling. "Dad, thanks for helping us out."

Toby was there, saying, "Grandpa!" his face radiant. Sam picked up the two suitcases. "Tell you what, Toby. You two get your coats, and I'll put your suitcases out in Grandpa's car. Okay?'

Before anybody said anything, he was outside in the blessedly cool and free air, carrying both suitcases.

Sarah said, "I'll try to call you the moment we're settled in if the damn phone's working."

He kissed her and said, "You sure you've got everything packed?"

She squeezed the back of his neck and whispered, "Not really, but I'm leaving all my frilly things behind for later... for another rain check."

Another kiss exchanged. "When it's all over, I'll come up to fetch you. The city'll owe me some time."

Sarah got into the front seat of the Oldsmobile. "Dad could come get us."

"I owe him too much already."

From the rear seat, Toby called out, "So I can go swimming? Really?"

"If your mother says so."

"Good," his boy said, and then, "Dad? Make sure my models are okay, will you?"

"Sure, Toby," he promised. "Nothing will happen to them."

He closed both car doors and walked up to his father- in-law. "Larry, thanks. I mean it. Thanks."

"Always nice to know I can fill in when you can't. Just need to discuss—

"

For the benefit of his wife and boy watching from the Oldsmobile, Sam smiled up at his father-in-law. "Let's not keep my wife and boy waiting. All right?"

Lawrence said, "Just one moment, that's all. Look, I understand you've taken my advice. To become more active in the Party."

"Maybe, maybe not."

"I see." Lawrence's voice turned frosty. "But I've been told you're probably going to become more active under the sponsorship of Marshal Harold Hanson."

"Look, can we get into this some other time, because—"

"No, we don't have to go into it some other time. You've made your choice, and you'll have to live with it. You've tossed your lot in with the marshal. That's fine. And when budget time comes, don't think you can come to me looking for help if your position in the police department is eliminated. When it's eliminated."

"Is that a threat, Larry? What, you think I'm your slave? Someone you can order around because I owe you?"

"Owe me? For what? Taking my daughter and grandson up to Moultonborough?"

"You know what I mean," Sam said. "Everyone knows how I got my inspector's job. You pulled some strings and talked to the Police Commission and—"

Lawrence laughed. "You stupid little dope. Whatever gave you that idea?"

"It was common—"

"Some smart inspector you are. I lobbied *against* you, you numbskull. Even knowing it might hurt Sarah. It would have been worth it to see you fail and stay a sergeant. Got that? And I still don't want you to make it—a punk like you, son of a drunk and brother of a criminal, with my only girl. And having you active in the Party... besides everything else, I just wanted you somewhere I had you by the short hairs. That's all. And now that you're sponsored by that fool Hanson, I know you're going to fail. I'm going to enjoy every damn second of it." Sam took a breath, thinking of the secret he knew about this man, the one he had pledged he would never divulge. "The only thing I'm looking for now is to see you get the hell off my porch."

Sam went in and closed the door, then stood at the window to see the Oldsmobile back out of the driveway and head away. He watched until it made the corner, turned, and his family was gone.

He didn't bother going to the police station after his family left. Instead, he headed straight to the Rockingham Hotel. Two army MPs stood at the entrance, clipboards in their hands. Their khaki uniforms were pressed and their boots and helmets gleamed. So did their Sam Brown belts and the holsters for their Colt .45 pistols. Their faces were lean and serious, as if they spent a lot of time saying no to people.

"Sorry, pal," the MP on the left told Sam. "Place is closed for the duration."

"I'm sure, but I'm here to see Agent LaCouture of the FBI."

"Name and identification?" the MP on the right said.

"Sam Miller. Of the Portsmouth Police Department." He showed his inspector's badge, his police identification card, and just for the hell of it, his officer's commission in the New Hampshire National Guard. All three were scowlingly examined by the MP on the right while his companion checked the clipboard and nodded. "Yeah, he's on the list. ID check out all right?"

"Sure enough," the other MP said, passing the identity cards back to Sam, who pocketed them. The lobby was chaotic, with piles of luggage, army and navy officers in full-dress uniform, and newsreel and radio reporters all thrust up against one another. He slipped through the crowd, went upstairs, and knocked on the door of Room Twelve.

Agent LaCouture opened the door, dressed for the day in shirt and tie and seersucker suit. Groebke was sitting at the room's round table, a pile of papers in front of him. The Gestapo man was dressed plainly again, in a severe black suit with a white shirt and black necktie.

"Glad to see you, Inspector," LaCouture told him. "You're early."

"Want to get a jump on the day," Sam answered. The room smelled of cologne and stale tobacco and strong coffee. He wondered what the two of them talked about when they were alone together. Did they trade war stories about the Kingfish and the Fuhrer?

LaCouture went to the desk, picked up a set of papers. "Here," he said, handing them over. "Your task for the day. Here's a listing of restaurants, hotels, and boardinghouses in your fair city. I want you to go to each of them, see how many people they can feed and house on a daily basis, get a master list together, and be back here by five o'clock. Got it?"

Sam looked at the papers. "This looks like something a clerk can do."

"I'm sure, but this particular clerk I'm looking at is a police inspector and thereby knows everybody he'll be talking to. And this particular clerk will know if someone is bullshitting him. So yeah, Inspector—a clerk can do this job, but I'm giving it to you."

Sam said nothing, just folded the papers in half. The Gestapo officer was grinning. LaCouture said, "You don't like it, do you?"

"I've had worse jobs," Sam replied.

CHAPTER TWENTY-NINE

The day became a long slog of going through most of Portsmouth. As much as he hated to admit it, LaCouture was right: Anybody else would have been faced with some bullshit talk about availability and prices, but such crap wasn't going to fly with him today. From the Irish landlady to the White Russian exile to the descendant of the first family into Portsmouth from 1623, he knew all of the lodging house owners, and he got the information he needed about the number of available rooms.

He was chilled at how quickly the checkpoints had been set up. It was like a newsreel from occupied Europe: soldiers with rifles over their shoulders, standing in the streets, mobile barriers made of wood and barbed wire blocking intersections and sidewalks. Several times he saw people held apart at the checkpoints as their papers were checked and rechecked by FBI or Department of Interior agents in dark suits with grim faces.

Now, having given the list to LaCouture, who appeared to have a phone receiver permanently attached to his ear, with Groebke sitting next to him, scribbling furiously with a fountain pen...well, he could now head home.

But home to what?

He went back to the police station, back to what he knew was ahead for him, another long night.

He had a dinner of fish chowder and hard rolls at his desk, watching the clock hands wander by, waiting and waiting. He had tried to call Moultonborough three times through the New England Telephone operator, and each time the call was interrupted by a bored male voice: "All long-distance phone calls from this county are now being administered by the U.S. Army Signal Corps. Is this an official military phone call?"

"No, it's a call from—"

Click, as the line was disconnected.

Two more tries, using his police affiliation, got the same result.

So he gave up.

The marshal's office door opened and Harold Hanson came out, his suit and shirt wrinkled, eyes puffy behind his glasses. "Time to ride, Sam," he said quietly. "Let's go."

Sam got up from his desk, wiped his hands on a paper napkin, and followed the city marshal to the station's basement. He smelled gasoline and fuel oil from the department's maintenance garage on the other side. There was a crowd of off-duty cops, all wearing civvies, talking in low voices. Large cardboard boxes were set by the near brick wall.

Hanson stepped up on a wooden box, held up a hand. "All right," he told them. "This isn't going to be easy, but it's something we've been ordered to do. This is a National Guard action. We're heading out in a few minutes."

"Boss," came a voice. "What the hell's going on?"

"The summit's taking place in a few days. We're under orders from the White House to clear out all undesirables in the city. This place has to look perfect for the radio, newsreels, and newspapers."

The basement was silent. Sam thought about that hobo encampment, bulldozed and burnt to the ground. What about Lou Purdue? Where in hell had he gone, with what he knew about a witness? One more loose end about Peter Wotan...

"So that's what we're doing." Hanson's voice was hesitant, unlike his usual style. "We've got flophouses and other places to check out. Anyone who's a refugee, anyone who doesn't belong in Portsmouth, we've got to remove. That's orders straight from the White House."

"Remove them to where, boss?"

"Not our problem. The army will have transports set up, and they'll be taken out to a resettlement camp." He rubbed his eyes. "Look at it this way, guys. We're just following orders. All right? Just following orders."

From the cardboard boxes, military gear smelling of mildew was hauled out: old-style round metal helmets from the last war *(Like one Dad probably wore,* Sam thought), canvas web belting, wooden truncheons, and green cloth armbands that said guard in white block letters. He put his gear on, feeling as if he were dressing up for Halloween, and joined four other cops—Pinette, Lubrano, Smith, and Reardon—in an old Ford cruiser that took three tries to start up. He sat in the rear, silent, with the helmet in his lap. There was joking and laughing from the others about being in the Kingfish's army, but he didn't join them.

Lubrano said to Reardon, "You know, I've always wondered how we got so many Jews and refugees in town. Bet you they paid off Long and his buds to look the other way when they got smuggled in."

Reardon laughed. "Too bad they can't get their money back after tonight."

They pulled up at Foss Avenue, a narrow street about a block away from the harbor, with sagging buildings of brick and wood, dirty trash bins on the crooked sidewalks. Sam knew the street well: taverns, flophouses, and boardinghouses. A place for people struggling to make a go of it. The luckier ones moved on to better neighborhoods. The others never left except in ambulances or funeral home wagons.

There was another reason for remembering this place, for something Sam had done on Thurber Street, two blocks over, just before he and his very pregnant Sarah had bought their house. Thurber Street. Even being this close to the street made him uncomfortable. He turned away. There was a wooden and barbed-wire barrier overseen by two regular National Guard troops in uniform, gear spotless, boots shiny, Springfield rifles hanging from their shoulders. Sam noted their grins as he and the others got out of the cruiser with their surplus gear. The real National Guard and the play National Guard.

Sam hung back as other cops dressed in helmets and gear approached. From the gloom came a man in a dark blue suit, Confederate-flag pin on his lapel, carrying a small flashlight and a clipboard stuffed with papers. "Eddie Mitchell, Department of Interior," the man said. "Listen up, okay?"

Sam and the others gathered in a semicircle around Mitchell, a tall man with glasses who spoke with a soft Tennessee accent. "The other end of this street is sealed off, and we've got the alleyways covered as well. Y'all gonna be used as chutes. There's a place down there, the Harbor Point Hotel. In about"—he put the flashlight beam to his watch—"ten minutes, we're gonna have that place raided and trucks backed up to take the undesirables away. Y'all just gonna be flanking the front entrance. Just make sure nobody gets away. Got it?"

A murmur of voices, but Sam kept quiet. He wished he was in his empty home, taking a bath and having a beer. Any place else than here.

A rumble of approaching truck engines, and Mitchell waved a hand. The regular National Guardsmen pulled the barrier aside. Two army deuce-and-a-half trucks growled by, canvas sides flapping, diesel fumes belching. Mitchell yelled, "Let's go, boys. Follow 'em!"

The more eager of the bunch followed the truck at a half-trot. Sam pulled up the rear, walking at a brisk pace, truncheon in hand, helmet hard and uncomfortable on his head. Ahead, voices were yelling, and there was a throng of people in front of the hotel, some wearing uniforms, others not. Flashlights were being waved around, and there were other guys in suits directing the flow of people, blowing whistles. The place was three-story, wooden, with a rotting porch out front, a blue-and-white wooden sign announcing harbor point. One of the trucks backed in, the tailgate rattling open. Sam took a position by the porch as lights blazed, as the other officers in helmets and webbed gear made up two lines leading to the truck.

Amazing, too, was what followed. Wooden tables were unfolded, chairs lined up. It was strange, like seeing a voting booth set up in the heart of a riot. Then people started filing out of the grandly named hotel. They were old and young, the men clean-shaven or bearded, some women wearing colorful kerchiefs on their hair, some holding children by the hand. Most carried small suitcases, as though they had always expected this night to come.

He heard a jumble of voices—French, Polish, Dutch, British—but the faces all looked the same. Pale, shocked, wide-eyed, as if they could not believe this was happening to them in this supposed land of liberty. All had the look of having been put through this before, but with soldiers in gray uniforms and coal-scuttle helmets, soldiers with crooked cross symbols on their vehicles, not white stars.

A woman in a thin black cotton dress stared at him as she went by. She called out in a thick accent, "Why are you doing this? *Why?*"

He looked away. He had no answer.

At the nearest truck, a line had formed by the wooden tables. Paperwork was being checked, clipboards consulted. The men manning the tables shook their heads, made a motion with a thumb, and up into the rear of the truck the people went. As if they had practiced it before, the younger undesirables helped the older ones up.

"Shit," someone whispered. "This is like those damn newsreels from Europe, you know?"

"Yeah, I know," Sam replied. "I guess we're all Europeans now."

A motion caught his eye. A man came down the wooden steps alone, using crutches, one leg usable, the other cut off at the knee. RAF Lieutenant Reggie Hale, the guest of Walter Tucker. Staring straight ahead, moving slowly and deliberately, heading over to the examining table. Sam watched, hardly able to bear seeing the slow progress of the crippled pilot. Walter probably hadn't gotten to him in time. When Hale got to the desk and started talking, the thought came to him of how the poor bastard would get into the rear of the truck.

That was what did it for him.

Sam left the line and went over to the desk, where Hale was speaking low and proper. "Old boy, I tell you, someone must have stolen my papers, because they were in my coat just last week."

"Yeah, fine, that's only the sixth time I've heard that in the last five minutes," replied the bored National Guard clerk. "Come along, up on the truck and—"

"Hold on," Sam said.

The RAF pilot swiveled on his crutches, his face expressionless. The clerk said to Sam, "Fella, get back where you belong, all right?"

Sam handed over his badge, not using LaCouture's card, wanting to keep the FBI man out of this. "I'm Inspector Sam Miller of the Portsmouth Police Department. This man is Reggie Hale, right?"

The clerk glanced down at his clipboard. "Yeah, so what?"

"Hale is a material witness in an ongoing investigation I'm conducting. He's to stay here."

"Hey, Miller, I don't need—"

"The name is *Inspector* Miller, pal," Sam said. "And Hale stays here. Or I'll go get the rest of the Portsmouth cops and leave, and you can see how well you do your job with twenty or so fewer men. How does that sound?"

The clerk had a little Clark Gable mustache that twitched some. He handed back Sam's badge with a clatter. "Fine, take the fucking limey. I'll put your name down as the guy I let him go to. In case he shoots the governor or something, it'll be your neck. Get back where you belong."

Sam walked back to the line, then glanced behind to see if Hale was following, but no, the RAF pilot had limped away and faded into the shadows.

Well, he thought, how about that.

One of his fellow cops said, "Sam, what the hell was that?"

"That was a lesson," he answered. "Sometimes you do a favor and you don't get anything in return. Except pissed-off people."

"Ain't that the truth."

He stood there, the wooden truncheon cold in his hand, as the arrests continued, as the trucks backed up with their growling diesels, the children crying, the whistles blowing, seeing it all, not wanting to see it, not wanting to hear it, but forcing himself to do it just the same.

After about an hour of watching the refugees get processed, the coffee he had drunk earlier had percolated through his kidneys and bladder. He said to Lubrano, "Hey, do you know anywhere a guy can take a leak?" Lubrano shrugged. "Dunno. There's an alley back there I used a couple of minutes ago."

Sam left the line of police, found the alley. He went down the narrow stretch between two tenements, stinking of trash and urine. He found a couple of ash cans, propped up his wooden truncheon against the far wall, and unzipped his pants, did his business. Damn, what a night. After he was done, he zipped up his pants and—

Someone was singing.

There was a sharp moan of somebody in pain.

He picked up his truncheon, went down to the other end of the alley, heard some laughter. On the sidewalk, a streetlight illuminated a scene that froze him. A man lay on the sidewalk cowering, dressed in tattered clothes. Standing over him were two younger and better-dressed men, kicking him, laughing. Both wore short leather coats and blue corduroy pants. Two of Long's boys hard at work, handing out their brand of street justice. The pair from the Fish Shanty, the guys whose car tires had been slashed.

"C'mon!" one yelled. "Let's hear ya sing, ya drunk mackerel snapper!"

The other man laughed, too. "C'mon, sing! You know how to sing, don't ya? Sing our song!"

The first one tossed his head back. " *I wish I was in the land of cotton, old times there are not forgotten, look away, look away, look away, Dixie Land.* ' "

The man on the ground cried out, "Please, please, stop... I'll... I'll try! Jesus.. .just give me a sec... ow!"

It seemed as if time were passing by at a furious pace, with no time for thinking or reflection. Sam stripped off his helmet and his armband, dropped them on the ground. With his truncheon, he hammered the skull of the nearest Long's Legionnaire, dropping him like a sack of potatoes. The other one looked up, startled, scared, and the astonished look on the Southerner's face brought Sam joy.

"Here," Sam said. "This one's for you."

He slammed the wooden truncheon into the side of the man's skull. The Legionnaire stumbled and Sam followed, hitting him twice in the stomach. The Legionnaire tripped over his companion and stayed down. Sam helped up the old man they had been tormenting.

His face was bloody, his hair white and stringy. "Ohhh... ohhh... thank you, thank you, I—"

"Go. Get going." Sam gently pushed him away.

The man stumbled down the street. Sam went back to the Legionnaires. He gave them both a swift kick to the ribs. Both yelped in pain.

He couldn't resist one. He sang to them: "Yes, we'll rally round the flag, boys, we'll rally once again, shouting the battle cry of freedom!"

Then he left them, like trash on the street, and picked up his discarded helmet and armband.

CHAPTER THIRTY

When Sam got home, exhausted, all he wanted to do was grab a beer and take a hot bath and let the dirty memories of the night soak away. If he had been lucky, all those Southern clowns saw was some guy with a big stick. All right, a pretty stupid stunt, but still, he felt good about it. He felt even better about letting that hobo get away. A beer to celebrate sounded pretty fine.

But when he got through the front door, the radio was on in the darkened living room, "Sarah?" he called out, confused.

"Nope, 'fraid not," came a voice, and Sam thought, *Oh, great.* After hanging: up his coat, he flicked on a switch, lighting up the room. Tony sat on the couch, muddy feet splayed out in front of him.

"Thought I left the house locked this morning."

Tony grinned, "Learned a lot of skills in labor camps, Sam. How to take your time cutting down trees. Best way to stow your gear without one of your bunkmates stealing it. And how to break into a house, even one belonging to a cop. You should have better locks."

"And you should have better sense. What the hell are you doing here?"

Tony crossed his feet. "Man, there's so many feds and National Guard troops crawling around, I had to get someplace safe, even for a little while, and this was it. You know, when we were kids, it'd take about ten minutes to get to this neighborhood from Pierce Island at a good trot. Tonight it took me almost an hour. Can you believe that?"

Sam took a chair, sat down heavily. "Yeah, I can believe that. You must have learned some skills up there, to miss all the patrols."

"You wouldn't believe some of the things I learned." He looked around and said, "Toby and Sarah coming back soon? I'd love a chance to see 'em, I really would."

"They're gone for a few days. I stashed them up in Moultonborough, at her dad's place. Too many chances of something bad happening while

Portsmouth gets crowded with every nutball in the region."

"A good idea. Too bad there aren't enough safe places like that in the state for people who need them. Or the country. Or the world."

Sam stretched out his legs. "Jesus Christ, do you have to make everything into some goddamn symbol of the times or something?"

"Why not? That's the world we're living in."

"So says you," Sam said, tired of it all.

From the radio came a familiar voice, that of Charles Lindbergh, speaking at some rally. In his Midwestern high-pitched tone, he said, "It is not difficult to understand why Jewish people desire the overthrow of Nazi Germany. The persecution they suffered in Germany would be sufficient to make bitter enemies of any race. No person with a sense of the dignity of mankind can condone the persecution of the Jewish race in Germany. But no person of honesty and vision can look on their pro-war polity here today without seeing the dangers involved in such a polity both for us and for them. Instead of agitating for war, the Jewish groups in this country should be opposing it in every possible way, for they will be among the first to feel its consequences. Tolerance is a virtue that depends upon peace and strength. History shows that it cannot survive war and devastations. A few farsighted Jewish people realize this and stand opposed to intervention. But the majority still do not. Their greatest danger to this country lies in their large ownership and influence in our motion pictures, our press, our radio, and our government."

"Can you believe that rube?" Tony motioned to the radio. "The war's all about Europe, all about the Jews. Just stay home between the two oceans and mind our own business and beat up the Jews ourselves and we'll all be happy little children."

Sam said, "Some would say the man makes a point, even if he has a lousy way of making it, of staying out of Europe's war."

"Yeah, some point. Just because you know how to fly a plane doesn't mean you know shit about politics and history. The next hundred years of what kind of people we're going to be, what kind of world we will inhabit, is being fought out in the steppes of Russia, small towns in occupied England and Europe, and our sainted Kingfish has just cast his lot on the side of the invaders."

Sam felt his blood rise. "As opposed to what, Tony? Helping Joe Stalin and the Reds? You say you know so much. Ever hear of a place called the Katyn Forest, in Poland? Russians took over the eastern half of Poland back in '39, as part of the Stalin and Hitler peace pact. When the Krauts overran that part in '41, they found thousands of dead Polish soldiers and officers buried in pits, hands tied together, shot in the head by the NKVD, the Russian secret police. The Krauts invited reporters there, newsreel guys, showed the world what the Russians had done to those Poles. That's the kind of people we should be helping?"

Tony glowered at him. "Just like you can't choose your family, Stun, you can't choose the ones to help you in a desperate fight."

Lindbergh's voice kept on coming, almost whiny. "I am not attacking either the Jewish or the British people. Both races, I admire. But I am saying that the leaders of both the British and the Jewish races, for reasons which are as understandable from their viewpoint as they are inadvisable from ours, for reasons which are not American, wish to involve us in the war. We cannot blame them for looking out for what they believe to be their own interests, but we also must look out for ours. We cannot allow the natural passions and prejudices of other peoples to lead our country to destruction."

"Come on, Tony, what do you say? Should Long make an alliance with Stalin, help him fight the Germans, is that it?"

"The Germans gassed Dad, put him in an early grave. And the Navy Yard thought so little of him and the other workers that they didn't care when he started coughing out his lungs. Don't you ever think about that?"

"Sure I do, but having one doctor or six at the Yard wouldn't have made much difference," Sam said. "And you know what? I'm sure we go back far enough, we'll find some English lord or gent made life miserable for the Millers back in Ireland. Does that mean we hold a grudge forever? Christ, that's what they do in Europe, and look where it's gotten them."

"So we just give up?"

"Christ, Tony. What the hell do you want me to do? Buttonhole Long or Hitler in a few days, give 'em the point of view from my escapee brother? Is that it?"

Tony stayed silent for a moment. "No. I... I expect you to do your job, Sam. That's all. Just do your job and do the right thing."

It now made sense. "Tony. It's no coincidence you're here now. What's going on?"

"Doesn't matter."

"Oh, yes, it does," he insisted. "You just told me to do my job. And that's what I'm doing. My job. So why are you here? You've been a prisoner for a couple of years, you finally escape and end up in Portsmouth just when Hitler's coming by for a visit. A hell of a coincidence, don't you think?"

Tony got to his feet, face set. "Sorry, brother. Time to go."

"You're not leaving. Tell me why you're here. The summit... what are you going to do? Make a scene? A protest? Tell me why you're here."

185

Tony stepped toward him. "You going to stop me? Arrest me? Pull a gun on me?"

Doing his job, doing what he had done with those two Long boys, that had been one thing. But his brother was something else. The room was still.

"Tony...."

"Still here."

"Leave, then. But get out of Portsmouth. It's too dangerous here. If you care for Sarah or Toby, get the hell out. Stop whatever it is you're up to, and just get the hell out."

"Good advice," Tony said, brushing past him, heading to the door. "But you know me when it comes to advice. I hardly ever take it. Even if I do care for your wife and boy."

The door slammed behind Tony and Sam wiped at his face with both hands. Such a goddamn day. He changed the radio station to some music, went into the kitchen, pulled out a bottle of Pabst Blue Ribbon beer, and emptied it before he headed for his bath.

INTERLUDE VII

When he left his brother's house, he circled around, went to the backyard, where it seemed like so many lifetimes ago he had sneaked over to place three rocks on top of each other. At the rear steps, there was another rock, larger and flatter. He picked it up, removed the slip of paper from underneath, and then walked to the shrubbery separating Sam's yard from the neighbor's. He reached into the shrubbery, took out a bag he had hidden there earlier, and then looked up at the lights of Sam's house.

He felt out of place here. He and Sam had never been close, had been rivals more than siblings, though he knew in his heart of hearts that Sam believed in the same things he did. But Sam was a straight arrow, believed in working within the system as much as possible, while he...well, he knew he was a hell-raiser, the proverbial bull in the china closet. He wished he could have told Sam more, wished he could have left him on better terms, wished he hadn't lied about why he had come to the house, but it had to be this way. Plans were in motion, things were happening, and it wasn't safe for Sam to know much. Even Sarah knew only her own small part of things, and he felt embarrassed, thinking of Sarah's words in the attic, how it seemed she had been looking for an excuse to betray her husband, his brother.

A betrayal. In a way he supposed he was betraying Sam, and he hoped that eventually Sam would forgive him. But for now, all he could rely on was Sam being Sam, and sometimes, that was even too much to hope for.

He walked away from the house, ducking into other yards and alleyways, the lights of the shipyard always out there, keeping an eye on him. He was torn, seeing them. That's where his other family was, the ones he had organized for, the ones he had tried to help, and eventually, that's where it all crashed down on him, with his arrest and deportation from his home state.

But now—now things were different.

Under a streetlight, he opened the slip of paper, read the address, the meeting time, and the code phrase. Memorized it all, then tore the paper into tiny bits and tossed them into an open storm drain, looked once more at the shipyard lights.

This time it was different. This time he would succeed, would go after that despicable man, would make it all worthwhile, not only for himself but for his family across the river and the family who lived in that little house just a few blocks away.

CHAPTER THIRTY-ONE

Sam listened to Frank Sinatra singing some swing tune on Your Hit Parade on CBS as he stared at the exhausted face looking back at him from the mirror and thought about what he had done to get this place for his wife and son. He didn't feel like thinking about Tony. He washed his hands, saw the flecks of dried brown blood from the old man circle down into the drain, and remembered.

Several years back, it had been a desperate time, trying to get the cash to make the down payment. Sam had borrowed and begged, had worked as much overtime as possible, but the cash just wasn't there. And he wasn't going to take his father-in-law's employment offer, not on your life.

So Sam had gone elsewhere—to Thurber Street—and there he was this cold March evening. He stood by a pile of dirty snow, looked at the row of boardinghouses stretching down almost to the harbor. Officially, these sagging wooden structures were places where sailors, shipyard workers, and fishermen rented rooms for a week, a month, or a year, but Sam knew better. Some of these buildings had illegal bars set up for all-night drinking sessions, and others had rooms that rented for thirty minutes or an hour.

Quite illegal, quite profitable, and so far, Sam's superiors hadn't done anything about it. No doubt some folding green was being passed around, but he didn't particularly care. He shifted his feet in the snow and ice, shivered. Far off, a church clock chimed three times, and he winced as he recalled the lie he had told Sarah, that he was working overtime tonight. It was almost true—he was working overtime for his family.

He looked up the narrow street, waited, his hands in his coat pockets. One pocket was empty, and the other contained a leather sap, filled with lead pellets. Out there was his target, and if he was very, very lucky...

There. Coming from the middle house, the one with the peeling yellow paint, a man shambled out, wearing a long raccoon coat and thick gloves and a sharply turned fedora. William "Wild Wily" Cocannon was a big man, broad in the shoulders. He owned most of these buildings, some legitimate bars and boardinghouses down on the harbor, and other businesses as well. Sam had followed him here and there for a couple of weeks, watching where he went, knowing that on these early Monday mornings after busy weekends, Wild Wily collected from his bars and whorehouses before going home to a nice little estate outside of Manchester.

Wild Willy rambled down the street, spotlighted for a moment by a streetlight, a plume of steam rising from his face in the cold. Sam stepped out and followed him down the sidewalk. Part of him still couldn't believe he was doing this, but in his panic the past few weeks, he had tried to justify it: Wild Willy was a criminal who was getting away with lots of crimes, week after week, and Sam was just going to deliver a little rough street justice.

That's all. His plan was a quick robbery and racing home with what he'd stolen.

He took out the sap, grabbed Wild Willy by the shoulder, and in a voice he couldn't believe was his own, growled, "Your money, asshole, and now!"

That was the plan.

But Wild Willy had his own plan.

The big man spun around and shouted, "Fuck you!" and a switchblade flashed in a gloved hand. Sam quickly backpedaled away, but not before the blade sliced across his knuckles. Sam punched back with the leather sap, catching Wild Willy on the side of the head, knocking his hat off. The large man cursed again and lunged at him. Sam stumbled back, slipping on the ice. Wild Willy was shouting, "You fucking little shit, you think you're going to rob me? Who the fuck do you think you are?"

Sam fell on his ass. He had never felt so terrified, so alone. Other times he'd been in trouble, he'd at least had other cops to back him up, but out here on this cold night, he was alone. And he had crossed a pretty big wide line, for he wasn't a cop at this moment, flat on his back, with Wild Willy coming after him. He was a criminal. He kicked out hard with his feet, caught Wild Willy in the shins. The larger man fell back, and Sam scrambled up and went after him again, slamming the leather sap into his shoulder, into his neck. As the knife came at him again, Sam struck down on Wild Willy's face.

Something went crunch, and Sam was now pissed off that he had to be out here, stealing money for a house, acting like a criminal because he didn't get paid enough, mad that Wild Willy was putting up a fight.

Sam straightened up, breathing harshly, like a racehorse nearing the finish line. Wild Willy was on his back, gasping, wheezing, flailing, making horrible gurgling noises from what used to be his face. Sam grabbed the man's arms, dragged him into the shadows of an alley. He knelt, wetting his knees in the snow, then went through the man's pockets, his hand shaking so violently he dropped the thick paper envelope that he found. He picked up the envelope, trembling, and then ran up the street, the cold air burning his lungs. He ran two blocks. That's where the shakes really hit him hard, and he threw up among some trash bins, heaving until all that was left was bile.

He got home to the cramped apartment about fifteen minutes later. He pushed himself into the tiny bathroom, washing and rewashing his hands, the brown blood from Wild Willy streaming into the sink. The water was cold, the water was always cold, and when he was done, he dried with some toilet paper, flushed it away, and opened up the envelope.

Seven hundred and twelve dollars. Two hundred more than what he needed. He put the money back in the envelope, hid it on a shelf in a rear closet, and stumbled off to bed.

A month later, when they looked at their house on Grayson Street, his very pregnant Sarah hooked her arm through his and said, "Sam, besides our wedding day, this is the happiest day of my life."

He couldn't say anything, for when Sarah had spoken, all he could hear was the desperate wheezing of Wild Wily, broken and bleeding, in that frozen alleyway.

So there. He looked at himself in the mirror, then at his hands.

They were clear of blood. All that covered his hands was his own skin.

He shook his head, ran the water some more, picked up the bar of soap, and started scrubbing again, knowing there were some things that just couldn't be washed out.

PART FOUR

Restricted Distribution

TO: R. F. Sloane, Regional Supervisor, Boston, Department of the Interior

FROM: W. W. Atkins, Department of the Interior, Camp Carpenter Transit Station, N.H.

RE: Interrogation of Special Interest Prisoner **#434**

The following is a synopsis of the interrogation conducted 10 May 1943 by this official of CURT MONROE, Special Interest Prisoner #434. (A full transcript is attached.) MONROE, a former employee of the Portsmouth Naval Shipyard, was arrested 09 May 1943 while attempting to cross into Canada via the border station in Newport, Vermont.

MONROE was advised that he had been under surveillance for a number of months and that it was known to this office that he was involved in a plot against the nation's interests with TONY MILLER, late of the Iroquois Labor Camp (see previous report, dated 07 May 1943) MONROE denied any such activities.

MONROE was subjected to a number of enhanced interrogation techniques.

Upon the conclusion of the first set of enhanced interrogation techniques, MONROE admitted he was involved with TONY MILLER and had been so since the two were employed together at the Portsmouth Naval Shipyard.

MONROE also admitted that MILLER is now in possession of a rifle and is still located somewhere in the Portsmouth area. MONROE was interrogated as to the possible target and placement of MILLER as a gunman. MONROE was also interrogated as to other participants in this plot, including MILLER's brother, SAM.

MONROE requested a brief moment to use a bathroom. Said facility was searched and secured, as was MONROE. MONROE visited the bathroom in lull presence of J. K. Alton, Interior Department Officer. At the time of using the toilet facility, MONROE distracted Officer Alton and removed an object from his mouth, said object to be a small razor blade. MONROE sliced veins in both wrists.

MONROE was declared dead at 1930 hours on 10 May 1943 by the on-duty medical officer at Camp Carpenter Transit Station, N.H.

CHAPTER THIRTY-TWO

The next morning was Sunday. Sam had a quick breakfast of tea and toast, tried to make a call to Moultonborough and was once again blocked by the U.S. Army Signal Corps, then drove to St. James Church for weekly Mass. He managed to catch most of the eight A.M. service. He sat in the back, listening to the ancient Latin phrases, ready to sneak out after taking communion. The parish priest, an elderly Irishman named Father Mullen, preached the Gospel about charity and faith, and despite all that was going on, Sam felt the soothing power of the old man's words. It was an odd world, he thought, where a hardworking parish priest like Father Mullen would labor in obscurity while a rabble-rouser and anti- Semite like Father Coughlin got a radio audience of millions.

Yeah, he thought, leaving quickly after receiving the communion wafer, an odd world where a Cajun thief was President of the United States.

After passing through the army MPs stationed outside the Rockingham Hotel, he went into the lobby crowded with luggage in piles in the comer and shouting men in uniform and out of uniform, pressing in on the overwhelmed staff. The shouts were in a mixture of English and German. Sam skipped the slow-moving elevator for the carpeted stairs. He checked his watch.

He knocked on the door of Room Twelve, waited, staring at the bright brass numerals. Voices came from the other side, but no one answered. He knocked again.

The door swung open. LaCouture stood there, phone to his ear, dressed in white boxer shorts and a dingy white T-shirt. "Yeah?" he said. Behind him, sitting at the table, was Groebke, sipping from a cup of coffee, reading a German magazine called Signal, glasses perched on the end of his nose. The Gestapo man had on a blue robe that looked like silk.

Sam said, "It's nine A.M. The time I usually show up."

LaCouture held the phone receiver to his chest, looked annoyed. "We're busy now. Come back later."

"When—"

The door slammed in his face.

Sam went back down to the lobby.

The noise and confusion of the lobby made his head throb. Sam went outside to the granite steps, near the MP guards, took in some deep breaths. He thought about going to the police station, maybe, coming back to the hotel in another hour or so.

But... after last night's raids, the station was probably crawling with friends and relatives of those seized, people desperate for justice or just a sympathetic ear. The thought of trying to explain to some Dutch woman who could barely understand English that her husband was in the custody of the feds and not the city—the thought of doing that all day made him queasy.

What, then?

He looked at the men in uniform, the army trucks rumbling by, the checkpoint just down the street, and it came to him.

What Tony had said.

He would do his job.

His real job, one he had overlooked for the past few days.

He stepped briskly down the steps on his way to his parked car.

CHAPTER THIRTY-THREE

The drive to the outskirts of the state's largest city, Manchester, took almost two hours along a poorly paved two- lane road heading west through small towns—Epping, Raymond, Candia—that looked like they hadn't changed much since the turn of the century. Little clusters of shops and buildings about the town center, the obligatory churches with white steeples and volunteer fire departments.

Along the way were billboards advertising the latest Ford model or a resort area up in the White Mountains. There were two billboards showing a grinning President Long, clenched fist raised up in the air. One billboard said EVERY MAN A KING and the other said SHARE THE WEALTH. Sam was pleased by the first billboard, for somebody had blacked out the last word and replaced it with another so that it said EVERY MAN A THIEF.

There were hitchhikers on the side of the road, standing either defiantly or in bowed exhaustion, arms and thumbs extended. Plenty of solitary men, faces hooded by battered hats. A few women with children, most of the time the kids hiding their faces in the women's skirts, as if ashamed to be out there. There were a couple of families slowly moving along, pushing their belongings in metal or wooden carts, heading from God knew where to who knew what.

He passed them all. He couldn't afford to stop. As he quickly passed through the little communities, he knew that by day's end, he would be in a lot of trouble, a hell of a lot of trouble. Somehow the thought cheered him.

But he didn't remain cheered for long. As he entered Manchester, he approached an intersection. There were two men in worn overalls and a woman in a faded yellow dress, staring at something on the ground. And then he saw what they were staring at: a shirtless man stretched out on the ground, facedown, his hands bound behind his back, the rear of his head a bloody mess.

A political, the first he had ever seen. As a sworn peace officer, he knew he should stop—but a political. He was already up to his chin in politics. So Sam kept driving, taking a series of turns he recalled from last year, having visited this location on official business, transporting a prisoner who belonged to the feds. Back then going to this place had been unsettling, like going into the basement of a haunted house, goaded into the shadows by your boyhood chums.

Now it was worse. Last time he had been here on official business. Today he was going into the belly of the beast itself, armed only with half-truths and lies.

Up ahead, a wooden sign, dark brown wood with white painted letters.

CAMP CARPENTER
U.S. DEPARTMENT OF THE INTERIOR
TRANSIT STATION
Official Visitors Only

He turned right, went down a road that was smooth and well paved, going to a sentry booth with a black-and- white wooden crossbeam across both lanes. On either side of the booth, a chain-link fence topped by barbed wire stretched off into the distance. There was a smaller sign as he approached: NIGHT VEHICLES DIM HEADLIGHTS. He stopped, and a National Guard sergeant stepped out of the booth, wearing a soft wide-brimmed hat, his face sunburned. He had a clipboard in one hand. "Yeah?" he growled.

Sam passed over his police identification. "Going to the Administration Building as part of an investigation."

The sergeant looked at the clipboard. "Not on the list. Sorry, pal. Back up your car and—"

Heart thumping, Sam passed over his National Guard identification with his rank of lieutenant. "Sergeant, you're going to open that gate now, aren't you."

The sergeant's mood instantly changed. "Sorry, Lieutenant," he said, passing back both pieces of ID. "Didn't realize that—"

"Sergeant, you're making me late."

"Just one moment, sir." The man went into the shack, came out with a thick cardboard pass, and said, "Place it on your dashboard, sir, all right?"

Sam took the pass, which said VISITOR --- NO ACCESS TO RESTRICTED AREAS

The sergeant gestured to someone inside the sentry booth, and the wooden arm was raised. "Take this main road a hundred yards to the secondary gate," he told Sam. "About a half mile after that gate, turn left. Keep your speed below twenty miles an hour and don't pick up anybody walking or hitchhiking. You see anybody walking or hitchhiking, report it to the administration staff. All right, Lieutenant?"

"Yes, thank you," and then he accelerated the Packard past the sentry booth, moving fast so the sergeant couldn't see his hands trembling.

He drove the indicated hundred yards, and the thumping in his heart increased as he saw the gate up ahead. He knew his bullshit story wouldn't work for this National Guard crew, but a phone call from the sentry booth must have been made. The gate was open, and two National Guard enlisted men, .45-caliber Thompson submachine guns slung over their shoulders, waved him through. The fence on either side of this gate was higher, with more rolls of barbed wire, and floodlights and guard towers were spaced along the fence. He passed through the gate and down the road. Ahead was a cluster of buildings; there was another sign, ADMINISTRATION, and he took a left.

The building was wide, one-story, with a porch. The place was built with logs and rough-hewn wood. Army trucks and jeeps were parked to one side, and he found an empty spot. He got out of the Packard and walked up to the building on a gravel path. The porch steps creaked and he went through the front door.

Another National Guard sergeant, his uniform tight against his thick body, looked up at Sam from behind a wooden desk. Behind him were desks manned by uniformed clerks. On the near wall hung a framed photograph of President Long. Sam pulled out his police and National Guard identification and set them on the desk.

The sergeant picked up the cards with blunt fingers that had chewed fingernails and asked, "Well, Inspector— Lieutenant—what can we do for you?"

"I need to talk to someone here. A prisoner. Taken from Portsmouth a couple of days ago."

The sergeant slid Sam's identification back across the desk. "You got clearance? An appointment? Some paperwork?"

"No, Sergeant, I don't. This is... a matter of some discretion."

The man smiled, showing tobacco-stained teeth. "A dame?"

"No, not a dame. Look. I need to see whoever's in charge of the prisoners."

The sergeant scratched an ear. "Not sure if I can be much help."

Sam picked up his National Guard card, held it front of the man's face. "The rank is Lieutenant, Sergeant. I want to see an officer, somebody in charge, who can locate a prisoner. Now."

The sergeant got up, still looking bored, and ambled back into the office area. Sam stood there, quiet. If it went well, then who knew what might happen. And if it didn't go well, then he might not be leaving any time soon. He'd always thought he might end up here because of Sarah and the Underground Railroad. Not because of his own bullheadedness.

The sergeant came back, motioned with his hand. Sam followed him past the occupied desks to a glass-enclosed office with a frosted glass door. Painted on the door were the words CAPT. J. C. ALLARD, COMMANDANT. A brief knock and the sergeant opened the door and Sam walked in.

The office was cramped but tidy, with framed photos of soldiers and artillery pieces on the paneled walls. A balding officer in a pressed National Guard uniform was sitting behind a bare wooden desk. Knowing he was on thin ice indeed, Sam stood straight and said, "Sir, Inspector Sam Miller, Portsmouth Police Department. I'm grateful you've agreed to see me."

"Have a seat, Inspector," the captain replied crisply. "Or is it Lieutenant?"

Sam sat down in the wooden chair across from Allard. "Well, sir, it's going to be whatever it takes for me to see someone who's in custody here."

"I see." Allard leaned back, putting the fingertips of his thin hands together. "That would be me, Inspector. What can I do for you, then?"

"You have a prisoner, name of Sean Donovan, an employee of the Portsmouth Police Department. He was taken into custody two days ago. I'd like to see him."

"Of course you would," Allard said, his voice soft and soothing.

A pause, the air heavy and warm. Sam felt he had to sit still, that he was being observed, so he stared back.

Allard gave a brief shake of his head. "No. You can't see him."

"Captain, he's involved in a—"

Allard held up a hand. "Inspector, I've got a hellish job here, probably the crappiest job in the state. You know why? Because we're the funnel where all the creeps, hoboes, dissidents, shitheads, and illegals get dumped. We process them, give them paperwork, and then ship them out to New York or Montana or Nevada. Day after day, night after night. And if this hellish job isn't bad enough, you know what makes it worse?"

"Sir, I'd like to point out that—"

Allard continued, "Every day I get people like you streaming in here. They say it's always a mistake, always an oversight, papers got lost, stolen, eaten by the family dog. You wouldn't believe what has gone on in this office ... why, once I had this housewife come in, her husband had been smuggling Jewish refugees north into Canada, and she opened up her coat and there was nothing on underneath, and she—"

Sam said, "Captain, with all due respect, shut the hell up."

The captain's face colored scarlet right up to his bald spot. "What did you just say?"

"I said shut up." Sam kept his voice sharp and to the point. "You moron, don't you think I know that? Don't you think I know it's irregular to come here without paperwork? Fool. I'm here without paperwork because of the sensitive nature of what I'm involved with. So shut up already or your ass will be on a boxcar before the day is out."

Allard's breathing quickened, making his nostrils flare. "I cut you some slack coming in here, you being an inspector and a Guard lieutenant, but consider that slack gone. Your ass belongs to me, mister."

Sam pulled a card from his coat pocket, tossed it across the desk. "Then read that, Captain. We'll see whose ass belongs to who."

Allard picked up the card and said, "FBI. How sweet." He reversed the card and read aloud, "'Bearer of card detached to federal duty until 15 May.' Yeah? So?"

Sam forced himself to smile. "Card says it all, Captain. I'm not just up here on a whim, trying to get somebody out. I'm here on official duty, detached to the FBI."

"That doesn't impress me, pal. All that means is that—"

"Yeah, right, you're not impressed. Look at the agent's name again, Captain. LaCouture, one of President Long's trusted Cajun boys, up here to work on the summit. You know about the summit, don't you? Or is your head so far up your ass that you can't hear the radio?"

"I just might give this guy a call," Allard said, but his voice wasn't as cocksure.

Sam pressed on. "Sure. Go ahead. Call him. He's probably figuring out what kind of table President Long and Herr Hitler are going to sit at. Or reviewing their menu. Or about a thousand other things. I'm sure he's going to want to drop everything for the privilege of talking to some National Guard flunky so dumb he's running a transfer camp. Oh, that'll impress him. Make the call."

Allard examined the card as if looking for proof it was a forgery, then gently slid it back across the table. "You could have told me this at the beginning."

"Yeah, I could have." Sam picked up the card. "But then I would have missed all this charming conversation."

The captain took the remark as a joke and managed a smile. "Yeah. Well. There you go." He opened the center drawer and came up with a pencil and a scrap of paper. "The name of the prisoner again?"

"Name's Sean Donovan, from Portsmouth. He was arrested two nights ago."

The captain scribbled something and yelled out, "Sergeant Sims!"

The sergeant came through the door in seconds, Sam thinking the guy had been outside, eavesdropping. Allard passed over the scrap of paper. "Locate this prisoner. Pass him over to... Lieutenant Miller here."

"Yes, sir," the sergeant said. As he left, Allard leaned back in his chair and said, "Always glad to assist the FBI and their people."

Sam said, "Thanks, Captain. I'll make very sure that goes into my report."

CHAPTER THIRTY-FOUR

About fifteen minutes later, Sam sat in a small cabin that was bare wood, beams and rafters, with a table and four chairs set in the center. Light came from three bulbs dangling from the peaked roof. The door opened and a pale Sean Donovan was led in, handcuffed, wearing a worn dungaree jumpsuit with the white letter P stenciled on each leg and on the chest. Two National Guard soldiers in white MP helmets with blue brassards on their shoulders flanked him, and as one uncuffed him, the other told Sam, "Sir, this prisoner is now in your custody. We'll be outside waiting. When you're through, you'll knock on the door and we'll retrieve him."

Sam stood up. "No doubt you will be at the door, but Mr. Donovan and I won't be here."

The older MP said, "Sir...?"

"I'm going outside with the prisoner." He stepped out and saw a picnic table in a grove of pine trees about fifty yards away. "That's where we'll be, in plain view."

The younger MP protested, "Sir, this is highly irregular, and I can't—"

Sam showed them his National Guard ID, thinking how useful that stupid piece of cardboard had turned out to be. "That's where we're going. And tell you what: If either of us makes a break for the fence, you have my permission to shoot us both."

"Why the hell did you want to sit out here, Sam? Warmer back in the cabin."

Sean looked awful. Heavy bags of exhaustion were underneath the record clerk's eyes, and one cheek was puffy with a bruise. His red hair was a greasy mess. Though he had been gone only a few days, it looked like he had lost twenty pounds.

"I'm sure it's warmer back there, Sean," Sam said, sitting at the picnic table. "I'm also sure it's bugged with microphones and wire recorders. I don't want our conversation to be overheard."

Sean shook his head. "It's real good to see you, Sam, but don't screw with me. You're not here to get me out, are you?"

"I wish I was. I'll see what I can do, but you know how it is."

"Ha. Yeah, well, thanks. It's a fed beef they've got me here for, and when it comes to that, there's not much anybody can do. Even your cop coworkers."

"So what's the charge?"

Sean gave a short, nasty laugh. "You want the official or the unofficial charge?"

"Both."

The air was cool and smelled of pine. Sam had a quick twinge of nostalgia, remembering camping out in the White Mountains, he and Tony in the same Boy Scout troop, rivals but not yet enemies. Where in hell had it all gone wrong?

"Official charge is that I released classified information to a third party without the government's permission."

"What the hell kind of classified information is that?"

Sean looked sheepish. "My wife's brother is a stringer for the newspaper up in Dover. I heard the FBI was staying at the Rockingham Hotel, and I told him. Big fucking mistake. Here I am, looking at a year cutting trees in a labor camp."

"That wasn't too bright."

"Shit, I know that, but to think LaCouture's name and hotel room number was a big damn secret... it must be, because that's what they're hanging me out there for."

"And the unofficial charge?"

"You got any smokes?"

"No, I don't. Didn't know you smoked."

Sean folded his arms tight against his chest, as if trying to stay warm. "I don't. But cigarettes are the unofficial currency around this joint. Be nice to buy a little protection until I get assigned to a boxcar."

"You'll get some before I leave."

"Thanks. Anyway, the unofficial charge. I was in the wrong place at the wrong time."

"Where was that?"

"My desk, if you can believe that. Look, remember I told you earlier the FBI guy and his goose-stepping buddy were snooping through personnel files?"

"I do."

"Okay, they came back, and that time looking for arrest files. With the summit coming up, makes sense, huh? There was a list of people they wanted—and guess who was on the list?"

"Tony?"

"Bingo." Sean sighed. "So you think I was dumb enough to ask the FBI and the Gestapo why they're requesting your brother's arrest file? The hell I was. And his file is a special one, since it ended with him going to the labor camp. So I was a good little boy and got the records they wanted, and they told me to leave them alone, which I did. Except..." Sean paused, looked to where the two MPs were standing at attention, watching. He lowered his voice. "Except I left a file on my desk. One that was on the list. Shit, I suppose I should have waited for them to come back. But I figured if I brought the file over, that would get them out of my hair that much quicker. So I hopped on over, and that's when I got my crippled ass in a sling. They were both pawing through this file, and I heard what LaCouture said to the Kraut. Then LaCouture looked up and saw me standing there, and that was that."

Sam thought back. He said, "That's when you told me you needed to see me. The day before the summit was announced. Because LaCouture and Groebke were looking at Tony's file."

"Yeah." Sean looked tired, shrunken.

"And what did LaCouture say to Groebke? What did you hear?"

"I'll tell you, but Christ, it doesn't make sense... something like that to get me in a labor camp."

"Sean, what did he say?"

He shrugged. "The FBI guy said something like 'Right from the start, he's our man.' "

" 'Right from the start, he's our man'? That's what he said? What in hell does that mean?" Sam asked.

Sean said, "If I knew, do you think I would be here?"

They talked for a few minutes more, with Sam trying to jiggle something, anything from Sean's memory of what he'd overheard. But the records clerk kept insisting the same thing: Right from the start, he's our man. Sam looked at the MPs, ready to take Sean back. And if ordered, ready, no doubt, to take Sam prisoner as well.

He asked, "How's it going here? How are you treated?" Sean had one dirty hand on top of the other on the picnic table. "There's been stories, you know. In Life and The Saturday Evening Post. And movies. I Was a Fugitive from a Labor Camp. But that's all bullshit. Nothing like the real deal, my friend."

Sam was silent.

"The real deal is, you get picked up and then tuned up slapped around, that kind of shit. Driven out here, dumped in a compound. Lined up, names checked, and first lesson you get, some of the older prisoners, they're on the other side of the fence. They whisper to you, 'Hey, toss over your watches, your extra shoes, food packages,' that sort of thing. The guards will confiscate everything you've got. So some of the guys—hell, some are just kids—they toss stuff over just like that. You know what happens next."

"They never see their things again."

"Of course. And then you get shaved, deloused, showered, and given these lovely clothes. Another tune-up here and there, and you meet your bunkmates. Oh, really trustworthy fellows. What wasn't taken at the fence is stolen during the night. Off to work the next morning... chopping wood, making furniture, waiting for your billet for a train out west... oh yeah, you learn a lot. Food is rotten, the bunks have fleas, and it's every man for himself."

Off in the distance, a burst of gunfire followed by another. Sean winced. Sam said, "What the hell was that?"

"Officially, weapons practice. Unofficially, guys decide that being here in a transit camp is their best chance to get out before being sent out west. Most of 'em have relatives in easy driving distance. So you get the occasional breakout attempt, the occasional shot-while-trying-to- escape. All unofficial, of course."

"Yeah."

Tears welled up in the record clerk's eyes. "Other thing you learn, Sam, is what kind of coward you are. All the talk of being brave and not knuckling under our new government order, it's all bullshit. You get dumped here, pretty soon all you care about is a good sandwich for lunch, hot water for a shower, and being able to sleep without getting beaten up. Stuff like freedom of speech, freedom of assembly, that's all crap. Just keeping your own ass well fed, warm, and safe. That's all you care about."

The wind shifted, and instead of hearing gunfire, Sam heard a man's scream. It seemed to go on and on and then gurgle off. Sean looked at him and said, "Bad, I know, but at least it's not as bad as the other camps."

"What other camps?"

"Shit, I think I've said too much already."

"Come on, Sean. What do you mean? What other camps?"

"Word is, there are other camps out there. Not officially part of the system. Highly restricted. Here, at least, and the regular labor camps, you get in, you're serving a sentence. These other camps, they work you to death."

"Where are they?"

"Mostly in the South, from what I hear, but Jesus, the rumors are something else. If you step out of line, just for one second, you're shot on the spot."

"Who's in these camps?"

"Who the hell knows? Not regular political prisoners, that's for sure. Word is, there are special trains that take the prisoners to these camps."

"What the hell do you mean, special trains?"

"Sealed. With markings painted on the side, so they get priority through all stations and sidings."

That damnable memory of when he was a patrolman, hearing that train roar through with no identifying marks save the yellow stripes painted on the side, hearing the screams and moans from within...

"Another thing, Sam. The prisoners in those special trains... they're tattooed. Numbers on their wrists. Can you believe that? Tattooed, like fucking cattle."

CHAPTER THIRTY-FIVE

Sean was looking at him expectantly, but Sam couldn't say a word. He was thinking furiously.

Peter Wotan.

Special trains.

Tattooed wrists.

He had to leave.

Had to leave now.

Sam stood up and motioned the MPs over. As they started walking toward them, he said softly, "I've got to go, Sean. But I'll do my damnedest to try to get you out."

Sean said, "Don't make promises you can't keep. And remember this. You get their attention, both you and your family are targets. Not just you. My wife and her brother—they're not here, but they're on a list. One more screw-up and they'll be right here with me, chopping wood and scratching flea bites."

The warning chilled him as he thought of Sarah and Toby. Sam told the MPs, "I'm finished with this prisoner. You can bring him back to his quarters."

"Very good, sir," said the older MP who still looked displeased at having been told to stay away. The younger one produced a set of handcuffs. Sam said, "Oh, I need something from you both. Give me your smokes."

The MPs looked at each other and then reluctantly reached into their shirt pockets. Full packs of Camels and Lucky Strikes were brought out. Sam passed them over to Sean, who made them disappear into his jumpsuit. The MPs didn't look happy.

Sean put his hands out, and as the handcuffs were clicked into place, Sam said to the MPs, "I know you don't like what just happened. But if I get word that this man's been mistreated, I'll have both your asses. Got it?"

Allard looked up at Sam, a sharpened pencil in his hand. "Was the prisoner cooperative? Did you get what you needed?"

"Yes, sir, on both counts," Sam said.

"And you'll make note in your official report of the cooperation you received here today?"

"Yes, sir, I will."

Allard tossed the pencil to the desktop. "Very good. Now, mister, get the hell off my post."

From the captain's tone, Sam thought a salute might be in order, but since he was in civilian clothes, he didn't know what to do. So he got the hell out of the building. A black Chevrolet sedan was parked next to his Packard.

As Sam went down the steps, two men in dark brown suits emerged from the sedan, putting on gray snap-brim hats, and went inside.

Sam went to his Packard and stopped when someone called out, "Inspector? Inspector Miller?"

He turned. Someone was sitting in the back of the Chevrolet. Sam went over, saw the rear window halfway down. The shape moved closer to the window, and Sam stopped, shocked. It was Ralph Morancy, the photographer from the Portsmouth Herald. His right eye was swollen shut, a bruised streak along his jaw. The photographer looked like he had been weeping.

"Ralph... what the hell happened to you?"

"Hazards of the job, I suppose. Took photographs that I shouldn't have, of trucks with prisoners heading out of one of the poorer neighborhoods in town. Two Long's Legionnaires and an officer from the Department of the Interior took offense. They ordered me to stop, told me to turn over the film, and I said fuck you and mentioned the First Amendment. One of the Long boys, he slugged me, told me he didn't know shit about the First Amendment. Here I am." Ralph edged closer to the open window. "Inspector, please. I only have a minute or two before they take me in and process me. Can you help me out? Please? For the love of God, I can't believe I'm being sent to a labor camp for doing my job... for taking photos... God, what's the world coming to..."

Sam looked up at the building's closed doors. "Ralph, I don't know what I can do."

"You're a cop. You could tell them I'm your friend. I'll pay you. You could say it was all a mistake, a misjudgment, I'll do anything they want. Please, can't you help me?"

Sam's mouth tasted of old pennies. Go back in there? Plead Ralph's case while he was here on a pretense? He lowered his head, turned away. "No, Ralph, I can't help you."

Ralph called out, "But I can't go with them...your brother, I've got to tell you something about your brother—"

There were more yells, but Sam got into his car, and the engine started up after the third attempt. He ground the reverse gear as he backed up, suddenly sweating. One phone call... Allard had to feel grumpy enough to make one phone call to LaCouture, and then he'd never leave this place except in a boxcar stuffed with straw, shit, and sweat. Never to see Sarah or Toby again.

In the rearview mirror, he saw the two men come out and go to the black Chevrolet, saw them drag Ralph Morancy out, the poor man's legs giving way as they went up the steps, carrying him like a sack of cement.

He forced himself to look straight ahead as he accelerated. Poor Ralph, sweet Jesus... and what was that babbling about Tony? What had Ralph been trying to pull? He didn't know. But he now knew something: The FBI and Gestapo were interested in his brother. More important, he also knew more about Peter Wotan. He wasn't sure how and why the man ended up dead in Portsmouth, but he sure as hell knew where he had come from.

Special camps that worked people to death, populated from sealed trains traveling at night with no identifying marks, just a few swabs of paint...

He kept the speed down as he approached the first gate, where the MPs stood. One held up his hand and he slowed. He rolled down the window and the MP leaned over and said, "Vehicle inspection, sir. I'll have to ask you to step out."

Sam put the car in idle, engaged the parking brake, got out into the late-afternoon air. Working quickly and professionally, no doubt having done this hundreds of times, one MP searched the car, going into the trunk, lifting up the rear seat, even checking the undercarriage. The other stayed motionless,, submachine gun ready in his hands. He tried not to think of what Ralph was going through now, what was happening. He had gotten close enough to the photographer to smell the stink of fear on him.

What had he done? What in God's name had he done back there?

A matter of minutes, and then the one doing the searching stepped back and the other went to the gate. "Very good," the tall MP said. "You're clear to leave."

Sam climbed into the Packard, conscious of how moist his back was against the leather seat. The gate swung open and he released the parking brake, put the car into first gear, and drove out on the road, heading for the last gate.

The sentry box. The only obstacle between the camp and the outside world. The outside world, where at last he could work on this damn homicide, a case he had been ignoring—

The black-and-white crossbar was raised, one MP was talking to another, it looked pretty damn clear, and he let the speed increase a bit—

The guards were looking at him.

A gentle push on the accelerator.

The Packard sped up.

One of the guards stepped out. The man still wasn't out in the road...

Twenty, thirty feet and he'd be out of the camp. Just a few feet, really.

An MP was now in the middle of the lane.

Holding up his hand.

Caught?

Caught.

Either Allard had made that phone call, or Ralph, in his terror, had shouted out something that had gotten their interest...

He braked, rolled down the window.

This was it, then.

The MP leaned down. "Sir?"

"Yeah?"

"Your vehicle pass. We need it back."

"Oh." Sam reached to the dashboard, grabbed the piece of cardboard, almost dropped it as he thrust it through the open window.

The MP took the cardboard and dipped his chin. "Drive safe, sir." He smiled.

"Thanks."

Sam drove out to the country road, turned left, and drove about two hundred feet before stopping and letting the shakes come over him.

Then he got over it and got the hell out.

CHAPTER THIRTY-SIX

Nearly an hour away from Camp Carpenter, Sam turned in to the Route 4 diner in Epsom. The lot was packed dirt, and there were two Ford trucks parked at the far end, black and rusting. The diner's aluminum siding was light blue and flecked with cancerous rust spots. Stuck in one of the windows by the doorway was a faded poster of President Huey Long. Underneath his fleshy face was the decade-old slogan: EVERY MAN A KING. The ongoing motto of the true believers, or those pretending to be true believers to get along.

Sam got out the car and looked around. No kings in sight. The story of his country, he thought.

Inside, he sat at the counter and ate a dry hamburger and drank a cup of coffee that tasted like water. He ignored the waitress and the cook and the truck drivers and thought about what he had learned about Sean and LaCouture and Groebke and his brother, Tony.

And more than anything else, the story of the hidden camps. The ones that held tattooed prisoners supplied by secret trains. Somehow one of those prisoners, Peter Wotan, had ended up murdered in his town.

He finished his meal, left a dime tip. Near the doorway was a public phone box. He pulled the glass door shut, pumped in some nickels, and got the long-distance operator. At least in this part of the state, in a different county, he could get through without that damnable Signal Corps oversight. On the floor was a copy of the President's newspaper, The American Progress. Someone had left a muddy bootprint on the first page.

That other thing Sean had said...about family. An idea was coming together about what to do next, and he had to make new arrangements. Had to. The phone at his father-in-law's cottage in Moultonborough rang and rang and then—

"Hello?"

He leaned against the side of the booth. "Sarah?"

"Oh, Sam, I was hoping it was you! I can't believe I—"

"Sarah, there's a problem."

"What is it?"

Sam turned, made sure he wasn't being watched. "You've got to leave. Right away."

"You mean... back to Portsmouth?" Her voice was puzzled. "Are you going to come up and—"

"No, not Portsmouth," he said, thinking fast. "You've got to go somewhere else up there. A neighbor, a friend, anyone who can put you and Toby up for a few days."

"You've got to be kidding me. What do you mean I—"

"I don't have time now. Trust me on this. It's very important. You've got to get out of there. With Toby. Do you understand?"

Even across the crackling static, he could hear from her voice that she was trying not to cry. "Oh, Sam—"

"Can you do it? Can you?"

"I could go to—"

"Don't tell me who," he interrupted, thinking of wiretaps. Who knew where the FBI could be tapping. "Don't tell me a thing, Sarah. Just take our son and be safe. We'll figure out how to get together once this summit is done. But you and Toby, you've got to go now. I mean it."

"All right. I understand."

She hung up. He stood there, holding the useless receiver in his hand.

Outside, as he was walking to his dust-covered Packard, he heard something clattering around the side of the diner, where there was a small wooden porch. Underneath the porch were cans of trash and swill. The lids to the metal cans were chained shut. Two old women were there, in tattered cloth coats, shoes wrapped in twine, wearing filthy kerchiefs over their gray hair. Both gripped rocks as they tried to break the locks.

One noticed Sam and said something to the other, and they both looked at him, cheeks wrinkled and hollow, mouths sunken from no teeth. Their eyes were filmy and swollen.

Sam slowly reached past his coat to his wallet and slipped out some bills. He had no idea how much money he was leaving.

He knelt down, put the money under a rock, and left.

CHAPTER THIRTY-SEVEN

The time driving back to the coast seemed to fly by, for he was thinking things through, knowing what he was going to do, what had to be done to make it all right. When he got back to Portsmouth, he passed through one checkpoint without any difficulty, then drove to the police station and parked nearby. Run in, see if there were any important messages, and run out. It was going to be a long and dangerous night.

In the lobby, he gave a quick wave to the desk sergeant, who was talking to a drunk hobo going on about how he'd like to join the George Washington Brigade overseas and fight those Bolshies, and why couldn't he sign up here, there was good money and hot meals and so forth. There was also a slight woman in a long coat and pink scarf about her head, speaking with a British ac-cent, trying to get the sergeant's attention.

By the stairs, Clarence Rolston was sweeping. "Sam! Am I right? Sam, good to see you."

Sam knew the seconds were slipping away, but he stopped. "Good to see you, too, Clarence. How are you?" Clarence blinked and smiled, a dribble of saliva escaping. "Doing good. And thanks about that other thing. I didn't get into trouble. Thanks a lot. Stun."

"Glad it worked out. Take care now, okay?"

Sam sprinted up the stairs. The door to Marshal Hanson's office was closed. He looked up at the clock. Nearly seven PM. He went to his desk, saw a pile of yellow message slips, all of them in Mrs. Walton's neat cursive, and all saying the same thing: Agent LaCouture of the FBI needs to talk to you. The messages were an hour apart. He flipped through to see if there was anything else, like a phone call from Lou Purdue, but no.

Just the FBI. He would take care of LaCouture later.

He crumpled the message slips, tossed them in a trash can.

The door to Hanson's office swung open. He came out, staring at Sam. "Inspector," he said tonelessly.

213

"Sir," Sam said, cursing himself for being stupid enough to get caught like this. Dammit, the man was getting ready for the Long-Hitler summit, of course he'd be working late.

"In my office, if you please."

Sam walked in, and Hanson gently closed the door behind him.

Hanson went around his desk, sighing loudly and running a hand across the top of his hair. His eyes were red-rimmed, and he sat down heavily. "How's it going, Sam?" he asked.

God, what a question. And what kind of answer? Sam said, "It's been a busy day."

"I'm sure. Look, do you smell anything unusual?"

Sam waited just a moment. "No, I don't."

Hanson said, "Well, you should. You should smell something charred. The phone lines between here and the Rockingham Hotel have been burning up all day with the damn FBI and his Gestapo buddy looking for you. What the hell is going on?"

Sam said, "I'm doing my job."

"Your job right now is doing what the FBI tells you to do."

"Which is what I've been doing," Sam replied. "LaCouture told me this morning he was busy. He told me to come back later. He didn't say when."

Hanson stayed quiet, gently rocking his chair. Then he said, "So what were you working on? Besides being a wiseass."

"Other cases. Trying to catch up. As you've instructed me.

The room was so quiet, Sam thought he could hear a clock ticking somewhere else in the building. Hanson seemed to stare right through him.

A slow creak-creak as Hanson moved his chair back and forth. "Then it's your responsibility to tell the FBI where you've been today. Not mine, is it?"

Sam thought, Nice job, Harold. Sam was the FBI's boy now, and Hanson was all hands-off. If he was going down for anything he did today, Hanson wouldn't be next to him.

"That's right, sir."

"Very well. When this summit is over, you're going to catch up on your casework. In addition, you're going to run for the district council for the Party later this month, and you'll win."

Sam bit at his lower lip. "I... I'm not sure I'll have the time to be more active."

"You're going to find the time," Hanson told him. "Let's avoid all the bullshit, all right? Sam, you've caught some people's attention. People you don't want to irritate. Some Legionnaire officers find it curious that two of their people in Portsmouth had their car vandalized, and the same two were

214

later beaten up. Both events happened when you were in the vicinity. Do you have anything to add to that?"

Sam looked evenly at his boss. "Not a thing."

"Glad to hear it," Hanson said. "But if these same officers see an enthusiastic, active, and respectful Sam Miller involved in the Party, it would ease their concerns. It would also be helpful to me and not helpful to your father-in-law. Do you understand?"

"I don't want to understand," he said. "I just want to do my job."

"You're going to keep doing your job, and you're going to be active in the Party, and you're going to succeed at both. You know why? Because you've shown me what you can do. You ignore rules when you don't like them. You go out on your own. And when push comes to shove, you're not above administering a bit of street justice. All skills that the Party could use. Tell me I'm wrong."

"You're wrong," Sam said. "Absolutely one hundred percent wrong."

Hanson smiled. "You may fool yourself into thinking that, but I know better. So when the summit is concluded and you've caught up on your casework, you're going to take a little time off. There's a special training session for up-and-coming Party members down in Baton Rouge. And when you come back, I'll make sure you win the council election. How does that sound?"

"Sounds like nonsense," Sam snapped. "I'm not leaving Portsmouth, I'm not going to Baton Rouge, and I'm sure as hell not becoming a whore for the Party."

"Too bad it sounds like nonsense," Hanson said evenly. "But in the end, it's going to sound very good to you, your wife, and your son."

"Leave my family out of it."

Hanson's eyes bored through him. "I'll leave your family out of it if you will."

"What the hell do you mean by that?"

Hanson said slowly, "You know exactly what I mean, and we're going to leave it at that. That way we both can deny later that we discussed such a forbidden topic, even though your promised report on the demise of the Underground Railroad station hasn't yet reached my desk. A subject I know that you're intimately familiar with. Care to say anything more?"

Sam knew exactly what Hanson meant. The Underground Railroad. The marshal knew. Had always known. "No," he said slowly. "Not at the moment."

"Very good." His boss nodded. "And when the summit is over, I expect and will receive your enthusiastic participation in the Party, correct?"

Hating himself, Sam said, "Yes. Correct."

Hanson opened his top drawer, reached in, and tossed something across at Sam, who looked down, saw the despised Confederate-flag pin. "And you can start by showing your loyalty, Probationary Inspector Miller."

Sam picked up the pin. He looked over and saw the marshal's suit coat hanging on its rack, the same pin on its lapel.

With his fingers trembling, he put the pin in his lapel. "There," he said. "Satisfied?"

"Quite. Now get the hell out of here and make the fucking FBI happy, all right?"

Sam did just that.

He barely made it down the stone steps of the police station before ducking into an alleyway. The spasms were hard, sharp, and the lousy diner meal splattered against brick. When he was done, Sam pressed his forehead against the cool brick. Busted. The marshal and the Legionnaires knew about the Underground Railroad station at the house, had known for some time.

So why hadn't it been shut down? And Sarah and he arrested?

Because they wanted more. They wanted a compliant and obedient Sam Miller, son-in-law to a connected politician, someone they could use for more important things down the road, helping out the Nats, disrupting the Staties in the Party structure.

He took out a handkerchief and wiped at his lips and walked out onto the sidewalk. He looked down at his lapel. Now an official member of the oppressors. How delightful. Sarah would be so goddamn proud.

There was singing. Across the street, four Long's Legionnaires stumbled along, laughing, drunk. They were spread across the sidewalk, bumping people—hell, neighbors who paid his salary—out of the way as if they were worth nothing. Any other night, he'd chase after those clowns, pull them up short, and show them what the law was all about, what they couldn't do in Sam's hometown. Make them go back and apologize to everyone they had bumped and jostled.

Any other night.

He looked down at his lapel.

But on this night, he was one of them.

He got into his Packard, started the engine. Waited. Before coming to the station, he had plans.

Yeah, plans, he thought. But the good police marshal Harold Hanson had plans of his own.

So what now?

Go home and be a good boy?

Or...

He reached up, gently undid the lapel pin, and dropped it in his pocket. He shifted the Packard into reverse, then into first gear, and went back to being a cop.

Just a goddamn cop.

It took a few minutes of driving in an upscale section of town before he found what he was looking for, a turn-of- the-century Victorian house with light yellow paint. He parked in front and went up to the front porch, turned the doorbell, and waited.

A man opened the lace-curtain-covered door. Pat Lowengard, manager of the Portsmouth office of the Boston & Maine railroad.

"Oh," Lowengard said, crestfallen, as though he'd been expecting anybody but Sam. "Inspector Miller."

"Pat, you don't look like you're happy to see me."

"We're about to have supper, and my mother is visiting, and—"

Sam stepped in, forcing Lowengard back. Sam said, "I need a few minutes of your time. Then you can go back to supper and your happy family."

"Can't it wait until tomorrow?"

"It certainly can't. Now, we can talk here, or I can drag you down to the station. Your choice."

A woman's voice called out. Sam couldn't make out the question, but Lowengard yelled, "It'll only be a minute, Martha! Just a bit of business to take care of." Lowengard closed the door. "This way. My office."

The station manager led Sam down a carpeted hallway. Sam looked at the nice furniture, the framed photos on the wall, and a thought came to him—that old phrase about how the other half lived. During these tough times, it was more like how the fortunate few lived.

At the end of the hallway was an open polished wooden door, and inside the small room were bookshelves, a desk, a typewriter, and two leather chairs. On the bookshelves were a collection of model trains and some leather-bound volumes, and on the floor was a small leather suitcase. After Sam entered the room, Lowengard closed the door and sat down and said, "Inspector, please, make it quick. What do you need?"

"You know trains, Pat, am I right?"

"Yes, I know trains. Is that why you came here? To ask me a stupid question like that?"

"Special trains."

"What?

Sam put his hands on top of Lowengard's desk. "Special trains. And don't bullshit me, Pat. I'm talking about trains that don't officially exist, trains that have no outside markings, save some yellow stripes. Trains that move at night—trains full of people. What are they?"

Lowengard's face seemed to pale, as though the blood had suddenly stopped flowing to the skin. He licked his lips and said, "Sam, please... I could end up in a camp. Or someplace worse."

"The other camps, right? The ones that are worse than the labor camps. Where are they? You must have an idea. The trains, where do they come from?"

"I... I can't say anything, Sam. Please. I'm begging you..."

This close, Sam couldn't help himself. He struck Pat across the face, the sound of the blow sounding sharp and loud in the small room. Pat gasped and brought his hand up to his cheek, and Sam said, "I'm investigating a homicide. And you're impeding my investigation, which is a crime. Now. You may or may not get into trouble by telling me what you know, but I can guarantee you a shitload of trouble right now unless you talk to me. It'll make me very happy to drag your fat ass out of this nice, com-fortable house and toss it in a county jail, or a state jail, or, if I get enough dirt on you, a labor camp. Think a guy in your shape will like cutting down trees at sunrise every morning?"

"Sam, please—"

Sam reached into his pocket, took out the flag pin, stuck it on his lapel. "Check it out, Pat. Know what this means? It means I'm part of something that's not a goddamn club like the Elks or the Kiwanis. Something powerful. Something that can put you in a world of hurt if I just say the word. So. Should I say the word?"

Pat slowly rubbed his cheek, looking like a chubby child who could not believe what Daddy had done to him. "I... I'll talk. Just for a few minutes. And you never tell anyone you talked to me, and we're done. All right?"

Sam nodded. "Yeah. We're done."

Pat blinked, and Sam saw tears in his eyes. "The trains... they started a few years ago. Top priority, we had to clear tracks and sidings for them, no delays, no questions. They departed from navy installations up and down the East Coast. You hear things, you know? In this business, you hear things."

"Was the shipyard one of the departure points?"

"Yes, but not often. Maybe two, three times."

218

"Who are in the trains?"

Pat shook his head. "People. That's all."

"Where do they come from? And where do they go?"

"Transport ships, that's all I know." Pat rubbed his cheek. "From there, they mostly go to small towns down south. A few out west. And just a while ago, a place in upstate Vermont. That's it. The trains go to these towns, and poof, they disappear. As if Mandrake the Magician made them go away."

"What's the name of the town in Vermont?"

"Burdick. Up near the Canadian border. I know a couple of the special trains went there in the past year. And that's it, Sam. I swear to God, that's it."

Sam looked at the plump station manager, could smell the dread coming off of him. Something inside felt sour as he remembered how thrilled he'd been to be named an inspector, to better fight crime. And here he was, slapping a scared railroad manager, a man who had done nothing save what he could to keep his job and support his family.

Sam said, "I'm leaving. But only if you can get me a round-trip ticket out to Burdick as fast as you can."

The man was almost pathetic in his eagerness as he picked up a pen and scribbled something on a slip of paper. "Of course, Sam, of course. Give me a call, seven AM. tomorrow, and you'll be all set."

Pat put the pen down and then burst into tears. He swiped at his eyes, embarrassed. "Sorry... it's just that... when I was a kid, I loved trains. My uncle worked at B & M in Boston, managed to get me a job as a luggage clerk, and I worked my way up. God, I loved trains, and look where I am... and what I have to do." He fumbled under the desk, came out with a handkerchief, honked his nose. "Look at me. A job I should love... and I hate it, Sam, hate it so much. Nobody loves trains anymore. They're crowded, dirty, and share tracks with trains full of prisoners. See that?" He pointed to the suitcase by the door. "It's gotten so bad, I've got a suitcase packed, just in case. Like every other station manager I know, one foul-up, one bad decision on my part, and I'm riding one of the trains I'm supposed to love to a labor camp."

He wiped his eyes and his nose with the handkerchief. Sam heard the voice of Pat's wife calling. Ashamed at what he had done to the woman's husband, he left as quickly as he could.

Fifteen minutes later, Sam stood in front of a three-story tenement building surrounded by others, all with light gray paint that was flaking and peeling.

The air smelled of salt air and exposed mudflats, and radios blared jazz and swing from the windows, and somewhere, a baby was wailing. Clotheslines spanned the alleyways. There was shouting in the distance and a sharp crack as somebody fired off a revolver. He jumped a bit at the sudden noise, then ignored it. Another shot in the dark to be overlooked unless it was reported, and he was going to ignore it. He had more important things to do.

Sam went up the front door of the building, which was open, the doorknob having been long ago smashed out. A single bulb, dangling from a frayed cord, illuminated the interior of the hallway and a second door. He went up to the door and knocked on it.

No answer.

He pounded with his closed fist. A muffled voice from inside, then the snapping sound of locks being undone. The door opened an inch, then two inches, held back by a chain. A woman in a dark red robe, her hair bristling with curlers, glared at him. "Yeah?"

"Need to see Kenny Whalen. Now."

She said, "He's not here," and started to close the door. He jammed the toe of his shoe between the door and the frame and pulled out his leather wallet, showed the badge to the woman. "Kenny Whalen, dear, or if I think you're lying, I break the door down, tear the place up, looking for him. And then you can ask the city to reimburse you for the damages I cause, and they might get back to you. By 1950 or thereabouts."

She muttered something, turned, and yelled, "Kenny! Get over here!"

Sam spotted Kenny coming over, buttoning a flannel shirt over a soiled white T-shirt, his hair uncombed. "Ah, shit, hold on, Inspector."

Sam said, "I pull my shoe back, that door better be open in ten seconds. Clear?"

"Oh, yeah, Inspector, I don't want no trouble."

Sam pulled his shoe back, the door clunked shut, and there was a tinkling sound of a chain being worked. Before the door opened, Sam took the lapel pin off. Party membership, to a guy like Kenny, wouldn't mean shit. Kenny stood there, managing a smile, but on his face the expression looked as inviting as that of a mortgage officer reviewing a foreclosure.

"Inspector, what can I do for you?"

"I need a few minutes to talk to you. In private." Kenny glanced back toward the living room. "Dora has ears the size of saucers. Let's go out in the hallway, okay?"

The two men stood in the hallway, a breeze making the dim lightbulb sway. Kenny said, "Well?"

Sam thought about lines crossed, about what was to be done, and why he was doing it, and thought of that dead man, dead and alone and cold in his city's morgue, with that tattooed wrist. Branded like fucking cattle, Sean had said. Why?

"I need you to make me some documents. Official identification."

Kenny stared at him in disbelief. "Shit, I don't know what's going on, but no way. I don't know what the hell you're doing, but it sounds like entrapment to me. No way in hell."

It was as if somebody else were mouthing the words, for Sam couldn't recognize his own voice when it answered, "You do this for me, and I'll knock off one of those felony charges for uttering a false instrument. Get you to serve in the county lockup instead of state prison. Sound fair, Kenny?"

"Sounds crazy, that's what. Couple days ago, you almost arrested me for requesting the same thing. What's different?"

"Times have changed. That's all you need to know." Kenny stared at him for a moment. Then he said, "You mean that, right? You'll broom one of those felony charges, let me get a lesser sentence?"

"That's right."

"Shit...All right. What kind of papers you looking for? A check? Birth certificate? Union card?"

"I need FBI identification. And something sharp and good, Kenny, something that will pass muster."

"Are you nuts? The FBI? Jesus Christ... and whose mug should I put on it? Huh?"

"Mine."

Kenny burst out laughing. "Hey, Inspector, feel free to put that felony charge back on my sheet, 'cause there ain't no way I'm messing with the feds. Do you think I'm a loon? I get caught making paper like that, that's a federal beef, that means my ass gets in a labor camp, and that's it, story finished. Good night. And I'll see you when my trial starts."

The forger turned back toward the door. Sam blocked him. Kenny stopped.

"All of it," Sam said, still not believing what he was saying.

"What do you mean, all of it?"

"All of the charges. They get dropped. Swept away. You never serve a day in jail, don't even have to face a judge." Kenny kept on looking at him, blinking. "Man, you must need this something awful."

"I do."

"Why?"

"None of your goddamn business."

"Then you got yourself a deal, Inspector. Let's get to work."

Work was in the crowded and dark basement of the tenement, in a comer that had been blocked off by a wooden wall that swung out on hidden hinges, revealing an area of about twelve feet by twelve feet, with a dirt floor and walls made of fitted rocks. There was a long workbench, a small printing press on top of another table, rows of cast-lead letters, bottles of ink, and cameras and tripods. Kenny brought Sam into the room and sat him down on a stool and said, "Just to be clear here, Inspector, what you see here... it's um, going to stay here, right?"

"Yes," Sam replied. "Everything I see here will stay here."

Kenny rubbed his hands. "Very good. We'll get to work," and then he laughed.

Sam Said, "What's so funny?"

"Funny? What's so funny is that I was right last time we talked. You told me you couldn't be bought, and I said you had a price. Lucky for me, you came up with a price." The forger busied himself, gathering up film and camera lenses. Sam bit his lip. Then he said, "Kenny, you say anything like that again, I'll break your nose. And then you'll still make me that FBI identification, but you'll be doing it through a broken and bloody nose. Okay?"

"Oh, of course, Inspector. Now, if you need this tonight, let's get to work." Kenny sounded apologetic, but there was no missing the glee in his eyes.

CHAPTER THIRTY-EIGHT

About twelve hours after Kenny had produced an FBI identification card that looked as good as the one Sam had seen earlier in LaCouture's pudgy and manicured hands—"Lucky you're in a grim mood, so I didn't have to take another picture," Kenny had said—Sam sat in a passenger compartment on the Green Mountain local, going up into Vermont. His train travels had begun in Portsmouth, then to Boston, then to a train going west, to Greenfield, Massachusetts. From there, he caught the local, heading north, one of the stops being a small town called Burdick. Before leaving Greenfield, he had rented a small locker at the B&M station, where he had placed his real papers and identification. Now he was traveling with his new FBI identification, which named him as Special Agent Sam Munson.

Kenny had helped him choose his new last name. "One of the many things I have learned over the years, Inspector, is that a false name should be similar to real one," he had advised.

Sam cupped his chin in his hand, watching the rural landscape rush by. What a world he now lived in, where he was following advice from a forger he had promised to keep out of jail. What a world.

The train car was mostly empty, the other passengers farmers and a few traveling salesmen, and one heavyset woman with two young boys sitting in front of her. The boys were barefoot. She wore a coat made out of a gray wool blanket. There were just a few pieces of lonely luggage in the overhead racks. Sam sat alone, hungry, for he hadn't the urge to take breakfast. All he cared about was getting up to Burdick, and then...

That was a good question. What then?

He continued looking at the small farms, the forests, and the distant peaks of the Green Mountains, the sisters of the White Mountains in his own home state. He thought about the special trains that had come up here, carrying its secret cargo of tattooed people. How had one of them escaped and ended up in Portsmouth? Why?

The train shuddered, slowed, as they entered a town, a few automobiles here and there, even some horse- drawn wagons. The train shuddered again and, with a great belch of steam and smoke, came to a halt. There was a station out there, even smaller than his home, and a wooden sign dangling beneath the eaves.

BURDICK.

He got up from his seat, grabbed his hat, and walked down the grimy aisle. The pavement outside was black tar, cracked and faded. He looked up and down. Nobody else was getting off. Nobody, as far as he could see, was getting on. Smoke and steam streamed from the engine. He felt an urge to climb back on the train.

He waited.

The train whistle blew.

Another shuddering clank.

The train started moving.

He watched the cars slide by.

He could still make it if he wanted to. Just climb up and get inside, find a conductor, make arrangements for a return trip to Greenfield, then Boston and home to Portsmouth. If he was lucky, he could be home tonight. Sam stood still.

The track was empty.

It was time to move.

He walked into the station, found it deserted. From his coat pocket, he took out the lapel pin, snapped it into place on his coat. There was a counter at one end, and he walked up to an older man working behind it. The man was wearing a stained white shirt and a black necktie that barely made it down his expansive chest, a black cap with the B&M insignia. He was doing paperwork with the nub of a yellow pencil and barely glanced up as Sam stood before him.

"Yep?" he finally asked.

Sam put his hands on the countertop. "Is there a taxi in this town?"

"If Clyde Fanson answers the phone, I s'pose there is."

"Then I need a cab."

"Where ya goin'?"

"To the camp," Sam said.

At that, the man looked up, his eyes unblinking behind his black-rimmed glasses. " 'Fraid I don't know what you're talkin' 'bout."

Sam pulled his new ID from his pocket, silently displayed it. The man swallowed. "You fellas... usually, you have your own transport, you know? Usually."

Sam put the identification away. "This isn't usual."

"Guess not," the man said, reaching over to a black phone. "I'll make the call to Clyde, he should be outside in a few minutes."

"Thanks."

"Don't mention it."

He walked outside into the late-morning sun. From here it looked like he could make out all of Burdick: a service station, a brick town hall, a white clapboard building that announced it housed the Burdick Volunteer Fire Department, and a grouping of two-story wooden buildings. A horse-drawn wagon clomped by, carrying scrap metal. He couldn't imagine a train dumping its load of scared people at this station. There must be a spur farther down. Would it have made more sense to go that way, to walk the line?

No, he decided. Who knew how long a walk it could be and what he would find at the end.

An old Ford Model A came down the street, rattled to a halt. On its black doors, someone had painted in sloppy white letters FANSON LIVERY & DELIVERY. A small man came out, dressed in white shirt, necktie, and overalls, his brown hair slicked back. He looked over the hood of the Model A and asked, "You the fella needing a ride?"

"I am."

He pointed to the passenger side. "Then get yourself in."

Sam opened the door, sat on the worn and torn leather upholstery. Clyde Fanson shifted and the car engine coughed, stalled, and then caught as Clyde made a U-turn and started out of town. He glanced over at Sam. "First time here?"

"Yeah."

"Good for you."

Sam thought about peppering the guy with questions about the camp and decided it was too risky. Sam was an FBI agent. He should know what was going on. Too many questions could make this taxi driver suspicious, and a suspicious driver could make a phone call or two, and then this little quest would be over before it started.

Now they were out of the town, climbing a poorly paved road up into the hills. Pine trees and low brush crowded against the narrow road. Sam said, "What goes on here?"

His driver hacked up some phlegm and expertly spat out the window. "Not much of anything, but for a while, it was stone. Marble. Granite. Had some of the finest quarries in this part of the state. Now... well, you know."

"Sure," Sam said, thinking of all the horrors that had emerged from the Crash of '29. "I know."

The road widened, and Clyde pulled over on the right to a dirt road that led up into the woods. He let the engine rumble a bit and said, "Here ya go."

Sam tried to hide his surprise. "You sure?"

He spat again through the window. " 'Course I'm sure. Right up that dirt road."

"The road looks pretty good. Why don't you haul me up there?"

"I'm no fool, pal. You're a fed and all that, which is fine, but we know enough to stay away. 'Nuff people over the past months got into lots of trouble, pokin' around, never to be seen again, so I won't be goin'. It's up to you."

"Okay," Sam said. "I understand. How much?"

"Twenty-five cents."

Sam passed over a quarter and a nickel. As he stepped out, Clyde called, "Hey, hold on." He passed over a slip of paper. "I know how you feds work. Expense account and all that crap. Your receipt."

Sam took the torn piece of paper. "Thanks," he said, but Clyde had already pulled out and sped up the road, as if even being at the entrance to whatever was in the dark woods would bring him bad luck.

Sam adjusted his hat, started walking.

After about ten minutes, he could hear the sound of machinery up in the distance. While the dirt road was well maintained, there was evidence that lots of heavy trucks or equipment had passed through. By now the heat was getting to him, and he loosened his tie and unbuttoned his jacket.

The rumble of machinery grew louder, and then there was a wooden sign up ahead.

RESTRICTED AREA AUTHORIZED VISITORS ONLY
U.S. DEPARTMENT OF THE INTERIOR
TRESPASSERS SUBJECT TO IMPRISONMENT
USE OF DEADLY FORCE AUTHORIZED

He paused, licked his dry lips. A hand went to his pocket, where his fake ID rested. It had been good enough to fool a B&M railroad clerk. He would soon find out if it was good enough to fool whoever was beyond that sign.

He kept on walking, the weight of his revolver no comfort at all.

CHAPTER THIRTY-NINE

The dirt road circled and widened to a small wooden gatehouse painted bright white, with chain-link fence. Another gate, another barrier. The chain-link fence had barbed wire around the top, and the center of the fence was on metal wheels, serving as the gate. Two men stood in front of the guardhouse, watching him. Sam kept his face impassive. The men weren't local cops or National Guardsmen; they wore the leather jackets and blue corduroys of Long's Legionnaires. They also weren't the kind of young punks he had seen in his hometown: They were lean, tough-looking, and hanging off their shoulders were Thompson submachine guns with drum magazines.

One stepped out from the shadow of the guardhouse. His face was freckled, and his hair was a sharp blond crew cut. "You lost, boy?"

Sam said nothing, walked closer. The other guard came out. His hair was black, slicked back, and parted in the middle. "He asked you a question, boy." His gumbo- thick accent was the twin of his companion's.

Sam kept quiet. The closest guard unshouldered his gun. "On your knees, now, boy!"

Sam stopped about four feet away from the two guards. "Names."

"What?" the blond guard asked.

"I want your names. The both of you."

The second guard muttered, "The fuck you say."

Sam said, "No. The fuck you say. I want your name and your buddy's name. This whole day has been a fuckup since 1 came to this little shitty town. Both of your names are going in my official report when I get back to Boston."

The two Cajun guards looked confused. The one with the crew cut demanded, "What the hell are you talking about?"

"I'm talking about the report on my trip here, starting from when I got to the station and there was no automobile waiting for me." Sam kept his voice low and determined. "I had to arrange for a taxi up here, in a piece-of-shit Ford that nearly broke my back. And once I got here, I get you two morons ready to shoot me instead of finding out who I am."

"Who the hell are you?" the second guard asked, his voice not as harsh as before.

Now, Sam thought, now comes crunch time. He opened up his wallet and flashed his fake credentials. "Sam Munson, Federal Bureau of Investigation. I've spent the better part of a day on a train coming up to this little dump. I was told when I started that I'd have full cooperation for my investigation. So far all I've gotten is crap."

"We weren't told anything 'bout an investigation," the first guard protested.

"Fine, glad to hear that," Sam said. "But I don't give a shit. Right now I want both of your names, and after, I want that gate open and a car to get me up to the administration building. Or whatever you call it."

The guard with black hair said, "The name's Clive Cooley. This here is Zell Poulton."

Sam made a show of taking out his notebook, writing down both names. He cocked his head and said, "Well?" Zell went into the guard shack and lifted up a phone, while Clive went to the gate and slid it open with a satisfying clank and rattle. Sam waited, arms crossed, willing his legs not to shake, knowing he was close, oh, so close. A memory charged into his mind, of skating one winter on Hilton's Pond with Tony, going farther and farther out on the ice, hearing it creak and moan, knowing with cold hands and colder heart that he was so close to falling in.

There came the sound of a motor, and a dusty Oldsmobile appeared around the corner. It stopped, and another Long's Legionnaire stepped out. Clive went over and talked to him, then called out, "Agent Munson? This way, sir. I'm gonna drive you up to headquarters."

Sam walked up to the car, hearing within his mind the sound of ice cracking once he passed through the gate.

The inside of the Oldsmobile was surprisingly clean, and Clive climbed in, putting his gun on the rear seat. He made a three-point turn and said, "Hear me out, will ya?"

"Sure," Sam said. "I'll hear you out."

"Don't put no blame on me or Zell, okay? We were just doin' our job. If we knew you was goin' to show up, we'd've taken care of it. But we didn't get told now, did we? Minute you showed us your badge and stuff, we cooperated, didn't we?"

"That's right," Sam agreed. "You cooperated. I'll make sure I mention that."

Clive looked back at the road. " 'Kay, that's fair enough, then."

The road rose up and then leveled off. Even over the car's motor, Sam could make out other sounds, of engines working and tools pounding on stone. There was another gate up ahead, but this one looked ceremonial: just wrought iron with an arch. In the arch was a series of letters. Sam made out the words as they drew closer:

WORK WILL MAKE YOU FREE

Sam said, "That's some kind of slogan."

"Yeah," Clive said. "Some kind of bullshit, if you ask me."

The far slope of the road suddenly fell away, clear of brush and trees, opening to a wide hole in the ground, bare rock and dirt. Looking over, Sam realized that it was deep, very deep, with terraced rocks and roads, cranes overhead, smoke and steam rising, the cranes raising great blocks of stone. A quarry, he thought. "What kind of rock are they cutting out down there?" he asked.

"Marble," Clive said. "Supposedly the best in the country. Ships all over the world. Real pricey shit, get lots of money for it."

Then he saw the workers. Long lines of men in the distance, dressed in white prisoner clothing with thin blue stripes, wearing flat cloth caps. The road swerved to the right, and Sam wondered what he had just seen. They weren't dressed like the prisoners at Camp Carpenter— they were different. Like Sean had said. A camp beyond the camp. Up ahead were buildings, and then another line of men, carrying pickaxes over their thin shoulders, overseen by two Long's Legionnaires at either end, riding horses, pump-action shotguns at the ready. Sam stared at the prisoners as they went by. They were gaunt and they shuffled, as if each step was as hard as lifting a hundred pounds. .

To a man, they looked as though they could be brothers of Peter Wotan.

Clive said, "See you lookin' at our guests."

"What?"

Clive said, "Guests. You know what I mean, right?" Sam thought quickly. He was FBI. This sight shouldn't be strange to him. "Sure, I know what you mean."

He resisted an impulse to turn in the seat and look at the men again.

CHAPTER FORTY

Clive braked hard at the largest building, where white poles out front flew an American flag, what looked to be the flag of Vermont, and the standard of Louisiana. "That there's the camp director's building. They'll take care of you in there. Just 'member, okay? Me and Zell, we cooperated."

As he opened the door, Sam replied, "I'll remember. You cooperated."

He went up the wide steps. There was a bulletin board posted beside the doors, but he ignored it. Unlike his visit to Camp Carpenter, he didn't have to force his way past a waiting sergeant. Another Long's Legionnaire—this one wearing a leather Sam Browne belt with a holstered pistol—was already waiting for him as he went through the double doors. Offices and desks spread out from behind the lobby, but the man, short as he was, dominated the place. He had thick hair, slicked back and combed to one side, a prominent nose, and an equally prominent five o'clock shadow. Unlike those of his counterparts at the gate, his uniform seemed tailored and well made. Silver stars gleamed on his collar tabs.

"Agent Munson?" His Southern accent was smooth and polished.

"That I am," Sam said, shaking the man's hand.

"Apologies for not havin' things set up for you. The name is Royal LaBayeux, Burdick commandant. I understan' you've got somethin' you're investigatin', so why don't you come into my office."

Sam followed him through a set of outer offices with other Long's Legionnaires at work, filing, typing, talking on the telephone. It looked so formal and clean and efficient, and yet he couldn't shake the memory of those gaunt men in the striped uniforms, trudging along the dirt road just outside.

The office held leather chairs and a couch, a wet bar and bookshelves. Windows, the drapes closed, dominated one wall. The desk was wide, with intercoms and telephones, and LaBayeux sat down in a black leather chair. On the nearest wall were photographs of President Long. Two of the photographs, Sam noticed, were of the President standing next to a beaming LaBayeux.

"Always willin' to help out one of Hoover's boys," LaBayeux said. "Whaddya got?"

Sam withdrew two photographs. He set them on the polished desk and watched as LaBayeux picked them up and examined them.

"First photo is of a man found dead a few days ago in Portsmouth, New Hampshire," Sam told him. "The locals didn't know what to make of it. Further investigation revealed he was traveling under the name of Peter Wotan, which we believe is fake."

"I see," LaBayeux said. "And why do you think this... man has anything to do with us?"

Sam pointed to the second photograph. "Tattooed numbers on his wrist. And your facility is the closest one. To see if anyone's missing, and to find out his real name and how he ended up in Portsmouth."

LaBayeux picked up the second photograph. "Central Registry couldn't help you?"

"Excuse me?"

"The Central Registry. They couldn't trace the tattoo number for you?"

Sam had no idea what the man was asking. "You know how bureaucracies work," he said, improvising desperately. "First they deny they can do anything. Then they say maybe. And then they say check in next week. But we don't have time. We have a tattooed dead guy in Portsmouth, where the President and Hitler are going to hold a real important meeting. Dead men raise a lot of questions. We want this cleared up as soon as possible. Which is why I'm here."

"Yeah, I can see that," the Southerner said. He let the photo drop and picked up a phone receiver, clicked a button on the intercom. "Jules, come in here a sec, will ya?" A plump man came in, the blue corduroys tight around his thick legs. LaBayeux passed him the photograph of the tattooed wrist. "Jules, run this number through Records. See if this yid belonged to us, and if not, let's help out the FBI here and see if y'all can't get Central Registry on the line to give us a hand. All right, son?"

"Absolutely, sir," Jules said, backing out of the office and closing the door.

LaBayeux leaned back in his chair, put his hands behind his head. "You look a bit peaked, Agent Munson. Bet you haven't eaten or drunk much since you been travelin'."

"No, I haven't," Sam said.

LaBayeux eased the chair forward. "Then come along. The grub here might not be much, but it's ours."

Sam couldn't think of anything he'd rather do less than to leave this man's office, but he got up and followed him outside.

LaBayeux kept up a running commentary as they headed to the mess hall. "Not bad duty, but it can be a chore, 'specially when cold weather socks us in. I'm from the bayous, and let me tell ya, we never have cold weather like this."

"I'm sure," Sam said. The buildings were clean, neat, painted white, and looked like they belonged to a military reservation. But always there was the noise, of the machinery thumping, the crane engines whining, and cutting tools biting into stone. Sam could think of dozens of questions he wanted to ask the camp commandant but knew he was walking through a minefield of danger. Any hint of ignorance would raise suspicion, and he could soon be down there in the quarry pit, cutting stone with those skeletal men.

Up ahead was a wide, low building. Sam followed LaBayeux through a set of swinging doors. It was a dining facility with long rows of tables and benches, and LaBayeux spoke to a cook in soiled white pants and T-shirt. Then he took the nearest table, and Sam sat across from him as the camp commandant stretched his legs out. "Like to get out every now and then. This gives me a good excuse. Bet you like getting out of the office every now and then, too, am I right?"

"That's for sure," Sam said, desperately wanting to change the subject. "Tell me, how long have you been here?"

LaBayeaux shrugged. "Just over a year ago, when the Department of the Interior seized the quarry and the surrounding lands. I got here with a boxcar of lumber, shingles and nails, and a couple of dozen camp inmates from Nevada and got to work. Muddy, rainy, mosquitoes biting your ass, but we got the place set up 'fore the first train got here. Hell of a thing when that train got here, though, all these people stumbling out, hardly a one of 'em speaking English. Hell of a thing."

"I guess it was," Sam agreed.

"Yeah, built this place from nothin', one of the first set up in the Northeast, and a year later, we're one of the most productive. So there you go. You been with the feds long?"

"Looks like our meal's coming." Sam was happy to see the cook approaching with a tray. "Long enough."

"So it is. Shit, I hear that some of our guests down there cuttin' stone are world-class chefs, but who am I to say? 'Sides, with our luck, the cranky bastards might put ground glass in the pots. Lord knows, as it is, we have our share of docs and engineers and other professionals down there. Ah, here we go."

The plates were heaped with fried ham steak, mashed potatoes, beans, and chunks of white bread. The cook brought mugs of coffee. As they both ate, the camp commandant kept up a running commentary. Sam was thankful that LaBayeux was a man in love with his own voice.

He sliced off a piece of ham and frowned. "Nothin' like the cookin' back home. Tried lots to get a real chef up here from Baton Rouge or New Orleans, but they'd rather stay home and stay warm, and who can blame 'em?" LaBayeux put the ham into his mouth. "Mmm, not bad. But what I would give for some shrimp gumbo. Yum, that would be something."

Sam ate quickly, wanting to get what information he could about Peter Wotan, then get the hell out of this place. The ham steak could have been made by a Waldorf chef, for all he cared; the stuff was practically tasteless. So far, he knew these camps were real, more secret than the run-of-the-mill labor camps, and full of foreigners. But why was Long taking in refugees from Europe? And why were they being worked like this?

The plump Long's Legionnaire strolled in. He handed a sheet of paper over to LaBayeux and went out again, his corduroy pants making swish-swish noises. LaBayeux wiped his lips with a napkin. "Well, lookee here. Your dead boy didn't come from our camp—which I was pretty sure of from the start, we keep a close eye on our guests, though they do try to slip out—but the Central Registry came up with a hit. What did you say your man's name was?" "Peter Wotan."

LaBayeux shook his head. "Fake. Real name was Petr Wowenstein. Originally from Munich, transferred to a place over there called Dachau, then sent here nearly two years ago, out to New Mexico. Worked in some sort of research facility, reported missing just over a week ago." He put the paper down. "Congratulations, Agent Munson. You've got your man. Just like the Mounties from up north."

Congratulations, Sam thought. He now knew who his dead man was. Knew where he came from, knew where he had been. But still didn't know why. Still didn't know what Wowenstein was doing in Portsmouth, why he was killed, why—

LaBayeux started picking at his teeth with a toothpick. "Now what?"

Sam wiped his hands on the napkin. "If I can impose upon you, I'd like a ride back to the railroad station. I need to get to the Boston office, compile a follow-up report, and my report will include the fine cooperation I received from you and your staff."

LaBayeux grinned. "That's pretty white of you. If you're finished eatin', let's go."

Sam got up, heart pounding, the lunch just rolling around in his stomach, thinking, Almost there, almost there, let's just keep it cool and get out of here.

He didn't it make it past the dining hall.

CHAPTER FORTY-ONE

Six Long's Legionnaires stood watching him. LaBayeux grabbed his right arm and said quietly, "Now, whoever the hell you are, I know you're carrying a piece. Probably a revolver in a shoulder holster. Get it out with your left hand, drop it on the porch."

Sam looked at the ring of faces about him, all of them staring, unfriendly, waiting. With his left hand—and part of him was proud that his hand wasn't quivering—he reached in under his coat and grabbed the butt of his revolver. He let it fall to the porch steps.

LaBayeux said, "Okay, now kick it off the porch."

Sam did that, watching his weapon clatter to the ground. Oh, what a mess, what a goddamn mess.

LaBayeux twisted his arm, and Sam grunted in pain. The camp commandant leaned in and said, "What, you think we're from the South, we're stupid, son? Huh?" Another twist of the arm, and Sam was silent this time, not wanting to give the man any satisfaction by asking him to stop. LaBayeux said, "Minute you got in this camp, the phone calls started up. You ain't from the Boston FBI office. They don't got no one comin' up here to check on us. So who the fuck are you?"

"I'm a police inspector from Portsmouth, New Hampshire."

"You Sam Munson?"

"No, the name is Sam Miller."

"Why the fuck are you here, Sam Miller?"

"Because of Wotan... Wowenstein... he ended up dead in my hometown. I'm a cop. It's my job. To find out why he was murdered there."

LaBayeux let his arm go abruptly. "And it's my job to do what my President tells me to do, and keep it secret, and keep shit asses like you out of the way if I have to."

"You said earlier, do I think Southerners are dumb?"

"And?" LaBayeux had a merry grin on his face.

235

"No, most Southerners I meet are okay guys. Not dumb."

LaBayeux's grin got wider. "Nice to hear."

"So why don't you be an okay guy and let me out of here so I can do my job?"

"Guess I don't feel like being an okay guy today, Yankee."

LaBayeux punched Sam in the face, and after he fell to the ground, the kicking started.

After a few long minutes the kicking stopped, and then he was picked up, ears ringing, nose bloody, ribs aching, and LaBayeux called out, "Process him, boys, take 'im away and process 'im. His ass is now ours."

And so he was processed.

He was dragged off the porch, and he struggled, fighting, and cried out as two burly Legionnaires twisted his arms back and cuffed him, then threw him on the ground. He tried to get up and was kicked in the head. He fell flat, eyes blurry, spit running down his chin. A car came up, and more hands grabbed him, threw him in the rear, his head and torso on the floor. A Legionnaire climbed in and Sam winced, feeling cold metal at the back of his head.

"Move or fight me, bud, and then what little brains you got are gonna be splattered o'er this fine leather, got it?" came a thick Southern voice.

Sam closed his eyes, thinking, God, what a screw-up, what a total and complete screw-up. "Look, I'm a cop... okay? Get ahold of my boss, this'll all be straightened out."

The pistol barrel pressed into his skull. "Shut up. Last month I had to clean blood 'n' brain off this leather, don't wanna do it again."

He shut up.

The car sped along, taking corners and dips, and Sam was thrown back and forth. The car stopped, words were exchanged, and the car sped up again, then quickly braked.

The door flew open, hands came in, and dragged him out, stood him up. He was in a fenced-in area, facing a building, concrete and stone, letters on a wooden sign outside: PROCESSING—NO TALKING.

"Let's go," and he was shoved in the back, then half dragged, half propelled into the building. He was slammed through an open door and was halted on a concrete floor with a drain in the center and gray metal benches on either side of the stained plaster walls. Before Sam was a metal counter with a slim man sitting on a stool, a leather-bound ledger open before him. Bare lightbulbs hung from the concrete ceiling.

The thin man coughed, picked up a fountain pen. His Legionnaire's uniform hung off him as if it had once belonged to a heavier man. "Name?" he said, his voice reedy.

"Sam Miller. Look, can I see LaBayeux again, the commandant, there's been a mistake—"

A slap to the rear of his head. He tried to turn, but the Legionnaires held on to him vise-tight.

The man with the pen laboriously wrote something down in the ledger. "Son, just to make it easy for you, these be the rules. I ask you a question. You answer. You give me more than an answer, then Luke back there, he'll whack your thick head. And each time he'll whack you harder. You keep it up, you'll be on the cee-ment down there, bleedin' from your noggin. So let's go on. Address?"

"Fourteen Grayson Street, Portsmouth, New Hampshire."

"Occupation?"

"Police inspector, city of Portsmouth."

The man looked up. "Religion? You don't look Jewish. What be you, then?"

"Catholic."

The man scribbled again. "Thought so. All right, fellas, you know the drill. Get 'im through."

His arms were twisted up, and they pushed him past the counter. Sam thought sourly of how many times he had brought prisoners to be booked back in Portsmouth, back when he was in charge, back when the prisoners weren't people, weren't anything save the offenses they had done: public drunkenness, brawling, petty burglary. Sam's offense? A simple one, a new one, of being in the wrong place at the wrong time.

A smaller room, also made of concrete and soiled plaster, stinking of chemicals, another drain in the center of the room. Lockers and laundry baskets and another blow to the head. "Here. Strip."

Sam didn't move.

Another, harder blow. His knees sagged and then the cuffs were freed, and he was lifted back up. A Legionnaire said, "You're gonna be naked here in a sec, and your choice whether you're gonna be bleedin' hard or not." Sam fumbled at his buttons while three Legionnaires watched him, and he had a quick, sharp memory of his first time in a locker room in high school, his first time being naked in front of other men, feeling awkward, shy, embarrassed, like everybody was staring at him.

He stripped. Stared at a brown spot on the far wall that looked like old blood spatter. His legs started shaking. "Stand still," and a hand on his shoulder, the hum of an electric razor, and his hair was on the floor. "Keep still." A man with a hose in his hand stood in front of him, laughed. "Poor bastard's hung like a hamster," and sprayed him with a cloud of dust. Sam coughed, his legs shaking harder, and some clothes were tossed at him. Thin cotton, not even thick enough to be called pajamas, striped blue and white, and his shoes fell at his feet.

"Feeling generous today," one of the men said. "You get to keep your shoes."

"But no socks!" another one called out. "Don't want people think we're goin' soft."

Sam awkwardly put his bare feet into his leather shoes. "Guys, let me make one phone call, to the FBI, a guy named LaCouture, and—"

The Legionnaire who had disinfected him raised his truncheon. "Shut up or those new clothes of yours, they're gonna be stained. Now let's go. And it's your lucky day, asshole, our tattoo man is gone for the day. So no number on your wrist. Tomorrow."

Aches and pains everywhere, Sam walked out into the cloudy sunshine, the sound of the equipment thumping in his brain. Up ahead, a gate opened at a fence, and he was pushed in.

"Barracks Six, your new home. Work hard, and you'll have a nice life."

More laughter, and he walked unsteadily forward, by himself knowing he was no longer Sam Miller, police inspector for the city of Portsmouth. He was cold, he ached, and his ribs and jaw hurt. He was inside the camp for real, in an area filled with barracks, the ground packed dirt. In the distance the walls of the quarry rose up on three sides, smoke and dust in the air. He stood before one of the barracks, shivering, the thin clothing providing hardly any protection. He rubbed at his eyes, crusted from the stone dust in the air. Barracks Six, the numeral painted in dark blue. It was made of rough-hewn wood and built on square concrete piers. His new home. He opened the door. It creaked.

Darkness.

Strong stench of unwashed bodies, other odors as well.

He took a step in, his eyes adjusting to the weak light. There were bunks crammed tight, floor to ceiling, four beds up. Movement as well, as men turned to stare at him, raising their thin shaved heads. He took a step forward, winced at the sharp pain in his ribs and hips.

"Hello?" he said.

Voices murmured in his direction. He took another step forward, the boards creaking underfoot.

The heads turned away. He kept on walking, trying to breathe through his mouth, to block out the stench that seemed to surround him like an old blanket as he went deeper into the barracks. Two small coal stoves with chimneys going up through the roof, more bunks, and in the very rear, what had to be the latrine, for the stench was thicker there. By the latrine was an empty bunk. He saw a bare mattress, a single blanket folded at the end, and a threadbare pillow.

One man unfolded himself from a nearby bunk and came over, favoring one hip. "You new, eh?" the man said. "Yeah, I am," Sam said.

"Thought so. Look too clean, too fresh. American?"

"Yeah."

The man was about six inches shorter than Sam, his head close-shaved. He had a thin dark beard and a prominent Adam's apple. His prison uniform hung like old laundry on his thin body. "My name is Otto," he said. "I'm Sam. Are you German?"

Otto shook his head. "Netherlander. Dutch. Though originally German. Are you Juden?"

"Excuse me?"

"Juden. Jew."

"No, I'm not."

Otto looked nervous. "Ah. So why are you here?"

"Because I was in the wrong place at the wrong time and asked the wrong questions." Sam looked at the faces and said, "Why are they staring at me?"

Otto glanced back and said, "They are nervous. You are clean, an American, and you say you're not a Jew. They think you are a spy. An informer. Who can blame them?"

"And you?"

The Dutchman cocked his head. "Not sure. Maybe I'm more trusting. Who knows, eh?"

Sam said, "Look, are you all Jews here?"

"Of course."

"From where?"

Otto shrugged. "Everywhere. Germany. Poland. Holland. Even some English in another bunkhouse, all Jews."

"How did you get here?"

Another shrug. "How else? We were taken from other camps, brought into trains and then ships. Ships across the Atlantic. All of us got very sick. And then to a military port. Virginia, I think, and then another train here."

Sam could barely believe what he had just heard. "You mean you all came here from Europe?"

"Yes, of course."

"But why are you here?" Sam asked.

Otto smiled, his lips twitching mirthlessly. "We all volunteered."

"Volunteered? To come here to this camp?"

Otto's smile remained. "Of course. Why wouldn't we?"

"I'm sorry, I don't understand. Why would you volunteer?"

"America. We were told we would come to America to work, to survive, and even if we came here to work, who would not want to come to America?"

Sam looked to the man's wrist.

It bore a series of tattooed numbers.

CHAPTER FORTY-TWO

Sam was in his bunk, breathing in the stench, listening to the wheezing and snoring from his bunkmates. Every now and then somebody would crying out in a dream in a foreign language. His shoes were off and tied about his neck—earlier Otto had warned him, "Thieves everywhere, so keep your shoes close"—and he stared up into the shadows.

At last he knew the secrets of the camps. Refugee Jews from Europe were being transported to America to work in quarries, mines, and forests. Slave labor, long hours, long days, and all they got was poor food— supper had been oatmeal and chunks of stale bread— and a place to sleep. They had all volunteered to come here.

Petr Wowenstein had escaped from a research facility in New Mexico and had been murdered in Portsmouth.

But why?

Sam rolled into his pillow, his shoes striking the side of his face, trying to get comfortable and failing.

Did it matter anymore?

Petr Wowenstein had escaped from a camp and ended up in Sam's hometown.

Investigating his murder had brought Sam to the same kind of camp. But as a prisoner, not an investigator.

He woke with a start, hitting his head on the overhead roof frame, the shoes nearly strangling him. Men were shouting, banging gongs, yelling, "Out! Out! Raus! Raus! Everybody out! Jeder heraus!"

He dropped out of his bunk, pulled his shoes off his neck, and struggled to put them on his swollen feet. The bunkhouse was still unlit, so he bumped into his bunkmates as he moved outside into the assembly area. The morning air was frigid and he started shivering, rubbing at his arms. He

241

could not believe what he saw. Long's Legionnaires were there, overseeing the rows of prisoners, but they had been joined by German soldiers... No, not soldiers. Their uniforms were black, with polished black boots, caps with skull symbols in the center. SS. German SS were there, helping the Legionnaires, laughing and joking, carrying short whips.

"Bunkhouse Six, Bunkhouse Six, at attention!" yelled a tall, thin Legionnaire who was joined by an SS trooper who yelled out, "Bunkhouse Sechs, Bunkhouse Sechs, an der Aufmerksamkeit!"

The Legionnaire counted out the number of prisoners before him, making notes, and Sam kept on shivering, thinking, This can't be real, cannot be true, German SS and Long's Legionnaires, stormtroopers from each side of the Atlantic, cooperating and working together as one in the mountains of Vermont. There had been a few news reports of Long's Legionnaires traveling to Germany to visit their compatriots, but never had there been mention of the reverse. It was like some nightmare that his upstairs neighbor would be writing for one of those fantasy magazines.

The Legionnaire yelled something to a camp official, and then Sam joined his bunkmates as they marched out to the quarries, flanked by Long's Legionnaires and SS stormtroopers.

His job was simple. By an area where cutting tools and drills made incisions into the marble wall, he had a shovel to scoop up marble chips that were processed later for some other use. The stone reared above him for scores of feet, and other prisoners scrambled up and down scaffolding, carrying tools. Only a few Legionnaires and SS men watched, content to sit in wooden chairs and gossip among themselves. Sam's hands quickly blistered as he shoveled marble chips into open wooden wagons. Once during the morning, he had a few words with Otto, who was carrying lengths of wood scaffolding.

Sam said, "You volunteered for this?"

The man laughed. "It is easier work than before, over there. The food, not good, but enough. And here, the guards are forbidden to shoot us unless we try to escape. We may be beaten here and there, but to live, we are living here better than in the camps in Germany and Poland. And you? Why are you here?"

Sam shoveled up some chips. "I'm a cop. From a city called Portsmouth. In New Hampshire. Came here investigating a murder back home."

Otto said, "You should have stayed home, eh?"

Sam coughed, leaned on his shovel. "Maybe so. What about you?"

Otto's face darkened. "Ach, we are the lucky ones. You see there are no women and children here, eh? Only we capable of work were allowed to leave. Our family members, left behind. For them, who knows how they are..." The Jew scurried away. Sam picked up his shovel and went back to work.

Breakfast came after two hours of work, a soup wagon pulled by a tired horse, ribs showing, plodding along. Thick oatmeal, cold toast smeared with foul-tasting margarine, and a mug of weak coffee. It was filling but something Sam would have sneered at earlier.

God, he thought, earlier. He went back to the marble chips, picked up his shovel, waited a moment. Look at what doing his job had gotten him. Right in the very heart of hell. His brother, Tony, would probably bust a gut laughing. Tony the hell-raiser, the criminal—Tony was a free man. And his Eagle Scout and high school football star brother, his Goody Two-shoes brother, he was in a camp, a place worse than Tony's, a place where—

The blow to his back knocked him to the ground, the marble chips shredding his clothing, bloodying his knees. He got back up quick, shovel held up, facing the SS officer who had just belted him with his whip. The officer had fair skin, blond hair, and a sharp nose, and snapped, "Zuriick zu Arbeit, Juden!" Beside him was a Legionnaire wearing glasses and a thick mustache, his uniform muddy and worn. Sam choked out, "I don't know what that fucking Nazi just said."

The Legionnaire laughed. "Man, I guess you're not from away, 'cause no guy here would raise a shovel to a Kraut. He said, 'Back to work, Jew,' so I suggest you do that. Even if you are an American, you ain't an American here."

Sam was going to say that he wasn't Jewish but didn't. He lowered his shovel.

Lunch wasn't as rushed as breakfast. The prisoners were allowed to sit and stretch their legs and eat from metal bowls of stew with water and chunks of stale bread. Again Sam found himself next to Otto, who was leaning up against a pile of lumber. Sam said, "What did you do before the war?"

"Before the war? Ran a business in Amsterdam. Nice, safe, boring job. Someday I hope to be picked for my skills and get away from this stonework. They do that, you know. If they have a need—electricians, plumbers, university professors—they get picked and sent where they're

243

needed at special camps."

"How long have you been here?"

"Eight months. Before that, I was somewhere in the South. Very hot. We cut trees in the swamps. Lots of bugs, too."

"And before that?"

He shook his head. "Don't want to remember that. It was a camp in Poland, very bad. Then one day an officer came in with an American in a nice suit. Volunteers for labor in America. Who would go? All of us, if we could, and here we are."

Sam shoveled in a few more spoonfuls of stew. "What happens to the marble? Or the wood that was cut? Where does it go?"

"Trains," Otto told him. "Loaded on trains. And why do we care? We work, we survive, we even get paid."

"Paid? Money?"

"Yes, one dollar a week. We can use the money to buy things at a camp store on Sunday. Like soap. Razors. Tea."

Sam finished his stew and wiped the bowl clean with a piece of bread. "Otto, have people escaped?"

"There have been attempts, yes. But how far can someone go, someone who is a stranger here? Eh? And dressed like this?"

"Have any attempts succeeded?"

Otto stared at him. "Are you thinking of escaping then, eh?"

Sam thought for a moment, not sure he could trust this fellow prisoner. "Just thinking aloud, that's all."

"Then think about this, my friend. If someone escapes from our barracks, everyone is sent to the cooler for punishment. Water only, no food for a week. And then one man from the barracks, he is chosen by lot and shot. For it is thought by the guards—helped by the Germans, of course—that shooting one from a barracks will discourage the others. It works. Most time."

Sam kept quiet, stopped eating.

"So I ask you, my new American friend, is that what you will do? Try to escape? To sentence me or one of my bunkmates to torture and then death?"

Sam said, "I don't know what I'll do, but I need to get out and—"

"We all need to get out." The voice was harsh. "We all want to leave. But where to go, eh? To be a Jew in this world now... there are no longer any safe places. None! So we live to live another day, and that is what we do. And here we are reasonably safe. Do you understand?"

"Yes, I do."

"No, you don't," the Dutchman shot back. "Here. I will tell you a tale.

Mmm, no, not a tale but a true story. In the South, cutting trees, I knew a schoolteacher from a village in Poland. His name was Rothstein. One day, months after the invasion, special German police units came to his village and took out all the Jews and brought them to the town square. There, in the hot June sun, they made them sit still. No water. No shade. No food. And the Germans laughed. And they took photographs. They told the Jews, 'You move, you will die. Understand?' An old man, he couldn't help himself. He tried to stretch his cramped legs. They shot him. A woman screamed. They shot her. Near Rothstein, his two-year- old nephew, he squirmed out of his mother's firms, tried to run away, and the mother cried and a German policeman, he picked up the boy by his ankle, dangled him before everyone, and put a pistol to the child's head and shot him. Rothstein, he was splattered with his nephew's blood and brains. That happened in a place where Jews had lived for hundreds of years in safety and sanctuary. Now... nothing. Even here, in your America. We are no longer safe. So tell me, are you going to have me killed? Or one of my bunkmates? Are you so important that this will happen?"

Sam didn't reply. Otto said, "And about your Jews. They have moved themselves to ghettos, haven't they, afraid of what might happen to them. We know that news as well. Your Jews have not been rounded up, eh, not yet the pogroms and the arrests. But will their time come? Like ours?"

A whistle blew, sending them all back to work, ensuring Sam didn't have to come up with an answer, for he had none to give.

CHAPTER FORTY-THREE

The afternoon dragged by, monotonous and backbreaking work, splinters from the shovel handle digging into his palms, blisters breaking into blood and pus, keeping his head down, just shoveling, trying not to breathe in the stone dust kicked up by the drilling and cutting. When the whistle blew again, he trudged back to the barracks with his new bunkmates, and he understood the look of those prisoners he had seen. It was the look of hopelessness, of giving up and knowing one's place. What was real was what was before one's nose, and nothing else. To live was to get through a day without being beaten, without being shot, and to eat as much food as possible, all to live one more day.

That was the life inside the wire.

And to get out, to successfully escape, was to doom some stranger in his barracks to death. Up ahead was Barracks Six, and the line of men moved in. A Legionnaire he recognized from yesterday was standing by the door; he crooked a finger at Sam's direction.

"You, cop." The Legionnaire's face was pockmarked from old acne scars. "Time to finish some business."

The Legionnaire grabbed Sam's arm and pulled him out of fine. Sam's bunkmates cast their eyes down, as if afraid that by paying any attention they, too, would be dragged away. Sam shook off the man's arm and the man laughed easily. "All right, pal, just come along and there won't be no problem."

He walked with the Legionnaire, each step heavy and painful, seeing a wooden and wire gate ahead of them open up, with watchtowers on every side. Now they went to the right, to a small concrete building that stood next to yesterday's processing facility. Inside it smelled of chemicals and sweat, and an older man in a white coat and with wavy gray hair sat at a wooden table, glasses perched on the end of his nose. Nearby were bottles of ink and shiny instruments. The old man looked up and asked in a

German accent, "He's not a Jew, is he?"

"Nope," the Legionnaire answered. "But he's a guest here, just the same."

The old man laughed. "Knew he wasn't a Jew. Can always tell. All right, bring him over."

At the man's elbow was an open thick leather-bound ledger, and Sam saw rows of names and numbers. It was as if icicles were tracing themselves up and down his back. He knew what was planned for him. He was about to be branded as a hunk of meat, like the poor bastards around him, like his homicide victim.

"Hey, now," the older man instructed. "Hold your wrist out. And be quick, I'm late for my supper."

Sam didn't move.

The Legionnaire slapped him. The pain shot through him. The Legionnaire urged, "Now, boy, hurry up!"

Sam glared at the Legionnaire, then rolled up the sleeve on his left arm. He held his wrist out, the man pulled a humming metal instrument close, a tattooing needle at the end of a handle, brought it down to Sam's wrist, and he felt the harsh sting as the painful marking began, branding him forever as a prisoner—

Sam balled his other hand into a fist, punched upward, caught the old man under the chin. The old man grunted in shock, and Sam heard the Legionnaire call out. Sam grabbed the needle, seized the man's right hand, pulled it forward, took the needle, and slammed it into the hand. The man howled and then the Legionnaire was on him, beating him, and Sam hurt as he punched and kicked, and through the pain, it all felt good.

He had fought back.

CHAPTER FORTY-FOUR

Hours later, Sam lay on his side, breathing shallowly, his ribs hurting. He had been dragged from the tattoo room to a place called the cooler, and damn, that was a good turn of phrase, because it was fucking freezing. It was a concrete cell block without a mattress pad, blanket, or pillow, just a covered bucket in the comer for shit and piss, and right now, even though his bladder was screaming for release, he couldn't drag himself the four or five feet to the bucket.

But he was smiling. Even through the blood and the bruises and the throbbing pain, he was smiling. He had fought back, had caused the German tattooist some serious pain. Sure, maybe someone else would be along eventually to finish the tattoo, but at least Sam Miller, Portsmouth police inspector, hadn't been completely branded like some barnyard animal.

He tried to shift again, groaned as something stabbed in his side. So, in under two days as a prisoner, what had he learned? A lot. In remote areas of the nation, Jewish refugees were at work, clearing wood, mining ore, cutting stone. Among these refugees, one Petr Wowenstein—aka Peter Wotan—had lived and worked until successfully escaping.

The refugees—how and why did they end up here?

Another intake of breath, another moan.

Yet Sam smiled, for even though he didn't have all the answers, he had found out a lot. He wondered if ol' Marshal Harold Hanson would be proud of his probationary inspector. After all, not only had Sam properly identified the city's latest homicide victim, he had also uncovered a national secret.

Damn, if that wasn't worth passing probationary status, what would be? Maybe even help him in the Party. Who knew?

He coughed.

Damn, he hurt.

Somehow he had managed to doze, and when he woke up, he stumbled over to the bucket, aimed into it. Daylight coming through a high barred window allowed him to see that his urine wasn't stained with blood, which was a good sign. He held up his left wrist. There. A blue numeral three. A permanent reminder of the horror he and so many others were living in. Sam lowered the sleeve and replaced the cover to the bucket and sat down, grimacing at the thudding pain in his ribs.

He looked around the small cell. Something was near the bottom of the wall. He looked closer, saw a set of initials—R.S. —and a Star of David carved in the stone.

A noise, a slight thump.

Something was on the floor. He crawled over, saw it was a hunk of bread with a string wrapped around it. He undid the string, saw the bread open up, and among the smears of margarine was a note:

From O. Good luck.

Otto. The Dutch businessman from Barracks Six.

Be damned.

He ate the bread, wincing as his sore jaw worked, and then he tore up the note and ate that as well. The piece of string went into his bucket.

He sagged against the wall, feeling just a bit better, trying to think of what he could possibly do next.

Survive, he decided. Do what the Jews here were doing. Stay alive. Somehow get out and get back to Portsmouth and—

Condemn a man to death, then? Is that what you're thinking? To escape and condemn someone, hell, maybe even Otto, who befriended you? Is that what you're going to do? Kill him on the off chance that you can get through the fences and wire and past the guard towers and—

The door was being unlocked. Two Long's Legionnaires came in, staring at him, wooden truncheons pulled from their belts.

One said, "Get your ass up, come with us, or we'll beat you somethin' awful. Got it, boy?"

Sam got up, hurting but happy he could hide his pain from these two thugs.

They escorted him to a building set apart from the rest, a wooden cottage that wouldn't look out of place at a lake resort. About him were the sounds of the quarry at work, the growl of the cranes, the thump of the drills, the whine of the cutting tools, and—underneath—the shouted voices of the

249

guards and overseers.

At the cottage, both men stopped. One pointed to the front stoop. "You go on up there, boy, and there's someone to see you. You step lively, and if you run out by yourself, jus' so you know..."

The man jabbed an elbow into Sam's ribs, making him gasp. The man went on, "Up there, at the southwest guard tower, there's a man with a scoped rifle, and if you come out of that there cottage by yourself, he's gonna blow your head clear off. You understand?"

Sam said nothing, shook off the other guard's grasp, and went up the steps. It was cold, and he could feel shivering starting in his legs and arms. He took hold of the doorknob, wondering what was on the other side.

He opened the door, stepped into a tiny foyer with stained Oriental carpeting and a bureau and lamp. Through an arched opening was a living room with a thick couch and two easy chairs, the arms covered with dainty doilies. A picture window gave a view of the distant fence line, and way beyond that, the tree-covered peaks of the Green Mountains. A man in a military uniform—it looked to be army—was standing with his back to Sam, looking out, his hands clasped behind him.

"Well," the military man said, and turned around.

Sam stood stock-still, as if someone had nailed his feet to the floor.

Before him, in his Army National Guard uniform, was his boss, Marshal Harold Hanson.

"Sam," Hanson said, shaking his head. "What the hell have you gotten yourself into?"

CHAPTER FORTY-FIVE

Sam closed his eyes, then opened them right up. "I... I was doing my job."

Hanson stood there, hands on his hips. "Look at you. Christ, how in hell did you end up here?"

"The dead man... by coming here, I found out who he was—"

"Dammit, Sam, you were told several times to leave that case alone. You know it belongs to the FBI and the Germans."

"Still my case, sir. No matter what you say or what the FBI says. It's still my case, and I found out where he came from. I know his real name, and—"

"Do you have any idea the problems you've caused?" Hanson interrupted. "What kind of trouble you're in?"

Sam ran a hand over his shorn head. "Yeah, I guess the hell I know what kind of trouble I'm in. Sir."

Hanson's face flushed. "That's enough of that, then."

"What else did you expect me to say? Or do?"

"I expected you to be smart, for one," Hanson said. "And you're lucky I'm here."

Sam said, "How did you know where I was?"

His boss said, "Allow me some intelligence. One reason I became marshal is because I keep my ears and eyes open. You don't think I knew about the deal you cut with Kenny Whelan to get a false FBI ID? He called me just after you left his apartment. Pat Lowengard sold you out, too, the minute you went out the door. That's our world. Spies and snitches everywhere. It was a simple matter of tracking you from Portsmouth to Boston and then to Burdick, Vermont. Knowing what's in Burdick, I knew you were going to get into serious trouble."

Even in this pleasant room, Sam could still hear the thudding of the stonecutting equipment, could still smell oil and stone dust. "Why are they here? All these Jews? Here and New Mexico and other places across the country? There must be thousands, am I right?"

Hanson said, "You don't need to know what's going on here."

Something sharp sparked inside of him. "The hell I don't!"

"Sam, look—"

"No," Sam insisted, "I've been beaten, stripped, and worked as a slave. I came close to getting a tattooed wrist like the rest of the poor bastards out there. I've got a right to know, and you've got to tell me. I demand it."

Hanson folded his arms over his uniform. "You don't look like you're in a position to demand anything." "Maybe so, but I think this would prove embarrassing for you, sir. After telling people in the Party you're sponsoring me for bigger and better things, having me imprisoned in Burdick wouldn't look good for you. But tell me, and you'll be thrilled at what I'll do for the Party and you if I get out."

Hanson stared at him, and Sam wondered what was going on behind those evaluating eyes. Then the marshal said, "What makes you think I know anything?"

"You're here in full National Guard uniform in order to gain access. That means you have pull in a place that doesn't officially exist. Which means you must know why it's here."

That brought a thin smile. "Thanks for your vote of confidence." Hanson waited, let a breath out, and said, "It's a couple of years old. It started small and then grew once it became apparent it was a deal that worked to everyone's advantage."

"Must be one hell of a deal," Sam said. "How did it start?"

"Why should I tell you?"

"Because I deserve to know, that's why. And you know I'm right."

A pause. "It began in occupied Paris, with a trade delegation led by the Secretary of the Treasury, Morgenthau. Probably the smartest Cabinet officer Long's got. He's also done his best since the war to get more Jewish refugees here, with no success. Too much resistance from Congress and everybody else. Nobody wanted them here, competing for jobs and housing. But in Paris, Morgenthau and some businessmen came upon a train shipping French Jews out to the east. There was a confrontation, and the ranking SS officer said to Morgenthau, 'Fine, you're so concerned about the Jews, take them.' Which is what he did. They got off the train and found their way here."

Sam said, "The news I saw before I came here said Morgenthau couldn't get any more Jews into the country. He's been trying and trying."

"Sure, publicly," Hanson said. "But he and his friends in industry have been doing it secretly for years. All that stuff you hear on the radio or see in the newsreels about him fighting Congress is all a lie. He makes a fuss in public, while in private, he makes it happen."

"How do they get here?"

Hanson said, "After England was defeated, the Germans took possession of one of the largest merchant fleets in the world. English ships, crewed by Germans and a few American overseers to make sure the Jews arrive here alive, bring them over. They land in military ports, so security is maintained."

"That's unbelievable," Sam said.

"When you get right down to it, the Germans want the Jews out of Europe, by either expelling them or killing them," Hanson explained. "Hell, even the guy running the SS, Himmler, said something like that in a book a year or two back, about sending all the Jews overseas. They're only doing worse to them because they can't ship them out easily."

"But the expense..."

"Sam, the Germans are locked in a death struggle with the Soviets. Once the offer was made for us to take the Jews, what made sense to them? To use their army and their train systems to ship Jews to concentration camps out to the occupied east, or to use their army and their train systems to supply the eastern front against the Russians?"

"And the Secretary of the Treasury went along with this?"

"Morgenthau eventually came up with the arrangement, as tough as it was. The Jews would come here secretly, not as refugees but as labor. The Nazis get their Jew-free Europe, and we get workers."

"Slave labor, you mean."

"They get paid."

"A dollar a week!"

Hanson said, "Which is more than they got back in Europe. A few thousand came out here at first, to work in some copper pits in Montana, and it started succeeding. They're hard workers, Sam, happy to be here and not there. They clear lumber, work in mines, quarries, and even some scientific facilities and shipbuilding. So money was made, and you know how President Long operates. He gets a kickback on everything, just like when he was governor. Donations were made to his campaign funds as well as the program grew."

"Money? This is all for money?"

Hanson nodded. "Yes, money, as crass as that might sound. For Christ's sake, this country is broke. It's been broke for years—even with Long's nutty wealth confiscation and redistribution plans and everything else, we're broke. We've been in this Depression for over a decade. So the country needs money. These laborers make money for exports. Hard currency. Money we couldn't get if those jobs went to the regular workforce at regular wages."

"Why can't the money be used to put people back to work?"

Hanson had a grim look on his face. "What's worth more to Long and the Party? Free Americans working at real jobs, or Americans on the dole who have to sign a loyalty oath to get relief money, who'll vote the right way when the time comes?"

"Sweet Jesus," Sam muttered.

"Some of the money goes to other things as well. You're a smart fellow, Sam. Look around your hometown, you'll see where it goes."

Sam didn't know what Hanson was getting at, and then it came to him. The Navy Yard. The fleet expansion. The new buildings, cranes, docks...

"For the military? That's it?"

"Mostly," Hanson said. "But it goes to other places as well. Some relief. Road and bridge work. The President and his boys get their cut, as well as the Party. Sam, Long is a fat, drinking, whoring criminal who happens to be our President and will be our President for the foreseeable future. But the future has something else waiting for us, and it's a man with a funny mustache and an army uniform. Once Hitler crushes Russia and takes a breath, he's going to look across the Atlantic. Maybe his slant-eyed friends in Tokyo will look across the Pacific at the same time. So we need to be ready."

"This summit deal coming up with Long and Hitler,"

Sam said. "There's more than just money being made. We're going to get our aircraft and arms factories up and running so we can be ready down the line—is that it?"

Hanson said, "True. And these poor Jews, they're our seed corn. Our way of funding what we can... and there's the humanitarian side."

Sam laughed. "Humanitarian! Are you out of your mind?"

"No, I'm not. Every Jew here is a Jew that's saved."

"Some saved," Sam said. "Worked hard, barely dressed, barely fed—"

"But saved nonetheless, compared to what awaits them in Europe," Hanson insisted. "Morgenthau doesn't like it much, either, even though he's running the program, but...it's better to be here, overworked and underfed, than to be back in Europe, slaughtered."

Sam kept quiet. He didn't know what else to say. Hanson sighed. "Look, Sam. You're in a very dangerous position. You now know one of this country's deepest and darkest secrets. And you need to tell me: What do you plan to do about it if you get out?"

Sam said, "Nothing." He waited, then added, "For the moment."

Hanson said sharply, "What do you mean?"

"Just what I said," Sam said, not liking the smooth way Hanson was talking, how comfortable and clean he looked in his uniform. Sam was sure his boss had eaten a good breakfast before coming here. Sam went on. "Maybe I'll keep quiet. Maybe I won't. Maybe the American people need to know what the hell their government is doing and how they're treating refugees here. Maybe they have a right to know these poor bastards are being worked nearly to death."

"Who gave you that right to say anything?"

Sam said, "I'm a free American, that's all the right I need."

Hanson shook his head. "Maybe that was right years ago. But not now. And you're making an assumption. That you're getting out of here."

"You didn't put on your dress uniform and travel a couple of hours by train to just to have a talk with me, did you?"

"That's exactly what I did. To have a talk with you and see how smart you are. Let's say Sam Miller, crusader of the truth and defender of whatever, convinces the Boston Globe or New York Times or New York Herald Tribune to break this story. What happens then?"

"I don't know."

Hanson reached into his uniform jacket, pulled out a sheaf of black-and-white photographs. "I'll tell you what happens then. Chaos. Violence. The camps are discovered, and maybe some of our jobless, they break into these camps and beat up or kill the Jews because they're stealing jobs at slave wages that they feel belong to true Americans. Maybe the ghettos in California and New York and Miami are attacked, and there's a pogrom here in the United States. That's one thing. The other is that the deal between Hitler and Long to ship the Jews here, the deal is dead. It only works if it's kept a secret, and with the secret out, Long will drop it like the proverbial hot potato. Then the Jews stay in Europe. No more cargo ships across the Atlantic. This is what awaits them. Look. I got these photographs from a friend of mine in army intelligence."

The first photo showed a country landscape, a hillside overlooking a ditch. There were German soldiers, laughing, rifles in hand. The next photo showed a line of people herded into range. Men with long beards, young boys, grandmothers, women, some of the women carrying children, and young girls as well.

They were all naked.

Another photograph, Hanson silently dealing them out as if they were some obscene set of playing cards. Most of the men, desperately trying to be modest, cupped their genitals with their hands. The women held one open hand below their bellies, others holding an arm across their breasts, some of the women using the infants to shield them.

Another photo. Sam forced himself to look. The Germans had lined up in good military order, rifles up, and were shooting at the line of naked men, women, and children.

Shooting at them all. The rustling sound of photo paper was all that Sam could hear. Most of the naked men and women had fallen forward into the open ditch, but others had crumpled to the ground. An officer holding out a service pistol was standing in the pile of bodies, aiming down to shoot the nearest ones in the head.

The final photo. One German soldier, grinning widely, was kicking at the body of a bloody infant, as if kicking a football.

Hanson held that last photo out the longest, then put the photos back in his pocket. He wiped his hands together as if they had been soiled.

Sam looked away, bile in his throat. Hanson said softly, "We can't save them all, Sam. But we can save a lot, and we can continue to save a lot. This truth gets out about the camps here in the United States, and the deal is done."

"Deals?" Sam forced himself to speak, even though he felt like throwing up. "We're making deals with a government and army that can do that?"

"We deal with who we have to, even if it's the devil himself," Hanson replied. "You saw those photos. If we hadn't brought over the refugees working in this quarry, that's the fate waiting for them."

"But we're better than that."

"Maybe so, but none of us have clean hands. None of us."

Sam said, "Speak for yourself."

Hanson said carefully, "I like to keep a close eye on all my officers, both on duty and off duty. I don't like surprises. The Police Commission doesn't like surprises."

"I'm sure." The nausea had been replaced by something harder.

"So you know, there's a limit to our interest, you realize. We know what's on the streets of Portsmouth, the temptations, the flow of booze and money. We do what we can, and as a sergeant, you were pretty straight and narrow. But then there are circumstances that get to the level of us paying close attention."

Sam looked out the window.

Hanson said, "Do you have any idea how many cops can afford a home on their own? With just a few years on the job? And with a pregnant wife to boot?"

Sam looked back. "I saved a lot. Worked overtime when I could."

"Certainly," Hanson said. "But a few weeks before you bought your house, there was an amazing coincidence. William Cocannon. Never made a formal complaint, but he let people know that somebody whacked the shit out of him early one March morning, stole several hundred dollars, just about the time you managed to scrape together enough money to get your house. I know the president of the First National. He told me you were short for the down payment, and then the day after Wild Willy got whacked, you showed up with enough money to make up the difference."

Sam felt the room getting colder. Hanson said, "So have I made my point? Or do I need to talk again about your wife and her friends?"

"You've made your point."

Hanson said, "Good. So there's no misunderstanding. I'm getting your sorry ass out of here, though a lot of strings are being pulled, favors are being called in, and I'm getting you back to Portsmouth. Where you'll resume your duties as probationary inspector, including working as a liaison with the FBI. Who, by the way, claim that they miss you very much. Which is one of the reasons I came out to fetch you. To keep the FBI happy."

"And the department's Log... who gets to write about what just happened to me? Or you?"

Hanson said carefully, "The Log will be correct. It'll say you and I were in a small town in Vermont as part of an investigation. An investigation, I'll remind you, Probationary Inspector Sam Miller, that is closed. Forever. Do you understand?"

"But I know who he was. And where he came from. And—"

"Sam." His voice was sharper. "Drop it. That's an order. You promise me it's dropped, and you're back in Portsmouth tonight. You say anything else, and so help me God, you'll be back on the other side of the fence in sixty seconds. Do you understand?"

"Sir... it's a homicide. In your city. Our city."

Hanson said, "A refugee from New Mexico, previously from Europe, who had his neck snapped by someone and got dumped from a railroad car passing through our city. That's all it was. All right? Leave it to the FBI. Or you can stay here."

Sam wiped at his face, looked at his boss. Maybe it was the hunger or the exhaustion or the bitter realization that he was giving up, but for a moment or two—or maybe longer—it seemed there were ghost images on his boss's chest, as if Sam could, through the fabric, see the photos again. The German soldiers lined up with rifles, smiling. The Jewish men and women, forced into a line. The shooting. The German soldier at the end, kicking at a baby's corpse as if it were a delightful sport.

Sam struggled to gain his voice and said, in almost a whisper, "The case is dropped. You have my word."

"Good," Hanson said, coming over, slapping him on the shoulder. "Like I said earlier, when this summit is all wrapped up, you've got a bright future in the Party, even with these stunts you've pulled."

Sure, Sam thought. A bright future tattling on my father-in-law for your benefit, for the benefit of the Nats against the Staties.

Hanson said, "Now. One more thing. You realize that whatever I tell you here stays here? Do you understand that?"

"Yes, sir, I do."

Hanson shook his head. "No, I don't think you do. What I mean is, everything stays here. Nobody else gets told. Not any other cop, not your wife, no one. If it's ever found out that you've blabbed about this place, then you and anyone else you've talked to—even if it's your boy, Toby, by mistake—you come back here. Forever. Now. Tell me you understand that."

In answer, Sam rolled up his left sleeve, showing the numeral three. "And this? How do I explain this to Sarah?"

"You'll think of something," Hanson said. "A drunken late visit to a tattoo parlor off the harbor, I don't care. But the secret of Burdick remains a secret. Understand?" "Yeah. I understand it all."

"Good." Hanson took a breath. "Let's get out of this dump."

There was a moment when the guilt struck him so hard that he almost turned around to go back into the camp. Now, dressed in his civilian clothes—which felt odd and constricting after the few days in the striped clothing, except for his hat, which was loose on his shorn head— and walking with Hanson, he saw a line of prisoners heading off to another part of the camp. The starved men stared him. He stared back and recognized his bunkmates, one face in particular. Otto, the Jew from Holland, the man who had risked so much to toss in a chunk of bread to Sam.

Otto stared at Sam in disbelief, and Sam could just imagine what was going through the prisoner's mind. Sam must have been a spy. Sam must have been a turncoat. Now everyone in Barracks Six was at terrible risk, for the friendliness shown an American who was going to betray them all.

He thought of shouting something to them, but realized it was a waste of time. Instead, he watched the line of men shuffling away to their work, and then he returned to whatever freedom awaited him.

PART FIVE

The Office of the Commandant Department of the Interior Burdick, Vermont

Sir,

As a follow-up to our phone call earlier, I am compelled to yet again protest in the most serious terms of the release of the prisoner Sam Miller of Portsmouth, N.H., on 10 May. Due to the intercession of others and the presence of Harold Hanson, Colonel, New Hampshire National Guard, Miller was released into the custody of Hanson at this duty station on the above- referenced date.

However, I still strongly believe that the release of Miller seriously jeopardizes the security of this facility. Notwithstanding this concern, I do understand that Miller's release was also due in part to his importance to the upcoming Portsmouth summit. I therefore recommend, upon the completion of Miller's duties of the summit, that

a)   Miller be arrested and returned to this facility forthwith and;

b)   That within the next twenty-four hours, the occupants of Barracks Six, which worked with Miller, be turned over to German authorities for immediate deportation to their respective internment facilities in Europe, so that security is maintained here as well.

Respectfully submitted,
Royal LaBayeux, Commandant

x Approve   Disapprove

Royal, wait until the summit is over before deporting those yids. Things are complicated enough without taking this step. But agreed, let's get Miller back where he belongs; sticks in my craw that a mere flatfoot got away with this. Tom

CHAPTER FORTY-SIX

Sam's front door was open.

His hand fumbled as he reached down for his revolver, liberated that morning from the Burdick camp. "Sarah?"

Nothing.

Thinking, he said, "Tony?"

Still no answer.

He pushed a switch to turn on the light.

Disaster.

Before him was the living room, with the chairs and couches that Sarah had so carefully picked from her father's showroom, jumbled, fabric ripped and stuffing torn out.

"Oh, Sarah," he whispered. His feet crunched on broken glass from shattered picture frames. Books and papers were tossed in a pile, the torn pages looking like crumpled leaves. In the kitchen, plates and saucers and cups and glassware were broken. Their bedroom... clothes ripped, the bed tossed on its side, the bureau drawers broken open... .

Toby's room. Something harsh clamped in Sam's throat at what they had done to his boy's room. Toby's precisely made models, most constructed with Sam's help in the kitchen, working carefully over sheets of the *Portsmouth Herald*, paint carefully applied... his son's proud models had been yanked from the ceilings and crushed. His chemistry set, his collection of fossils, even the model police car with the Portsmouth police markings destroyed. He tightened his jaw, remembering the promise he had made to Toby seemingly a century ago when he was leaving.

He heard footsteps in the living room and strode out, revolver in his shaking hands, ready to shoot, ready to do violence, ready to—

"Sam? Is that you?"

From the gloom, his upstairs tenant gingerly walked forward. Sam let a breath out. "Walter. Damn. Yeah, it's me."

BRENDAN DUBOIS

Walter looked around, his eyes wide from behind his glasses. "My word, I heard the noise down here, but never did I—Sam, I am so deeply sorry."

It took two tries before Sam could put his revolver away. "When did they come?"

The older man folded his arms tight across his chest, as though trying to prevent himself from running away. "Two days ago. It was a squad of Long's Legionnaires. The bastards came upstairs and looked through my belongings, but not like this. They were brusque, they were cruel, but they didn't... do this. What in the world were they looking for?"

"I don't know."

Walter peered closer. "Sam, what happened to you? Your hair's nearly gone, and it looks like you've been in a fight."

Sam was silent.

"Sarah?" Walter said. "And your son?"

"Out of town for a while. Until the summit is over."

"I see." Walter shifted his feet and said, "I'm sorry to say this, and it isn't a good time, but... Sam, I'm sorry," he continued, his voice plaintive. "The Legionnaires... they frightened me. Frightened me so much I was afraid I was going to soil myself. When they left, I decided I never wanted to be that scared again."

Sam looked at his tenant and kept quiet.

"I hate to do this to you and Sarah, but I'm moving out next week. You've gotten the attention of Long's Legionnaires, and that scares me. They might come back and put me in a labor camp."

Sam kept his eyes on the mess that used to be his living room. He knew what he was about to say wasn't fair, but suddenly, he didn't care. "What about all that talk about being brave, protesting, a dissenter?"

"Look, be reasonable. I... I'm a coward, we both know that. I'm going to move out, and I'm really sorry about the rent money. I know how you and Sarah depend on it, and I—"

"Walter, you can shut up. I get the idea."

"I'm sorry, Sam," Walter repeated feebly. There was a crunch as his heel snapped a shard of glass. "Well, one other thing. I heard you helped my friend Reggie Hale escape the clutches of the National Guard. You have my thanks and gratitude."

"Sure," Sam said. "Whatever you say."

Another pause that lengthened in the shadowy room, then Walter said, "I must be leaving. Again, so sorry. But Sam... Did you hear the news tonight?"

"No," Sam said brusquely. "My radio's not in good shape."

"Yes, yes, of course. It's just that they've arrested Winston Churchill in his hotel room in New York City."

"What the hell for?"

"Official reason, a number of violations of the Neutrality Act. Unofficial reason, it's a gift from Long to Hitler to help grease the summit, make it even more profitable for Long and his cronies."

Sam thought of Burdick and that damn camp. Walter opened the door and continued, "Churchill can be so many things. A drunkard, a blowhard, a knee-jerk defender of the Empire and its old Victorian ways. But the man's voice... his writings... he kept it alive, you know. The idea of a free, independent Europe, supported by a United States that still lived by its Constitution. And now that he's arrested... when he's executed, the resistance in England and elsewhere, it will collapse. Who will speak for freedom then? Long? Our collection of idiots and misfits in Congress? Our ward heeler Vice President? Our public spokesmen, a collection of isolationists and Jew-haters like Lindbergh? Father Coughlin?"

Sam looked to his tenant and said sharply, "I know one thing. It won't be you, Walter."

INTERLUDE VIII

In Curt's attic again this stifling morning, he rolled over on his side, thinking that even with the heat and dust and wooden floor, this was a much better place than the Iroquois Labor Camp. He remembered, back at the camp, how a group of men he knew and trusted—hard men who not only had contacts with the outside, but had contacts halfway across the globe—had come to him with a proposal, something that would get him out of the camp and into a mission that would change the world.

In the dim early light, he recalled with a smile his answer: *Shit, of course. Where do I sign up?*

He remembered as well, when Phil had asked him, whether he was tough enough to do his job, to kill one of the most guarded men on the planet.

Yeah. Tough enough. So far he had been.

So here he was.

There was the sound of a large engine, then the screech of tires as a vehicle braked to a halt.

He rolled to his knees, went to the window, and saw a Black Maria stopped on the street below. He froze, thinking no, he couldn't go through the house, too much of a chance to get caught in the stairwell, no, he'd go to the window on the other side of the attic, smash it through, and—

The doors of the Black Maria flew open; two men with hats and long coats got out and started running.

Not to Curt's house. To a house across the street.

He took a breath of stale air. Watched it unfold beneath him. The front door of the small house broken open, the men rushing in. Just a few seconds passed and the two Interior Department men emerged, one escorting a handcuffed man, the other leading a handcuffed woman, both prisoners only partially dressed, feet bare. The man's head hung down in despair while the woman was yelling, twisting against her captor's grasp. The pair were dragged across the street, the rear doors of the Black Maria van were opened up, and—

More screams. He bit his lower lip as children ran out of the house in pajamas, two girls and a boy, racing after their mom and dad. Could he get there in time? Could he? The Interior Department men wouldn't expect an ambush, somebody like him emerging from Curt's house, maybe with a hammer or a club. Whacking the shit out of them and then getting those parents free and back to their kids, telling them to run for it, run now...

He shuddered, moved away from the window. Sat on the sleeping bag. Heard the doors to the Black Maria slam shut, the engine start up, and the squeal of tires as it raced away.

No, stay focused. Concentrate. He had to think of the mission, what was ahead of them.

He put his hands against his ears, stared down at the dirty wooden planks beneath him. Oh yeah, stay focused, but that was so hard to do, with those terrified children out there, screaming and sobbing for their disappeared parents.

Maybe he wasn't that tough after all.

CHAPTER FORTY-SEVEN

Water was rushing up his nose, he was drowning, he was being tortured by an SS officer and a Long's Legionnaire, laughing at him, holding him down under the water—

Sam woke up.

He had fallen asleep in the claw-footed tub. The water had long ago gone tepid. He coughed and took a washcloth and ran it across his face, then gently touched his bruises and scrapes and the old blisters on his hands. He felt cold. Up in Burdick, they would be in the cold barracks, hungry, unwashed, shivering, wondering what tomorrow would bring, Jewish prisoners held here in the supposed land of the free—

Sam held up his wrist again. The number three. He was now marked for life.

What kind of life, he didn't know.

The phone rang.

Sarah?

He stumbled out of the tub, counting the rings for the party line—

One long ring followed by three short rings.

The Connors again, just down the street.

It wasn't for him.

Before going to bed, he went back to the living room, saw the little mound of books with their covers torn off. Some of them were from the Book-of-the-Month Club, from a flush time a couple of years back when Sarah could afford the monthly mailings. And there was his Boy Scout handbook, the one he had used to confirm Tony's signals, mutilated.

He flipped through it, seeing the merit badges, his first official fist of accomplishments, of what he had been able to do. He had gotten scores of merit badges on his way to becoming an Eagle Scout. Not like Tony, who had given up after only three. Tony's three versus his own thirty, the number needed to reach that magical pinnacle of Eagle Scout.

He tossed the torn handbook back into the pile. Some accomplishment, some record. Eagle Scout, quarterback, cop, sergeant, probationary inspector, and a freed inmate from a secret concentration camp.

It was time for bed.

In the morning Sam got dressed slowly, ignoring the raw marks on his hands. He thought about Barracks Six, going to work in the icebox confines of the quarry. He was hungry and surprised at how deep he had slept. No nightmares this time, just a sleep so deep that he woke up tired, not refreshed at all. When he was dressed, he did one more thing, as much as it disgusted him: With chilled fingers, he put the Confederate-flag pin on his lapel.

Breakfast. Sam looked around the mess of a kitchen and decided not to stay. This place should be filled with the laughter and smiles of his Sarah and Toby. No, he didn't want to be here. He'd go out and quietly do his work for LaCouture and Groebke, members of governments who could torture, imprison, and kill Jews with all the difficulty of someone buying a newspaper or ordering breakfast.

He went out the front door, didn't even bother locking it behind him, and took two steps before he saw someone was waiting for him.

Hans Groebke, leaning against the fender of Sam's Packard, a paper package at his elbow, on the car's mud-spattered hood.

Sam's first instinct was to charge over and punch out that smug face in a series of hammer blows, but he wondered if he was strong enough. If he wasn't, what then? He started for his revolver, to shoot the Nazi son of a bitch right then and there, but there was something in the man's eyes that stopped him. A look that didn't belong. Sympathy? Concern? What was it?

Groebke straightened, performed his courtly, tiny bow. "*Guten tag,* Inspector Miller."

"What the hell are you doing at my home?"

The Gestapo man said, "Things have changed since you went away. At midnight a new—how you say— *permit process* has been implemented." From his coat pocket, he removed a square of cardboard gilted on the edges. "All vehicles must now have this pass. Without it, you would have not been able to go work for us today, which would be unfortunate."

"How did you get here?"

"Herr LaCouture drove me here on his way to the naval shipyard on some sort of inspection."

"A favor? You're doing this to me as a favor?"

A brief nod. "Something like that, yes."

"Do you know where I've been these past few days?" Groebke studied him for a moment. Then he said, "Against orders from your own boss, you have been investigating the matter of the dead German found by your railroad tracks. You left town as part of this investigation. That's all LaCouture and I know. And eventually, you will be punished for that... oversight."

"Even with that, you want me?"

"Yes, we do. We have come to depend on what you can provide for us."

"That's bullshit," Sam said.

"Excuse? Bull what?"

"Crap, nonsense, that's what I meant. Any cop on the force can do what I'm doing for you. Which is why what you said is crap."

Groebke reached over to the package. "You may call it whatever you like, Herr Miller, but there is work to be done. And here. Some breakfast for you."

Sam took the paper bag, looked into it. A cardboard container of coffee, a plain doughnut. Groebke said, "After being with your police after all this time, I think I know what you like, am I right?"

Sam looked at Groebke, the smooth features, the blue eyes, the blond hair. In his mind's eye, he saw other things. The SS men at the Burdick camp. The newsreels of German troops burning and slashing their way through Europe and Russia. The photos he had seen yesterday of the massacre of the innocents.

Sam dropped the bag at Groebke's feet, the coffee spilling through the brown paper. "You don't know shit."

The scent of Groebke's cologne was strong in the confines of Sam's Packard as he drove to the Rockingham Hotel. Groebke said, "Your punishment—has it begun with your haircut?"

"No," Sam said, holding the steering wheel firmly with both hands, feeling self-conscious for a moment, that his sleeve may slip and reveal the tattoo.

"I see. And why did you get this haircut, then?"

"None of your business." Sam slowed for a checkpoint up ahead. There was a striped wooden barrier across the road, two MPs and a Portsmouth cop he recognized as Steve Josephs, one of the newer guys on the force. The MPs saw the cardboard pass on the dashboard, lifted the barrier, and waved the car through. The streets were nearly deserted.

After a bit, Groebke said, "Such a drive, with not much to say."

A flood of memories started churning through Sam, all tinged with the memory of that sickening fear of being in the camp, of not knowing if he would ever get out, would ever get to see Sarah and Toby again.

Sam said, "There's not much to say to someone like you. The Gestapo. Secret police. Torturers, killers." Groebke scratched at his clean-shaven chin. "Oh, yes. How we're portrayed in the cinema, in books. But we are mostly cops, Herr Miller. Enforcing the laws."

"What do you know about cops?"

"That's what I was years ago," the German said reflectively. "A cop in a Bavarian village, taking complaints, investigating burglaries, part of the *Kriminalpolizei*. That's all I wanted to do, eh? Be a cop. But in 1936 changes came—all of the police forces came under the rule of the state, under Himmler, and the *Kriminalpolizei*, we were absorbed into the Gestapo. That's what happened to me."

"Sounds ordinary. But however you call it, you're still Gestapo."

Groebke said mildly, "Yes, still Gestapo. The stories about torture, killing, it's just a minor part. The rest is police work. Do you understand? Just cops doing the job of their government. It's what I do. It's what you do."

"Sure," Sam said, hearing the bitterness in his voice. "And what about the Jews? Being slaughtered by the tens of thousands, branded, dumped into camps. Is that just a job?"

Another checkpoint, with two cars ahead. Groebke pointed to the left. The city's sole synagogue was there, boarded and shut, covered in posters of President Long. "Your Jews...no longer here, eh? In ghettos in New York, Miami, California. So let us speak of death, then, Sam. Who slaughtered the red Indian last century, who stole their lands and put them on reservations? Who is shooting auto workers in Detroit, fruit pickers in Oregon, strikers in Manhattan, yes? Your own hands, how clean are they, Herr Miller? Did you not participate a few days ago in a... a *cleansing*, is that the word? Of refugees and undesirables? And are these people not on their way to camps because of you? Of your job? Yes?"

The first car moved, then the second. Sam eased the Packard to the checkpoint. Groebke continued, "I do not judge you for what you do. I may judge your government, but not you. We are similar, you and I. Our nations. We each have made empires on the back of other peoples. We each have destinies. Even our symbols are the same. The eagle, yes? And our Führer, he is a great admirer of your industry, so much that his private train, it is called *Amerika*. Amerikan Eagle, both of our nations, so similar."

Sam kept quiet.

"So, our nations—so similar, like you and I. So please extend me some courtesy, *ja?*"

The MP waved them through, and Sam shot forward so fast he almost ran over the man's booted foot.

As Sam and Groebke walked toward the Rockingham Hotel, Groebke lit a cigarette with a gold lighter and said, "You know, I so love your tobacco. You cannot believe what we are forced to smoke back home—street sweepings, leftovers from France and Turkey. It's a good thing our countries will become friends, eh?"

"Don't count on it lasting," Sam said. "Long isn't one to be trusted. Also, we remember what Hitler did with Stalin. Peace treaty in '39, invasion in '41."

"You believe, then, no honor among thieves, eh?"

"Sure seems that way."

Up the granite steps of the hotel, with MPs checking everyone's identification, and as Sam displayed his police ID, he thought of what Groebke had said earlier.

They needed him.

The FBI and the Gestapo.

And the Portsmouth Police Department. His own boss in full-dress uniform as a colonel of the National Guard, had come out—or was he sent?—to retrieve Sam from Burdick.

Why? Why was he needed?

Groebke put his identification away as they went into the crowded lobby. "So it is, eh? Paperwork and records, such is the way we all must operate," he remarked.

Paperwork.

Records.

What had Sean said back at the labor camp?

Everything. They know everything about you, all of your records, everything.

Some records, as he went with Groebke up to the second floor, he was sure his records—

Tony.

What would be in Tony's records?

His arrest, of course, and his time in the illegal union at the shipyard, trying to make it all right after Dad's death, and more, of course. The Gestapo and the FBI, they were relentlessly thorough. He had no doubt that they had pawed through his files all the way back to high school, grammar school, hell, even the Boy Scouts! Tony's three merit badges. Sam remembered each of them, remembered how he had teased Tony about being such a lazy son of a gun, until one night Tony had slugged him in the coal room, where they had gone to get a bucket to keep the furnace going.

First aid. Astronomy.

And the third one, the one Tony had delighted in most, a craft he had continued to enjoy years later and which he still missed. Hell, hadn't Tony even told him so during their last talk?

Sweet Jesus, he thought. Sweet holy Jesus.

"Come," Groebke said, "let's get to work."

He followed the Gestapo man into Suite Twelve. LaCouture sat at the round desk, his feet up, the polished black shoes and white spats looking as if he had just stepped off an MGM soundstage. He was looking at some papers and raised his eyes as they entered. "Glad you could make it, Inspector. Tell me, did you enjoy your time off? I hope so. For Christ's sake, you've gotten us behind. And shit, look at that haircut of yours." He glanced back down at the papers.

Sam walked over to the desk. LaCouture looked up. "Didn't you hear what I said, boy?"

"I did, and I don't particularly care."

"And why's that?"

"Because I'm done here. I'm no longer an errand boy."

LaCouture grinned. "Pretty bold talk for a boy who's been AWOL a few days, comes back with his hair trimmed and bruises on his face. Somethin' bad happen to you, boy? Hmm? You go somewhere you weren't suppose to, got tuned up a bit?"

"None of your business," Sam shot back.

"Everything's my business, Sam. You'd be surprised at what I know. Like where you live. Like that commie ex-college professor illegally livin' at your house. Shame, your house gettin' broke into the other night. Some of Long's Legionnaires, it looks like, figured you were a shithead and decided to pay you a visit. You piss off any Legionnaires lately? Still feel like you're not an errand boy, Inspector?"

"I know why you're here," Sam said. "I also know why I've been picked to work with you."

LaCouture's smile didn't falter. "You do, do you? Why don't you tell us?"

"You're here because of my brother. He's escaped from the Iroquois Labor Camp. You're looking for Tony." There was a brief look between the Gestapo agent and the FBI agent. LaCouture said, "What makes you say that?"

"Because you hammered a file clerk from my police department who knows you were looking at his records. Because you said something about Tony being right from the start. Meaning you were looking at his paper trail from way back when. When he got his merit badge for marksmanship, when he was head of the shooting team in high school. He's good with a rifle, he's been a hunter all his life, and I'm sure you know he's here in Portsmouth, right ahead of the summit."

LaCouture's eyes stayed locked on his. Sam continued, "And here you are. An FBI agent and a Gestapo agent. Why the Gestapo? To protect Hitler, that's why. And you're here to follow me to Tony."

The words scalded Sam's throat, but he said them. "My brother... he's going to assassinate Hitler tomorrow, isn't he?"

LaCouture looked to the Gestapo man, looked to Sam, and then set his papers down and straightened in his chair. "Very good, Inspector. Welcome aboard. You're no longer just an errand boy."

CHAPTER FORTY-EIGHT

Groebke muttered something in German, and LaCouture replied. In English, LaCouture said, "All right, where is he?"

"I don't know."

"But you've seen him."

"Twice since he escaped. Once in a city park and another time at my house."

"Did he say what he was doing here?"

"No, of course not," Sam said. "He said he was just biding his time. Ready to go someplace else once the summit was over and the heat died down."

Groebke spoke up. "You kept this a secret from the authorities? Even though it is a serious offense?"

Sam tried to ignore the Gestapo agent. "He's my brother. What else was I going to do?"

The German persisted. "This brother of yours. He is intent upon killing the most important man the German nation has ever produced, and you chose not to help us?"

Sam said sharply, "Just a few minutes ago, on my own, I determined Tony was here to kill Hitler, genius. If the two of you had let me in on what was going on, maybe I could have helped you. But you decided to keep your secrets. Why's that?"

"Procedures, policies," the FBI man said. "We were told to keep an eye on you, to keep you close, but I guess it's not a secret. Speaking of secrets, why give him up now? Why not keep it to yourself?"

"Because I've seen what's out there. All those cops, National Guardsmen, Interior Department goons—I don't want him killed on some stupid suicide mission."

"Aren't you being the good brother." LaCouture said. It wasn't a question.

Sam ignored his condescension. "Whatever you say. But an assassination? Who's behind it?"

Groebke said something quick in German and LaCouture listened, cocked his head for a moment, then told Sam, "A variety of troublemakers, we're sure. Communists, either homegrown American Reds or NKVD agents sent here from the Soviet Union. It's impossible to get at Hitler on his home turf. Many have tried, and all have failed. But in the States, it's easy for someone to blend into a crowd. So probably the Russians. But maybe the Jews. Or the Brits, French, Poles... Christ, the guy's pissed off enough people, could be any of the above!"

"And my brother?"

"An ideal choice," LaCouture said, and once the FBI man started talking, Sam knew with a sick feeling how right he was. "A good hunter. A union organizer in jail for opposing the government. Someone whose hatred of Hitler and the quote, oppressors, unquote, is well known. And someone who knows Portsmouth like the back of his hand. An ideal combination, wouldn't you agree?"

Sam could only nod. LaCouture said, "We have no doubt someone helped get him out of Fort Drum. There's been an FBI squad up there for weeks, interrogating prisoners. And he had help getting to Portsmouth. We know there's a conspiracy, we know who the shooter is, and we know the target. Now we must stop it."

LaCouture picked up his cup of coffee. "Your little city and the Navy Yard are now the most tightly controlled and secure area in North America. In addition to your fine police force"—LaCouture's voice dripped with sarcasm—"we have the New Hampshire State Police, the Maine State Police, the FBI, the Secret Service, the Department of Interior, the navy, and oh, yes, a contingent of marines from the Navy Yard. Not to mention the Gestapo, the SS, the SD, the RSHA, and all those other German-alphabet security forces. All of them here to protect President Long and Chancellor Hitler. There's no way your brother will get close enough to do any harm. Not in a million years. However..."

Groebke leaned forward and spoke again in German, but LaCouture ignored him. "However, this is still a delicate time, having the summit in Portsmouth. Besides your nutball brother, we have Jews, Communists, labor leaders, the press, and every asshole that thinks he has a grudge against Long or the Nazis planning to be here. Fine."

LaCouture put his cup down, clattering it in the saucer. "But what's not fine is your brother, who knows this city backward and forward, making trouble and bad press. Trust me, Inspector, the President knows exactly what kind of press he wants for these next couple days. He wants a new era of peace and understanding between the Long administration and the Third Reich. He wants trade agreements that put millions of Americans back to work. And if it helps crush the Bolsheviks, than that's just a nice bit of extra credit, isn't it?"

"I see," Sam said, looking to Groebke. "First killing the Jews, then killing the Bolshies. Some credit."

Groebke smiled. "Nobody cares. That's what I read in your newspapers, hear on your radio broadcasts. It's Europe's business, not yours. We can do anything we want and the world doesn't give a shit. Except the Reds."

LaCouture frowned, "You're off point, Inspector. I agree with Hans. Europeans have been slaughtering each other in creative ways for thousands of years. Why should we care how they're doing it this year? We care about *us*. All the closed banks and businesses, all those damn hobo camps. With a few signatures and a trade agreement, all that's gonna change. You and me and Hans here, along with everybody else guarding this town, are going to make sure your brother doesn't fuck that up. Got it?"

Sam said, "Yeah, I got it. But one condition." LaCouture crossed his legs. "Not sure if you're in a position to ask for conditions, but go ahead. Amuse me."

Sam knew it was a long shot, but still he had to say it. "I don't want Tony hurt or killed. Just pick him up and bring him back to the labor camp. Let him serve out his sentence."

LaCouture laughed. "That was two conditions."

"One condition, two conditions, I don't care," Sam said. "That's what I want. Nothing bad to happen to Tony."

LaCouture said. "Interesting offer. Here's my counteroffer." From the paperwork on his desk, he pulled out an envelope. He slid out a black-and-white photograph and tossed it over. "Take a look. Even though it is a government photo, you can see the faces pretty well."

From the time he reached over to the photo, Sam could sense it all go wrong in an instant, like riding alone on a snowy night and feeling the Packard's wheels slip on the ice and snow.

The photograph showed Sarah standing with her arm across Toby's shoulders, pulling him tight to her. Her face was almost empty of emotion, gaunt with some terrible burden. Toby's head was buried in her waist, as though he were hiding from the bogeyman.

On either side of them were frowning National Guardsmen. All four figures were standing by a gate. It shouldn't be familiar, but it was. The photo blurred then, as his eyes stung with tears.

His wife and son were at the Camp Carpenter Labor Camp.

CHAPTER FORTY-NINE

LaCouture's smile was sharp, as if he were a happy predator facing a bleeding and three-legged prey. "So here's the deal. Nonnegotiable, of course, since I hold all the cards, from the deuce to the ace of spades. We're looking for your shithead brother. So far we've come up with squat. And you're going to help us find him."

"Why... why are Sarah and Toby there?"

"In federal custody pending the outcome of an investigation."

"They didn't do anything!"

"They never do, do they?"

Sam's hands started shaking. He put them in his lap to hold them still and out of sight. The FBI agent went on. "This is the deal. You find your brother. That is your sole job. Nothing else matters. How your son and wife are handled, how much food they get, how your wife is... treated all depends on you."

Sam said hoarsely, "How long are they going to be kept there?"

LaCouture shrugged. "Up to you, boy, ain't it."

"And Tony..." Sam felt like the room was slowly closing in on him.

"If you can get him to us with no fuss or muss, he'll be on his way back to Fort Drum with a few more years tacked on. I've looked at his file, and a few more years won't make much difference. Hell, with your new haircut, you even look like the traitor. But I'll tell you this, Inspector Miller, if there's any problem at all, any problem whatsoever, we're not playing around. We're here to protect Hitler, protect this summit. If we have to cut down your brother to do that, then we will."

Groebke shifted in his chair, said something in German. LaCouture replied in German. Then in English he said, "Enough chitchat. So. What's it going to be, Inspector?"

"Like you said, you've got all the cards, Agent." LaCouture grinned. "Then let's get to work." From his sheaf of papers, he tossed over a gilt-edged cardboard pass. "Temporary pass for the next two days allows you entry through all checkpoints. Better than the one Hans gave you this morning. This pass gets you through checkpoints controlled by our German friends, even in the

Navy Yard, where our esteemed leaders will be meeting tomorrow."

Sam picked up the pass. "All right. But one more thing. I get Tony to you, you get my wife and son out of that labor camp. If they're hurt in any way, I'll kill you, LaCouture. You hear me?"

"That's threatening a federal officer. You be careful."

"No," Sam said, his voice low. "*You* be careful."

There was silence, and then LaCouture, his face reddened, said, "Get the fuck out and go find your bastard brother."

At his desk, Sam went through a small pile of phone messages and dumped them all in the trash. There was also a note from an Englishwoman who wanted to make ah appointment to help find her lost husband. That note went into the trash, too. He had to find Tony. A scent of lilac overpowered him. Mrs. Walton was there, frowning. "Here," she said, holding out another slip of paper. "Will you please call him back?"

"Who?"

She slapped the message on his desk. "Dr. Saunders. He's called three times for you since you went on your... investigation." She stomped back to her desk, started typing away, attacking the keys as if their very presence insulted her.

Sam looked at the message, written in Mrs. Walton's precise handwriting: *3rd call from Dr. Saunders re: your John Doe case.*

He stared at the slip of paper, and what he saw was a photograph of Sarah and Toby stranded at Camp Carpenter. He noticed Mrs. Walton looking over at him, her thin hands poised over the keyboard. He crumpled up the note and tossed it in the trash. "Mrs. Walton?"

"What?" she snapped.

"If Dr. Saunders calls again, tell him I'm out of the office. Forever."

She scowled. "I can't tell him that."

"Oh. Okay. Tell him this: I'm the fuck out of the office. Forever. Got that?"

Mrs. Walton returned to pounding the keyboard, but the back of her neck was scarlet.

He rubbed his head, feeling the unfamiliar bristle. The door to Marshal

Hanson's office was closed, but he could hear voices inside. He thought about going in there, pleading his case, but no. Wouldn't work. It was all his now, and he had only one thing to do, to be a good investigator, be a good Party member, and find his brother. Find Tony.

The phone rang. "Miller. Investigations."

"Inspector Miller? Sam Miller?"

"That's right." He couldn't identify the male voice. "This is Sergeant Tom Callaghan from the Dover Police Department. I'm conducting an investigation, was looking for your help."

Sam rubbed at his eyes. Dover was the next city up from Portsmouth, whose school his team had defeated in the state championship so many centuries ago. The two cities had always had a friendly rivalry, especially since that city was known for its leather and shoe mills. One of the sayings from when he was a kid: "Portsmouth by the sea, Dover by the smell."

"Yeah, sure, Sergeant, what is it?"

"We pulled a body out of the Bellamy River yesterday. Hobo, no identification or anything. Except one thing: He had your business card stuck in a pocket. It was pretty soaked through but legible enough."

Sam stopped rubbing his eyes. The sergeant went on, "So we were hoping maybe you know this guy, can give us a lead on him, how he ended up here."

Lou Purdue, he thought. Lou from. Troy.

"Inspector?"

"Yeah, right here."

"Can you help us?"

Sam looked at the door to the marshal's office. Saw lots of other things as well. Sarah and Toby at the labor camp. The secret camp at Burdick. Promises and threats made by his boss here, and his other boss, the one at the Rockingham Hotel.

"No," he said. "No, I can't help you. Sorry. My card gets passed around a lot, and I don't remember giving it to some hobo."

He could hear the sergeant sigh. "Too bad. You see, the guy drowned, but we're pretty sure it was foul play. The guy's fingers were broken. Like he had a secret and somebody wanted him to talk."

Sure, Sam thought. *The ones behind Petr Wowenstein's murder.* Eliminating a witness to the death of that mysterious, well-dressed man standing by the Fish Shanty that rainy night.

"Sorry, Sergeant," he said. "I wish I could help you. Good luck."

He hung up, sick at what he had done, what he had to do. He got up and left.

Several hours later, stomach growling and feet hurting, he took a break for lunch at a restaurant by the harbor called, in someone's fit of imagination, the Harborview. The place was packed with reporters, government officials, shipyard personnel, and military officers, but his identification got him a small table in the corner that was probably used for piling up dirty dishes but on this day was being used to squeeze every dime and dollar from the visitors crowding Portsmouth. As he took his seat, he tried to keep focused on the task at hand and not think of a drowned and tortured Lou Purdue, killed because of one of the oldest stories, seeing something he shouldn't have seen.

Sam ordered his lunch from a waitress who seemed to chew gum in time with writing down his order; the girl's young face reminded him of another waitress, his friend Donna Fitzgerald. He hoped she and Larry were keeping low during this circus. For some reason, thinking of that sweet, innocent smile cheered him for a moment. To have a life and love so simple... He looked around at the customers. So many new faces in his little city since that damn summit was announced. He recognized a newsreel reporter, a couple of U.S. senators, and by the windows overlooking the harbor, a cluster of German *Wehrmacht* officers, their boots polished, eating and apparently enjoying the view of the Navy Yard.

He wondered what the Germans were thinking. In just under four years, they and their comrades had turned the world upside down. All of Western Europe flew their flag, and their armies patrolled from the Arctic Circle to the Mediterranean. In the Atlantic Ocean, U-boats still prowled, as did other warships of the *Kriegsmarine,* while the U.S. Navy tried to maintain some sort of presence. But the Germans—hell, they had even set up a tiny base in a couple of French-owned fishing islands up near Quebec, and they had bases in the Caribbean, in Martinique and Aruba and the British Virgin Isles.

They were in other places as well, in Burdick and other secret camps, helping the Americans with their knowledge of imprisoning, torturing, and exploiting the Jews. A secret deal that was to benefit both countries: one dumping the enemies of their state to a faraway land, said faraway land making a tidy profit from their slave labor. Fascist Germany and fascist America, soon becoming twins themselves, while nearly nothing stood in their way.

Except for Russia. Russia was still hanging on, not buckling under, not giving up.

As for giving up, he'd almost done so it a couple of times today. The whole of Portsmouth had changed, had locked down to a place he barely recognized. Every few city blocks, there were barriers manned by National Guard troops, accompanied by men in suits who were FBI, Department of the Interior, German security. Squads of Long's Legionnaires slapped up posters with Long's toothy grin and unruly shock of hair. Sam had begun by checking out the tallest structures in Portsmouth— where better to station a marksman like Tony?—but every building in the city had a security contingent at the door.

Every building!

Even with his own set of passes, he had been scrutinized as he went into the warehouses down by the harbor, just to see how tight the security was, and at the top of each roof, he found U.S. Marines from the barracks at the Navy Yard, keeping watch with binoculars and communicating with one another through handheld radios.

Just walking from block to block, he'd been stopped three times by roaming patrols of National Guardsmen and Interior Department officers, and it was only thanks to his own identification that he wasn't extensively questioned.

Once he had seen a couple of Long's Legionnaires arguing with a man in a doorway, poking at him with their fingers, and he had recognized the cowering figure as Clarence Rolston, the police department's janitor. The Legionnaires had left him alone when Sam had produced his identification, and Sam had told a weepy Clarence, "Better stay inside for the next couple of days until this clears up."

The janitor had wiped his dripping nose with his hand, complaining, "It's not fair, Sam, not fair... I just wanted to get some chocolate milk. That's all. It's not fair." Then he had gone back into his walk-up apartment, blowing his nose in a handkerchief.

Sam's fried-shrimp lunch arrived, and he picked up a fork and dug in. As he started to eat, his left sleeve slid back, revealing the fresh blue numeral three. He pushed the sleeve back and ate his lunch quickly, with no real appetite, wondering what Sarah and Toby were eating, what his former bunkmates were eating, while he dined in a restaurant.

Where to find Tony?

He looked out the window at the narrow expanse of river and Portsmouth Harbor and, across the way, at the shipyard, the place where Tony had once worked.

The Navy Yard.

Where Tony had once worked. Where Tony gotten arrested for his union organizing.

The Navy Yard—not the city.

He threw down a dollar bill and ran out of the restaurant.

CHAPTER FIFTY

He retrieved his Packard and drove out to the Memorial Bridge, a drawbridge connecting New Hampshire to Maine that spanned the fast-moving Piscataqua River. The bridge had been built to honor Great War veterans, no doubt including poor old dead Dad. The drive across usually took under five minutes; today it was nearly an hour, and as Sam crawled across the bridge in heavy traffic, he saw marines and armed sailors standing along the bridge, one every six feet or so. Hanging from the bridge were American and Nazi flags, secured on both ends, flapping in the breeze. He wondered what his bunkmates back at Barracks Six would think, seeing a Nazi flag honored in America.

On entering the state of Maine, he turned onto Route 1 and made his way to the main gate of the Portsmouth Navy Yard, built on an island in the center of the river. The island was claimed by both his home state and

Maine. A marine guard in formal dress khakis halted him at the entrance, glared at his identification collection— his inspector's badge, his National Guard commission, the business card from Special Agent LaCouture, and the gilt- edged pass he had just received—said, "Who are you seeing, sir?"

"Twombly. Head of security."

The guard checked his clipboard. "Sir, you're not on today's list for visitors."

"I know," Sam replied. "But this is time-critical. I have to see Twombly concerning the summit."

The marine's face was young, and pale under his uniform cap. "Very well. Pull over to the side, sir, and please wait inside the car."

Sam did as he was told, leaving the engine running. About him were the brick buildings of the administration and engineering and design offices of the shipyard, and beyond, he could make out cranes and temporary scaffolding. Men passed him wearing identification badges on their dungaree jackets, carrying lunch pails, wearing hard hats. There were piles of wooden beams, steel plates, rust-red chunks of metal. He tapped the steering wheel. This was where his father had worked out his life after serving in the Great War, and this was where Tony had gone and had... well, had gone where? Had entered the twilight world of union organizing at a time when unions were slowly being squeezed to death. Tony. Arrogant, pushy, self-righteous Tony. Seeing Dad cough himself to death, the doctor at the Yard not doing a thing to help him, and Tony seeking to avenge what had happened, now seeking to do so much more.

The marine guard strolled over, still carrying his clipboard. Sam rolled down his window. "You're cleared to see Mr. Twombly," the marine said. "Do you know where his office is?"

"Yes, I've been there before."

"Very good, sir. Please take a direct route to his office. He's expecting you."

Sam put the car into drive and headed into the shipyard.

The security office was in a row of brick buildings. Sam pulled in to a parking spot, and when he got out, he saw Nate Twombly standing in the doorway. He had encountered Twombly a half dozen times over the years for a variety of minor criminal matters involving shipyard workers.

Twombly ambled over, smoking a cigarette. He was just over six feet tall, his black hair shot through with gray, hollow-eyed and thin, as though he had just come out of the hospital after a month long liquid diet. "Inspector Miller. This better be good. Haven't had a good night's sleep in... shit, I can't remember."

Sam passed over the business card from LaCouture, and Twombly glanced at it, then passed it back. "Poor bastard. Working for Hoover's boys, huh?"

"Looks that way."

Twombly eyed his coat, spotted the flag pin. "See you're now part of the true believers, eh?"

"Just trying to get along." It hurt to admit it.

"Yeah," Twombly agreed. "Ain't we all. So, what's up? And please don't waste what I don't got enough of. Time."

"My brother—"

Twombly took a drag of his cigarette. "Tony Miller. Sure. Departed our fair shores a few years back for unauthorized union organizing here."

282

"Is there any authorized union organizing?"

Twombly gave him a pinched smile. "Don't ask dumb questions. Why are you here about Tony?"

"He's escaped from the labor camp at Fort Drum. He's been spotted in Portsmouth at least twice."

Somewhere, a series of horns blasted out a long tempo, echoing among the buildings. Twombly sighed. "And you think he might be back here on his old stomping grounds, with his working-class buddies?"

"That was the general thought."

Twombly laughed bleakly, reached into his pocket, pulled out a leaflet. He passed it over, and Sam unfolded it. Looking up from an old photo was Tony. The message printed under the photo said Tony was to be refused admittance to the Yard, and if he was spotted, to contact security at once.

"About a couple thousand of these have been printed up and passed around. Workers, administrative staff, naval officers, even the marines—every one of them has gotten this leaflet. Each guard station has it posted, too."

"Impressive." Sam passed the leaflet back. "When did you get word he was an escapee?"

"Two days ago. Like I need one more goddamn headache to worry about."

"Still—"

"Yeah, I know what you're thinking. Maybe he got smuggled by a sympathetic coworker. You can forget that crap. When your brother was sent up to Fort Drum, about a dozen other guys were fired and blacklisted. No offense, but if your brother shows up at the Yard, he should wish I get to him first. Come on, let's go for a walk."

Sam walked with Twombly while the security man started talking randomly, as though he needed a sympathetic ear. "Heard somewhere that summits like these, big-time meetings, usually take weeks or months to put together. And us lucky bastards got just under a week to put something together involving the goddamn President of the United States and Herr Hitler himself. Up there, see that building?"

The three-story brick structure ahead looked like an elementary school. Twombly gestured to it with his burning cigarette. "That's where it all happened back in 1905. Russians and Japanese did their thing here, with Teddy Roosevelt leading the negotiations. Building Eighty-six, the administration building. That's how TR got his Nobel Peace Prize the next year, for ending that war. Lucky for him, there's no process for revoking a peace prize. Seeing how the Russians and the Japs are both busily butchering thousands on a monthly basis."

In front of that building, Sam saw his first German flag on shipyard soil. Something inside of him chilled, seeing the swastika flapping in the breeze on an American military base.

"That's where they'll be tomorrow afternoon," Twombly continued. "Long and Hitler. See by the door? That's a plaque, commemorating Roosevelt's peace treaty. Think they'll put up another plaque when those two clowns finish their bloody job?"

Sam said, "No, not really."

"Yeah, that's a vote of confidence if I ever heard one." Two marines guarded the entrance. They looked ashamed to be standing underneath the flapping swastika.

"Come with me," Twombly said, leading Sam into another, taller, brick building. Twombly shut the sliding metal door, and the open-grill elevator made a rattling, hollow noise as it ascended four stories. At the darkened top floor, Twombly opened another door, and they went outside to a tar-covered roof.

A squad of armed marines stood in one corner, dressed in dungarees and fatigues. Their squad leader looked over at Twombly, and Twombly waved a greeting, took Sam to the edge of the roof.

From there, they had an expansive view of the shipyard, river, harbor, and Portsmouth itself. Off to the east, where the river widened, were the dark gray smudge of the Atlantic Ocean and the island community of New Castle. Before them were the cranes and docks and scaffolding, and Sam could make out the hulls of two submarines under construction. Nearby were the massive concrete and turrets of the Portsmouth Naval Prison, and there, across the river, rising above it all were the brick buildings of Portsmouth and the North Church spire.

"That's the way it is," Twombly told him. "Marines on every roof, observing everything coming and going. More marines and shore patrol in the buildings and on the grounds. It's the same over in Portsmouth. In a few hours, the day shift ends and the second shift is canceled. Only security and summit personnel will remain behind. Trust me, Inspector. Your brother may be somewhere around here. But he's not in my Yard."

It was cool up on the roof, a strong salt-tinged breeze coming in from the ocean. Twombly said, "Hold on a sec. Going to borrow something from these leathernecks."

He walked over to the marines and returned carrying a pair of high-powered binoculars. He brought the binoculars up and, after a few seconds, said, "Ah, there you are, you little bastard. Here, take a look. Out by the horizon, to the north of the main harbor entrance buoy." Sam took the binoculars. A passenger liner came into focus, at anchor by the shoals just outside of the harbor. From the stern, a large Nazi flag moved in the breeze. There were other ships out there, cruisers and battleships, off in the hazy distance.

"There he is," Twombly said. "Herr Hitler and his task force. The liner *Europa* and accompanying warships, including the *Tirpitz* and the *Bismarck*. Resting for the night...and tomorrow he and the President meet. See that dock down there with the bunting and the flags? That's where the motor launch is going to bring Hitler in. Fact is, I just heard Long might be coming into Portsmouth within the hour. Hell of a thing, don't you think? All this history happening in our fair little city and shipyard."

Sam kept the binoculars up to his eyes. From here, it seemed so peaceful, so innocuous. A passenger liner at rest just outside the harbor of his hometown. A passenger liner that held one of the most powerful and most hated men on the globe, a man Sam's brother was here to kill. And to save his own family, he had to save Hitler. "Penny for your thoughts," Twombly said.

Sam lowered the binoculars. "Wish the goddamn ship would weigh anchor and head back to Germany. Tonight, if possible. Would make a lot of things easier for me."

"Nice thought," Twombly said. "I wish you luck finding your brother. But I don't think you're going to find him here."

"Probably not, but thanks anyway, Nate."

"Sure," Twombly said. He took the binoculars back and raised them again. Sam wasn't sure, but it seemed as if the security chief sighed. "I do hope you find Tony. And that it all works out. Ever hear about my brother Carl?"

"No, can't say that I have."

"Carl was a couple of years younger than me. With youth comes ignorance, and with youth also comes passion. So when Germany invaded France and the Low Countries back in 1940, Carl went up to Canada and enlisted. Thought it was important to help England stand up against the Nazis. Lots of people thought like he did, but others, like me, thought we should stay out of it. Why was it our fight? Right?"

"Yeah, I know." Sam's wrist with the tattoo itched. He left it alone.

"Carl was with the RAF. Flew a Hawker Hurricane fighter plane against the bombers burning London to the ground. Nabbed a Heinkel bomber during one of his missions. And during the first landings, he was shot out of the air. A couple of Messerschmitts blew him up. Exploded in midair. No parachute. No chance of survival. So my little brother turned into burnt chunks of meat over the English Channel."

Now the binoculars came down; his voice turned bleak. "You said you wished the *Europa* would weigh anchor and go back to Germany. You know what I wish, Sam? I wish one of our submarines down there would go out tonight for sea trials and fire four torpedoes into the *Europa's* belly and send all those miserable bastards to hell. That's what I wish."

Sam kept silent, and Twombly shook his head and smiled ruefully. "That's what I wish—and what's my job? To make sure the Kraut bastard out on that boat gets here and leaves here safely and in comfort. Hell of a thing, isn't it?"

"Yeah, a hell of a thing," Sam agreed.

CHAPTER FIFTY-ONE

Back in Portsmouth, Sam parked his car at the police station and started walking downtown. Block after block, building after building, he looked at the doorway to each structure, seeing National Guardsmen or Portsmouth police officers or even state police officers standing guard. Tony. Where would he be?

One of these buildings? Doubtful, with all the security. And the shipyard was out.

He smelled coal smoke. He was approaching the Portsmouth rail station. More people were about him, a mix of residents and police and Guardsmen and reporters and military from both the United States and Germany, some Long's Legionnaires scattered through. He could hear a brass band playing a tune.

The President was arriving.

He let the crowd move him forward to the train station. At a lamppost he stopped, arm wrapped around the

metal to prevent him from going farther. Before him was the station, and to the left, a parking lot had been cleared. A new wooden platform, set with bunting and flags, had been raised there. At least there were no Nazi banners. A band was playing a Sousa march, and from his vantage point, he could make out the khaki uniforms of National Guardsmen and upheld rifles with bayonets attached. An honor guard, though he didn't see any honor out there.

Up on the platform, men were starting to appear, including a line of the Kingfish's good ol' Legionnaires. He hoped a couple of them still had bruises from the whomping he had given them the other night. Even at this distance, he could make out his father-in-law, fresh from his furniture store, and it was good the bastard was up there. How to explain to him what had happened to his daughter and grandson? The thought made him physically ill.

There was the deep whistle of a train. The whistle sounded twice more, and then, coming down the tracks, belching smoke and steam, rumbled the *Ferdinand Magellan,* the official train of the President of the United States. The train ground to a halt in a storm of steam, and another Sousa march started up. There were cheers and shouts and waves, and he looked around at his fellow citizens and thought, *Don't you see it? Don't you see what has come to us?* There was no difference between this man here and that man out on his ocean liner. Both crushed and imprisoned their opponents, both had bloody hands, both did what they wanted. Both had Jews behind barbed-wire fences.

Didn't these people see that?

There. Men filed off the train, and there was the familiar roly-poly figure with its florid face and shock of hair. President Huey P Long, the mightiest Kingfish in the world. When he raised both arms in greeting, the crowd roared.

No, Sam thought. *What they see is what they desire most.* Jobs, safety, and a way of keeping the bloody fields of death out there on the opposite side of the oceans. Just end this damn Depression, get people back to work, stay out of war, and right now, President Long was promising that.

His father-in-law, Lawrence, came up to a microphone and said a number of words, most of them drowned by feedback and over amplification, and then he shook the hand of Long, and the President came to the microphone as though chatting with an old pal.

"My friends, my very dear friends," he said in his rich gumbo-flavored voice, "I'm so very happy to receive this warm reception, even if you are a bunch of Yankees."

There was laughter and more applause. The President started talking in his seductive voice, but the words had a sour sound. More blather about the Rockefellers, the Mellons, the Carnegies, the moneyed interests he had fought ever since Winn Parish in Louisiana, and how the rich parasites had tried to sabotage him in all his years, in all he wanted to do, merely to serve the people.

More blather. Sam forced his way back out of the crowd.

He made his way back to the center of the city, the sidewalks emptying as he got away from the train station. He was there as the President went by.

First were the sirens, and then a brace of New Hampshire State Police motorcycles came roaring up, followed by three convertible black Ford sedans, the tops rolled back. It looked like staff or newsmen were in the lead and following cars, for President Long was in the center car, waving to the few people on the sidewalk, and Secret Service agents were on the running boards, two of them holding submachine guns. Taking up the rear were two more state police motorcycles. The sound quickly rolled on, dust and newspaper scraps spun up by the speeding vehicles.

Sam reached the police station, looked up at the old building, and realized there was nothing there for him. He went to his Packard, started it, and went back to the Rockingham Hotel.

LaCouture looked as though he were being held together by coffee and cigarettes. His usual dapper style had left him; his clothes were rumpled and stained. Even Groebke looked exhausted. There was none of the manly banter or ballbusting or usual bullshit. LaCouture just looked up from his eternal paperwork and said, "Well?"

"Nothing," Sam answered. "This place is so tightly sealed, I can't see him gaining access anywhere to make a shot. I even went over to the Navy Yard. If anything, it's tighter over there."

"Friends? Acquaintances?"

"None. Tony pretty much kept to himself. And the Yard security chief said Tony's not popular with most of the workforce. I just don't know—"

Groebke said, "You wouldn't be protecting him, eh, so that he could shoot our chancellor?"

"No, not a chance," Sam said, his voice biting. "Getting him gets my family free, and if that's what it takes, that's what's going to happen."

Groebke's pale eyes stayed on him. "Still, I know how you hate my country, hate my leader. I believe you would not mind seeing the Fuhrer get shot tomorrow, even if it means your wife and son remain in prison. Perhaps such an exchange, a trade, would be worth it. Eh?"

"You're right," Sam said, keeping his voice under control with difficulty. "I wouldn't mind seeing your Fuhrer shot tomorrow. Or stabbed. Or drowned. But I'm a cop, a cop assigned to you characters, and I'll do my job. Protecting Hitler, finding my brother, and getting my family free."

LaCouture yawned, waved a hand. "Go on. Go home or go out on the streets again, but get out of here."

"That's fine," Sam said. "What about tomorrow?"

"Come back at eight. We'll figure something out then." Sam stood there, tired and soiled, and he said, "My wife and boy. I want to talk to them. Now."

LaCouture shook his head. "Can't do it."

"Why the hell not?"

"Because I don't want to, all right? Because it doesn't suit me. Because I've got dozens of things to do before I get to bed tonight, and worrying about your family is not on that fucking list. What's top on that list is finding your criminal brother, so I suggest you get your ass out of here and find him if you want your wife and son out of that camp. Bad enough what can happen to a woman in one of those camps. I've heard stories about young boys and—"

Only Groebke leaping up and grabbing his arms prevented Sam, in a white-hot fury, from leaping onto the FBI agent. LaCouture kicked back his chair and stood up, nostrils flaring, and said, "That's right, son, you hit me and that might feel right, but your family will still be in that camp. I got the fucking lock that keeps 'em there, and your brother is the key. So find that key. Don't come beatin' up on me; that won't serve you none."

Sam broke free from Groebke's grasp. "You better pray they're okay. You got that, Jack?"

"I stopped prayin' to God above the day I got into the FBI, 'cause my savior then was the Kingfish, who got me there. Get out, Sam. I don't have time for you bullshit."

Outside, Sam was still shaking with anger. He strode over to the Packard and got in and slammed the door. He lowered his head, thinking about Sarah, frightened, imprisoned ... And poor Toby. Sam's heart ached so hard he was dizzy, thinking about his boy there, away from his home, his bedroom, his radio, his models.

He stared blankly out through the dirty windshield. All the models broken, shattered, by those thugs of Long's, breaking into his home without worry or legal warrant. The bastards.

He knew he should keep on looking for his brother, but for Christ's sake it was dark, and what could he do? Just flail around from one well-guarded building to another, going through checkpoints, hopefully not get shot by some trigger-happy National Guardsmen. And going home to that violated place, no, that wasn't an option. He put the Packard into drive and edged himself out on the streets, drowning in his troubles.

And then it came to him.

Where did he and Tony always go when they got into trouble?

That little island in the harbor. Pierce Island.

He was surprised to see two cars parked at the far side of the island's dirt parking lot. It looked like more people than he thought had those prized windshield passes. He got out and took his flashlight, played it around the interiors of both cars. One was empty. In the other was a man and woman in the backseat, so busy that they didn't even notice Sam's presence.

He scanned the lot. Called out, "Tony? You out here?"

He moved down the path, the flashlight beam slicing a wide area ahead of him, and then—

A noise. He whipped to his left, let his light play out.

A man stood there, trying to move away.

"Freeze! Portsmouth police! Don't move!"

He drew his revolver, held the flashlight out, saw a man standing there, his back to him.

Another man scrambled to his feet before the first man, holding a hand up to his face to block the fight. He wore the dress blues of a sailor. "Hey, pal, get the fight outta my face, will ya?" came the sheepish voice, with a thick New York accent.

Sam saw the other man adjust his pants and shook his head at what he had just interrupted. He lowered the fight. "All right, sailor, beat it."

"Uh..." The sailor backed away, "Not sure how to get back. This fella gave me a ride."

"Oh, Christ, the both of you just beat it. You, turn around."

Now something was familiar, something was wrong, for he knew this man, knew him very well.

The mayor of Portsmouth, his father-in-law, the honorable Lawrence Young. With his pants around his knees.

"Sam." His head was tilted so he wasn't looking at the man who had married his daughter.

"Pull your pants up, all right?"

Lawrence bent over, yanked up his trousers, drew the zipper up, and fastened the belt. "Look, this isn't what you—"

"Larry, you never gave a damn what I've thought, so why start now?"

"It's just the pressure, you know? The summit and the President coming and— Just a onetime thing, that's all. Something to take the pressure off."

Sam edged the flashlight beam back up to his father- in-law's face, knowing he couldn't tell the bastard anything about Sarah and his grandson, for LaCouture had made it clear: Only by getting Tony would they get out of Camp Carpenter. Bringing in Lawrence... Christ, who knew how that could complicate things? But there was something else that had to be said.

"Larry, you ever hear of a street over in Kittery called Admiral's Way?"

"Perhaps... I'm not sure... Why?"

"Cut the crap. Some months ago I went along with some Maine state troopers and Kittery cops on a raid at a whorehouse on Admiral Way. Nice, quiet Victorian house. I was just observing, but you know what? Something I observed was you coming out in handcuffs. How the hell did you think you got freed that night? Because of your voting record? No, I asked a favor from one of the Kittery cops. So he went over and uncuffed you."

Lawrence's face was ghostly white, and he was trembling. Sam added, "Oh, and another thing I observed was the staff of that particular whorehouse. Young boys dressed as girls." His father-in-law rubbed a hand across his face as if hiding his eyes. "So don't tell me lies, okay?" Sam said.

"Look, can I get the hell out of here?" Lawrence's voice was raspy.

"Yeah, you can go. And you know what? Don't come back. Ever. I never want to see you at my house."

"Why? Because you know one of my dark, deep secrets? Is that it? You too good to have secrets you're not proud of, Sam?"

Sam clenched the flashlight tighter. "Go. Get out of here."

"Some inspector. You think you know everything about me, everything about how I think and work. Kid, you know shit—"

Lawrence pushed past him, heading back to the parking lot, and Sam spent a fruitless hour longer on the dark island, looking for his brother.

INTERLUDE IX

He waited outside the Laughing Gull, one of the many bars near the harbor. The windows were blackened, and the wooden sign dangling outside was cracked and faded. Even with the summit crackdown, business was doing all right at this bar and its neighbors. Every time some cops or guys in good suits strolled by, he made sure to stay in the shadows. He waited, watching, in the spill of loud jazz music, the smell of beer and cigarettes and cigars. Sailors in dress whites came stumbling down the cobblestone lane, and when the laughing and singing group of men passed on, a man was standing at the street corner. He watched as the man took a cigarette out and tried to light it three times with a lighter that didn't catch.

He walked across the street, offered him a book of matches. The man looked at him and said, "Thanks, mate." His accent was English.

"You're welcome," he said. "That a Lucky Strike?"

"Nope, a Camel."

"I see."

The man lit the cigarette, gave him back the matches, took a drag, then dropped the lit butt on the ground. "C'mon, let's talk private, all right?"

He followed as the man walked around the comer into another alley that stank of trash and piss. The Englishman said, "Not much time, so here it goes. Tomorrow's the day."

"I figured," he said. The words seemed as heavy as stones coming out of his mouth.

"Good on you," the man said. "But there's been a change for tomorrow."

The whole damn street seemed to tip on its side, making him feel like he was going to fall over. "What kind of change?"

"Target change."

"The fuck you say."

"Bloody hell, mate, I'm just the messenger, all right? All I know is, it's got to be done, and I got to know, are you going to do what you're told? Because that's the deal you signed on for, right?"

He clenched his fists tight, then thought for a moment and said, "Yeah. That's the deal I signed on for. You're right. So what's the change?"

The Englishman said, "We go for a walk. We see someone. You get told there. All right?"

He thought again of everything he had planned, everything he had gone through to reach this point, to hear it was all being altered.

"All right," he said. "As long as what I'm doing tomorrow is not a waste."

The other man chuckled. "Oh, it might be something, but it won't be a waste. I got something going on as well... and I can't say more than that. Another thing— your brother."

"What about him?"

"You'll be briefed about him and everything else, just so you're not surprised."

"Thanks for the heads-up," he said, thinking, *Sam, poor Sam,* being part of something he knew nothing about.

The Englishman said, "C'mon, we've got to get moving. Look, can I borrow those matches again?"

"Sure," he said, passing over the pack. The man lit a match, let it flare up in the darkness, then dropped it. "What the—"

Suddenly, it all made sense. "A signal?"

"Yes, indeed."

"And if you hadn't lit the match?"

"That meant you didn't agree with the target change." The Englishman sounded apologetic. "And it meant that some nasty gentlemen watching from the other side of the lane here wouldn't have let you live."

"I see," he said. "Nice to see you're serious. All right, let's get going."

The Englishman led the way, limping slightly on one leg.

CHAPTER FIFTY-TWO

At the station, Sam went to his desk and, seeing the time, went to the basement, where fellow cops and National Guardsmen were bunking on army surplus cots with scratchy green wool blankets. He claimed an empty cot and went in search of supper. The evening meal was apple juice and spaghetti with lukewarm tomato sauce, served by women auxiliaries of the American Legion post. He ate off a metal plate, grunted one-syllable answers to anyone who spoke to him, then went back to his cot, the scents of gasoline and motor oil in his nostrils.

The lights were on, and some of the other officers and National Guardsmen were sipping bottled beers from paper bags while others smoked and talked among themselves. A radio in the corner was set low, dance music coming from some Manhattan club. Sam stretched out and pulled the blanket up over him. He stared up at the cement ceiling and tried not to think much, as the men murmured, as he inhaled the cigarette smoke. The lights were finally off at eleven P.M. and the radio was clicked off, and Sam was left there in the darkness and silence.

A coughing jag from one of his bunkmates woke him. Sam rolled to his side. A dim light showed the huddled and sleeping forms. Now that he was awake, he made out the snoring, the heavy breathing, the coughing from the sleeping men about him.

He wondered about Petr Wowenstein, the tattooed man. Forget about him. That's what he should have done days ago. Forget the whole damn thing. Close the case and move on. Think instead about Tony the marksman, rifle in hand, out there hunting for Hitler. Tony, the key to getting his wife and son free.

But where was he? The city, the Navy Yard, all were sealed tight, tight, tight. All buildings had somebody on guard, someone to keep watch, all buildings.

All buildings.

He sat up on the cot, let the blanket fall away.

But what separated Portsmouth and the Navy Yard?

The river and the harbor.

An old memory of Tony going down to the harbor— without Mom or Dad's permission, of course—and spending the day out there on a borrowed or stolen rowboat, fishing.

Hitler was coming to the shipyard tomorrow on an admiral's gig from his luxury liner, coming up to a dock- front reception.

That's how it was going to happen.

All the focus, the concentration, the attention on securing buildings and roadways and bridges.

But what of Tony, in a boat, under one of the docks, scoped rifle in hand, watching for the approaching gig flying a Nazi flag, a mustached man coming out on the dock...

One shot, maybe two...

A quick escape on the water, upriver to Eliot or Dover to a cove...

Sam sat up and quickly left.

CHAPTER FIFTY-THREE

On summit day, dawn was breaking when Sam got to the Rockingham Hotel, easily passing through the checkpoints, the National Guardsmen yawning and drinking from paper cups of coffee as they waved him through. Surprise of all surprises, when he knocked on the door of Room Twelve, both the Gestapo and FBI agents were awake, in dress pants, polished shoes, pressed shirts, and neckties. Their clean clothes belied the tension about their jaws, the shadows under their eyes.

LaCouture said simply, "Whaddya got?"

"I know how Tony is going to do it," Sam said. "He's going to shoot Hitler from the water."

An oval breakfast tray was on a side table with the scraps of a morning meal. LaCouture poured a cup of coffee from a metal pot and passed it to Sam, who sat down and said, "Do you have maps of the harbor?"

"Sure," LaCouture said. "Hold on."

Groebke pushed aside the papers and made room at the table as LaCouture unrolled a map and held it down with his manicured hands. Sam sipped at the strong coffee and pointed. "Look here. Piscataqua River comes down from Great Bay. Splits Maine and New Hampshire in two. Here's the harbor and the shipyard on the island. Now, the *Europa*, she's moored just outside the harbor, right? What time is Hitler coming in?"

Groebke frowned, but LaCouture told him, "Christ, can't be much of a secret anymore, not with the way the tides are running. He'll be here in three hours."

"What's the schedule like? Is he meeting the President at dockside?"

"No," the FBI man said. "The shipyard commander will receive him and then escort him to the yard's administration building. Hitler will meet Long inside. That's where the official reception begins."

Sam looked down at the map, at the little drawings marking buildings and docks and bridges. "Tony knows the harbor pretty well. Used to fish there a lot as a kid." He put his finger in the center of the harbor. "He's smart. He won't be in a building. Too secure. No, he's going to be on the water."

Groebke shook his head. "Difficult shot to make. Out there bobbing on water. Extremely difficult."

"He's a marksman," Sam said. "He'll make the shot. And the docks... he might have set up a sniper's nest somewhere down there." It came to him that he was setting up his brother, telling these men with their hard eyes and hard ways how best to capture him. But what else could he do?

He had to say the words, even though he had no bargaining power over these two. "Remember our deal—if possible, he gets captured. He doesn't get hurt. And my family gets out of Camp Carpenter."

LaCouture's lips thinned. "I remember the deal, Inspector. And I hate to admit, especially to a son of a bitch like you, but this is good information." He walked to the house phone and said, "Connect me with what's-his- name, Commander Barnes. Navy liaison officer over at the yard. Yeah, I'll wait, but not forever. Get on it." There was a long moment, and then LaCouture spoke. "Barnes? LaCouture here. We have late information that our shooter may be somewhere on the harbor. Or the river. Uh-huh. I don't care what you've already done or what's out there on the water, triple your efforts. We've got just three hours. I want places on and around the docks searched and any moored watercraft... uh-huh... I know the harbor's in lockdown, but this is what else you're going to do."

The FBI man paced back and forth. "Good... grab a pencil. You're going to have gunboats out there, right? Fine. Latest order. Any unauthorized watercraft out there, you're going to seize it. Don't care if it's Movietone, Dad and the kids out for a sail, or some forgetful lobsterman, and if the gunboats can't seize, they're going to sink. One warning from you and that's it—seize or sink and rescue the occupants. Don't want the newsreels showing us shooting swimmers... the President wouldn't like it, okay? Yeah, well, I know it's a bitch, being bossed around by the FBI, but handle it."

LaCouture slammed the receiver down. "We've got the joint covered. Inspector, you have a plan for today?"

"To do whatever I need to get Sarah and Toby out. That's my plan."

The FBI man said, "That sounds fine. I've got just the place for you." He reached over, grabbed a city map, and pulled it across the harbor map. "Bow Street generating station. You know it?"

"Of course."

"Nice tall brick structure, directly across the river from the shipyard. Our main observation point is going to be there, with watchers and gunmen. That's where I want you. You see anything out of the ordinary, you contact the duty communications officer and he'll contact me. Me and Hans here, we're gonna be at the shipyard."

"You just remember your promises. Both of them." LaCouture said, "With you whining all the time, how can I fucking forget?"

The Bow Street generating station was a five-story brick building that held coal-fired generators for Public Service of New Hampshire, the state's largest utility. After parking in a space between two army jeeps, Sam made his way through another set of checkpoints and guard stations. From one MP he got directions to the roof. There was no creaky elevator like the one from his visit to the shipyard, just a set of concrete steps going up and up and up. Along the way there was the sound of the generators, a constant hum that seemed to burrow into his ears. He felt out of time, out of place, wondering where his brother was, wondering how Sarah and Toby were doing, dreading what might happen on this supposedly historic day.

When he reached the roof, it felt as if his chest was going to explode, and he stopped to catch his breath as he took everything in. Amid piping and vent shafts, there was a group of men at the eastern side, closest to the river and the harbor. He walked across the tarpaper roof, his shoes making grinding noises among the tiny stones.

About a dozen men, mostly marines in fatigues and soft caps, kept watch over the harbor. A fat man with a sweaty face and a soft homburg pushed on the back of his head came over. His white shirt was sweated through, and his black tie fluttered weakly in the breeze. "You Inspector Miller?" he asked, his voice tired.

"That's right," Sam said, shaking the man's moist hand.

"Name's Morneau, Department of the Interior." He motioned Sam to join him. "For the rest of this day, this stretch of overheated paradise belongs to me and these poor leathernecks."

Binoculars on tripods were set up along the roof edge, and the marines were slowly transversing them, gazing out on the waters. Just about a hundred yards or so away was the Memorial Bridge, and from the rooftop, all of the shipyard and most of the harbor was visible. Nearby a metal table had been set up, and other marines sat in front of radio gear, headphones clasped over their ears. Two marines were sitting on the edge of the roof, chewing gum, scoped rifles in their arms. The rest of the squad sat a bit distant from them, as if they didn't like being so close to the snipers, hunters waiting patiently for targets.

Morneau blew his nose into his soiled handkerchief as a marine with sergeant's stripes broke away from the binocular stands and came over, his face friendly but bright pink, as though his blood pressure was twice that of a normal man.

"Sergeant Chesak," he said, and another round of handshakes ensued.

Sam said, "Can one of you tell me what's going on here?"

The marine looked to the Department of Interior man, and Morneau said, "There's about a half dozen observation posts here and across the river, most of them with overlapping fields of view. Our post has the most area to cover, which is why we've got the most spotters." He pointed to the binoculars. "Spotters look for anything that don't belong. Boats popping out of nowhere, people walking where they shouldn't, that sort of thing. Anything suspicious"—and he cast a thumb toward the radiomen—"gets put out on the net, and then it's taken care of."

"And those fellows?" Sam gestured to the two snipers.

Morneau grinned. "Only a handful of places where there can be guys with guns. We know those places. Our spotters find anybody else out there with a rifle or pistol or somethin' that don't look right, and me and the sergeant concur, and the snipers get to work. Those boys are from Georgia. Stone-cold killers, you can be sure. They see any guy out there with a gun who don't belong, they'll blow his fucking head off."

One of the spotters backed away from his vantage point. "Care to take a look, sir?"

"Thanks," Sam said. He pressed his eyes to the soft rubber of the eyepiece. The shipyard snapped into view, the buildings, the cranes, the sleek dark gray hulls of the submarines being built. Flags were flapping in the morning breeze, the red, white, and blue contrasting with the red, white, and black. With the high power of the binoculars, it was easy to make out the dock set up to receive Hitler and his delegation: The platform was practically overwhelmed with bunting and banners. White-clad U.S. Navy officers stood on one side of the dock, while another group—dressed in white pants and gray jackets, the Navy's counterparts in the *Kriegsmarine*—waited on the other.

He swiveled the binoculars, looked out to the harbor entrance, where he could just make out the *Europa*. On that ocean finer was a man set to motor his way into the United States and history, and waiting on the other end... Hard to even think it. His brother. Here to kill him. Sam backed away, looked to the spotter, a man in his late teens, thin and tanned, with a prominent Adam's apple. Sam gestured at the Nazi flags flying on the street corners and from the girders of the Memorial Bridge. "Hell of a sight."

The marine was wiping down the lens with a soft gray cloth. "What do you mean by that, sir?"

"Hitler and his Nazi buddies coming here, to an American navy yard. You must hate seeing that Nazi flag." "Don't bother me none." The marine bent, put his face to the binoculars again. "What bothers me... it's my ma and pa and younger brothers. I'm from Oklahoma originally, sir, and you see, the dust bowl drove us out of our farm. Grew up in a hobo camp in California, outside Salinas. A real shitty place. We got treated no better than dogs. Picking peaches and apples for fifty cents a day. I'm the oldest, so I got into the marines, send most of my paycheck home every month. If having Hitler and Long meet means my pa and my brothers can get jobs in those new aircraft factories, that's fine with me."

Sam folded his arms, said nothing, and the marine pulled his head back. "Sounds bad, don't it? I know what the Nazis done in Europe and England and Russia... and how they treat their Jews... but you know what? Me and my family, we don't live in Europe, we ain't Jews, and we need jobs. Simple as that."

"Maybe it's not that simple." Sam looked down at his sleeve-covered wrist, sensing the tattoo representing everything hidden and rotten about Burdick and the secret camps.

The young marine shrugged. "Maybe, but all I know is this: Me and my buds, we see a guy with a gun gonna screw up this deal, we'll kill him deader than last year's calendar."

My brother, Sam thought bleakly, walking away from the spotter. *My brother.*

INTERLUDE X

For the first time in a long, long time, he was walking in daylight, right on the sidewalks of his hometown. His back felt exposed, as though at any moment, he might receive a punch back there, or a gunshot square in the spine. He had on a suit and tie, and it had been years since he had worn anything so fancy, and the clothing itched something awful.

In daylight, Portsmouth looked nice enough, but there were too few people and too many cops and National Guardsmen, and men in suits and snap-brim hats with a hard-edged look about them.

A uniformed National Guardsman wearing a round campaign hat and a holstered pistol and Sam Browne belt stepped from a doorway, joined by a man in a dark brown suit. The civilian said, "Afternoon, sir, just doing a routine check. Can you show me some identification, please?"

He paused, put his hand slowly inside his coat jacket, pulled out a thin leather wallet, passed it over, thinking, *Well, we're going to see real shortly how good our people are.*

The civilian opened the wallet, glanced inside, looked up, and passed it back. "Sorry to bother you, sir. Go right ahead."

He smiled back, thinking, Yep, our people are pretty good, especially that newspaper photographer, and he kept on walking to the target building, saw a couple of cops and three National Guardsmen, and damn, one of the cops waved at him. What to do? Dammit, what to do?

He waved back, walked into the building as if he owned the place, and in a few more minutes, he was where he wanted to be, where he had to be. The floor was wooden and one of the planks seemed loose. He pried the plank up with his pocketknife, found a blanket-wrapped shape underneath. He pulled the blanket away, exposing a long cardboard box.

Fresh Flowers, the label on the box said in script. He undid the twine and paper, counted out the cartridges, picked up the rifle, and loaded it for the day ahead. He took the battery-operated radio out and dropped the wooden plank back in place. He switched the radio on, and after the tubes warmed up, he turned down the volume and listened to the day's news, knowing that if it all went well, his news would be the biggest of the day, week, month, decade.

CHAPTER FIFTY-FOUR

Morneau from the Department of the Interior said, "Word I got from the FBI is to give you cooperation. What do you need?"

Sam started to speak, then stopped. Now it made sense. LaCouture and Groebke and everybody else, they had it all under control. They didn't need him to identify

Tony. All LaCouture did this morning was shuffle him off, get him out of the way. These spotters knew their jobs, knew exactly what to do.

What Sam was going to do was to make sure those two good ol' boys from Georgia didn't have the opportunity to blow off Tony's head, so his brother could be spared, so Tony could be the key to unlock Camp Carpenter's gates.

Sam answered, "I'm here to observe, that's all. If you can give me a chair and a spare set of binoculars, that'll be fine."

Morneau nodded. "Yeah, we can do that."

In a few minutes he was in a chair that looked as if it had been borrowed from one of the PSNH offices below, and he was handed a pair of binoculars that were dented on one side. One lens was out of focus, meaning he had to squint with his right eye. The lousiest set of binoculars in the bunch but good enough for what he needed.

He scanned the Navy Yard and harbor again, taking everything in, the buildings, the people, the activity below. The naval officers at the dock had been joined by a brass band, and behind a rope barricade, newsreel cameras had been set up. There was also the drone of aircraft going overhead, P-40 Army Air Corps pursuit planes, it looked like. Sam imagined they would do some sort of ceremonial flyover at the propter moment.

During his surveillance, he tried his damnedest to listen to the spotters, to get a jump on anything if they saw Tony, but the spotters were quiet and professional. One would talk to the other, they would confer, and that would be that.

The farthest spotter said, "Man on the roof. Warehouse Two, Navy Yard. Something in his hand."

Another spotter moved his binoculars and said, "Dungaree jacket, dungaree pants. Confirmed."

"His hands. What's he got?"

The other spotter waited. "Length of galvanized pipe, it looks like."

Sergeant Chesak called over to one of the radiomen. "Tucker?"

"Sergeant?"

"Contact the Navy Yard, tell 'em to get that jerk off the roof of Warehouse Two before another spotter team sees him and shoots him dead."

"Aye-aye, sir."

Morneau was smoking a cigarette and the marine sergeant joined him, and then there was a burst of laughter. Sam tried his best to ignore them. He kept on looking and looking, though his hands grew heavy and his eyes ached from the strain. *Tony... Tony, you miserable fool, where the hell are you?*

Morneau's voice grew louder, and Sam heard him say, "But the best was in Los Angeles. Stationed there last year. Worked in a transit camp... man, some of those California girls, what they would do to get their men out. Had one honey, swear to Christ, built like a movie star, gave me the best head ever... it made my fucking toes curl..."

"Yeah?" Chesak asked. "Then what?"

Morneau laughed. "What do you think? Thanked her very much and sent her hubby off to Utah. What else was I going to do? Get my ass in a labor camp for a piece of tail? I don't think so."

Somebody chuckled, but Sam was pleased that it wasn't the marine sergeant. He was silent and went back to the binoculars. Perhaps sensing he had gone a bit too far, Morneau said, "Hey, how about some coffee? Been up late so many nights, hate to fall asleep now."

Silence again. Then Chesak said, "Yeah, some joe sounds good."

Morneau went to the communications table, picked up a phone, and started talking. Sam saw something at the farther reaches of the harbor. One of the marines said, "Sarge, looks like we've got an admiral's gig inbound to the harbor."

The sergeant swiveled his binoculars, and Morneau did too, and Sam was impressed by the professionalism of the other marines: They ignored the approaching boat and kept on scanning the Navy Yard and the harbor. In Sam's binoculars, the approaching boat bobbed into focus: a white craft with a canopied roof, flying the Nazi flag at the stem. Flanking the small boat were two gunmetal-gray navy gunboats, white numerals crisp on the bow, armed sailors both fore and aft.

"There you go," Morneau murmured. "Herr Hitler, coming in for a visit. Think the Kingfish is gonna make him eat shrimp gumbo 'fore the day is out?"

The marines laughed. Sam didn't. He was thinking of a desperate wife in California, giving herself away to try to save her husband, his own frightened family in a labor camp in Manchester, and a secret camp in Vermont, where half-starved Jews slaved under the eyes of fascists, both homegrown and imported.

The boat grew larger in view. Sam focused. Standing in the bow, hands folded before him, was Adolf Hitler. He had on a long gray coat and a peaked cap. The binoculars— damaged as they were—even allowed Sam to see the bastard's tiny black mustache. Black-clad SS officers were on the deck, some holding on to the canopy, but Hitler stood alone. There had been stories in *Time* and *Life* about how Hitler hated the water, but it looked like the son of a bitch was out there, almost defiant, to show that a will that could conquer Europe could also handle a twenty-minute boat ride.

All these American men were up here to protect a bloody dictator who had killed so many and was planning to kill and conquer more. Sam lost the admiral's gig and the accompanying navy escort, and as he was seeing the jumble of buildings and docks, something moved.

Something quick.

A small boat was darting out of the docks, heading straight toward the admiral's gig, its engine kicking up a tail of spray.

Sam froze.

The boat was moving fast. There was movement on board. He thought he recognized a shape, saw something protruding.

Tony, he thought, you miserable jerk.

He cleared his throat. Hesitated. One word from him and the boat might be halted, but this close, maybe the damn thing would be sunk and the people on board machine-gunned. If that happened, what would happen to his family?

"Sergeant," one of the spotters called out quietly. "From the south quay. Small craft, moving fast."

"Got it," Chesak said. "Tucker, raise the Yard, tell 'em what we got."

There was a murmur of voices from the communications table, and Sam's hands tightened on the binoculars as one of the gunboats flanking the admiral's gig put on a burst of speed, moving out to intercept the smaller craft. Sam quickly shifted his view to the intruder boat, looking for Tony, seeing what was at the bow, something on a tripod. A weapon? Pretty bulky to be a weapon.

"Newsreel," Sam called out. "It looks like a newsreel crew."

The smaller boat chugged to a crawl as the navy gunboat approached and came alongside. Three armed sailors leaped from the gunboat, rifles in hand, and then the navy gunboat churned back to its place, escorting the chancellor of Germany.

Morneau said, "Nice call, Inspector, but that's not a newsreel crew."

Sam was surprised. "It isn't?"

Morneau laughed. "Nope. It's the newest residents of a labor camp in Utah, about one day away from starting their twenty-year sentences. Freedom of the press, my ass. Morons."

Chesak said, "Lucky morons. If they had gotten any closer, they would've been sunk."

Sam put the binoculars on his lap, ran his palms across his pants, trying to dry them off. Oh, what a ball- buster of a day it was turning out to be. He heard a door open, footsteps on the gravel, and turned. Somebody familiar was approaching, in a Portsmouth police uniform. It seemed like a century ago when he had met Officer Frank Reardon and Leo Gray, poor disappeared Leo Gray, out there in the rain by the railroad tracks, examining the dead body that turned out to be an escaped Jew, escaping to God knew where.

Frank was carrying a paper bag, and a passing breeze brought the scent of coffee over to Sam. Frank said, "Hey, Sam. How's it going?"

"Not bad," he replied, remembering what LaCouture had said days ago about what the Portsmouth police would be doing on this historic day: directing traffic and fetching coffee. But if Frank looked embarrassed or humiliated at being a gofer, he was hiding it pretty well. Proudly pinned to his Portsmouth police uniform was the familiar Confederate lapel pin.

The cardboard cups of coffee were passed around, and when Frank approached him, Sam waved him off. "No, thanks. I'm fine."

Frank peeled the top off his coffee. "Suit yourself. I'll have yours, then." He made a big slurping noise and looked around at the harbor and the downtown. "What a goddamn circus. I'll be glad when everybody gets the hell out of here and goes home."

"Me, too."

"Yeah, and then it's back to work. Here and with the Party. Hey, congrats to you. I understand you've got a county position." Sam kept his mouth shut. There was another noisy slurp from Frank, and Sam was about to tell him to go away when the officer said, "Boy, you sure do move fast."

"What do you mean?" Sam said, now getting a much better view of Hitler and the SS and his cronies through the binoculars. A fat man by the side, there, who looked like Goering.

"Hell, you know what I mean," Frank said. "The North Church."

"I don't know what you're talking about."

Frank laughed. "Shit, play games if you want. You were there not more than ten minutes ago."

"I was?"

Frank looked confused. "Christ, yes. You were heading in there, flashed your pass at the guards, and went inside. Even gave me a wave. What kind of game you playing?"

"Just dicking with you, that's all," he answered, forcing his voice to stay even his mind was racing. He turned in his chair, looked a few blocks away. The white steeple of the North Church, rising above everything, everything in view.

A very good view.

No doubt that place was well guarded and sealed, like every other tall building .in Portsmouth. But a man dressed in a suit and looking professional and with forged documents, a man who looked very much like him, if he was quick and moved with confidence.

Tony. He was in the North Church steeple.

Sam looked back at everyone looking at the harbor, everybody looking at the Yard.

Frank had wandered off, was talking to one of the marines manning the radio gear.

If Sam said there was a gunman in that steeple, he knew what would happen. The two sleepy-eyed killers over there would trot to the other side of the roof and draw their weapons up, and at the slightest movement anywhere from the North Church, they would chew the place up with rifle fire. Maybe they'd get Tony, and maybe not, and who knew what would happen to Sam's family.

He stood up. And any pleas on his part, any attempt to tell LaCouture—

He dropped the binoculars on the chair. Started to walk away.

"Inspector?" a voice called out.

He said, "Gotta run out for a sec. Be right back."

He walked briskly but not without panic to the door. Don't let them see you run. You run, they get concerned, they start asking questions, they get excited.

He opened the door.

Stairwell. Concrete steps.

By the time he reached the fourth step, he was running hard.

INTERLUDE XI

It was lonely as he waited, but he knew he wasn't on his own. The spirit of Joe Hill was there with him, as well as those of Big Bill Haywood and Samuel Gompers. All men who had worked and bled and died for the workingman, fighting against the government, against the entrenched powers that be, the industrialists who saw men in the labor movement as nothing more than parts to be used and replaced. The same industrialists who supported the fascists and the union busters because the fascists promised fat contracts and trains that ran on time.

He listened to the radio. Picked up the rifle. It was getting close to time. He took a breath, knowing he would do the job no matter what. So many others out there were depending on him.

Some of those others were here as well, keeping him company in this supposed holy place. The Russian peasant with a rifle, fighting off the invader, making him pay with blood for every inch of ground. The French partisan, sabotaging panzer tanks along the Normandy coast. The British pub owner, secretly poisoning a pint of bitters for an SS officer.

He knew he was just one cog in one wheel, moving along, trying to change things, and as he gripped the cold metal and wood, he hoped those other cogs were doing their job. God knew he was about to do his part, and he supposed that should have scared him. Instead, it almost inspired him.

Someone was beating at the door downstairs.

He stood up, went to the hole he had cut out of the wood, allowing an opening for the rifle. Whatever happened, it would be over soon.

Somebody started running up the steps, calling out his name. He felt a sense of relief, recognizing the voice. It would all work out as planned. He lifted up the rifle, looked through the Weaver scope, waited for his destiny.

PART SIX

Top Secret

Partial transcript, radio communications between Senior FBI Officer in Portsmouth on 15 May 1943 and field agents under his command. Note: Due to technical difficulties, only the transmissions from the Senior FBI Officer were intelligible.

SFO: …what the hell do you mean, you've lost him? How in hell did you lose him? He was practically in your [expletive deleted] lap I Car Four, Car Six, do you have anything?

Car Four: *Unintelligible.*

Car Six: *Unintelligible.*

SFO: [expletive deleted] We've got the [expletive deleted] Fuhrer coming up the river, and no one knows where Miller is? Outpost Two, what do you have?

SFO: [expletive deleted] Comm shack, come in.

Communications

Office: *Unintelligible.*

SFO: [expletive deleted] Contact the Camp Carpenter transit camp immediately. Ii they don't hear from me in thirty—that's three-oh-minutes, the Hiller woman and the Hiller minor are to be shot. Understood?

Communications

Office: *Unintelligible.*

CHAPTER FIFTY-FIVE

Outside the PSNH building. Not much traffic on the streets. *Think!*

To his Packard, fumbling at the door, keys in hand. Don't drop the keys, don't screw this up, you've only got a few minutes, just barely enough.

The engine started with a roar.

He backed up, moving fast; a crunch as a rear fender clipped a telephone pole.

Somebody was shouting. A National Guardsman, rifle in hand, trotting from the PSNH building.

He shoved the column lever into first gear, popped the clutch.

Just a few blocks away. Just a few blocks away.

Tires squealed as he turned right, shifting again and then once more. Pedal to the floor. The Packard's engine roared. The steeple... one of the most prominent structures in town.

Just the other night, Tony was in his house.

In his house!

Stealing his clothes to fit in. No doubt the people behind Tony had the resources to fake documents, and sure, it could happen, hide a weapon in the church days ahead of time, before the security lid came down.

A checkpoint up ahead. Barrel through?

The Guardsmen were armed with submachine guns.

Able to tear through metal and glass and flesh in seconds.

Sam slammed on the brakes, screeched to a halt, rolled the window down, and flashed his inspector's badge and summit pass and yelled, "Get that goddamn barricade moved! Now! This is an emergency!"

Sweet Jesus, that was just what they did, they moved quickly back, dragging the wooden and barbed-wire barricade off to the side. He slammed the Packard into first gear, jammed his foot on the accelerator, and powered through, a front fender crumpling as it clipped the barricade.

Just two more blocks.

Tony, damn you Tony.

If I can get there in time and arrest your ass, my family could be home by tonight.

Market Square, center of downtown Portsmouth. Church on the left, more National Guardsmen, Portsmouth cops, some huddled around a radio with a long extension cord. He slammed on the brakes again, jumped out, and started running.

Shouts.

He ignored them, running toward the old North Church. Red brick and tall windows and three doors, spaced across the middle, high white steeple, and up there was his brother. He bounded up the steps, coat flapping, and a . Portsmouth cop—Curtiss, that was his name—said, "Sam! What's wrong?"

Sam yelled, "Get that door open! *Open it!*"

The cop muscled aside two National Guardsmen and opened the door, and he was inside.

A cool interior, scented with wax and candles. Empty pews stretching away. He looked around, heart pounding.

Door off to the left.

Opened it and went two narrow flights of stairs emptying onto the choir loft and organ, sheets of music on the chairs...

Dammit!

He swung his head around, hearing voices from downstairs—Curtiss arguing with the Guardsmen— looking hard, hoping not to hear the sharp report of a rifle from overhead.

Small wooden door, half hidden by a black curtain.

He ran across the choir loft, tore at the curtain, grabbed the door handle.

Locked.

Christ almighty!

He looked around.

A metal fire extinguisher hanging on the wall.

He pulled it off, tearing fingernails in the process, brought it to the door, raised it high, and brought it down.

The doorknob flew off and rattled across the floor. He dropped the fire extinguisher and pried the door open.

Worn wooden stairs, narrow and high, in a spiral. He started running up, his shoulders brushing against the plaster walls. There were voices in here too, from above. His .38 Smith & Wesson Police Special was in his hand and he went higher and higher, yelling out his brother's name.

To the top, just above the clock gears and machinery.

A man turned. The room was small and cluttered with boxes and rusting metal parts. A hole had been cut from the steeple in the direction of the harbor. The room smelled of dust and pigeon shit.

The man looked to him, holding a scoped rifle. "Hey Sam," the man said. He was wearing one of Sam's old black suits, the elbows and knees shiny from age, a suit Sarah had wanted to throw out.

Sam stood, legs shaking, arms at his side. "Put the rifle down. Come over here."

More voices. A battery-operated radio broadcasting a commentator with an excited voice, describing the approach of Hitler's boat. That's how it would work. The assassin would know when exactly to raise his rifle and pull the trigger.

Tony said, "Not going to happen, Sam."

"Tony. Get the fuck away from there and drop the rifle. Now!"

Tony had the impatient look of an older brother. "Sorry. Worked too long, too hard, sacrificed too much to get here."

Sam raised his revolver. "Drop the rifle, Tony. I don't care what you did at the Yard, don't care what they did to Dad. Look—Sarah and Toby have been arrested. They're in a labor camp. They get out if I bring you in! Do you hear me? I bring you in and they're free!"

Tony seemed to shudder, as though something had struck hit him deep and hard. "I wish you hadn't told me that, Sam." A pause, as if he were trying to regain his strength. "And you might be lying, for all I know."

"You numb shit, I would never lie about my family."

Tony said, "Sam, I love 'em both, more than you know, but they're soldiers, just like everyone else. Drafted but still part of the fight. And what I'm doing here, it's more important than them, you, or me."

"Tony!" he yelled, hearing loud voices in the steeple. "Leave me alone, Sam. I'm going to take care of that monster down there. Somebody should have killed the bastard years ago. He's long overdue."

Sam stepped forward. "Tony, he's a bastard, but just one bastard. You kill him, and so what? Another bastard will take his place. He's just one man. That's all."

Tony glanced out the opening. "No, that's not all. He holds it all together. Get rid of him and the whole rotten system collapses. One man can turn this world to hell. And one man can make it right. And that's gonna be me." The voice on the radio squawked, *"Now! Now the boat has docked, and I can make out Chancellor Hitler as he starts to step out..."*

Tony raised the rifle and Sam said, "Don't!"

His brother didn't turn. "Or what? You're going to shoot me? Why? Because it's your job? Your duty?"

Another step closer. "Yeah, it's my job and duty. And saving that bastard will get Sarah and Toby free. Now drop the rifle!"

Tony murmured, "We all got roles to play, and I'm sorry, mine is the more important. You can piss around the edges, host an Underground Railroad station, but when it counts, I'm going to make it all right."

The rifle came up to his brother's shoulder and the radio commentator said, "... the dock. Hitler is now on American soil for the first time, walking briskly to the Navy Yard commander—"

Tony's head lowered to the scope.

The sound of the shot was deafening, pounding at Sam's ears.

The revolver recoiled in his hand.

The rifle clattered to the floor, and Tony slumped over.

Sam ran to his brother and knelt as Tony looked up, disbelieving, his face white with shock. "You—"

"Tony, damn you," Sam said, his face wet. Sam fumbled at his brother's coat and shirt, and the radio was blabbering, and there were footsteps, racing up the stairs. Tony grasped Sam's wrist hard.

"You did it... I can't believe it... you actually had the balls to do it..."

Sam ripped the shirt open, buttons flying. "I aimed for your shoulder, Tony. You'll be okay. It's just a shoulder wound."

Tony grimaced, lips trembled. "Hurts like hell... shit, doing your duty. How true blue can you be?" Footsteps grew louder. He coughed and said, "Hope the hell you know what you did... one man... hope you know what you did..."

Sam said frantically, "I do. Look, you'll be okay, you'll see a doctor, and Sarah and Toby, you're gonna free them. You'll see."

A shake of the head, Tony's voice raspy. "Sam, you did good, guy, you did good. Tell Sarah and Toby...tell them—"

Before Tony could finish, the tiny steeple space was full of men in suits, and in front was Special Agent Jack LaCouture of the FBI. Sam turned toward him, starting to explain, when LaCouture drew out his revolver and shot Tony in the head, the sound of the report hammering at Sam.

CHAPTER FIFTY-SIX

Sam was yelling, screaming, spattered with blood, flailing, and the FBI agents grabbed his arms, disarming him- LaCouture shouted, "Get that body out of here! *Now*, dammit!" Amid the yelling and thrashing and tears, in just a matter of moments, Tony's body was taken away in the arms of the other agents, his limp bloody head bumping against the dusty floorboards, brain tissue and bone chips everywhere. LaCouture took charge as Sam struggled against two beefy agents, and then LaCouture said, "All right, leave us alone for a couple of minutes. Get out of here, all of you."

Sam broke free, sobbing and cursing, as the FBI agents obeyed, pushing through the narrow door. LaCouture stood there, revolver in his hand. He said, "Inspector, calm your ass down or I'll shoot you. Then you'll go into the history books as a co-conspirator with your brother. And your wife and son will grow old behind barbed wire. Your fucking choice."

Sam stood there, tears rolling down his face. The radio was on, blabbing away, and LaCouture kicked it with a polished shoe, breaking it, silencing it. "There," the FBI man said. "Damn chattering."

"You didn't have to shoot him! You son of a bitch, you didn't have to kill him!"

"Oh, sonny, I'm sorry, but yes I did. You see, there's not going to be a trial and months of headlines. There's just going to be a story about a failed plot to assassinate Hitler. That's what the world is going to know. And you're gonna play your part. The good brother who didn't know a damn thing. But if you say one word about what just happened, your wife and son ain't never gettin' out." Sam was shivering so hard he couldn't catch his breath. His hands felt empty without a weapon. He shifted, felt his foot touch something.

Tony's rifle, on the floor.

LaCouture said, "Nice going, leading us here. You did quite well, Inspector. Mind telling us how you figured out he was here?"

Sam forced the words out. "You were tracking me. All the time. Following me."

LaCouture nodded. "Yeah, especially today. Think those observers were busy just watching the harbor? Hell, no. They were also busy watching you. To see where you went. Boy, by the time you got to the church, I was hell-bent for leather, following you. You see, there was a moment when—"

Sam kicked at the broken radio, and LaCouture looked down long enough for Sam to drop to a knee, raise the rifle, catch the surprised look in LaCouture's eyes, slide his finger through the trigger guard, squeeze the trigger, and—

Click.

He desperately worked the bolt as an unfired cartridge flew out, spun to the floor.

Click.

LaCouture's smile flickered.

Sam stood up clumsily. He threw the rifle at LaCouture's feet.

"A setup. You filthy bastards. A setup. A loaded rifle that wouldn't fire."

The FBI man's nod was triumphant. "Your brother didn't escape from that labor camp. We practically gave him a get-out-of-jail-free card, made sure he didn't get picked up along the way, made sure he believed he was part of a conspiracy to assassinate Hitler. There were other people involved, fellow travelers, mostly domestic Commies with a couple of NKVD boys tossed in, and they're being picked up right now. Even me and Groebke, we played our parts—snooping around the police station, checking out your files and his files. Your brother was the perfect patsy, Inspector. Dumb bastard didn't even think of test-firing the rifle. It had a disabled firing pin. You filled your role, too."

"I led you right to him." The word seemed to choke in his throat. "Why?"

"Because when Hitler finds out that the Kingfish's FBI saved his Kraut ass, he's going to be in a better mood," LaCouture said. "Maybe make more treaty concessions. Buy more bombers, ships, guns, spend a fortune to kill Reds and put our people to work. A new era for them and us." LaCouture reached into his coat pocket, pulled out a small pair of binoculars with a long leather strap. He tossed them over to Sam, who caught them with one hand. "Go ahead, take a look," LaCouture said, motioning with his revolver. "Step over there and tell me what you see."

Sam walked stiffly to the cut-out hole and brought the glasses up. He looked out across the harbor, to the Navy Yard and the moored gig. People were milling about, and there was Hitler, striding past an honor guard of sailors and marines. At the end of the reviewing line, standing by his open convertible, in a surprise move, was the President.

"Come on, Inspector, what do you see?"

Sam turned. "Nothing. There's nothing I want to see."

LaCouture said, "Oh, no, what's there is the future. You've heard of Lindbergh's wife, Anne, and her book? There's a new wave coming, of strong countries and stronger men, to make things right. Parliaments and congresses and the people's, voice—forget them, that's all over. There's a new order coming our way, an order led by men like Hitler and Mussolini, and we're going to join with a man like Long."

Sam looked down at his brother's blood. "Count me out."

"No, we're all part of it, every one of us," the FBI man insisted. "You know"—his voice sounded dreamy, almost reflective—"last year I was sent to Germany, part of an exchange program, made some real good friends. They trusted me and I trusted them, and they took me on a long, long drive... someplace in what was once Poland... to one of their camps..."

Sam kept on staring at the blood, listening to the FBI man's memories.

LaCouture said, "The camp, what a place... so simple, really, so simple. Just a place to deal with your enemies. You never saw such terrible beauty. They wouldn't let me inside, but they told me what happened. These trains came in, filled with your enemies, and everything they had was seized, and then they disappeared. They just disappeared. Your enemies came in full and alive, and then they didn't exist anymore, and what a wonderful thing. We've barely begun here in the States, Inspector. We've just barely started to catch up to what the Germans can do, and they're going to teach us so very much in the years ahead."

Sam stayed silent.

"Do you understand now? Do you?" LaCouture pressed.

Sam looked up, thought of his tattoo, of Burdick, of Sarah and Toby, of his betrayed and murdered brother. "Yeah. I understand everything."

He swung the binoculars at the end of their leather strap, breaking LaCouture's nose.

LaCouture howled, brought both hands up to his bloodied face, and Sam dropped the binoculars, was back in high school, tackling the Southern son of a bitch, pounding him against the walls of the steeple, now on the filthy floor. He started punching the bastard in the ribs, in the jaw, in the ribs again, punching, flailing, getting punched in return, footsteps, shouts, and he was yanked up and off LaCouture, breathing hard, sobbing, one cheek bleeding, FBI agents holding him back.

LaCouture struggled to his feet, a lace-edged handkerchief against his face, smeared with blood. Sam wasn't thinking, was just trying to break free, to get at the FBI guy, the one who had killed his brother, imprisoned his family. LaCouture came up to him, speaking thickly. "Through... that's it... you and your family... they ain't never gettin' out of that camp, not ever, and you'll be with 'em before sundown, your wife and kid... they'll get beat up and raped, and it's all your fault, fool, all your stupid fault, asshole..."

Sam tried to get at him again, and LaCouture said, "Out. Get him out of here."

Sam tried to at least to spit in the FBI man's face, but two agents were already dragging him through the door.

CHAPTER FIFTY-SEVEN

He sat still, cheek bleeding, wrists aching, heart aching, everything aching. He was in the back of one of the FBI's Ford sedans, handcuffed, deposited there by the FBI agents who had dragged him down from the steeple. A brother killed in a supposed plot to assassinate Hitler, and here he was, in a parking lot near the North Church with other FBI sedans and army trucks, waiting. Arrested for assaulting an FBI agent, and not just any agent—the agent who had saved Hitler's life on this vital summit.

He shifted his weight, conscious of the pain in his body and of the tears that would not stop. His brother. Angry, committed, and blindly dedicated Tony. His burning sense of righteousness used against him in a plot he believed would set everything straight but in the end just made it worse. Sam could imagine President Long, bragging to Hitler about the plot, showing him the afternoon headlines, proving how dedicated the Americans were to this new arrangement, this new world order. Like LaCouture said, this new wave was about to drown the old ways of democracy and individual liberty.

Damn that Tony, ready to sacrifice Sarah and Toby to kill Hitler. What right did he have?

That bastard. Because of him, they would all be in a labor camp. He lowered his head. He couldn't stop crying.

The rear car door opened, and Sam looked over, bracing for another blow.

"Inspector," Hans Groebke said, his eyes emotionless behind his glasses.

"Come here to gloat?"

"Hardly." The Gestapo man held up a tiny key. "If you lean forward, I will release you."

Sam stared at the man. "Not a chance. Get me uncuffed, and then I'm shot while trying to escape. Oldest trick you clowns have come up with."

Groebke shook his head. "No, no trick. Lean forward, I will uncuff you.

And then we can talk for a moment before I send you on your way."

Sam struggled to gauge what was going on behind those quiet blue eyes, and then he gave up. He was just too damn tired. They'd finally defeated him. He had no fight left in him. He leaned forward. Groebke bent toward him, and there was a *click* as the cuffs were undone. Automatically, he brought his hands forward, rubbed at his wrists. Groebke said, "We shall speak, then, of deceit. And tricks. And appearances."

"Sure," Sam said bitterly. "You assholes used my brother as a tool, set him up. He had no chance at all. You got him out of the labor camp and here to Portsmouth, where he could get killed like a dumb cow at a slaughterhouse."

Groebke shook his head. He took out a packet of Lucky Strike cigarettes, pumped one out. "No, that was LaCouture's business. Not mine."

"Oh? What was your business?"

A wry smile as he placed the cigarette between his lips and lit it with a gold lighter. "To see that your brother succeeded. And in that, I failed very much indeed. I knew of many things, but not of the disabled rifle."

"What the hell are you talking about?" Sam demanded.

"Sorry, I thought I made it clear. Although I will always deny that this conversation ever took place. You see, I wanted your brother to succeed, to kill my chancellor. That's why I was here in Portsmouth, to make such things happen... to keep an eye on you... and to assist your brother if necessary. But I failed. He was contacted by LaCouture and his crew, the disabled rifle was provided, and now Hitler, that beast, will live, and many more innocents will die."

"But...you're goddamn *Gestapo!*"

"True. But first, remember, I am a cop. Just like you. A cop in a small Bavarian village, with obligations and duties, until I was promoted to where I am, eh? So what you see, what you think you see, may not always be the truth."

"Some goddamn cop!"

"But I am also a German patriot, Inspector," Groebke said quietly. "There are not many of us left, but we have tried to kill that monster. What he is doing to the innocents, in the camps and in the cities, he is doing in the name of the German people. If we lose this war, our name and our culture will be stained for a thousand generations times a thousand."

Sam was speechless. Groebke took another drag of his cigarette. "But there are other reasons. I had a brother, too. He was killed in the British landings. And for what? For the ravings of a madman who has the power to seize a people and their destiny."

The Gestapo man turned slightly, as if he were trying to see the shipyard through the nearby buildings. "Now my madman is meeting your madman, to divide the world between them, to make it a place for their visions and appetites. And the one chance we had today, that single chance, is no more." Groebke dropped his cigarette on the pavement, twisted a foot hard against it.

"Thanks for cutting me loose," Sam told him. "I owe you one. But I'm going to be in a labor camp before this day is over."

The German smiled. "It will be, as you Americans say, handled. Your FBI man, I have learned some things about him and his trip to my home country, and he owes me some things as well. Don't worry, Inspector. You won't be in a labor camp. He and I will no longer be in your lives."

"My wife and boy.."

"I will try, but I don't think I have that influence," Groebke said. "Maybe later, but believe me, it is safer for them to be there and not here. I wouldn't go to the camp to get them out by yourself—that would be far too dangerous. Too easy for you to get arrested there. Go back to your police station, Inspector. Your job here is done." Sam didn't move. His cheeks were still wet from his tears. "Why are you telling me all of this? What's the point?"

Groebke shrugged. "LaCouture and the others, they think of me as the perfect Gestapo officer, eh? But you— I wanted you, Inspector Miller, to know who I really am, so when I leave this country, I will have the satisfaction that at least one American knows the real Hans Groebke. This is for you as well."

The Gestapo man reached into his coat pocket and took out a revolver. Sam recognized it as his own. He took it and holstered it and wiped at his eyes, thinking of what Tony had said to him up in the steeple. "Yeah, my job. I did my part, too. As shitty as it was."

Then he climbed out of the car started to walk out to Market Square.

CHAPTER FIFTY-EIGHT

Except for a desk sergeant reading a pulp western magazine in the dingy lobby, the building was deserted. The police station seemed to be the only refuge left for Sam; he could not return home, not now. Upstairs he trudged to the city marshal's office, but that, too, was empty, as was Mrs. Walton's desk.

He sat down heavily in his chair and stared at the piles of paper and memos and file folders at his desk without touching them. All this work that awaited him. For the briefest of moments, he felt a stirring of anticipation, that with this whole summit fiasco concluded, he could go back to being a simple police inspector with a simple family, a simple life. If only he could get Sarah and Toby out, he could start again. It would be difficult, and it would take a very, very long time, but he just wanted it to be like it was two weeks before, before he found that dead body by the railroad tracks.

That's all he wanted.

He stretched out his legs, looked down at his shoes, and saw stains there.

From his brother's blood.

Sam put his arms on his desk, lowered his head, and wept.

Hours later, the piles had been sorted, some papers dumped, others reviewed, and some old case files reread. It had been routine, plodding work, and Sam almost cherished every moment. He had no idea what time it was; he didn't care.

There were footsteps behind him. He turned, and Marshal Hanson stood there, a bland expression on his face. "The prodigal son returns," Hanson remarked.

"If you like, sir," Sam said. "I've been released from my federal duty."

Hanson was dressed in a well-cut black suit. Sam saw that the man was swaying just the tiniest bit. Sam had never seen his boss drunk.

Hanson gently placed a hand on Sam's back. "Jesus, son, I heard what happened today. A damn, damn shame. I sure wish it could have ended in a different way.. .but there was no other choice, was there? Tony was trying to assassinate Hitler. It must have been a tremendous loss, but the summit had to be saved. In a way, it was a sacrifice—a hard sacrifice for the greater good."

Sam forced the words out, thinking how Tony had been betrayed. Some sacrifice. "That's true, and if you want a briefing of what went on, I'd be glad to—"

Hanson lifted his hand from Sam's back. "No, no, the FBI man in charge said I would get a full report later. I need to run along. Tell you what, you finish what you have to do and then go home. Okay?"

Sam wondered what in hell Groebke had on LaCouture, dirt that kept the FBI agent silent about the city's only police inspector breaking his nose. "No, I don't think so. I really want to get a jump on my work. I'll probably spend the night here."

Hanson said, "All right, but you won't be sleeping in the basement. Use the couch in my office. There are a couple of blankets in the closet."

"That's very generous of you, sir. And if I may talk about—"

Hanson swayed. "Yes, yes. Your wife and son. Not now, Sam. There's too much going on now. But I promise, once it settles down, we'll see what we can do. It's a federal beef, but I'll see if I can help." He rubbed his eyes wearily. "Sleep well! We're going to need you tomorrow, when this whole thing wraps up."

"It's done? So soon?"

"The summit's a success. Ended a day ahead of schedule. Agreement reached on a number of issues, so on and so forth, but bottom line, Hitler is going to get his arms, the Kingfish is going to get his full employment. Both of them are going to be safe in their jobs for a long time to come."

"And the Jews?" Sam knew he was pushing it, but he had to know. "Will they continue to come over here?"

Hanson looked about, ensuring they were alone. "Oh, yes. Hitler is eager to get rid of them, and Long is eager to put them to work. But Sam, no more talk of that, all right?"

"All right," he agreed. "So that's it, then."

"Yep," his boss said. "Hitler and Long, both heading home tomorrow, and Long is going to visit Berlin next week to seal the deal. There you go. History made again in our little Portsmouth."

Sam thought of Tony. His spirit must be furious. Not only to die in vain, but Sam was certain LaCouture had been right: Tony's death had made the summit a bigger success.

"Yeah," he told Hanson. "Our little Portsmouth."

CHAPTER FIFTY-NINE

It was a sign of his profound exhaustion that Sam slept deeply on Hanson's leather couch. After getting up, he went down to the basement, getting a bowl of oatmeal and some bacon for breakfast, again served by the American Legion's women's auxiliary members. He ate at a long table full of talkative and gossipy cops and feds, and he tuned them all out. He wanted to get through this day, do his work, and let the summit circus leave. Newspapers were passed around, with loud screaming headlines about the success of the summit, and buried in them were brief stories about Tony. If anyone said anything about his brother, he was certain he would punch out the first one, but no one did. They seemed to know enough to leave him alone.

If he was fortunate, in the next day or so, his family would be freed, through either Hanson or Groebke. If not, then the hell with what Groebke had said, he'd go to Camp Carpenter and demand to see the commandant and get his family out of there. Whatever it took, he would get them out.

At his desk again, he tossed aside the old message from Mrs. Walton to contact the medical examiner. As he dove through a pile of burglary reports, trying to find some pattern, some new angle of attack, a woman's voice said: "Inspector? Inspector Miller?"

He swiveled in his chair.

"Yes?" he said. "What can I do for you?"

"The desk sergeant. He told me to come see you."

He got up and dragged over an empty chair, trying to hide his displeasure. He hated these refugee matters. "Please, do sit down."

"Thanks," she said carefully. The women had blond hair cut in a bob, and her worn light blue cotton dress spoke of careful mending. She sat down and gripped a battered black purse in her lap. Her accent was British.

"So," he said, picking up a fountain pen and a notepad. "What can I do for you?"

"My name is Alicia Hale," she told him. "I'm looking for my husband. Your Red Cross helped locate him, so I know he's in your city, and I know who he's been seen with. Some kind of writer. This is the third time I've come here looking for help, and I hope you can do something."

From her purse, she took out a black-and-white snapshot of a smiling man wearing a British military uniform. Sam studied the photo and said, "Is it Reginald Hale?"

She smiled in astonishment. "You know my Reggie?" He handed the photo back to her. "I've run into him a couple of times. We have a mutual acquaintance. Your husband's missing a leg, correct?"

She placed the photo carefully into her purse, as if afraid someone might steal it. "Yes, he lost that during the invasion. We were separated soon afterward; Reggie was evacuated with some of the wounded, and I stayed behind. We've only managed to exchange a few letters over the years."

"Oh. And if I may ask, how did you get here?"

She frowned. "Through bribes, what else? The new government has been issuing travel visas for humanitarian reasons. Just a drop in the bucket, but it makes for nice propaganda. If you pay enough for them, the government grants them. The visas work only in North America. Mothers and wives aren't allowed to see the POWs in Germany, now, are they?"

"Prisoners are still being kept? I remember reading a story a couple of months ago saying the last of the POWs had been sent home."

"Ha," she said, and he noted how rigidly her hands were holding the purse. "A load of cod swollop, that is. Most of our boys are working in arms factories in France and Germany. Half starved and overworked, that's what they are."

He wondered what she would say if she knew what he had done yesterday to save Hitler's life and prolong the POWs' misery. He said, "So. You can't find your husband, is that it?"

"Not in this soddin' mess, can I? But I found out he spends time with this writer—"

"Walter Tucker," Sam supplied. Alicia Hale nodded and continued.

"I had to pay a taxi man a hefty fare to bring me to the man's flat, but he wasn't there, and the desk sergeant, he said maybe you could help me."

Sam asked, "Mrs. Hale, is it possible your husband's papers are no longer in order?"

"Who the hell knows? Does that make any difference?"

"Not to me, but it may explain why he's hiding out— with all the hoopla over this summit."

She seemed to shiver. "To think you Yanks are treating that bloody bastard like royalty! Should 'ave sunk his boat when it got here, you should 'ave."

"Maybe so," he said, not wanting to think any more of the summit, "but if we can find Walter, I'm sure we can find your husband."

"That would be brilliant."

He put his pen down, "Are you here to take him back to England?"

A violent shake of her head. "Not bloody likely. No, I've got a cousin who has a farm up in Manitoba. Once I get my Reggie, we're going there and never going back. Not ever."

"Good for you," Sam said. "Look. Let's go see if we can find your husband. I have an idea of where to start."

CHAPTER SIXTY

He took her to his Packard, dented and scratched from the previous day's desperate drive. A part of him was still mourning his brother and aching at the thought of Sarah and Toby behind barbed wire, but he forced his focus to the job, and he closed the passenger door after she slid in.

When he started the car, he asked, "What part of England are you from, Mrs. Hale?"

"London."

"Oh. What's London like nowadays?"

He headed toward the center of the city. The checkpoints had all come down. With the summit over and a success, it looked as though security had dissolved, although there were still armed National Guardsmen at each corner.

"Horrible, the city is, simply horrible."

"I'm sorry to hear that."

She sat properly and primly, purse again in her lap. "Parts haven't been rebuilt since the bombing and street fighting. Food, petrol, clothing, they're still rationed, but if you know your way around the black market, almost anything can be had. In *Reichsmarks*—the pound is worthless. People have to make the most awful decisions every day. Taking a government job or cooperating with the officials... are you being a collaborator? Or are you just a realist? Do you show allegiance to King Edward, even though he's only on the throne thanks to Herr Hitler. Or allegiance to the queen and her daughters marooned in Canada? The resistance—are they truly fighting for freedom? Or are they just terrorists and criminals? The interior zones, the unoccupied zones— some say that's the worst. At least in the occupied areas, the Jerries keep some sort of order... the miserable bastards."

He turned in to a bank parking lot and found an empty space. As he switched off the engine, she said, "Is it true, what I heard? That Churchill's been arrested in New York?"

"Yeah, it's true. Sorry."

"Don't apologize. I hope the Jerries hang the fat bastard and then shoot him, make sure he's dead. It's all his fault this happened."

She opened the passenger door but remained motionless. Sam, too, sat still and listened. "In '40, after France fell, there were rumors Hitler wanted an armistice, wanted a peace treaty," she continued. "It wouldn't have been all milk and honey, but we would have been left alone, for the most part. Drunk Winnie wouldn't sit still for it. That belligerent old bastard, fight them on the landing fields, on the beaches, blah bloody blah. Spumed old Hitler, he did. And after the invasion, the government collapsed and tried to make peace, but it was too late then. Too late for me and my Reggie."

As they walked, he grasped her elbow and leaned in to her and said, "Like I said, the trick is to find Walter. After that, we can find your husband."

Alicia looked around at the swelling crowds. "Going to take some luck, isn't it, then?"

"Walter is a regular when it comes to his writing. Once a week he produces a short story for one of the magazines, and every day he goes to the post office, always at about noon. And that's where we're going."

People swept by, some carrying small American flags, and from the bits of overheard conversation, he learned what was happening: President Long was motoring back from the shipyard after yesterday's triumph, and the local Party, doing a good job of grassroots efforts, had turned out this crowd to cheer him on. The Party... He shuddered at what would be waiting for him when the summit was over. Throwing his lot in with the marshal and the Nats, he thought.

The National Guardsmen had moved into the streets, rifles held up in a long, flowing honor guard. He found his fingers tightening on Alicia Hale's arm. "That's the post office," he explained. "Walter should be either entering or leaving in the next few minutes."

Sirens wailed and Sam said, "We'll wait for the motorcade to come by and then cross the street. We do it now, we might get run down."

She just smiled, and he felt a flash of envy for the wounded British vet, to have such a woman find the means and strength to cross the ocean and come to a strange city, to find her mate.

There. Could it be?

He leaned in to her and said over the approaching sirens, "Jackpot. There he is, going inside."

Sure enough, there was Walter trundling up the wide granite steps, worn leather valise in one hand. He disappeared into the building. The wail of the sirens grew louder.

Alicia had her hands up over her ears, squeezing them, her purse hanging off her wrist. "I hate sirens. Ever since the air raids."

Sam tried to give her a reassuring smile. The sirens yowled louder as the motorcade became visible, people waving their flags, cheers and applause. Three cars came up the road, Secret Service agents perched on the running boards, President Long in the rear seat of the last vehicle, waving his straw boater. Some of the crowd started chanting, *"Long, Long, Long!,"* but Sam heard another chant rise up at the same time: *"Jobs, jobs, jobs!"* Hearing those voices, looking at his poorly dressed neighbors, bad skin and bad teeth, poor shoes, patched suits and dresses, he felt the power in their cries. They had hope again, hope after so many years. He had a trembling thought that they would be betrayed again, that it was all a lie. Oh, for some there would be jobs, but those jobs would come with a price tag: devotion and blind adherence to the Kingfish. And for those on relief, the relief funded in part by the Jewish slave labor, they would pay the same price. These people would be asked to sign over their vote and freedom in exchange for a steady paycheck, and who could blame them if they did?

After the cars went by in a cloud of exhaust and dust, Walter came out of the post office, joined by a man who was walking with some difficulty.

Sam turned to Alicia. "Your husband, does he have a fake leg? A prosthetic?"

She raised her voice over the crowd. "Yes. He wrote me about it... an American charity group presented it to him last year. He doesn't need his crutches anymore." They were blocked in by the crowd, still clapping, still chanting *"Jobs, jobs, jobs!"* He watched Walter and Reginald talking and then the crowd shifted and he lost view. When he gained the view again, the British airman was gone.

Walter was still there.

Reginald was gone.

On two legs. Not a set of crutches like before.

People were jostling and bumping them. He pulled her to a nearby utility pole, pushed her against it, and said, "You stay here. I'll make my way across the street, talk to Walter, find out where your husband went."

"You're quite kind. It's been so very long since I've seen him."

Something in her voice touched him. "You must still be proud of him, a hero pilot and all that."

Tears were in her eyes, but her face was puzzled. "I'm sorry—what?"

"Your husband. Reginald. A pilot in the RAF. You must be quite proud."

She said, "You're quite wrong, Inspector. Reggie was never a flier. Not ever."

Now it seemed as though the crowd had vanished, that it was now just the two of them, staring at each other in disbelief. "You showed me his photo," Sam said incredulously. "In uniform. He told me he was a pilot. And so did Walter."

A firm shake of the head. "I think I bloody well know what my husband did in the service. He was not a pilot."

Sam stared into her determined face. "What was he?"

"Royal Engineers."

"Royal Engineers? Doing what?"

When she told him, he broke free, shoving his way through the crowd.

CHAPTER SIXTY-ONE

Running across the street, he almost got hit by a speeding Chevy as another motorcade roared by, this one carrying reporters and newsreel photographers. When he got to the post office, out of breath, Sam elbowed his way almost viciously through the crowds, feeling the same urgency and despair that had seized him yesterday when he was trying to reach his brother.

Where in the hell was Walter?

The writer had disappeared. Sam ran up the steps, looked around. There. Walter was going down the street, joining the streams of people, heading to the B&M railroad station to bid the successful President farewell.

Jobs, jobs, jobs. At long last, the Depression seemed to have met its match.

He rejoined the crowd, forcing his way through, holding up his badge, saying over and over, "Police business, move! Police business, *move!*" But it was like some damn festival, the people were so happy and wouldn't get out of the way. Elbows were sharply jabbed into his ribs, and once a heavyset woman stepped on his foot with a high heel, but by the time the station came into view, he was close.

He spotted the pudgy shape moving ahead. Sam took a breath, pushed his way past an older couple, almost causing the woman to fall.

He grabbed Walter's coat collar.

"Hey!" Walter called out, and Sam spun him around. A bout of nervous laughter came from his tenant. "Oh, Sam! Christ, what a fright you gave me. I thought I was being robbed. Or even arrested."

Sam had his hand on Walter's coat and dragged him to a hardware store and its doorway. He pushed Walter in and, breathing hard, said, "You've got one minute to tell me what the hell is going on here, or I'll turn you over to the feds. Let's see how your college background helps when they give you an ax and a fifty-foot pine to cut down."

Walter tried to laugh again, but the nervous sound seemed to strangle in his throat. His white shirt was wrinkled, and his red necktie was barely tied about his plump neck. He glanced around and said, "Really, Sam, I don't know what you're talking about."

"Walter, where's your valise?"

"My what?"

"Your valise. Your briefcase. Where the hell is it? It never leaves your side. You've told me that often enough."

"I suppose I left it at home this morning when I—"

Sam slapped his face. "Don't he to me!" he raged. "I saw you carry it into the post office, and you were carrying it when you left with Reggie Hale!"

Tears were streaming down the bewildered older man's face. Sam grabbed his shirt collar, twisted it, shoved him against the doorway. "He's not a pilot, is he? He's in the Royal Engineers. Bomb disposal unit. That's how he lost his leg. Not being shot down by a German fighter plane. Injured when a bomb went off as he was trying to—"

The valise was gone.

Reggie Hale was gone.

An expert in explosives.

Heading to the train station.

"You..." Sam left the sentence unfinished, and ran back out to the crowded sidewalk. Now Walter was there, desperately clinging to him, trying to hold him back. "Sam! Please! It's too late! Sam!"

Sam tried to punch Walter, but this time the ex-professor surprised him by ducking his head and then coming back up and pleading, "It has to happen! It has to happen this way! There's no other choice!"

"You... you're going to kill the President!"

In a stunning move, Walter struck him, and Sam rocked back on his heels. "No!" Walter shouted. "Not a president! A dictator, an emperor: A fraud who just pledged our lives, our sacred honor, to help one of the great monsters of our time to slaughter millions. That's what's out there, about to leave Portsmouth. Washington, Lincoln, Wilson—those were *presidents*. Not that freak of nature, that accident of circumstance!"

Sam broke free, plunged again into the crowd.

What to do?

A phone in this chaos?

He looked around. No cops. No National Guardsmen. Where the hell was LaCouture when you needed him? The crowd swept him closer. There was the platform, and the President stood up there, waving his hat, wrapping up a speech whose words couldn't be heard, and cheering. Sam felt his body go rigid, bracing for the platform to disintegrate in a cloud of flames and broken wood.

Bang.

He flinched.

The band started playing a Sousa march, the bass drum banging. There were more cheers, and then Long moved out of view and Sam's throat clenched up.

This was the man who had imprisoned his brother, had imprisoned and killed so many others, and whose thugs found great joy in using his brother as a pawn to be tossed away, destroyed when he was no longer needed. Walter was right. The man wasn't his President. He was a criminal.

And Sam's wife and son were in a prison controlled by this man and his people.

But let him die, to stand here and let it happen... A rush of emotions surged through him, led by revenge. Let the goddamn Kingfish get killed. Why not? The bastard deserved it as much as Hitler did.

He stood still, frozen, among the happy, jostling crowd.

And yet... and yet...

There were thousands and thousands of Jewish refugees alive in the United States because of Long. Tens of thousands of Jews who hadn't been killed, hadn't been gassed, hadn't been shot. And thousands more were on their way.

But Long was the key, as his boss had said. Without Long, there was no agreement. With Long dead—maybe things would improve. Maybe.

But with Long dead, thousands more—without a doubt—would die.

Sam kept moving, shouldering through the crowd, holding up his inspector's badge, pushing ahead, seeing in his mind's eye poor Otto, starved and beaten and away from home, Otto and his barracks mates, depending on Long's decision, depending on the Americans, depending on Sam, goddammit.

On the platform there was a knot of people at one end, waiting to get onto the *Ferdinand Magellan.* The Portsmouth cops let him through, thank God, and now he was on the platform, running, the stench of fear and burnt coal in his nostrils, and up ahead were men carrying submachine guns under their coats, other people, newsreel men, and waving a boater, President Long, whooping it up, laughing—

Joining the crowd, walking deliberately, limping, Reginald Hale, carrying Walter's old valise, walking straight toward Long and the crowd of people—

A Secret Service agent, large and wide in a black suit, shoulder holster visible under his coat, tried to block Sam, who shouldered him aside like the football player he once was, and he elbowed and spun—

"Hale! Stop! Right there!"

Reginald Hale turned at the sound of his name, his face suddenly white and frightened. He carried the valise with both hands. Sam pulled his revolver out, holding up his badge in the other hand, yelling loudly, "Bomb! He's got a bomb! He's got a bomb!"

Yells and screams and a phalanx of armed men grouped around the President, their submachine guns held up like spears of some old Roman guard. Hale was moving forward, too, the valise held against his chest like a prized possession, moving faster.

Sam shot once, and Reginald stumbled, fell to his knees. Men and women on the platform flattened to the ground, screaming as the guns opened up. Sam saw it all as the British army officer, his body jerking from the blows of the .45-caliber slugs, fell backward and rolled off the platform to the railway bed below, and as a couple of the braver guards stepped forward to fire again at him, the shattering *boom!* of the explosion tore them to pieces.

CHAPTER SIXTY-TWO

Sam sagged against a cement pillar, opening and closing his mouth, his ears ringing. A man came into view, kneeling next to him. Sirens were wailing. The man's suit was soiled with coal dust and blood. He mouthed something, and Sam said, "Huh? What?"

The man yelled into Sam's ear: "I said I need you to come with me."

"I can't move."

"You better move," he answered, "because you're putting the President's life in danger, you moron." The man grabbed Sam's arm, and Sam angrily shook it off and said, "Who the hell are you?"

"Parker. Agent in charge of the President's Secret Service detail."

"Is he okay? The President?"

"Oh, shit yeah, but he's had to change his underwear. Do me a favor and forget I told you that."

He helped Sam to his feet, Sam letting him. There were shiny spent cartridge cases and pools of blood, and by the platform edge, where Reginald Hale had fallen, there were two figures covered by stained white sheets. Expensive leather shoes poked out from under the sheets. Wooden police barricades were being set up, keeping screaming crowds and desperate photographers and newsreel men at bay. At the other end of the station platform, the *Ferdinand Magellan* was at rest, smoke and steam curling lazily up into the sky.

Parker gripped Sam's arm again and said, "Come on."

"What for? And why am I putting the President in danger?"

Parker looked at him as if he were a first-grader appearing in a high school math class. "The President wants to see you. The man who saved his life. And you're putting him in more danger because I want him the hell out of this town. Two assassination attempts on Hitler and Long in two days is too much. The quicker I get him back to Washington, the better, and that's why I need you."

Sam was half dragged, half propelled to the rear of the train, which had a wrought-iron railing about the stern car, complete with presidential seal. Secret Service and two of Long's Legionnaires stood guard there, all armed with pistols or submachine guns. "Do me a favor, okay?" Parker told Sam. "Do this thing and I owe you one, bud. Just go in there, let the President gush all over you, then get the hell out. Quicker you're done, quicker I can get back to my job. Oh, and you need to do something for me—your sidearm. Nobody but Secret Service and his Legionnaires see him with weapons."

Sam said, "I'm not sure where it is."

Parker grunted, flipped open Sam's coat, and pulled the revolver from the shoulder holster. Sam didn't even remember putting it back after shooting Reggie Hale.

He said nothing as Parker led him past the unsmiling men. As the door opened, Sam ducked in, his ears still ringing, his legs trembling. There were men crowded in the leather- and wood-lined train car. The window shades were drawn. A Southern voice, so familiar from radio and newsreels, boomed: "Everyone get the hell out, all right? I want to see this young man, this hero, and I want to thank him myself!"

In a matter of seconds, Sam was alone with the President of the United States.

Huey Long sat on a light yellow settee, plump legs sprawled out before him on the carpeted floor. He had on a bright red silk dressing gown and blue pajama trousers. His feet were clad in black slippers, and a thick glass was in one hand. Long was grinning, but his face was red, and Sam saw his hand was shaking, making the amber- colored liquor slosh back and forth in the glass.

"So!" came that familiar voice. "The man of the hour! My personal savior. Just who the hell are you, son?"

Sam stepped forward on the fine Oriental carpeting, trying to take it all in. Part of him couldn't believe he was here, talking to the man, and part of him was also aware of his stained and torn suit.

"I'm Sam Miller, sir. I'm an inspector with the Portsmouth Police Department."

"You're the one who warned us all? Who fired that first shot, eh? Against that mad bomber?"

"That's right, sir."

The florid face became suspicious. "You said your name was Miller. Dammit, didn't a guy named Miller try to kill Hitler yesterday? That man a relative of yours?"

"Yes... a relative, I'm sorry to say."

He waited, then the train seemed to stabilize as Long laughed and roared, "Damn, relatives can be a hell of a thing. If you knew what some of my relations back in Winn Parish were up to… I'm jus' glad you were here savin' my bacon at the last minute. How in hell did you know what was gonna happen, son?"

"Sir, it's a fairly long story, well, I think you'd want to get out of Portsmouth instead of listening to it. It's a pretty complex investigation."

Long laughed again. "Damn, boy, that's what they were tryin' to do to me—to get my ass out of town—but hell, I told 'em, first, I don't want to skedaddle out like some scared nigra hearing a haunt from the woods, and second, I want to meet the brave peace officer who not only saved me but saved his country."

The President's eyes narrowed as he took a healthy swallow. "You know that, right? You saved your country, son. Only the Kingfish could get that son-of-a-bitch housepainter over here to sign that treaty, and that treaty, son, is gonna mean millions of jobs for people at home. None of us got any taste to get into that fight over there in Europe, but if we can make some money off the deal, then why the hell not?"

Sam thought of Burdick, knew they and the others would survive with Long still alive. "That's a good point, sir. A good deal."

Long finished off his drink with a contented sigh. "It certainly is." He quickly got up and extended a hand, which Sam shook. His skin was cold and clammy. Long said, "This wasn't the first time someone tried to kill me, and it probably won't be the last. Hey, you wouldn't be interested in being in the Secret Service, would you? I sure could make it happen. You could be on the White House detail. Some travel but"—he laughed again—"I'm told there are some side benefits'."

"No, sir, thank you. I think I'll stay here."

It was an odd thing, it was as though a radio switch had been clicked somewhere behind those bright eyes of President Long; he had seemingly lost all interest in Sam. Tugging his robe closer to his ample frame, he said, "Well, son, thanks again for what you did, and for comin' in to talk to me. If you ever find yourself in D.C., by all means, stop by, and if there's anything I can do—"

It came to Sam like a flash of lightning from a cloudless sky. "Mr. President, there is one thing you could do for me."

"Eh? What's that?"

Sam took a breath. "Sir, my wife and son. They could use your help."

"How's that?"

"My wife, Sarah, and my little boy, Toby. They're being kept at the internment facility at Camp Carpenter, outside of Manchester. They haven't done anything wrong. They were picked up by mistake just before the summit. I've tried to get them out, but..."

Long pursed his lips. "Your wife, she didn't do anything?"

"Mr. President, she's just a school secretary. She's the daughter of the city's mayor. She's a supporter of yours for years now, and my boy, he's only eight. How could they be a threat?"

There was silence for a few moments, just the grumbling and rumbling of the steam engine. Sam could feel sweat trickling down his neck. Long stared at him. Then he nodded. "All right. You write down their names right there on that pad, and I'll check it out, and maybe I can get 'em sprung."

"Mr. President?"

"Eh?"

"Could you make it an official pardon? That way, my wife won't have to be scared about being picked up again. You know how mistakes are made."

Sam wondered if he had pushed too hard, if everything was threatened. But Long smiled and said, "That must be some wife, you're so desperate to get her home. All right, a pardon. I guess you deserve that after what you did for me and your nation. But I need the names, and they need to be checked out. Now, if you don't mind, Inspector..."

Sam didn't mind. He took out his fountain pen, scrawled Sarah and Toby's names on the notepad, hardly believing he had pulled it off. Long took it and headed to the far door, yelling out, "All right, you sons of bitches, I got one more piece of paperwork to take care of, and then let's get this train goin' the hell out of here!"

Sam went out the way he'd come in, and by the time his feet were back on the platform, the sharp shrill of the train whistle cut through the afternoon air. The *Ferdinand Magellan* glided away, the President, and current dictator, of the United States safe and sound.

Sam looked again at the sheet-covered bodyguards, and he shuddered, thinking of the bloody mess on the tracks below. Reginald Hale, killed in a foreign land, trying to murder a foreign leader.

He knew he should feel remorse at what had happened, regret for the poor man's wife, who had done so much in vain to free her husband. But as he walked down the bloodstained platform, he didn't care.

His family was coming home.

CHAPTER SIXTY-THREE

He spent several hours in Marshal Hanson's office, telling and retelling his story to Hanson, to the Secret Service, and even to a bandaged and angry Special Agent LaCouture of the FBI. And when it was over, LaCouture said to the Secret Service, "You heard what the man said about Hale and how he got here. I want arrests to start right away. We'll start with that writer tenant of yours, that Tucker."

Sam said, "Walter... he's just a science professor, a pulp writer, that's all."

LaCouture touched the bandage across his broken nose and snarled, "The hell he is. He's an accomplice to an assassination attempt."

Hanson intervened, "Sam, you know that's how it's going to be. I know he's your neighbor, but he's got to be brought in."

LaCouture glared at him and said, "Just be thankful I ain't chargin' you, too, Inspector."

Sam said, "You know, Jack, your nose really looks good. It truly does. Do you want me to rearrange it again?" LaCouture cursed and moved toward him, but Hanson and two Secret Service agents hauled him back, and Hanson said, "All right, all right. My inspector here has had a long day. I'm sure he can talk to you tomorrow if you've got any other questions. Okay?"

With that, the office emptied until it was just Hanson and Sam.

"Sam," Hanson said, going back to his desk. "You did something magnificent today, something historical. You saved the President's life."

"Tell you the truth, I didn't care about the President," Sam said bitterly. "I cared about those poor bastards in Burdick and everywhere else. That's what I was thinking."

Hanson took off his glasses, polished them with a handkerchief. "If you say so. Look, you're beat. Time for you to go home, take a few days off. Then you come back, and we'll clear all this up."

Sam was too tired to argue. "Sure. That sounds good." As he went to the door, Hanson called out, "One more thing—"

Sam turned and saw something flying at him. He caught it instinctively with one hand. He looked down at the thick black leather wallet, opened it up. The gold shield of an inspector. Not the silver shield of an acting inspector.

"Congratulations, Sam," Hanson said. "Now get the hell out of here."

Sam clasped the wallet and shield tightly in his hand and tried to remember when this scrap of leather and metal had once meant so much.

At his desk, he picked up his coat draped over the chair, the sleeve still damaged where that cig boy had tried to cut him the other day. Poor sweet Sarah. Never did get around to mending that sleeve. By his typewriter was the day's mail. One envelope stood out—from the state's division of motor vehicles. He recalled the request he had made so many lifetimes ago. He tore open the envelope, read the listing inside of yellow Ramblers belonging to area residents of Portsmouth.

There was only one. He read and reread the name and decided it was time to go home.

He pulled the Packard into his driveway, and he saw lights on downstairs. Lots and lots of lights.

Sam leaped out of the car, raced up the front steps, and opened the door.

Sarah. His Sarah, standing there, his lovely Sarah, looking at him, staring at him.

It was wrong. Everything was wrong.

She was standing there, arms folded. Her face was pale and looked thinner. Her hair hadn't been washed in a while, and her pale blue dress was stained and wrinkled.

Her silk stockings looked like they had runs, and her shoes were scuffed and soiled.

"Sarah," he said.

There was a pause. "You got a haircut."

"Yeah, you could say that," he replied, knowing nothing could be said about Burdick, nothing at all; that secret was terrible to keep but too terrible to share.

A voice from the kitchen, sobbing. "Mommy, look at what happened to my models! They're all smashed!"

Sam called out, "Toby! What's wrong?"

His son ran in, holding a cardboard box in front of him, the smashed pieces of his models sticking out. Sam's heart ached at seeing the tears on his boy's face. He said, "Toby, look, I'm sorry, we'll get you new ones."

"But Dad, these are *mine* We built them together!" Looking at Sarah stiffly standing there, Sam said carefully, "Bad men came into the house, Toby. Bad men came in and broke your toys. But I promise you, we'll either fix them or we'll get new ones."

"It won't be the same! It won't! Why didn't you stop them, Daddy? Why didn't you stop the bad men?"

"Toby, please..."

"You promised! You promised! I hate you! I *hate* you!" "Toby, back to your room." Sarah raised her voice, "Mommy needs to talk to Daddy."

Still sobbing, Toby tore from the room, carrying the broken pieces with him, as Sam looked to his wife.

"How long have you been back?" he asked. *I hate you,* the little voice had shouted. *I hate you...*

"Only a few minutes."

"How did you get here?"

She said, "A Long's Legionnaire who hadn't taken a bath in a month drove us back. We got home to this." Sarah gestured to the broken furniture, the piles of books, the debris of what their life had been.

Sam said, "Long's Legionnaires broke in, while I was away on the job."

"And you didn't have time to clean up so Toby and I didn't have to look at this when we got home?"

He ran a hand over his hair. "The past couple of days, I haven't had time to take a breath. I did the best I could."

"So I've heard," she said, lips pursed. "You saved the life of the Kingfish. Congratulations, I guess."

Something dark flared inside him. "Not *guess,* Sarah. You should say *congratulations.* It's because I saved Long that I was able to get you and Toby out. Nothing else was going to work. I saved his Cajun ass and in return, he got you and the boy out."

"Sure, I understand." Her eyes blazed at him. "Acting like a dictator or a Roman emperor dispensing favors because it suits him. I understand a lot. And I'm sorry about Tony, Sam. I truly am." Tears glittered in her eyes, and she wiped at them and then refolded her arms.

He stared at her, wondering what was going on behind those sharp brown eyes, and then he heard himself saying, "Why did you do it, Sarah?"

"Do what?"

"You know what I mean," he said, choosing his words carefully. "Why did you give yourself up to the FBI?"

"I have no idea what you're talking about. Toby and I got picked up while we were walking down one of the lake roads to a neighbor's house."

"That doesn't make sense—you and Toby being picked up like that, just walking along the road. Unless the FBI was following you, which I doubt. With the summit coming here, with all the resources being stretched out, I can't see why the FBI would spare the agents to tail you almost a hundred miles away."

She bit her lower lip again. Sam said, "But after I told you to get out of your dad's place, you must have made a phone call. You surrendered to the FBI. You wanted to be arrested. Why?"

Sarah didn't say a word.

He pressed on. "Doesn't make sense. You giving yourself up to the FBI. Unless you did that on purpose so I'd be blackmailed and would have to cooperate with them when they were looking for my brother. Somebody wanted me to look for Tony. Somebody wanted Tony to be found."

Her voice quavered. "I don't know what you're talking about."

"Sarah...you can do so many things with ease and grace, from taking care of Toby when he has the flu to cooking a Sunday meal... but you can't lie worth shit. And another thing—you lied to me when you said you didn't know anyone who owned a yellow Rambler. But your friend from school, Mrs. Brownstein. The one who helped you with the Underground Railroad. Your mah-jongg partner. She owns a yellow Rambler."

"How am I supposed to know who drives what?" she said carelessly. "What difference does it make?"

"The difference is that a Rambler was used to slow down the train the night that body was dumped. Like it was a setup. And it was. Wasn't it?"

Tears came back to her eyes, and Sam knew that the woman in front of him, his wife, his lover, the mother of his child, the high school cheerleader he had wooed for such a delightful time, was a stranger.

"Who was he?" No reply.

"Tell me Sarah," Sam went on. "The man on the train. Oh, I know his real name and where he was coming from. He had escaped from a camp in New Mexico. And what does he do? Does he go south to Mexico, to escape from America, or does he go west to California, where he can disappear in the crowds? No. He makes his way east, heading to the small port city of Portsmouth. Your friend slows the train down enough to jump off, and he ends up here, right? At the city's Underground Railroad station. A station that—"

A memory, incomplete but coming clear.

"This station.. .your station... gets wanted people up north to Montreal," Sam said. "That's the whole point of why he came here. To get to Montreal. And up in Montreal this week is a delegation from the Soviet Union. Not in

Vancouver, or Ottawa, the capitol. They were waiting for someone, weren't they? Why was he so important?"

"Please..."

"Sarah, who was he?"

"I don't know," she said urgently. "All I know is that he had to get off that train, get in our basement, and then get out the next morning. He had to be in Montreal. He just had to be. But he was murdered."

"And you didn't tell me any of this that day you knew he was murdered?"

She said, "Not my place to tell you that."

"Who killed him?"

"How the hell should I know?" she snapped.

"Because you know more than I ever imagined," Sam said. "And you surrendered to the FBI, didn't you? Betrayed me so I'd feel compelled to find Tony, to find him and set him up for his murder."

"Sam..."

"Dammit, that's what Tony told me just before he was murdered. That there was a grand plan and he and I were part of it. He knew all along he was on a suicide mission. He knew I would play my part as a cop, and you did your part as well."

Then something seemed to slam in the back of his head. "You used Toby, didn't you? My God, Sarah, you used our son!" Her face seemed set in granite. He had to catch his breath before he could go on. "Toby asked a lot of questions about spies. Told me he didn't like getting in trouble but sometimes he had to. That's right, had to. He was so scared he started wetting the bed. And when he got in trouble at school, he'd see the principal. Frank Kaminski. You know who his brother is. You used Toby as a courier, didn't you, Sarah? To pass along messages to Kaminski. And I bet you told him to get into trouble on purpose so he'd be sent to the principal's office."

He kept looking at the woman he once thought had no surprises for him. "Who's pulling the strings? Who's ordering you?"

She stared at him with an expression he had never seen before.

It was disdain.

"Sam... Toby's hero, so true and noble... and you can't even see what's going on right in your own house, can you, Sam? The Underground Railroad—you think that got in place by accident? Do you think thousands of us, hell, tens of thousands, aren't working day and night to defeat Long and crush Hitler? Do you?"

"Sarah—"

"Amateur revolutionaries, you called us. It's always been the amateurs who made things right, who fought against the evil and the powerful. But we're not amateurs, none of us, and we're working with our brothers in Moscow, London, and yes, even Berlin, to set things right."

He couldn't believe what he was going to say next, but it was the only thing he could think of. "Who's we?"

"Who cares? Its just labels, that's all. Progressive, liberal, Communist, socialist, even Republican... labels. Call us the resistance, if you like. But what counts is the fight, what people bring to the fight, and I've been in the fight for years. Sam, do you know what it's like to see children at your school, children in what's supposed to be the richest and safest nation in the world, wearing scraps of blankets? To see brothers and sisters take turns eating breakfast because there's not enough food at home? And who's helping them? *Nobody,* that's who! If that makes me a bad woman, someone who uses her family to help, then damn it all to hell, I'm proud to be a bad woman, a bad wife, a bad mother—"

"But what—"

She shook her head, furious. "So when I'm told to prepare for a guest from that scheduled train, I do just that. And when I'm told to give myself up to the FBI so that you do what has to be done for the greater good, whatever that is, then I do it. I'm sorry, and maybe you don't believe me, but I didn't know it was going to end with Tony being killed. And I didn't know Tony was going to try to shoot Hitler. I just knew he was in terrible danger, that he was part of something I belonged to as well."

"And what about Toby?"

She looked toward the boy's bedroom, and her sharp voice faltered. "He's a brave boy. A very brave boy... He did what I asked him to do, whether it was delivering messages or trusting his mother, and I wish he had a brave father to look up to."

"What the hell do you mean by that?"

Her sad eyes pierced him. "What do you think? From what you've told me, what I've seen in the papers, Tony was ready to sacrifice all to get himself killed in an attempt to assassinate Hitler to draw attention from what was being planned for that bastard Long, and there you are, *protecting* both Hitler and Long. Two fascists destroying what's left of civilization. I secretly saw Tony a few days ago. He said he was doing it all for Toby and what kind of life our son was going to have. Can you say the same thing?"

"I was doing my job," he countered, knowing how weak it sounded.

"That's some job you've got there, Sam Miller." She walked away from him, then turned, eyes wet with tears. "I'm going to my dad's place, Sam. And I'm taking Toby with me."

He was chilled, as if his blood had been replaced by salt water from the harbor. "For how long?"

"However long it takes for me to think things through. I need to be with someone committed to our fight, someone who wants to change things, to make things better. You're just part of the system, and... and I'm not sure if I can live with someone like that. Over the years, you've done some things here and there—giving money to refugee kids, looking the other way at our basement station, ignoring some of the stupid laws from D.C.—but I need more."

"Sarah, you've got to—"

"Sam, please," she interrupted. "I feel guilty about a lot of things, and one of those things is your brother. Right now I want Toby to be proud of his dead uncle, a man who sacrificed himself for everything, and I'm not sure what Toby has to be proud of when he sees you. And I don't like feeling that way."

"So your dad's place is the answer?"

Again a sad look that went right through him. "I don't see why not. I've always trusted Dad even when you've had nothing but contempt for him. I admire him, too. He's put everything on the line to do what's right."

Then it made sense. The visit to the store days ago from the man called Eric the Red. The encounter at the island: *You think you know everything about me, everything about how I think and work. Kid, you know shit.*

Sam said, "Your dad is your connection, isn't he? The one who told you what to do. On the surface, he's a full- fledged member of the Party. Underneath, he's something else."

"Very good, Inspector. You figured that out all on your own."

With his newly minted inspector's badge weighing in his coat pocket, he found he could not say a word. And what about Pierce Island, he thought, should he tell her about Pierce Island and her father and the sailor?

No, that would sound like cheap revenge and nothing else.

Again saying words he couldn't believe he was saying. "So you're off to be with your father, your resistance leader."

"For now."

He could hear the sobs from his son, weeping over his shattered models, crying over the broken dream that his father could protect him. *Sorry, kid,* he thought, *so very sorry.*

"Tell Toby... tell him I have to go out on a case, all right? I don't want to make a scene. Tell him I'll make it all right."

Her arms folded tight against her chest, she didn't reply. He went to the door, stopped. "You're pretty good at thinking you know what drives me and what I do, but in the past few days, I've seen things and done things I can't tell you about, Sarah. Important things that have made more of a difference than you and your friends could ever dream of."

"So says you," she said coldly.

"Yeah, so says me," he said. "And despite what you think now, we can work this out. It'll take time, but I know we can work it out."

"I'm not so sure, Sam. I'm really not. It would take a lot."

"Okay," he said. "I get the message. It'll take a lot, and that's what I'll do."

Outside, the damp air from the harbor chilled him.

CHAPTER SIXTY-FOUR

The day was cold and windy, and Sam stood by himself on a knoll at the Calvary Cemetery in Portsmouth, near the border of the small town of Greenland. The previous night he had once again slept in Hanson's office. He drew his coat closer, watching the ceremony finish up. There was a plain wooden casket, and a priest was saying prayers over the mangled body of his brother. Except for two cemetery workers standing by themselves, shovels in hand, this part of the cemetery was empty. The ceremony was supposed to be secret, but somehow the news had gotten out.

On the other side of the iron gates there were newspaper reporters and a couple of newsreel crews, all eager to record the burial of the attempted assassin of Adolf Hitler, but the priest—his parish priest, Father Mullen from St. James Church—had denied them entrance. Sam supposed he should have attempted to tell Sarah about the funeral, but he was going to let that rest for now. Sarah would have to mourn Tony at her own time and pace. And he wasn't surprised that he was the only mourner present. Being known as an associate of an assassin, someone who almost destroyed the summit that promised so much, was just too dangerous.

The priest finished, made a sign of the cross, and then came over, his vestments flapping in the breeze. Sam

shook his hand and said, "Thanks, Father. I appreciate that."

The priest nodded. "I knew your brother back when he was active in the shipyard, trying to make things better for the workers."

Sam felt the words stick in his throat, knowing his brother and what he had done. "Excuse me for saying this, Father, but he could be a pain in the ass. But sometimes he was a good man, wasn't he?"

"We're all good men, Sam. But these are trying times, and all of us sometimes make compromises, sometimes make decisions... It's not an easy time."

Sam watched as the cemetery workers came out and, with a set of straps, lowered his brother's body into the unmarked grave. He didn't answer the priest.

He stood there for a while, then started walking to another gate of the cemetery, where he could avoid the crowd of reporters. He saw a man standing near a solitary pine tree. The man was watching him, and Sam changed direction to join him.

"Hello, Doc," Sam said. "Sorry I've been avoiding you. It's been a shitty few days."

Dr. William Saunders, the county medical examiner, nodded in reply. "Yeah, it sure has. Sony about your brother."

"Thanks."

"Yeah, well, don't be so smug. I think you did a shitty thing, saving that asshole Long's life."

Sam replied evenly, "You and a bunch of others, I'm sure." The medical examiner kept quiet. Sam said, "Doc, don't play any goddamn games with me. I'm not in the mood. Why are you here? What's so important?"

Saunders looked over Sam's shoulder toward the downtown. "You know, we medical examiners, we sometimes pass along information to one another, little bits of professional knowledge that doesn't get out to the public. Especially for those of us working in cities that have a large refugee population. You tend to look for odd things you don't otherwise see in the course of your day-to-day work."

Sam said, "What did you find? And how did you miss it the first time out?"

Saunders sighed. "I'm old, and I'm tired, and things get missed. I didn't miss a damn thing on that autopsy. The poor guy's neck was snapped, he was malnourished, he had that damn tattoo, and oh, by the way, his blood work came back normal. No poisons or toxins in his system. But I did miss something in his clothing..."

He reached into his pocket and took out a metal cylinder, less than an inch wide and perhaps two inches long. Saunders said, "In these troubled times, refugees use these capsules to transport important things. Diamonds, rubies, or a key to a safe deposit box. Women—God bless them, they have two receptacles available to hold such tubes, while we men have to do with just one. Ingenious, isn't it? And when I was finally sorting through your dead man's clothing, I found this tucked away in his underwear. When a man—or woman—dies, the sphincter muscles relax, and what's up there, Inspector, will always come out."

Sam took the cylinder from the medical examiner, looked at it, and then unscrewed the top. He looked inside. "Was it empty when you opened it?"

"No."

"What was in it?"

Saunders looked at him; the scar on his throat was prominent. He said, "Sam... can I really trust you?"

"What do you mean?"

"Shit, I know that's a tough question to ask, especially these days. What I'm getting at... can I trust you to keep my ass out of a labor camp, and to do something important?"

"You can trust me to keep you out of prison, as long as I have anything to say about it. What's so important beyond that?"

The medical examiner coughed, a harsh sound coming from deep in his chest. "The last war, I spent months in those godforsaken trenches, trying to save the lives of men being gassed, shattered by shrapnel, and shot... and for what? To make the world safe for democracy. Corny, I know, but we believed it back then, and some of us, even in these worst of times, still believe it."

"Just tell me, what was in that cylinder?"

Another pause, and the wind seemed to cut at him even deeper. He pushed aside the thought of how cold Tony's grave must be.

Saunders said, "A special kind of film called microfilm. A process that reduces pages of documents to a single filmstrip."

"A courier," Sam said. "I'll be damned. What kind of documents was he carrying?"

Saunders reached again into his coat pocket, pulled out a business-size envelope. "That's for you to find out, Inspector. I processed the film, was able to make readable copies for you. I've looked at them, and I can't figure it out. But I'm sure you will."

"Was it another language?"

Saunders smiled. "Yeah, it was. But you're an inspector. Just do the right thing, okay?"

Sam held the envelope. Made of paper, it seemed to weigh a ton. "That I'll do. But Doc, after we talked last, just after that FBI guy and Gestapo guy met you, did you discuss the case with anyone else?"

"Nope. Not a soul."

Sam lifted the envelope again. "Thanks, Doc. And I'm sorry I didn't get to you earlier."

The medical examiner said. "It's okay, Sam. I'm sure it will work out."

Sam said, "I'm glad you are. I'm not."

CHAPTER SIXTY-FIVE

The day after Tony's burial, Sam stood in the football field of the Portsmouth High School, watching the FBI and the local contingent of Long's Legionnaires processing arrested people and conducting interrogations over the assassination attempt on President Long. The matter of the attack on Hitler was over and complete, Tony Miller being the designated patsy. But the investigation into the attempted killing of the President was still going on, and it was a chance for the Legionnaires and the FBI to conduct a nice purge of the surrounding towns, using the assassination as a cover to arrest anyone and everyone who had pissed off the government.

Temporary barbed-wire fencing had been strung around the perimeter of the field, and canvas tents had been set up. The turf had been churned into a muddy mess by all the feet trampling through. Sam used his newly minted ID to gain access to one special prisoner. And as he had walked across the chewed-up field, the finger he had broken back during that championship game started aching again, like a reminder of what had been, what had been lost.

He remembered how, days ago, the night the body was discovered, he'd recalled the sweet memory of winning that game... and immediately that taste of victory being overcome with a taste of ashes, of seeing his dad triumphant over Tony's acceptance at the Navy Yard, the bad son, the one who was always in trouble, the one always in Dad's favor. And now Mom at a rest home, Dad and Tony buried, and this field where Sam had first become someone, had done something to be proud of, had now been turned into something else, just another prison. Like this country, he thought, going from a nation of laws to a nation of labor camps. When he had been a senior at this school, it had been a more innocent time. It had all been so black and white. To defeat one's opponent, that's all. Just to win.

Black and white. No shades of gray. God, how he missed those days.

A dozen men were being herded along in front of him, their shoes and boots muddy, their eyes downcast, each with one hand on the shoulder of the man in front, as they were prodded along by Long's Legionnaires carrying pump-action shotguns. At the end of the line, a Legionnaire caught Sam's eye, and he didn't look away. He remembered that face. It was the Legionnaire who had strutted into the Fish Shanty so very long ago, the night he had first come across the dead man.

The Legionnaire grabbed the last man in line, brought him over to Sam. The Legionnaire grinned, breathing hard, his face bruised. "You're that police inspector. The one that saved the President."

"Yeah, I am," Sam said, looking at the prisoner. His suit was well cut, and he had a trimmed black mustache and haircut. Sam recognized him as a businessman from the next city up the coast, Dover. Woods, was that his name?

The Legionnaire twisted the man's arm, and Woods winced. The Legionnaire said, "Yeah, and you're the inspector that was in that greasy-spoon restaurant the night me and Vern had to get new tires on our car 'cause some asshole knifed 'em. Vern and me, we got ambushed and tuned up a couple of days later."

Sam said, "Look, I don't—"

The Legionnaire said, "You may be so high and mighty, boy, but remember this, me and Vern and everyone else like us, we're runnin' the show. No matter if you like it or not."

The young man pushed Woods hard in the small of the back. "Run, you son of a bitch, run," and Woods, stumbling a bit in the mud, started running after the moving line of prisoners. Sam saw what was going to happen next, started to yell out, "No!" In one smooth and practiced motion, the Legionnaire lifted his shotgun and fired at the back of the running man. The hollow *boom* tore at Sam's ears, and Woods crumpled to the muddy earth.

"So maybe you're a hero today, bud," the Legionnaire said, "but you and everyone else who don't fall in line, you're still shitheads, and you can still get shot while tryin' to escape, and there's nothin' anybody can do about it. Understand?"

Sam felt his face burning. He had just seen a first- degree murder right in front of him, and been powerless to do anything. Not a goddamn thing. He walked away.

He sat in one corner of a small green canvas tent smelling of dampness and mildew. Inside were a table and a couple of wooden chairs sinking into the soil. The flap of the tent opened, and another Long's Legionnaire peered in. "You Miller?"

"Yeah," he said, not wanting to see again in his mind's eye a man murdered to prove a point. That was all. A man dragged from his home today, accused of God only knew what, and because he was last in line and easy to grasp, he was shot dead.

"Your prisoner is coming," the Legionnaire said.

The guard seemed to be in his early twenties, with close-cropped blond hair and Legionnaire's uniform complete with Confederate-flag pin on the lapel. The look on his face seemed to indicate he would be equally comfortable in the uniform of the SS, just like his shotgun- wielding partner. "You the same Miller who saved the President?"

"I am," Sam said, looking out at the mass of prisoners.

"Then it'd be an honor for us to buy you a drink or six when the day is through, if you don't mind."

Sam fought to keep a friendly smile on his face. "That sounds great, but my schedule's pretty packed. I tell you what, you tell your friends here that I said hello. Okay?"

"Sure," the Legionnaire said, and then another arrived, holding a man by the elbow. The man had on a light brown tweed suit but no necktie. His shoes had no laces. His hands were cuffed, and the second Legionnaire said, "The cuffs are comin' off, boy, but you best behave. You got that?"

The man whispered, "Yes," and Sam noticed his left eye was bruised and swollen. The prisoner rubbed at his wrists as the cuffs were removed, and both Legionnaires left.

"Hello, Walter," Sam said.

"Sam, what a pleasant surprise."

"Have a seat."

The former science professor sat down in one of the chairs, breathed an apparent sigh of relief. "It feels good to be in a real chair. The interrogations... sometimes they ask you question after question and make you stand for hours...it doesn't sound like much, but do it for hours, and you'll see what kind of torture it is."

"I can imagine," Sam said.

Walter shook his head. "No, you can't. Unless you've been here or someplace similar, you can't."

Sam looked to his wrist, where the hidden numeral was tattooed into his skin, was. "Walter, I'm not here to debate."

His former tenant smiled wanly. "Of course, yes, of course. How in the world did you get in here? Lawyers and family are all being kept out while we stumble through our version of Hitler's Night of the Long Knives.

Remember that, back in the '30s? It was decided it was time for Hitler to kill or jail all his opponents, and they did. Oh, that was a time—"

"Walter, for once, will you shut the hell up?"

Walter did just that. Sam said, "I got in because I called in a favor from the Secret Service. Told them I needed to see you."

"I take it you're not here to free me."

"Hardly. I've got two things I want to talk to you about. Remember the night I was called out for the body by Maplewood Avenue?"

"No, not really."

"Of course you do. I had to come upstairs and unclog your sink. Who told you to do that, Walter? A couple of weeks earlier you had pulled the same stunt, clogging the sink with potato peels. You're scatterbrained but not that scatterbrained. So who told you? Was it Sarah?"

Walter blinked. "She asked me to do something to get you upstairs for a while."

"Did she say why?"

Walter squirmed in his seat, and Sam went on. "Sarah had a guest coming, right? Someone to go in the cellar, someone she didn't want me to know was there. And she wanted me upstairs at a certain time so she could sneak the man in."

"That's what I surmised." He wiped at his bruised eye with a soiled hand. "She didn't say it so plainly, but yes, I believe that's what she wanted. So who was that dead man?"

"Not your place to ask questions," Sam said curtly. "Only to answer them."

From his coat pocket he took out the papers the medical examiner had given him. "Take a look these, tell me what they mean."

Walter looked puzzled, but he did as he was told. He unfolded the sheets and examined each one, sometimes holding them close to his undamaged eye. "There are some serious mathematical formulas in here. Even with my teaching background, I'm not sure I can puzzle them out."

"You better try. I need for you to look at those equations and tell me what they mean."

"I'm not sure I can do that," Walter insisted, his voice plaintive.

"Then, dammit, tell me why they're important. Tell me why someone would be willing to die to protect these pages."

Walter stared at him a moment. Then he bent again on the pages, pursing his bruised lips. Finally, he gathered the pages together and pushed them back across the table. "Can I ask you where you got these?"

"No."

"Some research facility? A physics laboratory of some sort?"

"Walter..."

He moved in his chair, winced from something paining him. "A guess, that's all. An educated guess."

"I'll take that. Tell me."

And Walter told him.

Sam shoved the papers back in his coat, tired and cold and feeling as if he were climbing the slope of a mountain that kept on getting steeper and steeper. Walter put his hands together and said, "What now?"

Sam said, "I go back to work, and I'm sorry, you go back to your interrogators."

Walter shivered. "They caught me as I was driving up to Maine, Sam, trying to get to the Canadian border. I suppose a brave man would have raced through the roadblock, but I'm not. And later, when they brought me here, I had illusions of trying to resist, trying to be strong, trying to hold out as long as I could... I held out for five minutes before I started crying and answering every question they asked me. Do you want to know how they did it?"

"No, I don't," Sam said.

Walter ignored him. "They put you on a board, tie your hands and feet together, and then tip you back, put a wet cloth across your face, and pour water over you. They laugh as you think you're drowning. A nice little treat they learned from the Nazis. It worked, but still, the questions keep on coming." Walter cocked his head. "Is it true, what I've heard? That you got to Hale before he got to Long? That you shot Hale, and he blew himself up, but not close enough to hurt Long?"

"True enough," Sam said.

"You son of a whore. Do you have any idea what you did in preventing that monster's death?"

Sam got up, thinking of his tattoo and of his nameless camp companions, alive and spread out across the nation, thought about that dead businessman out there, dead on a muddy playing field, all because of him. "Yeah, Walter, I think I do."

When he left the tent, a young Legionnaire stood waiting, his red hair closely trimmed, patches of wispy orange hair about his chin.

"Mr. Miller?" the Legionnaire asked. "Somebody needs to see you right away."

The man took Sam's left arm, and Sam angrily shook it off. He thought about striding out of the camp, ignoring this young punk, but with all the shotgun-toting Legionnaires and angry-looking FBI agents about, how far could he go?

"All right," Sam said. "Take me there, but keep your damn hand to yourself."

The Legionnaire glared at Sam but kept quiet, and Sam kept stride with him as they went to a larger tent. "Right in there, sir," he said. Sam hesitated, then ducked his head and walked in. This tent had a canvas floor, chairs, a dining room table, a wet bar, and a desk with matching chair and a black metal wastebasket. Lights came from overhead lightbulbs, and a small electric heater in one corner of the tent cut the chill. Sitting in the chair was another Long's Legionnaire, older, his uniform crisp and clean, the leatherwork shiny, and on the collar tabs, the oak leaves of a major.

Sam took the chair across the desk. The Legionnaire said, "Sam. Good to see you."

"How long?" Sam said.

Clarence Rolston, the janitor and handyman for the Portsmouth Police Department, picked up a file folder and replied, "Years and years, of course. And damn long years at that. Pretending to be brain-soaked, slow and dense, takes a lot of work. Most Legionnaires are happy to do their work in public. It takes a special talent and commitment to spend years underground."

"Was Hanson in on it?" Sam had to ask.

Clarence's smile was thin-lipped. "Sort of defeats the purpose of being undercover if your supposed boss knows what's going on."

"You were very convincing," Sam managed to say, thinking of what Clarence must have overheard, must have seen, all the while toiling in the background of the police department. He remembered what the marshal had told him back in Burdick: *That's our world, Sam. Spies and snitches everywhere.*

"Thanks, Sam," Clarence replied, going through the folder. "Only the ones who desire to see the President and the Party succeed can be chosen for such a task. But you know what? I was proud of every second of my job." Sam thought, *Back there, dammit, should have taken that chance, should have taken off when that kid said somebody wanted to see me.* All those important papers he had... and his plans for them... oh, Christ.

He said, "Does your brother know?"

Clarence grimaced. "You mean my older brother, the honorable Robert Rolston, city councilor? He knows how to toss a vote for the right bribe, how to skim a city contract for money, and how to get booze and broads in return for city jobs. Other than that, he knows shit." Sam said, "I see."

Clarence said, "Let's get right to it, all right?"

Sam was startled at the sound of a shotgun blast coming from outside, but the firearm discharging didn't bother Clarence a bit. Sam said, "Sure. Let's get to it."

The supposed janitor put on a pair of reading glasses and said, "What I have here is a collection of documents, Sam, all implicating you in a variety of anti-Party crimes and activities. For example, I have a denouncement saying that at the last Party meeting, you wrote down the names of Long, Coughlin, and Lindbergh when you were asked to list the names of local undesirables. I also have a canvassing report from two Legionnaires who detected suspicious activity at your house when they arrived for a visit. And I have an interrogation report concerning your brother and other plotters against the President. This report strongly implicates your participation. Finally, I have a request from a facility in Vermont seeking your immediate arrest and internment because of activities threatening national security."

Sam stayed still, his ears roaring like tidal waves crashing over him, overwhelming him and everything in their path.

Clarence peered at Sam over his reading glasses. "Do you have anything to say about these documents, Sam?" "No, I don't."

"Do you deny the information contained in these reports?"

"No."

"Anything to say in your defense?"

Sam said, "Not a goddamn thing."

Clarence stared, then put the papers down. "Very well, then. I have no other choice, I'm sorry to say."

The Legionnaire lowered his hand, opened a desk drawer, and Sam watched as Clarence took out a— cigarette lighter. Sam was expecting a pistol, or handcuffs, or an arrest warrant.

Clarence took the papers he had read, held them over the wastebasket, and with a flip of the lighter set them ablaze. The flames quickly rolled up the sheets of paper until Clarence was forced to drop them in the wastebasket. Wisps of smoke rose to the peaked green canvas roof of the tent.

Clarence put the cigarette lighter back into the desk drawer, slid it shut. He took his reading glasses off. "Sam, you always treated me well all the years I was undercover. Every single time you saw me. Not like some of your fellow cops, who figured I was just a dummy, a moron they could ignore or tease or rough up... Anyway, how you treated me day after day, month after month, year after year, that tells me what kind of man you are. Not whatever was claimed on those sheets of paper— which, of course, no longer exist."

The Legionnaire picked up a fountain pen. "You're a good guy, Sam.

But get the hell out of my sight, all right?" Sam did just that.

Outside of the temporary holding areas on the football field, a small crowd of people had gathered against the fence, looking for friends or family members. A couple of the braver ones were arguing with the Legionnaires keeping guard at the gate. Sam slipped through and thought of the luck that had just graced him.

As he was going to his Packard, there was a touch on his arm and a familiar voice. "Sam? Sam?"

There was Donna Fitzgerald, face drawn, eyes puffy.

She had on a shapeless tweed coat. He said, "Donna... what's wrong?"

"Larry... he's been rounded up... and all I know is that he's in there somewhere."

"What are they charging him with?"

She wiped at her runny nose. "Who. knows? Who cares? He hasn't done a thing since he's been back from the camp, just sleeping and catching up on his eating, and now he's gone again. Oh, Sam," she sobbed. "Can you help me?"

His chest felt cold and tight. "Donna, I'm sorry, I'm just a local cop, and it's a federal charge he's up against. I can't do anything."

"But I saw you walk out of the compound with no problem."

Sam was tom, God, how he was tom. He wanted so much to help his old friend, but he had to keep moving. There were so many important things going on, things he couldn't talk about or even afford to think about too much.

"That was different, Donna. Police business. I'm sorry, there's nothing else I can do."

Her hand grabbed his. "Sam. Please... we've known each other for years... I thought I could rely on you..." "Donna—"

Tears were streaming down her cheeks. "Don't you remember when we were kids, how you saved me?"

He knew the look on his face said it all: He didn't remember. She went on. "I had. I had started to develop... you know? And a couple of the neighborhood boys, the Taskers, they wanted to see my boobies... they were holding me down, they were trying to pull off my shirt.

You were there, and you pulled them off of me, slugged them, and I ran home crying. You saved me, Sam, you saved me..."

She squeezed his hand and went on, faster. "I don't have much in the way of money, but I can make it worth your while. You know I can. Pay you back... for then and now..."

For the briefest of moments, he closed his eyes. Thought about the other desperate women he had heard of, offering the only thing they had to try to free their men. How had it come to this? He opened his eyes, took his hand back from her, and gently said, "Donna, I can't."

By then it made no difference. Donna turned back toward the closed gate, her shoulders slumped against the biting wind, her possible savior no help at all.

CHAPTER SIXTY-SIX

Sam spent the night at the station, having no desire to go back to the wood-frame building that had once been a home. He hoped being here would push away the thought of Donna, standing alone, betrayed by her government and by the man who had been a childhood hero. By now the National Guardsmen and the cops not on regular shift had gone home, leaving him alone with a desk sergeant who was content to sit in a wooden swivel chair and read the latest copy of *Action Comics*. Sam dragged a cot up to his office area and made a bed there. Before stretching out, he read and reread his notes and the medical examiner's report from those few first days when everything seemed possible, his very first homicide case, one that he would solve and get off probation and make everything safe and secure for his family.

Sarah. Toby.

The pages fluttered as he read them. He supposed he should have fought harder when she left with his son, should have made a scene, but there was too much going on, too much knowledge—his wife a revolutionary, her own father her contact, Toby a courier as well. He had just let her go.

Would Tony have done that? Just let her go?

He doubted it. Tony was a fighter, always a fighter, even going into a suicide mission with his eyes and purpose clear.

And Sam? What was Sam Miller?

He read the report one more time, saw what he had been looking for.

The papers shook in his hands.

Who was Sam Miller?

He was going to find out.

Later that night, he got up from his cot, padded down to the lobby in his stocking feet. As he had hoped, the desk sergeant was still in his swivel chair, but he was snoring, hands clasped across his belly. Even as the department's janitor, operating in the darkness as a spy, was probably busy signing arrest or execution warrants back at Sam's high school playing field. Sam went back upstairs, where a desk lamp was on, illuminating both his desk and Mrs. Walton's.

In his upper drawer he reached to the back. He pulled out a screwdriver that he used now and then to fix his own swivel chair. Not tonight. *Hell,* he thought, looking up at the clock, *not this morning.* He went over to Mrs. Walton's desk, which smelled of her lilac scent. He knelt and jammed the screwdriver into the lower drawer. The wood squealed, and a piece of metal snapped free, and then the drawer came out.

Sitting there in plain sight was the infamous Log, the record of every upper-ranking officer in the Portsmouth Police Department. Luckily, Mrs. Walton had prim schoolteacher handwriting, for everything was as clear as day. When he got to a certain page and a certain date, he stopped, sucking in his breath. He read the entries three more times before he was satisfied, and then he tore out the page, tossed the book back inside, and closed the broken drawer.

The page now folded, he stuck it in his pants pocket and stretched out again on the cot and stared up until the morning light came through the windows. Then he got up and did some work at his desk. After that he went into Marshal Hanson's office and propped a note on his desk blotter.

As he drove away in the early hours, he looked back one more time at the old brick building and thought, *I'm never coming back.*

At a small white Cape Cod house at the outskirts of Portsmouth, the county medical examiner answered the door after Sam spent nearly ten minutes banging on it. Saunders's hair was unkempt, and he had a dull green robe wrapped around him. Saunders looked at Sam and said, "What is it?"

"The other day, at my brother's burial, you asked me if you could trust me to do the right thing."

"I remember."

"The answer is yes," Sam said. "And now I have a question for you."

The doctor opened the door wider. "Come in and I'll give you the answer."

Resuming his drive just a few minutes later, he checked his watch and knew he was pushing it, since Hanson was always one of the first to arrive every morning. But there was one thing he had to see before he went on.

On State Street, he pulled up across from the brick building. The building had once housed the only synagogue within miles. It was shuttered and closed; the posters of President Long he had seen slapped up the other day were still there. Those who had worshipped here, who had raised their families here as Americans, had fled to other parts of the country during the unsettled months after Long's election. Self-ghettoization, it had been called. He tried to recall what he had thought about it at the time and remembered hardly a thing. It was just one of those unsettling bits of news that came across, and since you couldn't do anything about it, you kept quiet and went about your business.

For some reason, he recalled his high school days, a kid on the team named Roger Cohen, who was a halfback. During one of the training sessions, out on the football field that was now a temporary prison, someone had made a crack about Roger being a weak-kneed Jew, and Roger had practically flown across the grass to slug that other kid.

Good ol' Roger. Not one to take crap from anyone. He wondered where Roger was, if he ever thought of his days back here in Portsmouth, if anyone else even remembered him and his family.

Did anybody remember? When did they all stop caring?

He shifted the car into drive. But before he left, he looked at the shuttered synagogue one more time, and he saw that someone had taken the time to tear away some of the Long posters from the far wall of the synagogue.

That one sight cheered him as he drove away.

At Pierce Island he stood by the shoreline, looking across the harbor to the naval shipyard. The cranes and smokestacks and buildings were still there, as well as the hulls of the submarines under construction. The wind was biting, and his hands were in his coat pockets as he stared out at the shipyard. By the dock where Hitler had landed, the decorative bunting was still up, though parts of it were snapping in the breeze. *The circle closes,* he thought. This was where he and Tony had played and hidden as children, this was where Tony had come when he had escaped from the labor camp, and this is where he was going to try to make it all right.

The circle closed.

The rumble of a car engine reached him. A black Ford sedan clattered over the bridge and came to the parking area, where it pulled in next to his Packard. The driver's door opened and Marshal Harold Hanson got out, dressed in his usual suit and tie, his face puzzled.

"Sam... what's going on?"

He walked over to his boss. "You know," he said softly, "something I've always wondered about this little island."

"What's that, Sam?"

He looked around at the flatland and the scrub brush and trees. "This has always been a magnet for illegal activity, hasn't it? Every few months we get sent here to make some arrests, make some headlines, and after a while, the problems return. But you know what? Why isn't there a gate over there by the bridge? A simple gate, closed at dusk, opened at dawn, and instantly, you take care of about eighty, ninety percent of the problems."

Hanson said, "That's interesting, Sam, but what—"

"But there's never been a gate, has there?" Sam interrupted. "And you know why? Because this island serves a need; it's a safety valve. The mayor and the city council and the police commission, they'd rather have this place open so that any undesirables congregate in one place, make it reasonably safe and happy for the rest of the city."

Hanson didn't say anything, just stared unhappily at him. Sam said, "That's all we do, isn't it? We do the bidding of others, we do things either illegally or not at all, to make those higher up happy and content. Whoever the hell they are."

"I don't know what you're getting at."

Sam reached into his coat, past his shoulder holster, and took out his revolver. He cocked back the hammer— the click sounding very loud in the morning air—and Hanson held up both hands and said, "Whoa, wait a minute, Sam, what do you mean—"

"What I mean is this," Sam said, raising up his revolver. "Petr Wowenstein escaped from a research facility in New Mexico and made his way to Portsmouth. He was coming here to reach the Underground Railroad, a station that was going to help him get to Montreal, with something very important he was carrying. A station I know you're familiar with, with all those hints you've given me. Wowenstein was a courier with a package that meant the life and death of hundreds of thousands, maybe millions. But the package never got delivered. Just as he was coming into Portsmouth, just as he was about to leave the train, he was murdered. His neck was snapped, and he was tossed off the train like a piece of garbage."

Hanson said, "Well? So what?"

Sam held the revolver level and steady. "What's what is the truth," he said. "Harold, you were on the train that night. You were trying to get the package off Petr Wowenstein. And when you couldn't find it, you killed him."

CHAPTER SIXTY-SEVEN

He stared at his boss, wanting to see a reaction. Except for a quiver of the lips, there was nothing. Sam said, "No reply, Harold?"

"Sam, you've drawn a gun on me. You're making crazy accusations. What do you want me to say? And what the hell gives you the right to call me by my first name?"

"The right of someone who's no longer your errand boy. You were on that train, Harold, and you murdered Petr Wowenstein."

"Sam—"

"Then tell me it's not true."

"Of course it's not true!"

Sam took one hand off the revolver, went back into his coat pocket, and took out two pieces of paper. He tossed them in the direction of Hanson, where they fluttered to the ground. "Pick them up."

Hanson stared at him for a moment, then squatted down, picked up the slips of paper.

"The one with the blue lines," Sam went on. "You'll recognize it, I'm sure. It's a page taken from Mrs. Walton's log. You may run the department the way you see fit, but by God, Mrs. Walton demands to know where everyone is. No one dares to cross her by telling a lie. And the night the Boston express train came through, that's where you were. It says so right there in her writing. How did you get back and forth to Boston? On the train, and with your National Guard and police marshal IDs, you could ride for free, no paperwork. Right? But remember what you told me that morning I came to see you? You said you were in Concord the day of Petr's murder. Not Boston."

Hanson crumpled the paper, let it drop back to the dirt. "So?"

"Check out the other paper. It's a carbon copy of my report on my first homicide. My first homicide, Harold. Read the last two lines, will you."

Hanson, his voice dripping contempt, said, "Since you're holding a gun on me, I guess I have no choice." He brought the piece of paper up and read it: " 'According to Dr. Saunders, his autopsy results have not yet been finalized, although he is confident in his finding of homicide. No progress has yet been made on the victim's identification, although the investigation continues.'"

Sam said, "Sound familiar?"

"I guess."

"I've talked to Dr. Saunders. He said he never filed a follow-up report, and he never talked to anyone after he was visited by me, LaCouture, and Groebke. So how did you know Petr's neck was snapped?"

"What?"

Sam stepped closer, his revolver inches from his boss's chest, knowing he was taking a path that he could never, ever retrace.

"Back in Burdick, you told me to ignore the case, that it was just one refugee who had his neck snapped and got dumped off the train. But I never told you his neck was snapped. Dr. Saunders never told you his neck was snapped. None of my reports ever mention his neck. Nobody ever told you his fucking neck was snapped. So how did you know?"

Now he saw a reaction in Hanson's face. It was as if he had aged ten years from the time he'd stepped out of his car.

Sam knelt down, picked up a rock with his free hand, and tossed it at Hanson's head. The marshal ducked and brought up his left hand to block the flying stone. Sam stood up, breathing hard. "And another thing. The killer was left-handed. Just like you. So. How and why was the courier killed?"

The air was cold, still, and heavy, and then Hanson nervously cleared his throat. "It was an accident."

"How was killing him an accident?"

Hanson spat on the ground. "Because it was, dammit! The son of a bitch wouldn't give it up!"

"Give what up?"

"Whatever he was carrying, the skinny bastard," Hanson fumed. "I was just told to get on that train, find him, and get any documents he had. Whatever he had was vital. But he didn't have anything on him, nothing. I dragged him into the baggage car, started working him over, looking for a suitcase, a valise, anything, and he still wouldn't give it up. Then the train started slowing down. I thought we were stopping because someone saw me drag the bastard to the rear. I held him tight, told him to give it up, and shit, he was so sick, so skinny. Damn neck just broke in my hands. I didn't mean to kill him."

"After you dumped him, what did you do?"

"Got off a few yards down, by the Fish Shanty lot. And that was that."

"Where my witness, Lou Purdue, spotted you. A fine-dressed man standing in the rain. Lou Purdue, murdered up in Dover. Another loose end tidied up."

Hanson said, "I know nothing about that."

"So you say," Sam said. "Who told you to go to Boston and grab those documents?"

"What difference does it make? Someone from the Party in D.C."

"The Party, the Party... which faction, Nat or Statie? Who needed those plans?"

Hanson said, "There are factions, there are differences, but that didn't come into account here. I was given an order by the Party, and I followed it. That's what happened."

"You did all of this?" Sam's voice was shaking with rage. "And you threw this case at me, knowing right from the start what was going on?"

"What else was I going to do?" Hanson yelled back. "I was trying to protect you, you stubborn bastard. You could have just given it up after a day or two, filed it away, and you would have been fine. But no—you had to prove how noble and upright you were."

"Sure," Sam said. "If I had been a lousy cop, I would have been fine. But guess what, Harold? I wasn't a lousy cop. I was a good cop. And for the past several days, I've been a lousy man and a lousy husband, but that's all going to change." He unfolded the pages and held them up. "Here. Here, you Party whore. This is what you were looking for. Was it worth it, murdering an innocent refugee? Lying to me and everyone else in the department? Covering up everything connected with the case?"

Hanson's eyes seemed frozen on the handful of papers.

Sam had a strange feeling, knowing what he was holding, knowing it all would come down to the next few seconds. "How... where did you get those?"

"Got them off that poor bastard's body, that's where. You didn't look far enough, Harold. Refugees, they're experts at hiding things. These papers were produced from microfilm, hidden up in his butt."

"How long have you had them?"

"Not long enough, and that's why my place was trashed. Those Legionnaires weren't tossing my house just for the hell of it. They were looking for these. Want to know what they are?"

Hanson said, "What do you want for them?"

"That's for later. Right now these papers are what count. They're calculations, figures, plans for building a bomb. A super bomb that comes from splitting the atom. An atomic bomb. Here we are, just you and me, and we're going to decide where it goes."

"I don't believe it." Hanson's voice was barely above a whisper.

"I'm told that a bomb like this, something not so big at all, can destroy a harbor. A small city. A division of panzer tanks. And it was Jewish refugees, smart fellows from Europe, professors and scientists, half-starved and beaten but still alive in an American research facility out west, who came up with these plans, these figures. It's not the whole package, I'm sure. There's so much more work to be done. But they have the outline, the blueprints. And once they came up with it, who would they give it to? Long and his thugs? Or the Soviets? The Reds are the only ones left fighting the Nazis, who are busily killing their families and neighbors. They contacted people on the outside, people like my wife, who could get this refugee with the plans to the Soviets."

"Please, Sam, give me those papers."

"Why should I?"

"How can you ask that? We're going to need those calculations, so we can get ready when Hitler decides to take us on. You know damn well we're outnumbered and outgunned. If those papers are for real, that bomb can be an equalizer when the time comes. And you can believe Hitler's going to take us on one of these days, no matter how many trade agreements Long signs with him, no matter how chummy they get. Hitler had a whole bunch of trade and peace agreements with Stalin. Those agreements didn't mean shit when Hitler invaded in '41. Long may like all these new jobs, but he doesn't trust Hitler. Nobody does. They're not going to—"

"Oh, shut the hell up. The papers belong to me, and I'll decide what to do with them. Why shouldn't I give them to the Soviets? That's where they were intended to go. That's where the refugee scientists wanted them to end up. So why not the Russians?"

"But Sam—"

"Hell, maybe I'll screw everyone up and sell them to the Nazis. I'll get ahold of my new best friend, Groebke, and tell him what I have. Don't you think I could get a pretty price for these papers? Retire with my family to some sunny city in South America and watch the rest of the world go to hell?"

Out on the harbor, a whistle blew at the shipyard. Hanson's eyes were locked on the sheets of paper in Sam's hand. "I could also dump these in the harbor, Harold. So your murder would be for nothing. All that work—for nothing."

"Sam, don't—"

"So tell me this," Sam demanded. "Am I talking to the right person? Are you able to make a deal? Or do I need to talk to somebody else?"

"I can make a deal."

"Talk to me, then."

"How much money do you want?"

"Not a fucking dime." And Sam smiled.

CHAPTER SIXTY-EIGHT

"But there's still a price to be paid," Sam went on. "Do you understand?"

A pause. "Yes... I understand."

"Good," he said, taking a breath. "The camp at Burdick and the rest of them, all across the country. The conditions improve. Better food, fewer hours, clean quarters. The fucking Nazis, they get kicked out. And the Jews, they get paid a living wage. Everything can still be kept secret, that doesn't have to change. Long keeps on admitting them. And their family members."

Hanson said, "That's... that's impossible."

"Best deal you're going to get. Oh, and one more thing. My wife. Tomorrow you're going to take the two of us on a trip to Burdick. I want Sarah to see it, and I want you to explain to her why it's there, why Long is the key to keeping all those Jews alive, and what I've done here today."

"This is important? For your wife to see Burdick?"

The other day, the sadness in her eyes, the disdain in her voice, wondering where it had all gone wrong... It would take a lot, she had said, to make it all right. He was certain now that this would do it. The look in her eyes had tormented him. To see them shine again with happiness and love meant everything to him.

"More important than you know," Sam said. "I've lost her. And I'm going to get her back."

"Can I put my arms down?"

"Do we have a deal?"

"Some calls have to be made. You know what that's like."

He held the papers up, motioned to throw them into the choppy waters of the harbor. "Wrong answer."

Hanson spoke hastily, "Yes, Sam. We have a deal."

Sam kept the revolver pointed at him. "Believe me when I say this, Harold. If the deal doesn't go through, if there're changes, if it doesn't happen the way I want it, then I won't complain. I won't make a fuss. I'll just find you and kill you."

Hanson spat out, "A hell of a thing to say to your boss!"

"Boss?" Sam laughed. "You're not my boss anymore. Our relationship has changed. We're partners now, bound together for life. And here's a news flash for you and my father-in-law, your Party rival. You've all been pushing me to become more active in the Party, for all your different reasons, and guess what, that's exactly what I'm going to do starting this week. But like they say, be careful what you wish for."

"What do you mean by that?"

Sam offered a nasty smile. "Like I said—partners. I'm going to become active in the Party. You're going to be there, greasing the wheels, seeing that I become powerful and prominent. Maybe my father-in-law will help. Hell, being the official savior of the President won't hurt, either. And once I'm inside, in a position of power and influence, you're going to see some changes there, too. Just you watch. You know, a couple of guys these past few days"—he thought of his brother and his upstairs neighbor—"said to me that sometimes one man can make a difference. I plan to be that man, Harold. There are changes coming, positive changes, and I'm going to be leading that charge. No more hiding, no more sitting on the sidelines."

"Sam, please, can I put my arms down?"

"Go right ahead."

Hanson lowered his arms, then rubbed his hands together. "All right... the papers?"

Sam passed them over, and Hanson grabbed them like a child opening his first gift on Christmas morning. He flipped through the pages, then looked up. "This math is gibberish. How in hell did you figure out what it all means?"

"Had someone help me out." Poor Walter Tucker, not knowing how the plot and conspiracy had eventually paid off.

"These papers... they're numbered from one to fifty."

"Yeah, I know."

"But I only have twenty-five pages."

Sam uncocked the revolver, put it back into his shoulder holster, pulled his coat close. "Consider it a down payment."

"What the hell do you mean by that?"

Sam thought of his visit that morning to Dr. Saunders, where the rest of the papers resided and where other agreements had been reached. "You think I was going to give it all up just like that? Not likely, Harold. I gave you half of the equations, enough to show those calculations are for real. And once I see the progress being made in Burdick and other camps, the more of the other pages you'll get. My schedule, not yours. Any delays, any foul-ups, I get arrested or a rock falls on my head, the rest of the papers get destroyed."

Hanson kept on staring at the papers.

"Oh—and to use a favorite phrase of yours—one more thing," Sam said. "I've typed up a narrative of your involvement in the murder of that courier. So after you and your friends have all of the calculations, if you're tempted to have me run down by a truck, forget it. Anything bad happens to me, Harold, those papers I prepared go straight to the mayor. Just think of all the fun my father- in-law would have with you if that were to happen. My guess is, you'd be acquainted real quick with the inside of a boxcar heading to Utah."

Hanson carefully folded the sheets and tucked them in his coat. "You drive a hell of a bargain. And you didn't have to. You could have given me all of the papers, Sam. You could trust me and trust the President to do the right thing. This is America, you know."

Sam looked out to the harbor. Thought about the camps, the arrests, the censorship, the torture, the day- to-day humiliations, the mothers and fathers and sons and daughters hungry or homeless, his dead brother, the alliance with Hitler...

He turned back to his boss. "No," he said. "No, this isn't America. And it hasn't been, not for a very long time."

He walked back to his car, and Hanson called to him, but he didn't bother to listen. There was so much to do, so much to hope for, and he didn't know how much time he had left.

He got into the Packard, one hand on the steering wheel, saw the numeral three on his wrist. Three. Sarah and Toby and him. A lifelong reminder of what was important, what counted.

He started up the Packard and headed home.

AUTHOR'S NOTE

On February 15, 1933, Giuseppe Zangara, a thirty-two-year-old Italian anarchist, was at Bayfront Park in Miami, where he opened fire with a .32-caliber revolver at President-elect Franklin D. Roosevelt. Whether because of the unsteady chair that he was standing on or because a woman nudged his arm, his shots missed Roosevelt and instead struck Chicago Mayor Anton Cermak, who later died from his wounds.

Zangara was promptly charged with Cermak's death, put on trial, and executed just over a month later.

At the time of this assassination attempt, the Vice President-elect was John Nance Garner of Texas, Speaker of the House of Representatives, an opponent of Roosevelt's New Deal and an isolationist. Most historians find it doubtful that he could have provided the leadership the nation so desperately needed at the height of the Great Depression, when the unemployment rate soared to 25 percent and public commentators such as Walter Lippmann called openly for the new President to assume dictatorial powers.

Huey Long, governor and then senator from the state of Louisiana during Roosevelt's first term, made no secret of his desire to become President of the United States. In fact, he outlined his plans in the novel My First Days in the White House, published in 1935. Long was also an isolationist, and he often boasted that he never traveled abroad and did not care about the fate of other nations.

The novel was published posthumously, as Senator Long was shot on September 8,1935, in the statehouse in Baton Rouge, Louisiana, and died two days later. At the time of Senator Long's death, President Roosevelt considered him one of the most dangerous men in America.

The public statements made herein by Huey Long, Winston Churchill,

Charles Lindbergh, and Father Charles Coughlin are factual. Only the time and place of their comments have been fictionalized.

Walter Tucker's recollection of the visit to Harvard in 1934 of its alumnus, Ernst Hanfstaengl, Nazi Party member and head of the foreign press operations for the Third Reich, is based on a true event.

Even though refugees and escapees told of the true nature of the holocaust during the 1940s, their stories were not believed by government officials and the media until the Allied victory in 1945 and the subsequent liberation of the Nazi death camps. One of the little-known stories about the holocaust was the Madagascar Plan, a proposal by the Nazis to deport the Jewish population of Europe to the island of Madagascar. In May 1940, in his book Reflections on the Treatment of Peoples of Alien Races in the East, SS head Heinrich Himmler declared: "I hope that the concept of Jews will be completely extinguished through the possibility of a large emigration of all Jews to Africa or some other colony."

The Madagascar Plan was abandoned after 1940, since Great Britain remained undefeated and its navy was still a formidable foe to German shipping.

The mostly unsuccessful attempts by Treasury Secretary Henry Morgenthau, Jr., to convince the government to admit more Jewish refugees to the United States is a matter of historical record. So, too, is the bloody Memorial Day massacre of the Republic Steel strikers in 1937.

The city of Portsmouth, New Hampshire, is real, as are the naval shipyard and its vital role in the peace treaty signed by Japan and Russia in 1905 that led to President Theodore Roosevelt receiving the Nobel Peace Prize. However, certain geographical and historical aspects of Portsmouth and its police department have been changed for the purpose of this novel. Any errors of geography or history are the author's.

"This is pre-eminently the time to speak the truth, the whole truth, frankly and boldly. Nor need we shrink from honestly facing conditions in our country today. This great nation will endure as it has endured, will revive and will prosper. So first of all let me assert my firm belief that the only thing we have to fear... is fear itself... nameless, unreasoning, unjustified terror which paralyzes needed efforts to convert retreat into advance."

President Franklin D. Roosevelt, Inaugural Address,
March 4,1933

"People who are hungry and out of a job are the stuff of which dictatorships are made."

President Franklin D. Roosevelt, Address to Congress,
January 11,1944

ON THE USE OF PEN NAMES

So with a number of novels published and scores of short stories under my name, why did I decide to publish AMERIKAN EAGLE under a pen name back in 2011? There's a lengthy answer and a short answer, and I'd prefer to use the short answer. At this point in publishing in 2011, it was becoming increasingly common for some authors to submit novels under a pen name, in order to jump-start a career, or start a series of new novels under a new name, or to attract new readers.

At about this time, I had finished a new alternative history novel, similar in concept to what I did with RESURRECTION DAY. In RESURRECTION DAY, I wrote about what might have happened if the Cuban Missile Crisis of 1962 erupted into World War III. In AMERIKAN EAGLE, I took the little-recalled but true history of the attempted assassination of President-elect Franklin D. Roosevelt in 1933, and tried to look at what might have happened to the United States and the world ten years after his death. Imagine all the possibilities of what might have happened with the death of one man, at a time when a country desperately needed his knowledge and leadership. I had a lot of fun --- and experienced some terrifying moments --- in imagining a world in 1943 without FDR.

With this novel completed, I decided to give this new strategy a chance, which is why AMERIKAN EAGLE came out under a pen name.

Did this new strategy work?

Maybe yes, maybe no.

It's still hard to get a straight answer years later, but now, I'm just thrilled to re-release AMERIKAN EAGLE under my own name. No other books of mine have been published under the Alan Glenn pen name, and I can promise, none will in the future.

And what about this particular pen name? Where did Alan Glenn get his start?

Based on the fact that I'm a space and astronomy geek, with an interest in astronauts, I leave it to the reader's imagination to figure that one out. Thanks again for taking this look at AMERIKAN EAGLE.

Brendan DuBois of New Hampshire is the award-winning author of seventeen novels and more than 145 short stories. He is also a one-time "Jeopardy!" game show champion, and he was also a winner on the trivia game show "The Chase." "Blood Foam," his latest novel, was published in June 2015.

Writing as Alan Glenn, "Amerikan Eagle" was first published in 2011.

His short fiction has appeared in Playboy, Ellery Queen's Mystery Magazine, Alfred Hitchcock's Mystery Magazine, The Magazine of Fantasy & Science Fiction, and numerous other magazines and anthologies including "The Best American Mystery Stories of the Century," published in 2000 by Houghton-Mifflin. Another one of his short stories appeared in "The Year's Best Science Fiction 22nd Annual Collection" (St. Martin's Griffin, 2005) edited by Gardner Dozois

His short stories have twice won him the Shamus Award from the Private Eye Writers of America, and have also earned him three Edgar Allan Poe Award nominations from the Mystery Writers of America.

Visit his website at www.BrendanDuBois.com.

Made in the USA
San Bernardino, CA
02 April 2020